Rival Passions

Rival Passions

Zoë Miller

W F HOWES LTD

This large print edition published in 2012 by
W F Howes Ltd
Unit 4, Rearsby Business Park, Gaddesby Lane,
Rearsby, Leicester LE7 4YH

1 3 5 7 9 10 8 6 4 2

First published in the United Kingdom in 2011
by Hachette Books Ireland

A CIP catalogue record for this book is available
from the British Library

ISBN 978 1 47120 092 2

Typeset by Palimpsest Book Production Limited,
Falkirk, Stirlingshire

Printed and bound in Great Britain
by TJ International Ltd, Padstow, Cornwall

Dedicated with lots of love to Derek

PROLOGUE

This can't be happening; not now . . .
Yesterday, she thought she knew passion, from tenderness to desire. But in the beat of a moment, when she sees him strolling across the lawn, something flares inside her and everything changes. That's all it takes; one look, one pulse-beat, and she feels like laughing at the sheer craziness of it, only it's not really funny at all.

She tries to focus on everything around her rather than the man who is causing her skin to prickle and her heart to skitter. The tables under the oak trees are laden with rows of glistening crystal flutes and buckets of chilled champagne, beaded with moisture. Under the shade of the trees, silvery balloons bounce gently against the branches and prisms of sunlight flicker through the shifting canopy of leaves. In the foreground, Tamarisk Manor, the Georgian hotel, boasts a graceful facade and a pillared entrance flanked with ornamental trees in granite urns. Long sash windows face the south and reflect glimmers of light.

All of this is set against a backdrop of dramatic

mountain scenery. But there is nothing as dramatic as the pounding of her heart. When her eyes slide back to him as if drawn by a magnet, she feels giddy as if she's had too much champagne. He's achingly familiar, yet she's really seeing him for the first time. He smiles at her across the table and her senses pound with aching need while she fights for normal breath. She feels as though sparks are shooting from her limbs and disturbing the soft afternoon air.

People talk to her. She answers them. She hears herself laugh. Someone hands her a brimming champagne flute and her fingers tremble on the smoothness of the stem. Bubbly liquid catches in her throat. When he comes to her for a welcoming kiss, she knows, already, as though it's leaping in her blood, the scent of his skin, the taste of his lips and the touch of his breath on her face; warm, like a lover's caress.

She knows too, that the timing is all wrong and everything about this is forbidden.

CHAPTER 1

There was nothing like a sunny Friday evening in June to bring out the best in Tamarisk Manor, Serena Devlin decided, as she stood by the open window of her first-floor office. The inviting clink of cocktail glasses and seductive pop of champagne corks enhanced the laughter and chat drifting up from the outdoor terrace. Across the parkland, Ireland's latest supermodel strolled hand-in-hand with her beau, her white cotton maxi-dress fluttering against the velvet green lawns. Sunlight sparked off the bonnet of a silver-grey Bentley as it purred up the curving avenue of beech trees towards the hotel reception.

The weekend in one of Europe's hottest hide-aways had just kicked off to an ultra-perfect start.

Serena felt a small bubble of contentment in her heart. This was it; this was what she worked so hard for and moments like these made the sacrifices worthwhile. And at least, she told herself, ignoring the sudden lurch in the pit of her stomach, she was getting something right.

'Serena, you were looking for me?'

She jumped. She turned around to see Andrew, the senior manager, framed in the doorway.

'Yes, I was,' she said, stepping away from the window, thankful he had interrupted her thoughts before they nose-dived into murky territory and burst her fragile bubble. 'I want to make sure we're all set for Claudia.'

'We're more than sorted,' Andrew said. He sat down opposite her and brandished a clipboard full of green and yellow highlighted notes with a triumphant flourish. 'You should be down there on the terrace, celebrating with champagne, because this crisis is over.'

'It should be me, you and the rest of the staff,' she smiled warmly, sitting back and twirling her silver pen between her slim, manicured fingers. 'And if we all bunked off, who would look after our visitors?'

On Saturday morning, Claudia, an A-list diva and the darling of America, was arriving in Tamarisk along with her team of stylists, publicists and minders, seeking serious down time after an exhausting three-night, sell-out stint in the O_2 in Dublin. Her list of special requirements, however, hadn't been emailed through to Andrew until four o'clock that afternoon and he'd come straight to Serena. She'd dropped everything and called her key operational staff together for a quick briefing. This booking was too important to leave anything to chance, as Claudia had promised to recommend the hotel to her mega-rich celebrity friends if her visit was successful.

And of course, the opposite also applied.

'I can double check Claudia's requirements if you want to get on home,' Andrew said.

Andrew had worked in Tamarisk for over twenty years, working up through the ranks from bell boy in the days when the young Serena was setting tables and making herself useful in between school and homework. Now he was her right-hand man. 'I do trust you,' she said, 'but you know me, I'll only go home happy when I'm certain everything is under control for tomorrow.'

'You're certainly your mother's daughter.' Andrew shook his head. 'Diligent to the last.'

'I should hope so,' Serena grinned. 'Considering how successful she was at running the whole show, I've a lot to live up to.' But it was nothing she couldn't handle, she told herself as she turned to her laptop and scrolled to the email Andrew had forwarded. 'Right. What's first?'

Andrew consulted his clipboard. 'Top of the list is absolute privacy. Check. Claudia will not be disturbed by other guests. I've alerted Reception and Front Office as to her arrival time and all registration details will be efficient and discreet.'

'Her suite?' Serena prompted.

'The Premier Suite will be ready and waiting.'

Serena nodded. The ultra-luxury suite was completely self-contained, including a private dining room and a relaxation room for spa treatments. It was also sound-proofed, as were the five other suites and fifty bedrooms in Tamarisk Manor.

'Menus are sorted,' Andrew said. 'Kate has gone through the food and beverage list. Anything not to hand can be sourced at the farmers' market in the morning.'

Serena snapped to attention. 'In the *morning*?'

'Yes. She's already phoned through our orders to the suppliers,' Andrew said hastily. 'I've been assured everything will be delivered long before Claudia arrives. And we've just taken delivery of Claudia's specified humidifiers. We managed to get six,' Andrew ticked some green highlighted text on his notes. 'Whatever part of the suite she'll be in, her vocal chords will be preserved.'

Serena suppressed a grin. She had long ago stopped passing judgement on some of the more unusual requests from her guests. Business was business after all, especially in these challenging times.

'Organic dark chocolate. Check,' Andrew went on.

'Mineral water? Wine list? Champagne?' Serena asked.

Andrew nodded and ticked further items. 'And Accommodation has confirmed the arrival of cotton sheets with the specified thread count. The four-poster bed in Claudia's suite is being made up now.'

Serena shook her head. 'She doesn't know what

she's missing.' Irish linen, soft and pure and heather scented, swaddling you comfortably in deeply quilted, queen-sized beds, was one of the attractions of Tamarisk.

'The Spa manager has juggled the appointments rota for tomorrow afternoon and freed up two therapists. Three dozen orchids have just arrived and will be in place around her suite, pale-pink rose petals are ready to be strewn,' Andrew continued. 'Oh, and Ben & Jerry's low fat ice cream and it must be chocolate fudge brownie flavour and served slightly thawed. It's Claudia's one and only weakness,' he said.

Lucky Claudia, Serena thought, wishing the stain on her conscience was as trifling. 'What about hotel directions?' she asked.

Even though it was signposted, it was easy to overshoot the sheltered laneway that led to the hotel. Serena liked to think that being off the beaten track added to the ambience of pampered privacy and she knew it helped keep many a gossip-hungry social diarist from disturbing the celebrities and stars who flocked to the secluded sanctuary. Set in the heartland of the stunning Wicklow countryside, the chic, family-run hotel offered peace and tranquillity in beautiful surroundings. Serena, along with her twin brother Jack and the team of staff, worked hard to provide a package of unrivalled luxury combined with a homely touch, and, above all, a discreet anonymity that allowed celebrity guests to relax.

Guests could unwind in the quiet refuge of the Tranquil Garden, with its specially commissioned slate and granite water features, scented Wicklow heather, Connemara wild flowers and Irish-designed teak and wicker furniture. The hotel grounds were bordered by acres of hushed woodland trails that led up into the mountains. Serena had been quietly proud when the ambience helped to catapult the hotel into the shortlist of the most captivating hideaways in western Europe. Then in a recent edition of a travel magazine, she had been hailed as the bright star at the leading edge of Irish hospitality, because of the personal touch with which she managed her guest relations.

'Well done, darling,' her mother Charlotte had said.

'I guess it's in the genes,' Serena had replied, lightly.

'I'm very proud of you,' Charlotte had continued, 'and if your father was still alive, he would have been equally proud of you.'

'Do you think so?'

'Of *course*. And, Serena, this will help your profile to soar . . . if that's what you want.' Charlotte had looked quizzically at her daughter.

'Why wouldn't I want? I hope it'll bring Tamarisk closer to my goal of five-star classification.' They had been working towards this when, two years earlier, Charlotte had stepped back from the day-to-day running of the hotel after devoting almost thirty-five years of her life to it. Now Serena was determined to follow through and position Tamarisk where it deserved to be.

Instead of showing enthusiasm, Charlotte had given her a long look. 'I don't like to see you taking on too much. You work hard enough as it is. Sometimes, darling, I wonder why you're so driven to succeed.'

'Maybe that's in the genes too,' Serena had said.

When she'd glanced at the article again, the words had blurred in front of her eyes. 'Bright star'! God. Making sure that guests had the ultimate experience was as natural to her as breathing. Serena had been born to this and it was as much a part of her as the blood running through her veins. But behind her successful image, nobody knew her private life was anything but stellar, for she was falling far short of the kind of loving wife Paul expected and the devoted mother Harriet deserved. Sometimes she felt she was living two different lives, which were at terrible odds with each other and she didn't know how they could be reconciled.

'Claudia's arriving by helicopter,' Andrew was saying, once again rescuing Serena from her plummeting thoughts. 'The red carpet is ready to be rolled out to the helipad. I've checked the weather forecast and it's to be calm and settled for the weekend. That's it,' he said, rising to his feet. 'I'm here until eleven o'clock this evening with enough staff to take care of any last-minute requests.'

'Great stuff,' she said, 'Thanks a million, and

well done to everyone for pulling out the stops. I'll be heading home soon, but call me if you've any problems. I'll be here early in the morning to greet Claudia.'

'No bother, you know the staff would do anything for you.'

'I know, and their loyalty is important to me. Would you mind throwing your eye over this?' she asked, handing him a document. 'It's our submission outlining why Tamarisk should win the award of Exceptional Haven. I have most of it completed, but I just want to be doubly sure I haven't overlooked anything.'

Serena really wanted this. Exceptional Haven of the Year was one of a new set of industry awards sponsored by the recently formed Celebrate Ireland, a government body set up to strengthen the tourist industry and promote the unique Irish heritage and tradition of excellent hospitality. If Tamarisk was shortlisted, there would be an anonymous site visit, before the award ceremony. Tamarisk had already won awards under her mother's directorship, but this would be Serena's first attempt at gaining formal recognition and it would also be a wonderful stepping stone to the goal of upgrading their classification.

'Sure, I'll have a look,' Andrew said, attaching the document to his clipboard, 'but knowing you, I've no doubt it's word perfect.'

Serena smiled at him, before taking a deep breath. 'There's something else.'

10

He paused in the doorway, looking at her expectantly, alerted, she knew, by her tone of voice.

'Jack's arriving home from France this evening. So I expect he'll be back in the office next week. He wants no fuss, though. You can pass the word around.'

'That's good news, isn't it?' Andrew said, clearly uncomfortable as he gripped his clipboard, shield-like, in front of him. 'I hope he's feeling . . . well, I hope he's recovered . . . a bit.'

'I'm sure he has,' Serena smiled for Andrew's sake, 'but we'll have to give him time to get up to speed again.'

'Of course.'

As soon as Andrew had left, Serena sat back in her chair and chewed the end of her silver pen. Recovered? You didn't recover from the death of your loved ones, she thought, remembering her father's death and the myriad of feelings she'd had to work through afterwards – loss and sadness, regret for what might have been in spite of their flawed relationship. But whatever about losing a parent, it was surely far more traumatic to lose a wife after a few short months of marriage, the way Jack had lost Amy.

The tragedy, almost a year ago now, had devastated the Devlin family, happening so soon after Amy's miscarriage. The media frenzy hadn't helped either. 'This has pulled the luxury rug from under the Devlins' glitzy lifestyles,' one tabloid journalist had cruelly put it.

It had turned Jack's life upside down and Serena had been extra busy since then, taking up the slack in the aftermath of Jack's depression and gloom. It was the least she could do for him, he was her brother and she loved him and was terribly cut up to see him so upset. As well as that, Serena privately felt it went some way towards making up for her innate dislike of her sister-in-law, a dislike that had come back to haunt her in the weeks following Amy's death.

She had thought Jack was beginning to turn a corner, when, a couple of months earlier, he had decided to take time out in La Mimosa, their sister hotel in the south of France, which was even more exclusive than Tamarisk. As she closed her files and powered down her laptop, she could still picture Jack's pinched, white face when he had stood in her office.

'I need breathing space and time to get my head around it all,' he'd said, pacing the floor.

Time? Breathing space? Even though she truly empathised with Jack's pain, she couldn't help feeling a little hurt that her support hadn't been enough.

'I was starting to get my act together,' Jack had said, 'and I appreciate all your help, I really do, but last week I met Karen, you remember Amy's sister, and it brought it all back. A couple of weeks chilling in La Mimosa is just what I need.'

He'd seemed, she thought, more agitated than ever, a muscle in his cheek had flexed non-stop and his taut, shadowed face had spoke silent volumes about his long, sleepless nights. She'd felt a tug in her heart. No doubt seeing Amy's sister had set him back completely.

She'd reached up to kiss his cheek. 'Just come back in one piece.'

'You're okay with holding the fort? Mum's around if you need any help.'

'I'll be fine. I won't need to call on Mum,' Serena had said. It had been a proud day for her when her mother had handed over the reins – no way would she give her any reason to think she wasn't up to the job.

Jack's visit to La Mimosa had turned into a six-week retreat and Serena couldn't believe he'd stayed away for so long. He'd obviously been far more cut up about his wife's death than he'd let on. Thankfully, he was finally coming home, his flight due to land in Dublin later that evening. She'd offered to meet him at the airport, but he'd insisted he wanted no fanfare. Serena fervently hoped he'd be back to some sense of himself, both for his own sake and to support her towards the goal of five-star classification. He needed to take up the reins again on the financial side of things; the side she'd let slide a little in his absence, and which, she suspected, he hadn't given his usual attention to in the past few months.

Serena was putting away her laptop when her private mobile buzzed and her heart jumped. 'Hi, Paul.'

13

'Where are you?' Her husband asked.

'I'm in the office.'

'Still? It's after six o'clock.'

'Yes, darling, I'm just finishing up here, we had a slight emergency this afternoon but it's all under control.' When there was silence at the other end of the phone, she ran her free hand through her silky blonde hair and said, 'Is everything okay?'

'You forgot about Harriet. She's just left.'

Harriet! In the rush to sort out Claudia's requirements, she'd forgotten her promise to her four-year-old daughter to be home to wave her off as she left to spend the night at her best friend's house. The friend from her crèche who was more like a sister to her. The sibling she, so far, didn't have, Serena reminded herself guiltily.

No wonder Paul sounded cool with her, but he wasn't half as annoyed as she felt with herself. A familiar sense of failure washed over her. In her mind's eye, Serena saw her little daughter's flushed and happy face and the small overnight bag she'd packed enthusiastically the previous evening. It was her first overnight play date on the occasion of her friend's fifth birthday.

'I'm really sorry,' she said contritely. 'I hope she didn't mind too much. I'll make it up to her. How did she seem, going off?'

'She was so excited when Sophie and her mum called for her that she barely remembered to kiss me goodbye. To be honest, she didn't even notice you weren't around,' Paul said evenly.

14

Serena was silent for a moment. 'Just as well,' she said, swallowing hard. 'I hope she enjoys her night and has some fun.'

'What about us?' Paul said, sounding more upbeat. 'How often do we have a free night and time alone?'

'Hardly ever.'

'Let's make the most of it.'

'Maybe we could drive out to that new restaurant on the coast? I'd like to check out the competition.' She doubted if the food was in the same league as Tamarisk's superb Oakwood restaurant or more relaxed Maple bar, both renowned for the creative and nutritious menus based on fresh, locally sourced produce.

Paul huffed. 'What competition? I don't think you'll be losing sleep over it.' He paused, then went on in a different tone of voice, 'I had something else in mind. How about you getting your sexy ass home so that we can enjoy some ravishing baby making?'

Serena tightened her grip on the phone. 'Sounds good. I'll be home soon.'

'I'm ready and waiting. Impatiently waiting.'

After the call, Serena picked up the framed photograph on her table, taken during a weekend visit to Disneyland Paris the previous year. Harriet was giggling at the camera, the mirror image of Paul with her dark wavy hair and deep-grey eyes. Her arms were tightly wound around her daddy's neck, their two heads stuck close together, while a smiling Serena stood slightly apart. They looked like the perfect family unit.

Something clutched at her heart as she put down the photo and went over to close the window. She picked up her bag and left her office, pausing at the top of the curving staircase that led to the lobby. Her eyes automatically scanned the scene; the welcoming reception area with its tall vases of fresh floral arrangements, the comfortable sofas where guests were invited to complete their registration details, the Waterford crystal chandeliers and the elegant Connemara marble fireplace where a homely log fire glowed on chilly days.

In the lobby, she stopped to chat to Suzi and Helen, the receptionists, and Ross, the porter on duty, and then she walked towards the entrance porch, where a soft glow filtered through the graceful fanlight over the door. She stepped out into the forecourt and felt the warmth of the sun on her face as she walked across to her silver Saab.

Serena drove halfway down the beech-lined avenue and halted the car for a moment. She looked in the rear-view mirror at the play of early evening sunlight slanting across the facade of Tamarisk, and the purple haze of the mountains behind. The beauty of it caught at her heart and she could have stayed in that spot for ever, to let the peace and tranquillity soothe her troubled spirit. Then she took a deep breath, put the car in gear and continued down the avenue. It was time to go home to Maple Hill, where Paul was waiting for her.

Waiting to make babies, she sighed, and totally oblivious to what was really going on in her life.

CHAPTER 2

Jack Devlin felt a surge of relief as his sleek Mercedes convertible zipped around a sharp bend on the Moyenne Corniche and another spectacular vista on the French Riviera shimmered into view. He pressed a lever and the soft top lifted up and folded back on itself, enabling him to soak up the full brilliance of the late afternoon sunshine while the warm breeze tossed his dark-red hair.

He drove around an incline of steep charcoal cliffs, the thrumming engine fragmenting the still, drowsy air. The sea momentarily disappeared from view and from behind impenetrable walls and security gates, the upper storeys of villa after villa flashed by, a blur of pink and cream-stuccoed walls, basking sleepily in the sunshine. Each one was more ostentatious than the last, their billionaire owners indulging their lavish tastes. Not that he could scoff, Jack reminded himself. He'd just spent the last six weeks in the luxuriant extravagance of La Mimosa, the chic bolthole tucked into one of the most picturesque areas of the Riviera.

Then where the road once again ran parallel to

the coast, the glittering waters of the Côte d'Azur stretched out to infinity, flanked by the lush green arm of Cap Ferrat. Out in the bay, gleaming whitely against the sapphire sea, he saw a cruise ship floating towards the harbour at Villefranche. It was a sight that would normally send his pulse tripping with a frisson of excitement, but today he felt nothing at all.

He'd taken the scenic route on purpose; something inside him wanted to test his reaction to the explosion of sights and the stunning beauty of the landscape but, more importantly, he wanted to test the memory of the last time he'd driven this road. He'd been with Amy, her long, blonde hair flying in the breeze, her eyes concealed by oversized sunglasses, her mouth curved in a smile of childlike delight.

'This is perfect,' she'd cried out, craning her neck to absorb all of the view, her voice catching in the breeze.

'You like it?'

'Yeah.' She'd stretched her arms up towards the bowl of sky. 'Woohoo. This would almost make me believe there is a God. It's so heavenly . . . so fabulous, so beautiful . . .' Then, she'd unbuckled her seatbelt and, clutching the top of the windscreen, had stood up just as the car had veered around another bend, tyres squealing. 'Hey, this is awesome!'

Jack had immediately slowed down and put out a restraining arm. 'Amy, sit back.'

The picture dissolved in front of him. He wondered where she was in spirit, if she was free-wheeling somewhere around the universe, and if she believed in God now. He was relieved that he'd passed the test and that the fog of despair, which had given way to guilt and then anger, had been finally replaced by a resigned acceptance that would be easier to live with.

His only problem was that he'd cut it very fine to get to the airport in time for the evening flight to Dublin. A subconscious rebellion, he guessed. He rounded another bend at speed and Nice swung into view, a glimpse of red-tiled rooftops topping creamy buildings.

Jesus!

Jack jammed on the brakes – he'd almost crashed into a slow-moving school bus. Suitably chastened, he reduced his speed to a crawl and kept a safe distance from the bus as it trundled into Nice. When he stopped behind it at traffic lights, school-children in the back row twisted around and made faces at him out through the dusty window. Feeling a little silly, he lifted his tanned forearm in half-hearted greeting, and was so taken aback by the wildly enthusiastic response that he missed the turn for the airport and found himself driving into the city. When he was halted again in the thickly congested street, he realised he'd no chance of making his flight.

Serena will love this, he thought. No doubt his darling sis would good-naturedly fuss that he still needed looking after because he couldn't even get to the airport on time. Sometimes, she was far too bossy. Still, he'd never have come through the last year without her support.

He crawled through the sluggish traffic before parking his rental car in an underground car park, leaving his luggage in the boot. When he emerged into the sunshine, he decided to stroll as far as the Old Town for a cup of coffee. He'd text Serena, and stay the night at the Negresco, one of the most exclusive hotels along the Côte d'Azur. There was no point in returning to La Mimosa and, this way, he'd be nearer to the airport and couldn't miss another flight.

Feeling as though he was playing truant, he sat outside a pavement café on the Cours Saleya, drinking coffee and idly watching the world go by. He'd been away for six weeks – one more night wouldn't make any difference.

'Hey, babe, thank Christ you came. We'd have been rightly stuck if you'd said no.'

'Don't you know by now that I absolutely adore my job?' the girl said saucily as she came through the back door of The Anchor and deftly twisted and turned through a narrow gap in a pile of crates and pallets of shrink-wrapped bottles.

'And on your birthday and all . . .'

She paused, alert. 'How did you know it was my birthday?'

Her boss, Michael, picked up a crate of empty

21

beer bottles and smiled. 'I saw your CV and you're a Gemini, like my mum, that's how I remembered.'

She rolled her eyes. 'Yeah, lively and amusing . . . tell me all about it, why don't you?'

'I prefer adaptable and resourceful . . . and rising to the challenge in a crisis.'

'What crisis?' She eyed him suspiciously.

'Two of the waitresses have called in sick and you're the only one who's agreed to come in and cover – for both of them. Somebody less versatile than you might call that a crisis.'

'Told you, I love this joint,' she said nonchalantly.

'I'll make it up to you, promise.'

'You'd better. Any post for me?' she asked, keeping her voice light.

'Post? As in birthday cards, you mean?'

'Huh, I'm not that hard up for a card. It'd be more like a tax demand.'

'No, babe, nothing, lucky you.' Michael kicked open the door to the back yard and humped the crate through. 'Although I'm sure you couldn't get near your apartment door this morning with the avalanche of birthday cards.'

'Too right,' she laughed cheerfully. 'And then you had to spoil it all by looking for my services.'

'Ouch.'

'It's okay, I told you, no sweat.'

'The dish of the day is chicken korma,' Michael said. 'And there's a special beer promo as well. It's all on the blackboard.'

'Good.'

She went into the tiny room that served as a staff changing room, changed into her black top and put on her apron. She checked her face in the mirror, caught her hair back with two plastic butterfly clasps and told herself not to be too disappointed.

Her mum would hardly have sent a card to her work address. But having found her apartment post box empty, she'd wondered if it was some sort of sign when Michael phoned and begged her to come in on her night off to get him out of a hole. For a moment, she'd thought maybe it was fate, that her mum had forgotten the address of her apartment but had remembered where she worked from the postcard she'd sent her.

But there was nothing here either.

Oh, well. Maybe she wasn't getting any birthday greetings, but she'd nobody bothering her. She could do whatever she liked, even if it meant spending her birthday evening serving cheap and cheerful bar food and gallons of drink to the tourists on the Cours Saleya. She gave herself the benefit of a big, bright smile before sticking an order pad and biro into the pocket of her apron and going outside.

It was a long time since Jack had idly mingled with the locals and the tourists swarming around downtown Nice on a Friday evening, and he found himself observing the life going on around him. The Cours Saleya was a pedestrian area full of a vibrant jumble of bars and cafés that sat cheek by jowl, a variety of overhead canopies and different outdoor furniture being the only way to distinguish one from another.

Then he saw her. And once again, Jack felt his life change in a heartbeat.

She was clearing a table outside the adjacent bar, expertly balancing a pile of plates in the crook of her arm while scooping up cutlery and glasses. Slim and petite, her dark hair was short and choppy and was held back from her face by bright butterfly clips.

One of the barmen called out to her and she turned her head and laughed. For a millisecond, Jack wished she'd been laughing with him, at something he'd said, or maybe a joke he'd cracked. It seemed a long time since he'd had a woman laugh at his jokes.

Caught in that moment, he watched her, and there was something contained and sensuous about her that he found terribly attractive. He became aware of the warmth of the sun across his skin, the way it lit her hair and the soft curves of her face.

She must have sensed him watching, for she slowly turned her head to meet his gaze. For a long moment, they stared at each other before she smiled a carefree smile, her eyes mischievous. He found it refreshing after the stiff, embarrassed smiles he'd had to endure since Amy's death. He knew she probably smiled like that at all the tourists but Jack had the sense that someone had lobbed a tiny gemstone into the still, flat pool of his consciousness. She turned away and strutted into the dim interior of The Anchor, as though she was fully aware of his eyes following her, and, more pointedly, as though she liked his attention.

Her name was emblazoned in white lettering across the back of her T-shirt, under the name of the bar.

Jenni, he read.

CHAPTER 3

In Maple Hill, Serena put her car keys beside the crystal bowl on the table and dropped her Hermès briefcase inside the door of the study. She slid her feet out of her spiky Ferragamo heels before padding down the hall through her tasteful dining room with the ivory leather chairs and the solid cherrywood table, and across to the conservatory. Their spacious, light-filled bungalow had been designed to maximise stunning views of the Wicklow scenery and in the conservatory, floor to ceiling French doors framed the view of the mountain backdrop beyond the landscaped grounds. Paul was sitting in his favourite armchair, a gin and tonic on the table beside him. He had changed out of his suit and his dark hair was still damply spiked from the shower.

'Hi darling, mmm, you smell nice.' She went over to him, feeling as though she was tip-toeing across very thin ice. She bent down and kissed him, catching his fresh, clean scent. Then she sat down on a rattan sofa, putting her bag on the floor beside her. 'I'm really sorry about Harriet. I couldn't get away. Claudia's list of special requirements was late coming through and we had to drop everything. *Six* humidifiers were on the list, as well as cotton sheets with a certain thread count we had to rush from Dublin. Panic stations all around. But silly stuff really, it's hardly life or death.'

'Sounds exciting,' Paul said, 'but I wish you didn't feel you have to micro-manage every last detail. You shouldn't be afraid to leave your staff to manage from time to time.'

'Well it's all sorted out now, but I'm raging I missed Harriet going off.'

'Harriet was so thrilled that I didn't even get a look in so I guess you're off the hook this time,' he said ruefully.

'Yes, but it doesn't make me feel any better about myself.'

'Relax, Serena. Forget about it for now. Don't let it spoil our evening.'

'How was your day?'

'Fine. The usual. No last-minute excitements like you, I'm glad to say.'

Paul was a research scientist in a large pharmaceutical company. He did something very clever with experiments, the essentials of which Serena didn't attempt to grasp. He was quiet and unobtrusive about his work and, unlike Serena, who felt as though she was always on call and sometimes had to return to the hotel to sort out an issue, it was only very occasionally that Paul had to go back to the lab after hours. When he talked about problems with test trials, processing results, and analysing streams of data, graph pads and prisms, Serena listened and pretended to understand, even though he could have been discussing the various methods of freezing cauliflower for all she knew. But she did realise that his job was a lot more serious than hers. She and Jack were responsible for the large team of staff that worked in Tamarisk, including their welfare and salaries, before you even got to the guests, but Paul's work was important and a lot more significant than the thread count of cotton sheets or the melting point of ice cream. Through his fastidious and pains-taking work, he was helping to ease suffering and give people a better quality of life.

He was also a computer whizz and, the previous year, when they had upgraded the computer system and website for the hotel, Serena had been very thankful for his patience when he'd sat down with her and the admin staff and carefully explained every last detail, step by step, almost as though he was explaining it to Harriet.

He usually got home from work first – the laboratory in a modern office block in south County Dublin was just a forty-minute commute – which meant he was able to collect Harriet from the crèche in Glendoran, something Serena knew she was guilty of taking for granted a lot of the time.

She was so lucky to be married to him, Serena reminded herself. He was kind and considerate, and carefully protective of both her and Harriet, all the qualities she had sensed about him when they had first met. And he was great in bed. Now, six years into their marriage, he was thirty-nine, with flecks of grey in his dark hair, and he was perfectly toned and fit, thanks to his jogging sessions around the woodland trails in the Wicklow hills and the rugby he played for his university's senior team.

'You still look a little stressed,' Paul said. 'Have a drink. It might help you to unwind.'

'No, thanks, I'm going to have a shower first.'

'I should have waited and showered with you,' he grinned, his dark grey eyes sparking with lust.

Something pulsed inside her. 'I won't be long.'

'I can bring some drinks into the bathroom, if you like?'

'You must be very impatient,' she joked, rising to her feet.

'And why wouldn't I be impatient to make love to my sexy wife?' His smile was contagious and surprisingly warm. God, he was really hot for this, hot for her, her thoughts fluttered. She stood up and had just taken a few paces when she realised she'd left her bag behind. She turned back, cursing as she stubbed her toe against the table.

He looked at her for a long moment, then said, calmly and neutrally, 'Chill, Serena, take as long as you want. I promise I won't come in and jump on top of you.'

*　*　*

Serena went into their bedroom and walked past the super-king-sized bed with the cream lace cover and row of plump, silky cushions.

She stepped into her dressing room and put her bag on a shelf, jumping at her reflection as she passed by the floor-to-ceiling mirror. Paul was right. Caught off guard, her face looked tense and it didn't appear pretty in the mirror. She'd been fortunate to inherit her good bone structure, deep violet eyes and trim figure from her mother.

She took off her white silk shirt and John Rocha trousers and stood in her lacy bra and pants. She lightly shook her head so that her hair fanned around her shoulders. Now she looked less like a busy co-director and more like a sexy wife. In the en suite, she dropped her underwear into the laundry basket, selected her favourite aromatherapy shower oil and massage sponge, and stepped under the warm cascade of water. She closed her eyes and blotted out every-thing except the soothing feel of water running down her body and the circular movements of the sponge. When she came out, wrapped in a thick robe, Paul was sitting in an armchair. There was a glass of white wine on her bedside table. The blinds were drawn, enclosing the room in muted light.

'I guess you got a little impatient,' she said.

'Too right,' he said.

Serena sipped some wine before she went over and sat on his lap.

'I love when you're like this,' his voice throbbed against her skin. 'Still a little damp from the shower and all naked underneath.' He kissed the soft hollow beneath her collar bone. He coiled one hand in her hair and with the other, he loosened the belt of her robe, sliding his hand inside and cupping her breast. 'And as much as I'd love a brother or sister for Harriet,' he said, 'I'm enjoying the making of him or her even more. Even if it's taking longer than we thought.'

His fingernails gently grazed her nipple. It immediately hardened and caused an ache in her groin. She leaned into Paul as he kissed her. Eventually he pushed her to her feet.

'We have until eleven o'clock in the morning. I hope you're up for some fun.'

'Like melted ice cream and chocolate sauce? But our curfew is eight o'clock,' Serena said, putting her arms around his neck, still feeling a little muzzy after his kisses.

'Eight?'

'Yes, I've to be at the hotel in the morning,' she said, hoping he wouldn't mind too much.

He frowned. 'Harriet's expecting you to collect her at eleven. That was the plan. I'm training in the morning.'

Serena bit her lip. God. Something else that had slipped her mind. 'I'll ask Mum to pick her up and look after her for a couple of hours.'

'And what's so important that you can't be there for Harriet? Again?' Paul asked quietly.

31

'I want to greet Claudia when she arrives. It won't take too long.'

'You actually *want* to be there?'

Anxiety rose in her chest. She took a deep breath and pulled her robe around her. 'Look, darling, you know the personal touch is one of the reasons we're successful. I'm hoping it will help swing an award for us.'

'I'd love to know what your definition of success is,' Paul said edgily. 'Surely a business that's weathering the worst of the recession is more than successful? Don't you think that for once the management could look after Claudia without your expert supervision? And why do you think you need this award? What are you trying to prove?'

There was a silence.

'There's nothing wrong with having goals,' she said in a subdued voice.

'I agree, but dammit, Serena, in the past few months our home life has really suffered.'

'I know. I'm sorry I was caught in the office this evening.'

'Where's Jack? I thought he was due home by now?'

'He'll be home later this evening.'

'Good. You've been carrying the can for too long.'

'I didn't have much choice, did I?' Serena pointed out quietly.

'No, I suppose not,' Paul said, looking suitably sober. 'But, honestly, I've a feeling you've been drifting away from me in the past few months. I hope I'm just imagining it.'

Drifting away from him? Serena bit her lip. Being extra busy on account of Jack's absence had been a handy excuse and she had ploughed her energies into Tamarisk to blot out the secrets and shadows that constantly troubled her.

'I just want my wife back,' Paul said.

'I'm right here, so why are we wasting time fighting like this?' she asked huskily.

'I dunno. Why are we?'

She shrugged her shoulders and let her bathrobe drop to the floor. Naked, she stepped towards him and reached for the belt of his trousers. 'I thought we were supposed to be making the most of this evening,' she murmured.

'We were. We are,' Paul said and his dark eyes glittered as they roved across her curves. He stayed motionless, allowing her to open the belt, slide it out of the hooks and push down his jeans. He was already aroused, his hard erection straining against his Calvin Klein boxers. She peeled off his shirt and leaned against his broad chest, before sliding both hands inside his boxers, one cupping his silky hard erection, the other splayed against his muscular ass. That was as far as she got before he groaned and toppled them both onto the bed.

Her head fell back among the pillows and he cradled her face, kissing her forehead, her eyelids, her nose. He ran his hands through her hair and tenderly kissed the side of her face. Moving on down, he caressed her breasts, causing her nipples to tingle with his fingers and then his mouth. He sat up on his elbow for a moment and gazed at her naked body stretched across the bed, his steely, grey eyes heavy with sexual desire.

'I love you, Serena,' he said as his hand slid across her tummy, down to her thighs and into her soft wetness, stroking and teasing.

She wound her arms around his neck and caught him to her, feeling the breadth of his shoulders and the hard heat of his body on hers. She ached to feel the strength of him inside her, catching her breath as he moved between her opened legs, and deliciously filled her up.

Afterwards he turned towards her, brushing tendrils of her hair gently back from her face. 'You were fantastic, my love. And if that doesn't make a baby I don't know what will.'

Serena murmured something, feeling conscience-stricken. Tears pricked the back of her eyes so she squeezed them tightly shut.

God forbid Paul ever found out the truth. It would destroy their marriage and break his heart and mess up Harriet's life big time. They didn't deserve that.

Paul would never find out, she vowed, pressing her hot, damp face into the pillow.

CHAPTER 4

Jack strode across the elegant lobby of the Negresco. He'd lingered far too long over his coffee, but had felt unable to move, mesmerised by the sight of Jenni going about her job. He'd told himself he was nuts. At almost thirty-six, he should have more sense than to be caught up in a fizz of instant attraction – especially after all he'd been through. Soon he'd be back in Tamarisk and he'd pick up the threads again, and time would move on. Eventually, it would be as though his life with Amy had never been, the heartbreak would become a distant memory, and he'd have forgotten all about the girl with dark choppy hair who had put all sorts of mischievous notions into his mind, a mind he'd thought to be safely flatlined.

He asked the receptionist for a deluxe room.

'Oui, Monsieur, we have one available.'

'Fine, I'll take it.' Jack slid his gold credit card out of his wallet.

'For just tonight or . . .?'

'Can I leave that open?'

'Certainly, Monsieur, it is free until next Friday.'

Next Friday.

'Do you wish to reserve a table for dinner in the restaurant, Monsieur?'

Jack wavered. 'Yes, please. In about thirty minutes?'

'Certainly, Monsieur.'

His room was decadent, from the gold tub and matching twin washbasins in the bathroom, the beautiful regency furniture, to the fantastic view from his balcony overlooking the shimmering bay. He unpacked a few items, showered and changed into a pair of slacks and a shirt and tie before going downstairs to the Chanteclar restaurant where he ate a solitary meal. If his strong and beautiful sister was here now, she'd be busy making notes, too intent on analysing everything to relax and enjoy herself. He remembered that he hadn't let Serena know he wasn't on his way home. He took out his mobile and sent the text, before powering off the phone in case she decided to call him back to poke fun at him for missing his flight and ask him when he'd be home.

After his meal he did what he'd been subconsciously planning all evening. He went back upstairs and changed into a pair of denim jeans and a white Timberland top. He cleaned his teeth and took a quick peek at his face in the mirror. While Serena took after their mother, he'd inherited his father's dark-red hair, blue-green eyes, long nose and generous mouth. Suddenly he remembered the time Amy had told him that he was handsome in a Brad Pitt sort of way.

'You remind me a little of him. You could almost be his kid brother,' she'd said.

'Stop taking the piss,' he'd said. Brad Pitt? Bloody hell.

'No, really, Jack. If you grew your hair longer and got blond highlights, you could look like you've walked off the set of *Troy* . . . Some people think I look like Diane Kruger.'

'Who's she?'

'She was in *Troy* as well. I loved that film. All those naked thighs.'

For a long moment, he saw her stretched across their bed, smiling up at him with her cat-like smile and her blonde hair fanned about the pillows. What devil had made him remember? Surely he was finished with her ghost?

Jack glared at himself in the mirror. His hair was longer and now it curled around the back of his neck for the simple reason that he hadn't bothered to get it cut. And the Riviera sun had lightened some of his reddish tints – but it was still a far cry from Brad Pitt's blond mane in *Troy*. Amy had been having serious delusions.

Jack turned impatiently from the mirror. Leaving the hotel, he strolled down in the darkened evening to the Old Town and the Cours Saleya. He couldn't remember where he'd been sitting earlier that day as it all looked so different at night. The night was aromatic with tempting cooking smells, the vibrant scene lit up with rows of tiny bulbs, strung together and suspended along the edge of the awnings like lengths of bright, gaudy necklaces.

He strolled up one side of the street and halfway down the other absorbing the babble of different voices and the party atmosphere, and then he spotted The Anchor. As soon as he paused outside, a young woman came forward and proffered a menu.

'A table?' she asked in accented English.

Jack waved away the menu. 'No food, just beer, please?' he hazarded, wondering if he'd be refused a table as he wasn't eating.

'Just beer is fine,' she smiled, leading him across to a small table under the awning. He was conscious of a swirl of nervous excitement in spite of his foolhardiness. She disappeared into the bar and minutes later, Jenni came out with his beer. She recognised him immediately.

He was glad she remembered him. 'Sorry,' he put up his hands in mock surrender and smiled as disarmingly as he could. 'I'm not trying to stalk you or anything like that. I just fancied soaking up some of the party atmosphere. And maybe . . .' he hesitated.

'Yes?' She looked at him a little suspiciously as she placed the beer in front of him.

'Maybe saying hello, chat a little . . . that's all, honestly.'

She looked at him for a long time.

'I'm Jack. I'm from Ireland,' he went on hurriedly. 'I don't really know what I'm doing here. Oh look, it seemed a good idea at the time but—'

'Hey Jack-from-Ireland. Chill,' she said, smiling at last. 'It's no big deal. Why don't you just relax and enjoy your beer. I'm Jenni. And if I've time to talk, we'll talk. Okay?'

No big deal, he told himself, his eyes following her as she moved to the next table.

'Who's the guy?' Michael asked Jenni later.

'What guy?' Jenni feigned innocence.

'I've seen him chatting you up.'

'Come on, he's just a tourist who looks a little lonely.' She set down her tray and swiftly scraped leftover food into a basin, clattering the used cutlery into another container.

'Don't be falling for that lonely tourist spiel.'

'I'm not falling for anything,' she shrugged. 'A bit of friendly chat never did anyone any harm. It's part of the job.'

'And that's as far as it should go, a bit of friendly chat. For all you know, he's a knife-wielding psychopath.'

'Nah. His name is Jack and he's Irish.'

'Irish. God. Don't you dare fall for his charming tongue.'

'He might ask me for a birthday drink,' she said mischievously, testing Michael's reaction.

'You just be careful, that's all.'

'Now you sound like my mother.'

'So you *have* a mother? And there was me thinking you were all alone in the world.'

'Get lost, Michael.'

Humming underneath their casual exchanges about the night life, the tourists, the busy season, Jack felt as though some kind of connection was forming with Jenni. He watched the graceful, slightly self-conscious way she moved about the tables and from time to time put her hand to her butterfly slides or fiddled with the silver chain around her neck. Her eyes studied him from under her dark lashes and she threw him a sidelong glance when he wasn't expecting it. The silent but unmistakeable language of flirtation.

Eventually, things quietened down as tables became vacant and people moved on. 'What time do you finish?' he asked.

'Why?'

He floundered. He was used to fighting back advances from throngs of determined women and her question threw him. He'd obviously made an ass of himself. Not surprising, considering how long it had been since he'd chatted up anyone. 'I'd like to bring you for a drink,' he said, amazed at the words coming out of his mouth. All he knew was that he would be sorely disappointed if she turned him down.

'Okay, just the one,' she said. 'I should be through in about half an hour.'

When Jenni emerged at the end of her shift,

something sparked inside him. They strolled together through the Old Town in the warm night air, the top of her head just reaching his chin. They sat down outside a bar not too far from where Jenni worked. When their drinks arrived, another beer for him and a white wine for Jenni, she took out her mobile and said, 'I don't usually allow myself to be picked up at work and go for a drink with a man I hardly know. My boss thinks you could be a knife-wielding psychopath. So I've to send him a text soon or he'll send out a search party.'

'I'm afraid I'm not that exciting. And it's a long time since I asked someone to come for a drink on the spur of the moment,' he admitted.

'The spur of the moment?' she laughed softly, her brown eyes full of amusement. Her voice was tinged with merriment and had a distinctive English accent. 'I was sure you'd been planning this all evening.'

'How did you guess?' he said, meeting and holding her eyes. Then after a little pause he said, 'So why did you come?'

'It's my birthday. That's why.'

'Happy Birthday, Jenni. I know I'm not supposed to ask your age, but . . .'

'It's okay. I'm twenty-four.'

Twenty-four. Just starting out in life, no wonder she seemed so carefree. As they chatted, Jack found he couldn't take his eyes off her. The combination of her confidence and warm, devil-may-care smile that was constantly lurking around her mouth was beguiling. As time went on, he began responding to her, as though she had switched on a more light-hearted version of himself that he'd forgotten existed. Then before he realised it, his glass was empty and Jenni was draining the last of her wine.

'One drink, that's what you agreed to,' Jack said, unwilling to push his luck but privately hoping the night wasn't ending just yet.

She pushed away her glass and rose to her feet. 'Yes, that's right. One drink.' Then she gave him an impish smile. 'But you can walk me home if you like? It's about thirty minutes. Although I won't be asking you in for coffee, understood?'

He felt elated. 'Gotcha.'

As they walked out into the soft night, up along through the Masséna gardens and park, the musky perfume rose from the flower beds lending magic to the evening. As they approached the square, they came to a dip in the park, where the grass gave way to a large, circular flag-stoned area. Jack heard music playing and, as they drew nearer, saw that couples of all ages were dancing around, with many more sitting around the perimeter wall.

'Hey! Let's dance,' Jenni said, stalling suddenly.

'No way. I've two left feet,' Jack said, feeling foolish.

'That's no excuse. When was the last time you danced?'

The last time he'd danced? Jack faltered, his mind plunging backwards, an image of Amy flinging her arms around his neck and dragging him onto the dance floor, her body flailing against the length of his. They'd been at someone's wedding, a friend of Amy's, he couldn't quite recall who. All he could remember was the embarrassment of supporting her body against his as he led her around the floor; he'd carried her up to their room as soon as he could drag her away. That was the last time he'd danced.

'Hey, Jack, are you with me? Come on, it's my birthday and it's fun.'

Jack came back to the present, to the warmth of a mellow night. Jenni hitched up her shoulder bag and held out her arms.

Fun. It was a long time since he'd had some honest-to-goodness fun. And it was so, so different to all that had gone before that he felt like a drowning man suddenly breaking free from the deep, dark depths to the bright, glittering surface. He stepped forward, feeling as though he was moving away from the past, and took her into his arms. He wasn't sure what they were dancing to, just that the music was energetic. Jenni was light and sensuous in her movements. The air was imbued with warmth and the shadowy night-time lent an intimacy to everything. After a while, he realised that he didn't feel in the least bit foolish, rather he was full of an unexpected joy.

When there was a break in the music, Jenni said she had to get home. 'I'm on the early shift tomorrow and I need my sleep.' Together they

43

strolled down the Avenue Jean-Médecin, turned a couple of corners and then, outside a slightly shabby four-storey apartment block, Jenni said she was home.

'So if you're on the early shift tomorrow, does that mean you get off early tomorrow night?' Jack asked. One part of his mind wondered why he was even talking about the following day, when he should be out of here on the first available flight. But home meant the empty house with the silent rooms and that suddenly seemed unbearable compared to a joyful Saturday evening in Nice with Jenni. A free and unfettered recklessness made him reach out his hand and stroke her soft cheek. Then, he bent and kissed her lightly, taking her by surprise. Taking himself by surprise with the pleasure it brought.

'Just a birthday kiss,' he said.

Jenni smiled. 'That's allowed. I'm on split shift tomorrow which means time off in the afternoon before I go back for the evening. Same on Sunday. Why?'

'I was hoping to bring you somewhere for a meal. To celebrate your birthday properly.'

'I get free food in work,' she grinned, and he knew she was teasing him. 'But, hey, I could give it a miss and meet up with you instead, maybe have a picnic in the Parc du Château?'

'I've never been there,' he said.

She shook her head and said she'd have to fix that, and he should meet her at three o'clock on the corner down from the bar. Then, she slipped through the doorway, waving goodbye. Jack strolled back to the Negresco, thinking that a picnic in the Parc du Château sounded perfectly innocent – a flight home the last thing on his mind.

CHAPTER 5

O n Saturday morning, Charlotte Devlin
woke up far too early. She lay in bed
listening to the chorus of sparrows outside
and watched daylight brighten against the window
blind. Yet again, she found herself asking why the
beginning of the rest of her life seemed to be rather
slow in arriving. She was glad that Serena had
phoned her to ask her to collect Harriet from
her friend's house that morning. Looking after her
granddaughter for a couple of hours would keep
her occupied and take her mind off herself.

Her granddaughter was ready and waiting for
her and Charlotte's heart overflowed when Harriet
hurtled down the garden path of Sophie's house
and into her arms. Harriet was a joy, and at four
years of age was at that lovable and uncomplicated
stage when she had no inhibitions about allowing
you to pick her up and hug and kiss her. Charlotte
soaked up the feeling of the little body clinging to
hers. After she had strapped Harriet into the
booster seat of her Saab, they drove off, waving
at Sophie, and took the turn to bring them through
the village of Glendoran.

'Did you have fun, Harriet?' Charlotte's eyes met Harriet's in the rear-view mirror.

'Yes, Nana,' Harriet's dark eyes sparkled. 'We had face painting and I was a monster, then we watched the Disney channel and stayed up really, really late.' Harriet's high-pitched voice chattered non-stop about the treats she'd enjoyed.

It should really have been Serena enjoying the warmth of this unbridled excitement, this unconditional love, Charlotte thought. In a few short years, Harriet wouldn't allow you to make eye contact, or hold her hand in yours, never mind giving you a detailed rundown of the previous night's excitements. The early years were very precious and Serena was missing out. She'd returned to work too soon after Harriet's birth, throwing herself far too wholeheartedly into the renovation of the Spa.

But who was she to talk when it came to not having enough time for your children? Outside Glendoran, Charlotte drove up the narrow hill, past the tumbling gorse-filled hedgerows and overhanging chestnut trees, and, just past the bend in the river, she turned into the laneway that led to Tamarisk. If Serena happened to glance at any of the security monitors, she'd see her mother's car gliding through the entrance, the image captured by a camera that was so discreet it went undetected by the guests. And, even if she did spot them, it was highly unlikely that Serena would drop over to her mother's house to say hello – not until she was sure that Claudia was fully settled in and happy.

Charlotte drove up the avenue and around to the back of the hotel to where she lived in a renovated coach house tucked behind the Tranquil Garden. When Serena and Jack were young, the family had lived in a ground-floor wing of the hotel until the coach house had been restored and became the family home. She was parking in her garage when she heard the roar of Claudia's helicopter as it landed in the hotel grounds, a little later than scheduled.

By the time Serena called around, Harriet was asleep on Charlotte's sofa, worn out from all her excitements.

'You can leave her here if you like,' Charlotte offered, keeping her voice quiet. 'I'll bring her home later.'

'No, Mum, you've done more than enough. She'll be fine. Anyway if she sleeps all day, she'll be up all night.'

Serena was immaculately turned out as usual but Charlotte knew by the strained smile that didn't reach her eyes that her daughter was tense. 'Everything go okay this morning?'

Serena nodded. 'Yes, fine. Claudia and her steel ring of stylists and minders are already chilling out.'

'Good. You'll stay for coffee, won't you?' she said.

'Sorry, Mum, I can't. Lots to do.'

'Don't you ever give yourself a break?' Charlotte didn't mean the words to come out. 'Why don't you and Paul go out tonight? I've nothing on, I'll gladly babysit Harriet.'

'Maybe another night. I might ask you to look after Harriet for a weekend so that we can go away. As soon as Jack's home. You won't believe this, but after I phoned you last night he texted me to say he'd missed his flight.'

Charlotte was immediately concerned. 'You're joking? I hope there's nothing wrong.'

'He would have told me if there was.'

'I suppose . . . still, that's not like him.' Charlotte couldn't help a note of anxiety in her voice. 'Look, are you sure you won't have coffee?'

Charlotte was glad when Serena changed her mind. 'Well, okay. Just a quick cup. I've to go grocery shopping before I go home.'

Charlotte took mugs out of the press. 'One quick cup coming up. Did Jack sort out another flight?'

Serena shook her head. 'He hasn't been in touch since his text. I called him this morning but just got his voicemail. Hopefully we'll see him this evening or tomorrow.'

'He seems to have been gone a long time,' Charlotte said slowly.

Serena nodded in a way that told Charlotte she understood the subtext of her words. For in reality, Jack had been gone from them for a lot longer than the weeks he'd spent in La Mimosa. A year – correction, almost two years, if you count the way Amy had hogged him all to herself.

'I hope Jack's feeling better,' Charlotte said.

'So do I,' Serena replied. 'Anyway, how did you get on last night? Sorry if I interrupted anything with my phone call.'

Last night had been a late night for Charlotte. She'd been invited to a launch of a new signature restaurant in a boutique Dublin hotel. The invite had included a friend but she'd chosen to go alone.

'I'd a great night,' Charlotte smiled. 'And you didn't interrupt me. People were making the most of the free bar and harassing me to stay over, so I was glad of a cast-iron excuse to come home.'

Charlotte had passed on the generously flowing wine and champagne. She'd enjoyed the evening, but had been happy to leave before it got too late and drive home, soft music playing as her car effortlessly purred through the shadowy night, towards Tamarisk and home.

'Whatever about me, it's time you started going out more often and letting your hair down,' Serena told her.

'Yes, dear.'

'I mean it, Mum. You're still young and should be making the most of your good years.'

'You're right, Serena.' Charlotte smiled at her daughter.

She was sidetracked as Harriet woke, cranky and disorientated, and clearly still tired. Serena made a fuss of her daughter in a vain attempt to cajole her into a better humour.

After they had left, and faced with the prospect of an empty afternoon ahead and a quiet night in with nothing but her thoughts for company, Charlotte phoned the Spa in Tamarisk to book a massage.

'Most of the slots are full this afternoon thanks to Claudia's gang, and two of our therapists have been booked for her private facilities,' Rita, the Spa manager, said. 'But Trudi, our new therapist, is free due to a cancellation and she's highly qualified.'

'That's great, Rita, please book me in,' Charlotte said, knowing that Serena wouldn't dream of hiring anyone who hadn't got the best qualifications to join the Spa staff.

That afternoon Charlotte went across to the leisure complex. In the private changing room that Serena had incorporated for her in the ladies' area, she undressed, hanging up her Marc Jacobs trousers and red jersey top and, wearing just her knickers – lace trimmed and pink silk La Senza, as she'd always believed in luxury next to her skin – she donned the thick cream robe, monogrammed with the Tamarisk Spa logo, and slid her feet into matching slippers. Then she padded out into the Spa reception.

'Mrs Devlin? I'm Trudi, your therapist for this afternoon.' Her voice was tentative and very soft, overlaid with a west of Ireland lilt. Her face was full of anxiety.

'That's me, and please don't look so nervous, Trudi, I'm not going to bite you!'

'Sorry, Mrs Devlin—' Trudi's face flooded with colour.

'Please call me Charlotte,' she smiled kindly. 'I'm the same as any other customer. I'll let you in on a secret, my daughter's the one to watch out for around here.'

'Serena's lovely. She made me feel so welcome and part of the team.' As she spoke, Charlotte noticed that Trudi had the look in her eyes that said she'd already put Serena on a pedestal. As did most of the Tamarisk staff.

'I'm glad to hear that,' Charlotte said, before raising a conspiratorial eyebrow as though they were sharing a joke. 'She's the one who's in charge. Me? I'm almost beyond my sell-by date.'

Trudi looked surprised. 'I wouldn't exactly say that, Mrs . . . em . . . Charlotte.'

Charlotte only made the self-deprecating joke about her age to relax Trudi. Privately, she felt that, at almost fifty-eight, she was nowhere near her sell-by date. She could give Helen Mirren a run for her money in that famous red bikini shot, and do a couple of laps of the hotel pool without stopping for breath.

Aloud she said, with a short laugh, 'Well you won't find that many men queuing up to ask me out. Not at my age. I'm not even sure if they do that anymore, or if it's all done through text and the internet. Or this speed dating thingy I've also heard about. I must give it a go sometime.'

Trudi smiled faintly, and Charlotte knew she still felt unsure of her ground. It was a position she hated putting people in. She was no different from anyone else and had worked very hard to get where she was.

'A back massage?' Trudi said, checking the file that held Charlotte's details.

'Yes, I don't like too much pressure, although some of my knots might need a little ironing out.'

'You normally have lemongrass and orange oil for the massage . . .' Trudi read from the file, her voice trailing away.

'That's it, although I'm sure it's called something far more sophisticated on the treatment menu,' Charlotte smiled reassuringly, 'but it sounds about right.'

'I'll leave you to get ready and be back in a minute.'

Charlotte slipped out of her robe and slippers, and stretched out on her tummy on the treatment bed, pulling a heated, chocolate-shaded towel up to her hips. The candlelit room was peacefully designed in warm tones of taupe and cream and, in the background, music played softly.

After Trudi returned, she was soon gently massaging warm oil in slow, sweeping strokes on Charlotte's back, moving upwards from her hips, across her shoulder blades and into her neck.

'You seem to be holding a lot of tension in these

muscles,' Trudi said, her fingers and thumbs delicately teasing out the knots in Charlotte's shoulders. 'Tell me if the pressure is too much.'

'You're fine,' Charlotte said, feeling the pressure yet glad to notice a slight loosening up in response to Trudi's massage. 'I didn't realise I was so wound up.'

'It happens to us all. The general stresses and strains of life prevent us from relaxing our bodies properly.'

Charlotte felt herself relax as Trudi continued her massage and by the time she was finished, Charlotte had helplessly slid into another zone.

'Take your time getting up,' Trudi said. 'I'll be outside.'

'Well done, you were wonderful,' Charlotte told her, when she eventually gathered enough willpower to get up off the bed, put back on her robe and come through to the reception area.

'Thank you,' Trudi said shyly.

She handed Charlotte a glass of still water, necessary, she said, in view of the lymphatic drainage she'd just facilitated. When Charlotte had finished, Trudi ushered her towards the Quiet Room, the first-floor relaxation room that had a view across the woods to the Wicklow mountains and that promised to reinforce the feeling of pure, undiluted bliss after a treatment.

'I don't normally bother with this . . .' Charlotte began to say.

Trudi's face dropped.

'Maybe just this once, I'll indulge myself,' Charlotte said, not wanting to leave Trudi with a sense of failure. Half an hour or so wouldn't kill her.

'Can I get you anything else to drink?' Trudi asked. 'Or would you like music?'

There were oriental teas, fruit juices and chilled mineral water available in the Quiet Room, in addition to personal iPods with a choice of music.

'No, I'm fine thanks,' Charlotte said. 'And, Trudi, well done again.' Then, wrapped in her robe, Charlotte lay back on one of the ergonomic recliners and gazed out through the expanse of glass at the peaks and valleys of the stunning panorama.

Most visitors were refreshed and rejuvenated with their visit to the Quiet Room, but Charlotte found that she had no such mindless euphoria, for now that the sleep-inducing effects of Trudi's massage had evaporated, her brain was on the alert as she thought of her children. She knew that neither of them was happy and, deep in her heart, she felt she shared part of the blame.

Amy's death had devastated Charlotte. The problem was, she'd never really warmed to her, and from her capricious and unpredictable behaviour at family gatherings, Charlotte had also suspected that Amy had a drink problem. It was something Jack had done his best to gloss over, but it was a pattern of behaviour she'd all too easily recognised. She'd asked herself why her son had rushed into marriage with someone rather weak and wayward, and why he'd covered up Amy's drinking, but she knew she'd provided a role model for her son to follow, in the way she'd always covered up for her husband's drinking. She'd been surprised when Jack had bolted to La Mimosa. She'd thought he'd been slowly adjusting to life without Amy – obviously something had set him back. God knows what mood he'd be in when he came home.

As for Serena . . .

She wondered how Serena was getting on with a fractious Harriet. Charlotte had been delighted when Serena had started seeing Paul the year after her husband's death. Serena had taken her father's death quite badly and Paul had made her eyes sparkle again. Their wedding had been a sumptuous affair, held in Tamarisk, putting it on the map in a way it had never been before.

'This is the icing on the cake,' Serena had said, hardly able to contain her excitement as she'd spread glossy magazines containing photos of her wedding day across Charlotte's kitchen table.

'How does Paul feel about all this?' Charlotte had asked.

'He's pleased as well,' Serena had said, bursting with happiness and contentment. 'God, Mum, I really love Paul, he's my grounding force. Our honeymoon was blissful. And if I hadn't got him behind me, none of this would matter.'

Full of enthusiasm, and radiating love and

happiness, Serena had led an extensive marketing campaign, capitalising on her elevated platform. Before long, both Charlotte and Serena's BlackBerrys had been bulging with contacts, their post full of party invitations.

But although it had all seemed very exciting, Serena was now working harder than ever to maintain standards and make up for Jack being elsewhere. She was too proud to accept help from Charlotte, which meant that she sometimes neglected Harriet and Paul. Charlotte hoped she was imagining it, but there were times lately when her gut instinct was telling her that Serena seemed almost glad to be preoccupied, mirroring the way her mother had ploughed all her energy into running Tamarisk for most of her adult life.

Her thoughts were interrupted when two young women in their twenties sashayed into the Quiet Room and relaxed on recliners. Charlotte guessed by their exotic air that they were part of Claudia's cavalcade, so she closed her eyes and pretended she was relaxing. And the question she'd been avoiding all day popped back into her head, teasing and mocking her. Even Serena had pointed out that she should be making the most of her good years, so what was stopping her from moving on? She knew regrets were useless and living in the moment was all-important, but if you couldn't move on, maybe it was good to revisit the past and take a look back at what had shaped your life, like looking at an old movie reel, even if it was painful. It might help you accept the person you had become so you could tell yourself it was okay, maybe you had messed up, but, hey, you did your best.

She must have dozed off, because the next thing she knew, Trudi was whispering in her ear and gently shaking her. 'Mrs Devlin . . . Charlotte . . .'

Charlotte struggled into wakefulness. 'Gosh, I must have nodded off,' she said, feeling disorientated.

Trudi's eyes were anxious. 'Sorry to disturb you, but . . .' she hesitated.

Charlotte examined her face. 'I was snoring my brains out, wasn't I?'

'Well . . .' Trudi tried to look composed but her expressive face betrayed her.

Snoring in the Quiet Room. Serena would have had a fit.

'It's okay, Harriet's already told me that I snore when she cuddles up to me in bed. But the gentle kind of snore, not like her father's monster-like explosions.'

'Harriet?'

'My granddaughter,' Charlotte explained hurriedly. She glanced around to see who else had witnessed her faux pas. More guests had arrived while she'd been asleep. The two exotic girls were plugged into iPods and another client was engrossed in a magazine, but a man on the adjacent recliner had clearly heard every snore and the whispered conversation with Trudi. He was pretending to be chilling out and minding his own business, and his eyes were closed to small crescents, but there was an amused grin playing on his been-there, done-that face. He was tall. She knew this by the way the bathrobe only came to his knees. His silvering hair was cut quite short and he had a face that looked as though he took no prisoners, and she immediately guessed he was one of Claudia's personal bodyguards.

He must have sensed her glare and he gave up the struggle of pretence and opened his eyes. Charlotte immediately looked away, gathered her dignity about her before rising to her feet gracefully, making sure her robe was secure around her body. She had a jolting realisation that his close proximity and awareness of her had made her hotly conscious of her near-naked body.

She couldn't help smiling to herself. So there was something there, still, in spite of everything that had happened.

CHARLOTTE 1969–1973

Her darling papa told her to never look back. 'The future is what counts, Charlotte, your future. Nothing else matters to us, so make it worthwhile for your mama and me. We have closed the door on the past and all its sorrow. It is all behind us.'

It wasn't, though, not really. Her parents pretended they'd severed all connection with the past for Charlotte's sake, so that she'd grow up proud and strong, and, most importantly, free and American. But even though their lives in an underprivileged suburb of Chicago were a far cry from post-war Poland, she knew they were old before their time and saw the sadness at the back of their eyes, and when she heard her mother weep to the lyrics of Elvis Presley's 'In the Ghetto', she knew she was remembering Warsaw and the country she'd fled with her husband just after the Second World War had ended.

Charlotte had come into their lives several years later, and long after they'd given up hope of having a child. They lavished all their love, hopes and dreams on her. That was why she worked hard at school, and why, when some of her contemporaries skived off, heading to a music festival at Woodstock, Charlotte stayed at home and made herself indispensible in her first job in a downtown Chicago hotel. This, she determined, was only the start. Her sights were on New York and she'd get there eventually.

'In America, anything is possible if you work hard enough,' Papa said.

Two years later, she found herself in that glittering city, being interviewed by a man with horn-rimmed glasses. 'Now then, Miss – em Walcheck,' he said.

'It's Walczak,' she automatically corrected his mispronunciation and then berated herself for blowing her chances of a job she wanted with all her heart.

'Charlotte,' he smiled faintly at her. Suddenly he wasn't so terrifying after all. He said, 'Tell me in your own words why you'd like this job. Forget about what's written on your application form and the fifty others I have in front of me.' He sat back and looked as though he could have waited all day.

Fifty? He had to be exaggerating. She steadied herself, took her time, and then she took a deep breath and said, 'I'd love to work here because even though I was nervous coming for this interview, my heart jumped with excitement when I crossed the foyer. It's a magic ground that drew me in. It's so beautiful and busy, as well as important and exciting. New York is exciting and beautiful and this great hotel is one of its biggest landmarks. I would find it a joy to work here.'

She must have said something right, because she got the job and two weeks later, at nineteen years of age, she found herself working as part of the house-keeping staff in Fitzgerald's of Fifth Avenue. It was a whole new glittering universe and a big step up for the daughter of working-class Polish immigrants who were deeply proud of her.

Charlotte found it hard to grasp the sheer splendour of the hotel, from the lavishly appointed foyer, the corridors with carpets so thick you could sink into them, to the elegant bedrooms and sumptuous suites. She hadn't known such luxury could exist, or that women could own so many pairs of glamorous high-heeled shoes and luxury jars of face creams, as well as the crystal flagons of expensive scent that lined up on a dressing table, never mind have rails full of whispering, opulent gowns hanging in their wardrobes, so fine and exquisite that she was afraid to breathe near them. She couldn't imagine what other luxuries they might have in their equally lavish homes. One day that'll be me, she told herself as the first year slipped past as she conscientiously went about her duties, little knowing how it might come about.

At first she ignored the chit-chat in the staff canteen . . .

'He'd remind you of a Hollywood star.'

'Really? I heard he's Irish.'

'He's here for six months getting experience because he owns a hotel back in Ireland.'

'You mean it's owned by his family.'

'Yes, but he's the heir, same thing!'

Charlotte kept her mind on the job and only believed what her good friend Martha told her. She knew by now that the gossipy waiting and house-keeping staff were great for embellishing the truth. Every other boyfriend was compared to an actor or a singer. But the first time she saw Jamie Devlin she realised the rumours had not been exaggerated. He had thick, dark red hair and laughing blue-green eyes in a square-jawed, attractive face. He was surrounded by a bevy of off-duty waitresses, fluttering around him as though he'd possessed a magical aura, giggling at everything he said. The rumours were almost correct. He saw her looking at him and she turned away, feeling annoyed that she'd been caught staring.

She soon found out that Jamie had lashings of confidence, a quick-witted ability to find the funny side to everything and was possessed with a huge fondness for life. She seemed to bump into him quite regularly in the corridors and began to suspect that he was deliberately engineering their meetings, but she couldn't believe it when he asked her to accompany him to see *Jesus Christ Superstar* on Broadway. Then he brought her to see Stevie Wonder at Madison Square Garden. Soon, it was all around Fitzgerald's that they were practically engaged and Charlotte felt a mixture of excitement, embarrassment and a huge dollop of self-doubt. No one had ever entranced her like Jamie. But what could he possibly see in her?

'You've put a spell on me,' he said, holding her

close, his blue-green eyes smiling into hers. 'Your hair is like pale, golden silk, and the shade of your eyes reminds me of the lavender that grows in the walled garden back home in Tamarisk.'

'You've a great way with words,' she said to him, her heart hammering, afraid to believe what he was saying.

Martha had advised her to take little notice of what Jamie might say. 'The charm of the Irish is legendary. There's only one thing he's after,' she warned. 'Don't let him break your heart. Or get you into trouble.'

'He's going to break my piggy bank first,' Charlotte said. 'I'm running out of outfits to wear and I can only mix and match so often. If I spend any more time going through the bargain rails in Macy's to see what I can afford, I'll be arrested on suspicion of shoplifting. And he won't get me into trouble. No way.'

'You're my ice queen,' he said one night, 'but I'll melt your heart.'

She didn't mind being called his ice queen. It set her apart from the girls who flirtatiously followed him through the back corridors of Fitzgerald's, wearing their hearts on their sleeve. But she didn't know whether Martha or she was the more shocked when Jamie proved to be old fashioned in more ways than one and after their whirlwind courtship, he asked Charlotte to marry him and return to Ireland with him.

'You have to come home to Tamarisk with me,' he said. 'I see you there, walking through the park with the sunlight on your hair. It's a magic place.'

In spite of her misgivings she was intrigued. 'In what way?'

'It's beautiful, just like you, whether it's winter or summer. Sometimes, the mountains seem to be floating in the mist, other times they sparkle in the sun, but they always catch you by the heart, although not as deeply as the way you catch me.'

No one had ever spoken to her like this before.

'Do you love him?' Martha asked.

'Yes, of course! He makes me feel wonderful and very special . . . I never expected to feel like this, ever. I can't believe he wants me but I can't imagine being without him.'

'Have you gone all the way with him?'

'Martha! Of course not.' Charlotte felt her face reddening. 'Well, not quite . . .' she admitted, knowing already that her ice queen label was history thanks to Jamie's hungry kisses and the way he ran his hands over her curves, slipping his fingers under her clothes and whipping up her desire until she halted him. She might have had a disadvantaged upbringing in terms of material things but some things had been ingrained in her by her parents, and she was nobody's fool.

'Then I guess you got lucky, honey. Grab him with both hands.'

'I think I will,' she said, pinching herself at the

amazing turn her life had taken and the wonderful prospect of being Jamie's wife.

Jamie couldn't wait to be married. He wanted to bring her home to Ireland as his bride. His family couldn't travel for the wedding ceremony, so, on her twenty-first birthday, they had a quiet, registry office wedding in New York, followed by a meal in Fitzgerald's with Charlotte's parents and some friends. She and Jamie were going on honeymoon to Cape Cod, before flying to Ireland. Charlotte was intoxicated with the excitement of it all, although leaving her parents was a huge wrench.

'Be happy,' Papa said, when they had a quiet moment with her. 'We're overjoyed that you have such a lovely man and are blessed with a great future. It's everything we hoped for.'

Her mother hugged her. 'You'll have a great life in Ireland. It is a beautiful country. But be careful, darling, they have their troubles.'

Charlotte understood that her mother was concerned, but Jamie had impressed upon them that Wicklow was perfectly safe. 'I'll be back to visit,' she told them, knowing that visits would be few and far between and, most likely, short-lived. 'It's time for us to go and catch our train,' Papa said. 'We've said goodbye to Jamie and entrusted you to his care. So go on, Charlotte, turn around and go to your new husband and the start of your new life. And please,' he smiled, 'don't look back.'

She suppressed sudden tears and dug her nails

into her hands to distract her from the painful dart in her chest as she straightened her shoulders, turned and walked away – but she hadn't looked back.

CHAPTER 6

Harriet jumped in front of the trolley as Serena pushed it past gleaming freezers of ice cream.

'Mummy, we need these,' she ordered peremptorily, heaving open a refrigerator door with all the strength in her four-year-old arms and pulling out a carton of colourful ice lollies, which she dropped into the trolley.

'No, Harriet,' Serena said, looking at how many sugary treats Harriet had already lobbed in. Her daughter was having a field day. She'd sensed Serena's distracted state and was taking full advantage of it by slipping in bars of chocolate and packets of sweets among the organic fruit and vegetables, treats that were usually restricted. Serena picked up the carton and replaced it in the freezer.

'I *want* them!' Harriet jutted out her bottom lip. 'All my friends have nice things in the fridge.'

'No, love,' Serena said smoothly. 'You've already enough sweet things in the trolley. And I've got you some frozen yogurts.'

But there was no reasoning with Harriet. 'But I

need them!' She pushed her face against the glass of the freezer door.

Heads turned at the sound of her raised, childish voice. Then Harriet threw herself across the front of the trolley. 'You're *mean*, Mum! Ice pops, ice pops, I want the ice pops!' she chanted loudly.

Serena tried to push the trolley forward but Harried had looped one arm through the door handle of the freezer and the other was grimly clutching the trolley and supporting the weight of her body.

'Harriet! If you don't stop this I'll . . .' Serena hissed ineffectually.

The previous night, Serena and Paul had stayed in bed, making love again and again, Paul drawing out his foreplay unbearably slowly so that she was trembling on the edge of need and almost sobbing for release. At around nine o'clock, he'd wrapped her in the duvet, and she'd phoned Charlotte quickly while he put a pizza in the oven and opened more wine. Cuddled in bed, they'd watched a rom-com on DVD. After which, he'd brought in the chocolate sauce. Later again, they'd showered together.

Sometime during the evening, when Jack's text message had come through on her mobile to say he'd missed his flight, she'd ignored it.

She'd left for Tamarisk early that morning without waking Paul, tip-toeing out of the room, feeling like a big, huge fraud.

Now she felt caught in a bottomless pit of failure. She couldn't even handle a squabble over a few ice lollies. A rush of tears stung her eyes and her vision blurred. Dear God, this was ridiculous. She even looked ridiculous, shopping in her suit and heels. The manic business of supermarket shopping on a busy Saturday afternoon was anathema to her. Maria, her housekeeper, who came in four mornings a week, looked after Serena's house, shopping and doing laundry with a mixture of pride, affection and ruthless efficiency and usually filled up the fridge, freezer and larders on quiet Thursday mornings. Besides, Serena had a lot of her meals in Tamarisk when she wasn't going to dinner parties or out with Paul. But Maria was on holiday.

With pinpoint accuracy, Harriet gauged her change of mood. 'Mum, please?' she wheedled. 'Just these?' Her daughter gave a whoop of triumph when Serena nodded.

The checkout was a nightmare of packing her bags haphazardly, rummaging for her credit card, and momentarily forgetting her pin number, while Harriet jigged with glee at the number of goodies passing along the belt. She picked up the box of ice lollies and waved them triumphantly in the air. Then sticking out her tongue, she made a big drama of licking the outside of the box for the benefit of the young boy standing with his mother in the queue behind them. Serena hadn't even the energy to check her.

When they reached Maple Hill, Paul had just arrived home from his rugby match.

'Daddy!' Harriet called out, running into his outstretched arms, allowing herself to be picked up and whirled around the kitchen.

'Did you have a good time last night, honey?' he asked, putting her up on his shoulders so that her head almost reached the ceiling. Harriet squealed and held on tightly to him and searched for a suitable word. 'It was . . . it was *monster* good!'

'Oh wow. Sounds great. Mummy and Daddy had a monster good night as well, didn't we?' He winked mischievously at Serena. Her stomach did a double flip.

'Why, what did you do?' Harriet asked. 'We stayed up for *ages* and had . . . had *hundreds* of sweets.'

'Daddy stayed up for ages as well, didn't he, Mummy?' Paul's eyes met hers as they gleamed with satisfaction.

Serena felt able to ignore him as Harriet clamoured to get down and go through her haul of treats, rummaging in the shopping bags and lining them up on the limestone worktop.

'Jeez.' Paul shook his head. 'There must be enough additives there to send her into orbit.'

'Just as well Maria usually does the shopping,' Serena said. She moved around from fridge to freezer to larder as she put the shopping away, feeling that she was moving like some kind of stiff marionette.

'Are you okay?' Paul came up behind her as she stood by the kitchen worktop, folding the empty shopping bags.

'Yes, why?' She tried not to sound too sharp.

'You look – I dunno, a little frazzled.'

'Frazzled?' Serena frowned.

'Maybe you're just tired after last night.' He clasped his arms around her waist and dropped a kiss on the side of her neck. 'Some night, wasn't it?'

'Sure was,' she twisted around in his embrace and plastered a smile on her face.

'A warm bath for you and an early night tonight. How does that sound?'

She leaned back against him. 'Bliss.'

'I'll keep an eye on Harriet.'

'You're looking after her tomorrow, while I meet Kim for lunch. She's just back from celebrating her birthday in Spain,' Serena reminded him.

'I haven't forgotten,' he said, swatting her gently on the bum. 'I'm bringing Harriet to the seaside. Any word from Jack?'

'No. I phoned him this morning but it went straight to voicemail.'

'He could be in the air.'

'I hope so.'

But in that case, Serena grumbled to herself, why hadn't he texted his flight details? Jack's home, Garryvale, was on the other side of the village to Serena, and less than five minutes' drive from Tamarisk. Since he'd been gone, his cleaner had called in once a week to check everything and air the house. But the fridge and freezer were bound to be bare and if he'd responded to her voicemail, she could have dropped off some food for him.

Paul opened the weekend newspapers that she had brought home and spread them across the island worktop. She was putting away the shopping bags when he said, 'Serena, what's this?'

'What's up?' she asked him, her face flushing and guilty heart suddenly missing a beat. It was okay, she told herself. Calm down. He couldn't possibly know.

He looked up from the newspaper with a slightly puzzled expression. 'Don't look so worried. Did you know about this travel article? I quote: "We asked four celebrities to name their favourite, most romantic getaway. First up, Serena Devlin whose star is continuing to ascend . . ."' he read aloud.

'Oh, that,' she breathed a sigh of relief. 'They phoned me early this week,' Serena said, trying to sound smooth despite her fluttering pulse. 'What photo did they use? I sent over two file pictures.'

'What *photo*?' Paul asked, looking decidedly annoyed. 'Is that all you're worried about? Or have you been caught on camera somewhere you shouldn't have been?'

She laughed shakily. 'Don't be silly. What's your problem with this?'

'Number one, you're quoted as Serena Devlin.'

'I always use that name for business purposes, you know that.'

'Number two, you say your favourite romantic getaway is Tamarisk. *Tamarisk*?'

'Well?'

He looked disappointed. 'I thought you loved where we went on honeymoon, even if it was in the remotest part of Cork with a place name you couldn't even pronounce. Obviously it wasn't glamorous enough for you.'

'Paul, of course I loved it, but this is publicity.'

'Publicity? This article is supposed to be about the real you, Serena Taylor, the human person behind the successful hotelier front.'

The *real* her? They'd be lucky. No one got to see the real Serena Taylor, warts and all.

'I dunno,' Paul grumbled. 'Even though we're six years married you're still Serena Devlin and lots of times Tamarisk comes first with you. Sometimes, I feel I don't get a look in. Or Harriet.'

'You're being ridiculous,' she found herself snapping, aghast that fear made her over-defensive. 'It's only a stupid article,' she went on, pulling the sheets of newspaper so that they slewed across the worktop.

'Hey, calm down.'

'I *am* calm,' she fumed, clumsily folding the newspaper.

Paul said nothing, his silence goading her to continue. 'You know the past few months have been difficult. Of *course* you and Harriet come first and as soon as Jack is home, I'll be less busy at work. Let's not argue about a silly article.' Having made a mess of the newspaper, she wrapped her arms around herself.

'I'm not arguing about it,' Paul said evenly. 'Don't look so agitated. Forget it.'

Harriet had already gone off to her playroom clutching an ice lolly and a packet of jellies, and now Paul went in search of his daughter. Shortly afterwards, Serena heard the sound of Harriet's favourite *Monsters Inc* DVD. As she put away the rest of the shopping, she wondered why Paul was being so sensitive, and realised in the next breath that he was probably picking up on her undercurrent of anxiety.

She *had* loved their honeymoon, even though it had been different to anything she'd expected. Paul had arranged it all, keeping her in the dark about it until the last minute, merely telling her that it wasn't going to be a beach holiday, and to bring casual clothes, strong walking shoes and a couple of fleeces. Serena's vision of honeymooning in the Maldives had disappeared in front of her. But maybe Paul was trying to throw her off the scent? In the end she had packed a selection of everything, and told herself she could always shop at their destination.

'Where are we going?' she'd asked, two days after their wedding, as he'd driven south-west through the late spring countryside and sped in the opposite direction to Dublin airport.

'Somewhere we can totally relax, away from all the fuss,' he'd said cryptically.

Somewhere they could relax had turned out to be a rustic cottage in west Cork, set in a private woodland clearing, with the backdrop of a conifer plantation and a track through a meadow in front leading to a still, calm lake. It was situated two miles from a small, picturesque fishing village, with welcoming pubs and restaurants, and sailing, windsurfing and water-skiing all available in the harbour.

It couldn't have been more different than her glittering and prestigious wedding day or the on-show tropical honeymoon she'd expected. Yet within a day, Serena had found that there was a marvellous sense of freedom in spending most of her honeymoon in jeans and a T-shirt. There had been no need to maintain an appearance, it had been just herself and Paul enjoying their honeymoon in the most anonymous and relaxed way possible. Running like a glittering thread through those precious, easy days had been the warm glow that she was Paul's wife, and that he had vowed to love and cherish her. She had known she could trust him implicitly.

And now, whenever she remembered their honeymoon, she could still smell the resin of pine trees, hear the gentle sound of the wind and taste the tang of the breeze rippling in off the harbour; she recalled days when they'd strolled by the velvety lake and had found paths through the soaring, silent woods; evenings when they'd enjoyed impromptu music and convivial company in the nearby pubs, and above all, the deep, inky quiet of those west Cork nights when Paul had taken her to bed and they'd cuddled up and made hot, passionate love. Most of all, she remembered the sense of feeling totally renewed, body and soul, when they'd taken the road home after ten wonderful days and nights.

Serena sighed as she put the offending newspaper away. She walked down to the doorway of the playroom where Harriet was sitting on the mat in front of the television, engrossed in the DVD, her arm tightly around her big blue Sulley bear. Beside her, Paul was balancing on the bean bag. Folding her arms, Serena leaned against the door jamb.

'Daddy, look at this bit. Watch this!' Harriet shouted. She dropped her bear, jumped to her feet and began to act out the antics of the cartoon dragon on the screen, punching the air and hopping excitedly from foot to foot. Like Paul, she was honest and straightforward, but, unlike him, she was feisty and noisy, and spent her day asking an endless stream of questions. And unlike her mother as a child, she shunned dolls or anything remotely feminine and frilly, preferring karate lessons and swimming to ballet and tap dancing. Much to Serena's gratitude, Harriet had always loved going to her crèche, and had a small circle of friends there, with Sophie already her best friend.

But now and again, her daughter's tomboy

streak bothered Serena and, even though she knew it was ridiculous, the basket of neglected, dismembered dolls dumped in a corner of the playroom seemed to be a reflection of her own maternal instincts. For, thanks to her behaviour, she was failing Harriet just as much as she was failing Paul.

CHAPTER 7

On Saturday afternoon, feeling like an awkward teenager, Jack stopped by a deli in the Old Town and picked up crusty rolls filled with tomato, ham and chicken, and some light beer, water and orange juice. He couldn't remember the last time he'd done anything like this.

He'd ignored Serena's voicemail. What could he have said? I'm playing truant? I've met someone? No, I scarcely know her, but I want to see her again? Serena would surely have told him to get on the next flight. As he stood in the warm sunshine on a corner of the Cours Saleya close to The Anchor, he wondered if Jenni would turn up, if he would still feel the same about her – how *did* he feel about her?

But the minute he saw her weaving through the milling throngs of tourists, with a big smile on her face, he knew it was going to be fine.

'Hi,' he said.

'Hi, yourself.' She put her head to one side and studied him.

'What is it?'

'Just getting a good look at you in the daylight.'

'And?'

She grinned. 'You'll pass, I guess. Although I didn't tell my boss I was meeting you again.'

'Looking at me now, do you think he'd be worried about you?'

'Big time,' she laughed.

They got the elevator up to the Parc du Château and strolled around in the sunshine. The park was full of families and children. They picked out a spot under the shade of the trees, with breathtaking views across the sweep of the bay and the red-tiled rooftops of Nice, where they sat and chatted about the city, the tourists and some of the more unusual customers Jenni had encountered.

'So what part of England are you from?' Jack asked eventually.

She tilted a bottle of orange juice against her mouth and took a slug. 'London. Primrose Hill.'

'What are you doing in Nice?'

'Hey, this isn't twenty questions, is it?' she said in mock outrage.

'Sorry, just curious.'

'Hmm. I've been working here for about a year. How about you?'

'You could say I've deserted my post and I'm absent without leave,' he told her, pulling at blades of grass, his tone of voice light as though it was a great joke.

She gave him a steady look and then scrambled to her feet. 'Okay, deserter, let's go for a walk.

There's a great view of the harbour from the other side.'

Jack stood up and put aside all thoughts of home and Tamarisk. He soaked up the stunning scenery, the sight of Jenni's laughter-filled eyes, the sound of her voice and the soft touch of her skin when their hands or arms happened to brush together. It was all very casual, but underneath the surface, Jack felt he was falling deeper into something he couldn't get his head around.

'I'll be working late tonight,' she told him, when they reluctantly started the long climb down the steps to street level at the end of her break.

'I'll walk you home again, if you like?' He wanted to experience it all over again, his senses coming alive as he shared a carnival night with Jenni.

'I suppose . . . yes, okay.'

That night, they strolled among the crowds in the Place Masséna. For the first time, Jack noticed the street art exhibits mounted on top of tall steel poles, which were lit up in shades of yellow and red, purple and orange and leant a festive atmosphere to everything. At the southern end of the square, the Fontaine du Soleil thrust frothy spray skywards in a seductive, exuberant rhythm. Someone was playing the piano in the square and crystal clear notes flowed out across the night.

'That's Madeline,' Jenni told him. 'She plays here at the weekends to earn money for music college in Italy.'

'She must be very determined.'

'Yes, it's her dream.'

'Do you have any dreams, Jenni?' he asked.

'Not like that, no. I don't have any amazing talents or gifts. I just want to be happy and contented and make the most of every single day. And I don't waste any time doing things I don't want to do.'

'I think that's a gift in itself,' Jack said slowly, 'the ability to stop yourself from getting sucked into things you don't want to do.'

'Yes, sometimes it takes a bit of courage,' she said. Then she grinned. 'Problem is, not everyone might be happy with you.'

He looked at her intently, wondering what had happened to give her that insight, but her eyes were smiling their usual, carefree smile. They lingered for a while in the wonderful atmosphere, as if both of them were reluctant to break the magic spell that was being weaved around them. Jack wanted this warm, quirky and exhilarating Saturday night with Jenni to go on for ever.

'Maybe we could do lunch again tomorrow?' he asked outside her apartment, wondering, like a lovesick adolescent, how he was going to put in the hours until he saw her again.

'Sure. I prefer chicken by itself though, just butter and no mayo,' she ordered teasingly.

'Whatever you say.'

Another kiss goodnight. More leisurely this time, longer, deeper.

'That wasn't just a birthday kiss,' Jenni said, a little breathless.

'No.'

On Sunday, Jack was ready far too early, so he sat along the promenade for a while, watching the rippling sea, a sweep of milky-grey silk lapping gently against the pebbled beach. Down on the beach, sunbathers were lined up on towels and mats. Strollers and joggers, couples and friends, and families with babies and dogs filled the pavements. Jack had forgotten how beautiful the curving beach was, rimmed on one side with a graceful, tree-lined promenade and palatial hotels. Or maybe he was seeing it with different eyes. He watched an aircraft drone across the bowl of the sky following the contour of the beach as it dropped altitude and lined up for the runway in Nice airport. He closed his mind to the flight he was supposed to be taking home.

He breathed in the air, and the prospect of seeing Jenni again sent a giddy rush through his veins.

CHAPTER 8

Serena's wardrobe was full of Irish-designer labels from the dazzling Synan O'Mahony and the internationally renowned John Rocha to the soft and romantic Deborah Veale, but when she found herself unable to decide what to wear for Sunday lunch with Kim, she realised that she had to get a grip on herself.

She told herself that everything was cool. Paul had already left for the beach with Harriet and both of them were happy and upbeat. As she sifted through the rails in her wardrobe, she reminded herself that Kim had been her best friend since childhood. It would be a much-needed, relaxing, girlie catch-up.

Still, she had to make an effort and look good. Looking good would help her to feel good. As well as that, she never knew when she'd be caught on camera. A celebrity in her own right on account of her profile as Tamarisk's glamorous co-director, by now she was used to featuring in glossy magazines and diary pages and she was developing a reputation for promoting Irish labels. It was a reputation she was happy to foster given the glittering talent available on her doorstep.

Lunch with Kim called for something casual, Serena told herself as she put on an ivory silk blouse and pale-blue jeans, telling herself she looked great.

Sitting in the restaurant in Merrion Row at lunch-time on Sunday, Kim was wearing a beautiful embroidered jade shirt which complemented her tumble of mahogany hair and brought out the colour of her light-green eyes. Serena kissed her cheek and handed her a small gift bag.

'Happy belated birthday, Kim. You look fantastic, love the shirt.'

'Oh, thanks a mill, Serena. Can I take a peek?'

'It's not very exciting,' Serena said pulling out a chair and sitting opposite her. 'Just a gift card for Brown Thomas. I thought you'd prefer to choose your own thing.'

'That is exciting. I have my eye on a fabulous cream Karen Millen dress.'

'Good.' Serena passed a birthday card across the table, and then another pink envelope.

'*Two* cards? Don't tell me Jack actually remem-bered my birthday!'

'No, Jack's not home yet, the other card is from Harriet. She insisted on making one for you when she heard I was taking you out to lunch for your birthday.'

Kim smiled. 'Harriet! She's a dote. I love her!'

'She's just been at her first all-nighter. Her friend

85

Sophie invited her to stay the night but I don't think they slept at all.'

'An all-nighter?' Kim chuckled. 'God, you Devlins start rather young, don't you?'

Serena grimaced. 'Harriet's not a Devlin, she's a Taylor and, thankfully, Paul didn't hear you say that, he'd go mad,' she laughed and shook her head.

'Come on, it's in the royal blood, she's a Devlin through and through. Bright and clever, like her mum. So, what's happening? How are things?'

'Everything's fine. It's been a busy week, as usual.'

They gave their orders, Serena opting for a starter of Howth crab, while Kim asked about the Dublin Bay prawns. 'I only want them if they're big and chunky,' she said, keeping a straight face, as she fluttered her mega lash effect eyelashes at the good-looking, twenty-something waiter. Serena held up the drinks menu to hide her mortified grin.

He smiled good-naturedly. 'Yes, madam, I can guarantee they are.'

Kim beamed flirtatiously. 'Excellent. In that case, I'll relish them. And lamb cutlet to follow. I'll see if I feel like dessert afterwards.' Her gleaming eyes swept him from head to toe. 'I might fancy a large banana with tutti-frutti, or would that be on the menu?'

Serena snorted, grabbing a napkin and pretending to blow her nose. She straightened her face long enough to ask Kim if she wanted a drink.

'Just bring me a glass of Prosecco,' Kim smiled

at the waiter. 'I can't afford to get tiddly at lunch-time. God knows, I might jump on you.'

'You're a disgrace, you know?' Serena said when the waiter had left.

'Good,' Kim was unperturbed. 'I'm thirty-five, it's about time I was disgraceful. It's all right for you, you have Paul to satisfy your urges. Me? I have to make do.'

'How about Matthew?'

Kim shook her head vehemently. 'Don't put us together in the same bed.'

'Sounds bad. Are you sure you won't have anything more exciting to drink?'

'No, thanks. I'm going to a twenty-fifth wedding anniversary in the Four Seasons tonight. It might be as boring as hell, but it's networking and I don't want to arrive looking hung over. How about you?'

'Much as I'd like to toast your birthday with a couple of champagne cocktails, I'm driving.'

When their starters arrived, Kim gave the waiter a huge, appreciative smile.

'So how did your trip to Spain go?' Serena asked.

'Great. Mum and Dad embarrassed the hell out of me, they made such a great fuss of my birthday. The whole village was on standby awaiting my arrival. Seriously, Serena, you'd think they'd been living in Andalusia for ever instead of just five years. And they were asking for you.'

'I should go and visit sometime. I love them to bits.'

'Yes, they're special,' Kim agreed. 'I didn't really appreciate them until they uprooted and I saw them in a different landscape. Mum's still sewing away, and supplying the most amazing silks and cottons to the local markets, fair play to her, and Dad is busy with his carpentry.'

Looking at the glow on Kim's face, Serena found herself admitting, 'I don't remember much about my childhood. Lots of stuff seemed to fall through the cracks. But I do recall that sometimes when I was growing up I felt envious of you, with your parents.'

Her friend stared at her. 'What? You envied *me*? I must be hearing things. You were the one living in the fairytale manor with your successful, glamorous mother and easy-going father. Come on, Serena, I came from a cottage in Main Street, Glendoran, where my parents had to scrape a living together. You had the shiny, blonde hair and fancy-sounding name and I still remember the way you lit up the classroom in Glendoran, with your bright, sparky cleverness. Me, I was plain old Kim Mulligan, who couldn't see the point of school. It's a wonder we became friends.'

Serena grinned. 'Something else I remember is the way you drove all the teachers mad. You and Jack. You both got away with murder.'

'Whatever,' Kim's eyes gleamed. 'Only for your friendship and joking with Jack in the back row of the classroom, I don't know how I would have got through those years. Hey, did you realise it's

88

over thirty years since we started in the village school in Glendoran.'

'Have I really known you that long? You always were, and still are, my closest friend. I really appreciate our friendship – and I think you and your parents are the salt of the earth.'

Kim teased, 'Jesus, Serena, what's this in aid of? You haven't been given weeks to live, have you?'

Serena fiddled with her glass of water. 'Nah, I'm just in that kind of humour. A little tired and emotional, as the song goes.'

Tired and emotional? It covered her see-saw of feelings quite neatly, she congratulated herself.

Kim said, bluntly, 'What's up?'

Serena gave her a lopsided smile. 'Nothing, really. Think I'm just coming to my time of the month. I can be touchy beforehand.'

Kim made a face. 'My sympathies.'

'Although Paul will be disappointed,' Serena said, weighing her words carefully. 'He's hoping for baby number two, like, as of now.'

'Oh? And are you?' Kim asked shrewdly. 'I thought it took you a while to get back to yourself after Harriet.'

Serena stared out the window where Sunday afternoon shoppers were bustling past. That was one way of putting it, she supposed.

'Still, Harriet's four now, so you must feel it's time to go again,' Kim went on.

'It would be lovely to have a sibling for her,' Serena said smoothly.

89

'Speaking as an only child, it would be absolutely wonderful,' Kim said. 'I always wanted a sister or brother but it just didn't happen for Mum and Dad. Still, I was lucky to have had you and Jack. And you deserve the best, Serena. You've a gorgeous daughter, and hopefully you'll have another baby, or two. Then, there's your lovely husband, your fabulous career, your celebrity profile and your twin brother. You have it all, you lucky sucker,' Kim ended on a light note.

No, Kim would never understand where she was coming from. Serena gave herself a mental shake and vowed to keep her silence. 'I do appreciate what I have,' she said to her friend, 'but so should you. You have your independence, your own business and parents who adore you. Marriage and kids involve compromise and you know what they say about the grass being greener?' She looked down at the table and played with the condiments.

'Are you sure it's just your time of the month?' Kim probed.

Serena grinned. 'Yes, and there I go again. Don't mind me. Whatever way you look at it, we've all come a long way from the classroom in Glendoran, me, you and Jack.'

Kim helped herself to some steamed vegetables and passed the dish across to Serena. 'Speaking of Jack, I presume you've put out the flags for your beloved brother?'

'No, dammit, he missed his flight yesterday and I don't know when he'll be back.'

Kim put down her fork. 'Jack? Missed his flight? That's a first.'

'I hope it's not an omen. I need him to cut me a bit of slack for a change.' Serena bit her lip, conscious that she'd sounded a little rattled.

'Yes, you're long overdue a break,' Kim said. 'It's been full-on for you since Amy. It was a desperate time for you all. Jack must be on his way home by now, though.'

'That's the funny part, I haven't been able to contact him because his mobile is off.'

'Maybe it ran out of power. Men! He needs someone to look after him after what he's been through.'

Something in Kim's casual nonchalance alerted Serena. 'You sound like you could be volunteering? Mind you, I'd love to see you two getting it together.'

Kim laughed and her eyes gleamed as though Serena had cracked a great joke. 'Of course I love Jack to pieces. He'll turn up soon. Hopefully in time for next Saturday.'

'What's next Saturday?'

'I'm planning a garden party, as my newly renovated back garden is finished, and all the Devlins are invited to the opening ceremony, if Tamarisk will spare you, of course!'

'You mean the Devlins as in Charlotte and Jack, and the Taylor family.'

'There you go again, Serena. What's this? A crisis of identity? Since when did you become a Taylor?'

'Since I married Paul, of course.'

'Yes, but . . . oh, never mind. I don't care what you call yourselves, once you all turn up for the grand unveiling. This garden has had my head wrecked for the past couple of weeks, but it's finally finished. I'm dying to show it off. And even if it lashes rain, you'll all have to don your raincoats and wellies and look suitably impressed as you admire my trailing begonias, scented lavender and Donegal quartz slabs.'

'Sounds nice,' Serena said.

'It should be nice considering it's blown the budget by a hefty margin,' Kim threw her eyes up to heaven. 'I'm calling it my tranquillity garden and I might as well confess that I've modelled it on your Tranquil Garden at Tamarisk, but somehow a town garden in the middle of Dublin suburbia doesn't present the same scope.'

'I'm sure it's perfect,' Serena said.

'So pencil it in for next Saturday at five-ish. Oh, and let Jack and Charlotte know, will you? Hopefully he's up for it.'

'I'm sure he will be. I'll give you a buzz Monday or Tuesday. What delights have you lined up for next week?'

'I'm busy all week, and I've a couple of new clients to see. After tonight I'll hopefully have a couple more. I've even booked a blow dry for this afternoon. My mum would have a fit if she knew I was going to the hairdresser on a Sunday after-noon! But I don't want to turn up tonight looking like the Wicked Witch of the West.'

'As if,' Serena said stoutly. 'Your modelling days might be over, and I still don't understand why you pulled the plug on them so soon, but you could go out in a sack with no makeup on and you'd still look sensational.'

'That's what I love about you, Serena, you always see the bright side and bring out the best in me.'

'And you take me out of myself, if that makes any sense,' Serena grinned. 'Now are we having dessert? Only I don't think bananas are on the menu!'

'Oh dear, no tutti–frutti for Kim. Never mind. I think my sexy stud of a waiter is hiding in the kitchen anyway. I wonder what would happen if I accidently lost my way en route to the bathroom?' Kim smiled mischievously and Serena called for the bill.

They parted company outside the restaurant, Kim hugging Serena, and enveloping her in a waft of Kim's favourite fragrance along with her warmth. 'Give Harriet a hug from me,' Kim said, 'and tell that hunky man of yours you need some rest and relaxation.'

'I'm fine.'

Kim gave her a squeeze, and then she stepped back and studied her friend. She reached out and tucked strands of Serena's hair behind her ear in a motherly fashion. 'No, you're not. You look tired and hassled. I know you've been stretched lately with all that sad sorry mess, so I hope Paul is pulling his weight.'

'He is, of course.'

'He'd better be, or I'll talk to him. Don't forget I feel personally responsible because I introduced you guys.' Waggling her fingers in farewell, she walked down the street.

Serena drove out through the city centre and took the road for the south, remembering how she and Paul had met.

When Serena was twenty-eight, Kim's boyfriend had dumped her just a week before her cousin's wedding.

'I'm finished with men,' Kim had said, wiping her tears. 'I'm hibernating for a long time. I'm not even going to bother with Anna's wedding, because her fiancé plays rugby in his spare time and some of *his* friends are bound to be there.'

'Good. Surely that's all the more reason for you to put on your best face and your glitziest gown. If your invite includes a friend, I'll come with you for moral support,' Serena had insisted.

Kim had carried on in a muffled voice. 'You don't understand. I'm right off men for now, so I don't even want to run the risk of being enticed by a rugby player no matter how sexy he is.'

'I'll be there to save you from temptation,' Serena had smiled. 'I don't want to be enticed by anyone either – I'm off to Singapore for six months' work experience, remember?'

Little did Serena know what fate had in store.

As Serena drove home, she recalled, as though it were yesterday, the moment she'd been standing by the bar chatting to Kim at Anna's wedding when she felt herself under scrutiny.

Somehow, she had sensed he was different. The first thing she'd noticed was that his dark wavy hair was messy and his tie was off-centre. Her next thought was that he must have been rushing after a hard day at the office. Then she found herself imagining that he'd lingered in bed too long after a steamy session and got dressed in a hurry. He'd caught her eye, and the way his intelligent eyes gazed at her sent something smouldering through her. Serena had blushed furiously and Kim had laughed at the sight of her face.

'Interested?'

Suddenly, Serena had felt exposed. 'Jesus, Kim, do I look like I am?'

'Do I what? You look like you've stripped him naked. And vice versa. I think he's on the groom's side, but I'll find out. Definitely a rugby player to judge by that body.'

'Kim! Leave it! Don't make a fuss,' Serena had implored, darting him another glance, totally ruffled to find his eyes still on her.

'Hello, Serena, you can't ignore a guy who's not only Ireland's answer to the Emporio Armani ad, but looks as though he'd be very happy to drag you off to his cave and show off all his weaponry . . . inch by glorious inch. I'm going to find out all the goss on him – and then you can strut your stuff!'

Later, in the interval between the music, she'd

reported back to Serena. 'He's Paul Taylor, a friend of the groom and a force of energy on the rugby pitch. But—'

'What?'

'Quite shy when it comes to women. No track record of heavy relationships, so not much baggage until his Gucci belt. And I'm not sure if he's your type.'

'Why not?'

'From the sound of it, you're chalk and cheese. He's – wait for it – a research scientist. Very brainy, the strong and silent type. Reserved. Not much of a socialiser. Different to your usual outgoing restaurateur, hotelier or businessman date.'

'Opposites attract,' Serena had pointed out, glancing around the function room, excited to see that while he was in conversation with a group, he was watching her out of the corner of his eye, as he had been for most of the evening.

'And although this might seem like heresy to you,' Kim had gone on, 'I bet he's never heard of Tamarisk.'

'How did you find out so much about him?'

Kim had grinned. 'I got chatting to one of the groomsmen.'

'Great. How long will it take for word of your interrogation to get back to him?'

'I'll be amazed if it does,' Kim had said airily. 'The groomsman is three sheets to the wind after far too many whiskey chasers. I'd say he's forgotten about our conversation already. Besides, he only had eyes for my cleavage. And here comes my brand new cousin-in-law,' she'd said as the groom approached. 'I'll get him to introduce us.'

'Kim!'

'Relax, Serena, there's safety in numbers but I'll make myself scarce as soon as you give me the nod . . .'

Serena continued down the N11 and drove past the exit for Bray, recalling that Kim had made herself scarce almost immediately that night and, somehow, Serena had found herself floating away from the noisy wedding and out into the foyer, with Paul in tow. By tacit agreement, they had moved down the corridor to where it was quieter and had found deep cushiony armchairs looking out onto a shadowy courtyard. She had made small talk with this mannerly, reserved man, and hadn't been able to help but see that his dark-grey eyes had sparkled with desire as they met hers. What was he like beneath that calm, self-possessed surface, her thoughts whirled. What would it be like to linger in bed with him?

As they had chatted, Serena had discovered that Paul was into rugby, classical music and arty movies. And Indian food. In that order. He was also passionate about his research career. Serena, on the other hand, had liked walking, pop music and romantic comedies. And Irish cuisine.

Paul had looked at her thoughtfully, a look that sent a tingle down her spine. 'So where does that leave us, in terms of dates, as in movie watching and concerts?'

'I guess we'll have to compromise,' she'd smiled.

'Compromise?' He'd given her a meaningful look. 'There are some areas where I'm not into half measures.'

'Sounds promising,' she'd said. Then, unsure about where this was going or how long it might last, but feeling it was important to let him know, she'd ventured, 'Thing is, I'm off to Singapore in a few weeks' time.'

'Singapore? How come?'

'Work experience, to bring back to our hotel—'

'Your hotel?'

As Kim had guessed, he'd never heard of Tamarisk.

'Ancestral pile?' he'd asked, giving her a teasing grin and her heart had flipped.

'Sort of. An exclusive hotel and the family business, where I was born and bred, and it's also my passion,' Serena had said. She'd told him that her paternal grandparents had inherited the sprawling, run-down eighteenth-century mansion after the Second World War and had restored it into a profitable hotel, in turn passing the business onto their twin sons, Jamie and Conor.

'Conor, my uncle, took his share of the inheritance and moved to France to establish La Mimosa in the mid-seventies, when Jack and I were babies. It's our sister hotel over on the Côte d'Azur.'

'And Jack is . . .?'

'My twin brother. But Jamie, my dad, died last year,' she'd paused momentarily before hurrying along, anxious to gloss over the subject, 'my mother Charlotte runs the whole show. She's coping fine, and is a true force to be reckoned with. In a way, she's always been the one in control as Dad was happy to take a back seat and let her at it. Jack and I are second-in-command and learning the ropes. Mind you,' she'd given a careless laugh, 'I think I've been learning the ropes since I was about five!'

'I'm sorry about your dad,' Paul had said gently. 'My parents are still alive and well, as are my two younger sisters, and I have an adorable niece and nephew, so I can't imagine how awful it must be to lose someone you love.'

Serena had bit her lip. To her surprise and angst, his empathy sent a rush of tears to the back of her eyes. This man had looked as though he was genuinely interested in her as a person, that he was giving her his undivided attention, and not just self-centredly trying to work out the kind of impression he was making on her. Most of all, he'd looked as though he cared.

'It's not great,' she'd admitted, surprised that her normal guard was let down and she could hear a choke in her voice. 'Dad and I . . .' she'd gulped, 'well, I know he loved us but he wasn't always there for us in a meaningful way. After he died . . . it was difficult. It threw up all sorts of messy emotions.' Her hand had been shaking so much that she'd had to put down her glass.

Paul had taken her hand and laced his fingers securely through hers. 'Sorry if I put my size tens in it . . .'

'No, you're fine.' She'd been anxious to reassure him. 'I'm over the worst of it by now. I just never expected it to feel the way it did and sometimes it still catches me unawares.'

'I'm sure it does.'

He'd tightened his grip and she loved the way it made her feel. Precious. Secure. Up to now, she'd enjoyed the social whirl of the college years, when she'd studied hotel marketing in Dublin. And in between moving into a managerial role in Tamarisk, she'd worked abroad in a variety of world-class hotels, gaining knowledge and experience. Over the years, there had been plenty of dates and a few casual relationships with men who had moved in similar social circles to hers. But the longest of these had lasted eight months and most of them had been unsatisfactory.

'Well, what's the verdict?' Paul had asked.

She'd grinned. She might have known he'd suss she was checking him out. 'I have some free time before I go to Singapore . . .'

He'd smiled at her in a way that had lifted her heart. 'We'll have to make the most of that.'

They'd dated a few times, bonding over her choice of movie, his choice of concert, Serena standing on the breezy sidelines of the rugby pitch, Paul bringing her to his favourite Dublin restaurant, squeezing in time together before

Serena left for Singapore. Alone with him, she'd found him quiet and thoughtful, but had loved the way he gave her his whole attentiveness. He had also proved to be a very sensual lover.

'I thought you were supposed to be reserved,' she'd told him, after a marathon love-making session that left her totally breathless and delightfully sated.

He'd smiled and trapped her leg between his strong thighs. 'Who said that? I told you I wasn't into half measures. This isn't going to end here, Serena, because I'll be out to visit you in Singapore.' He'd trailed his hands across her tummy and down to where her sensitive nerve endings were still pleasurably sparking. She'd snuggled into the heat of his hard chest and closed her eyes, loving what he was doing to her.

She'd been in Singapore a month when he'd arrived out to see her, and in between her shifts at the hotel, they'd gone sightseeing, but had spent most of their time together in bed. He'd be back, he'd told her, as soon as he could get another week off work. Kim had also come out to visit and over Singapore Slings in Raffles had declared that Serena was in love.

Serena had almost choked on her cocktail. 'Me? In love? How do you know?'

Kim had smiled calmly, 'You haven't stopped talking about Paul since I got here.'

Serena had felt contrite. 'God. Sorry, I must be boring you to tears.'

'Relax, it's nice to see you all of a flutter for a change and I'm quite happy to bask in the glow of knowing I brought you guys together.'

'Have you – are you dating anyone yet?'

Kim had shaken her head. 'Nothing serious. But I'm enjoying that freedom. Well, I was until I saw the big grin on your face.' She'd plucked her pineapple segment from the top of her glass. 'I'm joking, of course. I might be the tiniest bit jealous but I hope you and Paul will be very happy and I'll gladly be your bridesmaid.'

'Hey, it mightn't come to that!'

'Yes, it will. You two might be chalk and cheese but, listening to you, it's obvious to me you're perfect for each other.'

Kim's words came back to Serena as she hit the accelerator and crested the incline outside Glendoran. When she'd come home from Singapore that December, tired and disorientated after a bumpy overnight flight, and had seen Paul waiting for her, his arms stuffed with red roses, her heart had jumped and her tiredness had melted away. The cold and chilly arrivals hall had been filled with magic. Kim had been right. She had, indeed, fallen in love with him. Four months later, just as a perfect spring transformed the Tamarisk parklands, and Serena had the feeling that life was bursting with promise, Paul had proposed.

Serena turned in at the entrance to Maple Hill. She slowed to a halt, tyres scattering the gravel. Right then, she sighed, everything in her life had been wonderful. When she'd discovered she was pregnant a year after their wedding, she'd felt her life was unfolding like a dream, and was almost too good to be true.

Unfortunately she'd been right. For after Harriet was born, and just when she'd least expected it, everything had come crashing down around her.

CHAPTER 9

'Kim! Darling! The very person I was hoping to see!'

Kim's guard automatically rose as a woman bore down on her with all the determination of an avenging angel. Being called 'darling' by someone she didn't know usually meant they were looking for a favour. The woman was wearing a fabulous Ben de Lisi cocktail dress, and she weaved through the crowds and waved a glass of champagne so violently that the socialites sipping cocktails and champagne in the Ice Bar instantly parted to give her a safe passage through.

Kim politely smiled as the woman stopped in front of her and caught her breath. 'Have we met?'

'No, but I'd recognise you anywhere, and I'm delighted to see you,' the woman smiled enthusiastically. 'I need your help.' She announced this in lowered, conspiratorial tones, her eyes avidly sweeping the throng of people as though she was afraid to be overheard.

'I'm Thelma, Thelma de Courcy. I badly need radical makeover surgery to my home before I have any more malfunctions.' She laughed at her own joke. 'You will take me on, won't you?' Thelma looked a little unsure. 'Money is no object even in these times. Within reason, of course!'

Out of the corner of her eye, Kim spotted Matthew O'Brien pushing through the crowd, looking tanned and fit after his stint in Dubai. The last thing she wanted right now was Matthew's attention or his attempts to pick up the threads of their off-again–on-again relationship. She put her hand on Thelma's arm and drew her away from the general hubbub. 'Tell me a little about yourself,' she said, feeling relieved when Matthew was sidetracked by a young and attractive BBC starlet.

'My husband has just got a *big* promotion,' Thelma said, with the emphasis on the word 'big', and Kim knew by the practised way she said it that most of her family and friends had been treated to the same information delivered in the same reverent tones. 'It'll mean entertaining at home, dinner parties and charity lunches, you know? The thing is, our home has kind of evolved over the years with bits and pieces from every decade, and now with the family reared, it badly needs a facelift. I'm not much good at throwing out stuff, and I don't even know where to start when it comes to choosing the right shade of paint as I can't figure out the difference between Farrow & Ball and Dulux. So I badly need someone like you to perform a miracle.'

Kim warmed to Thelma's honesty. She asked her

a few general questions, and opening her purse, took out a small business card. 'I might be a bit short on miracles, but here are my details. Why don't you contact me next week and we'll meet up for coffee and have a good chat, to see where we go from here?'

'Oh, thank you, Kim. You are a darling. They told me not to be afraid of getting you on my case, that you weren't the least bit up yourself but very approachable and understanding . . .'

'*They*?' Kim queried, slanting an eyebrow.

'Pierce and Jackie, our hosts,' Thelma nodded in the direction of the wealthy solicitor and his wife. 'I was in their house recently – pardon me, their mansion – and admiring the style and they told me that it was all down to you, and, better again, that you'd be here tonight.'

'I'm very pleased to have met you, Thelma, and we'll talk next week. But right now I'm afraid I'm in rather a rush,' Kim explained, preparing to leave as she felt the full voltage of Matthew O'Brien's white-teethed and blue-eyed smile radiate in her direction. He was making small talk to the starlet. She knew that smile. It meant he was already picturing them having rampant sex all through his penthouse apartment. No thanks. Not tonight. And not when she was patiently waiting for someone who meant the world to her. When Matthew's attention was momentarily distracted by the starlet's friend looking for an introduction, Kim slipped through the crowds, went out through the foyer, and jumped into a taxi outside.

'Terenure, please,' she instructed the driver, sinking back into the seat and turning off her mobile as they glided out through the hotel entrance. Although Matthew was great in the sack and she hadn't had sex in months, she was more than happy to pass up the opportunity. Especially now, when she was saving herself.

She stared out the window at the darkened Dublin city streets, now and again catching a shadowy image of her face in the passenger window, the face that had adorned the covers of countless glossy magazines, and a far cry indeed from the plain, tomboyish daughter of Michael and Margaret Mulligan, who had been reared in a small cottage off Main Street, Glendoran.

When Kim had been growing up, her father had been a carpenter who'd worked in a shed at the end of the garden, where the floor had been full of wood shavings that had stuck to the sleeves of his jumper and the soles of his shoes. Her mother had supplemented his small income by running up curtains and bedspreads on a sewing machine in a corner of the kitchen. Her apron had always been full of threads and pins stuck in a zigzag line around the edge of her pocket, and the kitchen radio had often crackled because of the interference the rhythmic whirr of her sewing machine had caused.

Her friendship with Serena and Jack, begun in

the chalk-scented village classroom, had been forged in the parklands of Tamarisk, which had been their magical playground. If at any time Kim felt overawed by the grandeur of Serena and Jack's childhood landscape, compared to her humble beginnings, it had quickly dissolved. Jack and Serena were the sister and brother she'd never had.

Jack used to call her tatty-head on account of her carroty hair, right from the time they'd joked together in the back row of the classroom. Kim would never have tolerated the name from anyone else. Then, in her teens, she'd grown almost as tall as Jack, her hair had become an attractive, rich mahogany mane and her face had lost its natural chubbiness revealing high cheekbones. It had been a metamorphosis. Just before she'd left school, and egged on by her classmates, she'd entered a local modelling competition. She'd been the runner up and her photo had appeared in the local newspaper and was spotted by a scout for one of Dublin's most exclusive model agencies. Before she'd known what was happening, she was having a portfolio prepared and she was signed up by the agency.

When Jack and Serena had gone to college and gained experience abroad in other hotels, Kim had found her feet in the world of modelling. In a short space of time she'd become one of Ireland's most sought-after models – instantly recognisable, with her porcelain skin, a scattering of freckles, light-green eyes and tumble of tousled hair. No exclusive VIP party had been complete without her presence. She'd regularly jetted abroad and stalked the catwalks of London, Paris and Rome. Life had been good, full of celebrity parties, charity events and black-tie balls, as well as boyfriends and lovers, and she'd regularly caught up with Jack and Serena, sometimes in Glendoran and other times in London or New York.

Then, three years earlier, she'd walked away from it all and turned her talents into interior style consulting.

'I don't think people really understand how tough it is being a model,' Kim had said at the time, when interviewed by a journalist for a magazine scoop. 'All that travel sounds exotic, but in reality it means early morning flights, sometimes dashing to London or Paris at the last minute, lots of hanging around, then by the end of an event you're sometimes far too tired for bellinis and oysters.'

'What do you see yourself doing in the future?' the interviewer had asked.

'I love fashion and style, but, most of all – and God help me if I sound like a contender for Miss World – I love dealing with people. I'm reinventing my career and launching my own interior style business.'

'Wow. That's a change.'

'Yes, it is! When I had my own home gutted and renovated a couple of years ago, I loved the project. I found I had a talent for putting style and texture together, making the most of lighting, and creating a mood.'

'You must be very talented.'

Kim had smiled. 'It runs in the family. My father is a carpenter of the old school tradition and my mother is a dab hand with a sewing machine, and used to run up curtains and soft furnishings for half the population of Wicklow, where they lived. They've now moved to a small village in Spain, where they are busy doing more of the same. I've already done my research and talked nicely to my accountant and bank manager. I'm taking a year out to gain some qualifications, and then I hope to begin building up a client list. Nowadays, people are renovating and improving rather than moving, but I plan to expand into the corporate area as well.'

'Sounds great. But as well as swapping the catwalk for other people's houses, you're cutting down on the travelling. Sounds to me, Kim, like you're thinking of settling down. Any romance on the horizon?'

'Not at the moment. I'm quite happy being single.'

'Sexy and single,' the interviewer had quipped.

'You're the one who said it!' Kim had laughed.

The taxi drew up outside Kim's stylish Victorian three-bedroomed house, situated on a quiet, tree-lined avenue in a choice area in south Dublin. She went in through the hall door and switched on her mobile; as expected, there had been two calls from Matthew wondering where she'd got to and saying that he'd be in the Ice Bar for another hour or so if she wanted to meet up. No way, babe, she mouthed, switching off her phone as she went down to the kitchen to get a glass of water.

Kim's house showcased her talents. It struck a fine balance between classic and contemporary with vintage accessories thrown in for quirky glamour. She showered and changed into soft fluffy pyjamas and slippers. Then went back downstairs for another glass of water.

Her new career had taken off. She'd hit the market just as people decided to upgrade their homes instead of their address. Thanks to her networking, her client base was continually expanding, and it included many of Dublin's A-list celebs and socialites. Business was good, even if she'd had to adjust her cost base and trim her profit projections as the recession had continued to get worse, but it didn't bother her if she had to take out last year's Dolce & Gabbana or Diane von Furstenberg for another airing instead of splashing out for every occasion. She was still a name that guaranteed a table at her favourite restaurant no matter how booked up it was, and a name that was on everyone's invitation list.

However, much to her anguish, her private life hadn't turned out anything like she'd expected or planned. No one but she knew how difficult it had been to deliberately step away from the camera and all the adulation that had accompanied her career. The interviewer at the time had hit the nail on the head when she'd asked Kim if she was interested in settling down. For it was the main reason she'd taken the drastic step to quit. She'd fallen in love. In a totally surprising, earth-shattering moment, she'd been swept off her feet by the last person she'd expected. Suddenly there was nothing she wanted more than to love, and be loved by, Jack Devlin. By making the ultimate sacrifice, she'd hoped to prove to him that she was ready for commitment and that her travelling days were over. But all her dreams had turned into heartache when he'd met and married Amy Skelly.

Then a twist of fate had brought her a second chance.

CHAPTER 10

Still caught in the thrall of relaxed sleepiness, Jack tried to turn over in bed but his inert body refused to budge and he felt a weight pressing on his arm. Even though his eyes were still closed, he knew by the quality of the brightness pressing on his eyelids that he wasn't at home in his bedroom in Ireland, nor in his suite at La Mimosa. In that state of drowsiness, he heard what sounded like a train chugging past. A train? What the hell . . . Gradually he forced his eyelids open and came to semi-wakefulness.

The room was small. There was a long window to his right that was partly open, through which sounds of near-distant traffic could be heard as well as the clang of a tram. Pale-blue curtains were half open and fluttering gently in a light breeze. On the wall opposite him, a rectangle of mellow evening light was shimmering like a filmy rainbow, and his brain hazily figured that it was caused by the sun reflecting off something outside and bouncing through a brightly coloured windmill stuck in the window frame. He heard the sound of another train picking up speed and gliding past at the same time as cool, naked skin pressed against his.

For a split second, he was back in time. His chest flooded with panic and he jerked wide awake. Then his heartbeat gradually steadied when he realised that everything was different now. It was Monday afternoon – and it was Jenni lying beside him.

On Sunday after their picnic, Jenni had brought him around to a waterfall in the Parc du Château, where sunlight had danced on a torrent of water, turning the droplets to spun silver as they hurtled out of the gap in the rock to the well below.

'You can make a wish,' Jenni had said, opening her bag and handing him some coins.

'I don't know what to wish for,' Jack had said, moving closer to the glittering waterfall so that fine spray misted his face.

'Whatever you want the most in life.'

'Ah well, that's easy,' he'd replied, bemused to realise that all he wanted was the girl standing there beside him. What was happening to him? Was it some kind of mini-breakdown after a year of angst and turmoil? Had he turned into a sex maniac? It was more than just sex, though. He wanted to lose every bit of himself in her. There was no point in trying to figure anything out, so he took her hand and led her back up into the park. They'd come to a small clearing where a picnic table had been set up under the shade of the trees; pink balloons, tied to the branches, were gently drifting in the light breeze. A young girl was having a birthday party, her family grouped around her.

Jack had said, 'Hey, they're copying us. We do this on the south lawn at Tamarisk. We have parties outdoors under the oak trees if the weather's okay and we tie balloons to the trees. My birthday and Serena's is in the middle of August, and Mum's is a couple of days later, so we have one big party and it's always great fun . . .' his voice trailed away as he'd remembered the year the party hadn't been such good fun, the time Serena had gone missing and he and Kim had found her over by the river, looking as though she'd been crying, but assuring them she was fine. Something about his sister's tear-stained, valiant face had always stuck at the back of his mind. 'It's a family tradition. For occasional celebrations, and every year, the birthdays. Except last year . . . when we cancelled . . .' he'd faltered as memory tumbled once more in front of his eyes, but this time it almost drained him with its powerful sadness.

'Jack,' Jenni had said. He'd heard her soft voice cutting through his churning mind and felt her hand pressing his. 'Who's Serena? And Tamarisk?'

'Serena's my twin sister,' he'd said, a little of his energy coming back. 'Tamarisk is our family home and our hotel, so it's our job, career, whatever. But we didn't celebrate the birthdays last year because . . .'

'Because?' she'd prompted.

He'd stared at her, not really seeing her. The bright day around him had flickered and darkened and all he could see was Amy lying like a rag doll, half in and half out of the bed, just as he'd found her when he woke that morning. He'd had a giddy sensation in his head, and something had roared in his ears and sliced across his chest. Then he'd heard the words coming out, falling away from his mouth with a life of their own, 'My wife had just died.'

He'd been sorry he'd spoken. He'd broken the spell around them. Now Jenni would be looking at him with pity in her eyes and choosing her words carefully. She'd be treading on eggshells in case she said the wrong thing, and feeling uncomfortable with him, something he'd had to put up with since Amy's death. Suffocating sympathy and cold reality would dissolve the sense of careless abandon and fun that had lifted him up and enclosed them since last Friday afternoon.

Then she'd said, in a soft voice, 'I can see it is making you sad.'

He'd tried to detect grating sympathy but instead she'd sounded tender and understanding, as though he wasn't someone pitiable or damaged but someone whole and strong in spite of the stuff fate had thrown at him. He'd looked at her face and she hadn't been afraid to hold his gaze with her brown eyes. It was going to be okay. *He* was going to be okay. Some kind of strength had flick-ered into life and flowed through his veins and from nowhere his voice had come out of its own accord, 'Let me tell you about the last time I danced . . .'

Sitting on a bench in the warm sunlight, with the vista of Nice spread before them, the rustle of the light breeze in the trees and the laughter of children floating across the afternoon, Jack had poured his heart out and told Jenni everything that had happened over the previous eighteen months of his life.

Afterwards she'd brought him back to her apartment.

'This might not be quite what you're used to,' she'd hesitated, throwing opening windows and moving a pile of clothes. Her studio apartment was small and poky. He heard trains gliding past outside and picking up speed. A child's windmill stuck into the window frame whizzed around in the draught of air. The kitchen was a tiny alcove, the bathroom minuscule. Jack had never seen anything like it in his life. And although he'd been with lots of women, he'd never experienced anyone like Jenni, as she held his gaze and unselfcon-sciously wriggled out of her T-shirt, plucked off her bra, slid off her shorts and stood in front of him in plain white briefs, proud and beautiful. Jack's mouth had felt dry. She took his hand and led him to the bed, and he sat on the edge of it while she sat on his lap and pulled his head to her breasts. He closed his eyes and held on tight like a drowning man clinging to a raft.

As the evening had melted into night-time, and the night-time into the dawn of a new day, Jenni's soft lips and body had spoken a language that words were not able to express. He'd tasted his own tears. She'd licked them away. Tentatively at first, then with more confidence, he'd found a new passion in himself and sparks of pleasure he'd never expected to feel again. And when a hand reached up and slid around the back of his neck, drawing his face down for a kiss, he realised that, right here, right now, everything was perfect.

'Hi, there, sleepyhead,' he murmured.

'Hi, yourself,' Jenni smiled up at him, her dark hair dishevelled. 'How do you feel now?' she asked.

'Peaceful,' he said. Very peaceful. Soothed. Whole.

There was very little room to manoeuvre as they were both lying in a tangle of sheets on her narrow single bed, which was jammed against the wall. They stared at each other for long minutes and when he saw the calm expression in her eyes he knew there was nothing to fear.

He kissed her soft mouth, her eyelids, the delicate hollow of her throat. He kicked off the sheets and put a hand under her hips and, easily scooping her up against him, he turned so that she was lying on top. Some kind of elation bubbled up inside him and he felt himself grow hard again.

'Did I just say peaceful?'

'You did,' she laughed. She wriggled a little, her high breasts rubbing against his naked chest and her hips teasing his. She paused long enough to unroll a condom and as her warm skin slid deliciously against his, and she straddled him, he closed his eyes and allowed himself to soak it all up and lose himself in the blissful pleasure she gave. She moved faster, tightly enfolding him in her warm, moist sweetness, and the sensation was almost unbearable.

'Shh, stay still, just as you are,' she murmured as he began to thrust.

'No, wait,' he said hoarsely. He kept her fastened to him and manoeuvred them both into a sitting position. With his back against the headboard, he held her face in his hands, pushed back her hair and began to kiss her. Their mouths crashed together and Jenni swivelled her hips back and forth until his groin felt as though it was on fire. When she collapsed against his shoulder, giving a small cry, he closed his eyes, finally let go and lost himself in sweet oblivion. Eventually he opened his eyes. Jenni was smiling at him with pink lips that were lush and ripe from kissing him, and those fabulous, soft eyes he wanted to drown in.

'Hey, what's been happening here?' he asked, his voice thick. His hand trailed across the swell of her hip. Her damp skin felt soft and velvety. It also felt like more, but he struggled to contain himself. He'd lost count of the number of times they'd made love since they'd come back to her apartment.

'I dunno,' Jenni said. 'This is not my usual behaviour.'

'Nor my usual behaviour,' he said.

She sighed and stretched her arms above her head and he kissed the smooth underside of those arms, before moving down to kiss her breasts, her nipples still red and swollen after the earlier ravages of his mouth.

Jenni sighed against the top of his head. 'I could stay here for ever, Jack, but I have to get up soon and go to work.'

'Work? No way,' Jack laughed, his arms trapping her.

Jenni wriggled out of his grasp and hauled herself off the bed. 'Sorry, but I bunked off last night, remember? I'll lose my job if I don't turn up tonight.'

'Tell them you're in bed with scarlet fever . . . tell them you have a highly contagious form of the flu . . . anything,' he leaned cross the bed, his hands flailing futilely in open space as she eluded his reach.

'I can't. No way,' Jenni giggled, 'although I've had so much sex in the last twenty-four hours that I don't know how I'm going to walk straight, let alone cope with being rushed off my feet all night. People will know what I've been up to just by my face.'

'Tough,' he said in a deadpan voice.

'It was worth it, though,' she grinned. 'Every single minute.'

He watched in amusement as her totally naked and perfectly proportioned slender body nimbly stepped over their abandoned clothes and hurried across the floor towards the tiny bathroom. Then he heard the drumming of the shower.

Jack leaned out of bed and picked up his watch off the floor. Five-thirty on Monday evening. He should have gone home on Friday night, back to cold, stark reality. He should have been showing up in Tamarisk this morning, buttoned into his suit and shirt, and meeting with Serena and Brian, the financial advisor, to get up to speed on everything. He should have been examining sales figures and projected forecasts for the next six months. Instead he was still in Nice, indulging in the most impetuous, impassioned, yet joyful behaviour he'd ever experienced in his life.

What in God's name had Jenni done? He scarcely knew her, but in a matter of hours she'd given him something that weeks of chilling out in La Mimosa hadn't achieved. During his time there he'd walked in the gardens and along the beach, swam in the pool, read newspapers and books, played golf with his cousin, and visited the wineries with him to choose the next stock of hotel wines. But in an effort to rid himself of the memories of Amy, including the long weekend they'd spent there, he'd locked away something vital of himself.

Now, in some inexplicable way, Jenni had stepped into his heart and he'd been able to tell her things he hadn't yet told another soul. Now he felt like a different person; more peaceful, lighter, free.

Beyond his Friday-night text to Serena, he hadn't been in touch with her or Charlotte to explain his delay. Something else that was unusual for him. He knew that his perfectly organised sister's patience would only stretch so far and there would probably be hell to pay when he got home.

But thankfully, not just yet.

He bounded out of the bed and made a run for the bathroom, his hurried footsteps causing excited shrieks to come from the small, curtained shower stall. Then he wrapped his arms around a wet and slithery Jenni and lifted her off her feet.

He insisted on walking her to work because he didn't want to let her out of his sight.

'How soon can you escape?' Jack asked, when they paused on the corner near The Anchor.

She wrinkled her nose. 'Probably midnight. I might get off earlier, depending on how busy it is.'

He kissed her, heedless of crowds swirling around them. He'd bring her to the Negresco. He could already see her bouncing on the ornate bed and laughing, exclaiming over the lavish extravagance of the suite, playing with him in the massive gold tub and doing something very sexy with the filmy material of the draped canopy. 'Call me the minute you know what time you'll be free. I'll be waiting here for you. I'd like to bring you back to my place.'

'Your place?'

'The hotel where I'm booked in.'

'Which is?'

'The Negresco.'

She laughed. 'Yeah, sure.'

Then she slipped out of his arms and was gone.

'Where were you last night?'

She knew Michael would be on her case immediately.

'I told you I was sick, I had a stomach bug,' Jenni said, hoping she managed to look contrite and pale-faced. Considering the amount of sleep she'd lost, she should look wan and tired. But considering the amount of great sex she'd enjoyed, she knew she looked sleek, glowing and all loved-up, right down to her fingernails.

'I hope it wasn't an Irish bug,' Michael searched her face.

Jenni reminded herself he was just looking out for her. The big, sometimes blustering manager was kindness personified and had taken her under his wing, treating her like a daughter when she'd first come looking for work, keeping a watch over her while she found her feet, got a small bedsit and stared to make friends with the other 'young ones' who worked in the bars and restaurants lining the Old Town.

123

'I hope you're feeling better, Jenni,' she said pointedly.

'Well that too,' he conceded. 'But I don't want you falling for any fly-by-night tourist who's trying to fill you with his charm.'

Jenni hid a grin. Jack had filled her with a lot more than his charm. He was big and beautiful. She'd been amazed at his staying power and the way he couldn't get enough of her. She'd been amazed, too, at his skill, for he was far better than anyone else she'd had sex with, taking the time to make her come again and again. She'd had a feeling from the very first night that they'd end up in bed, but she hadn't expected the surprising way it had come about or the sad story that Jack had poured out.

And she was surprised at herself, for she'd never gone off with a tourist like that before. But there was something about Jack that had drawn her in, that made her feel happy, that made her feel that she, Jenni Anderson, was a good and important person.

She tied her apron around her waist and, listening to the sound of Lady Gaga coming through the speakers, she checked the menu and saw that the house special tonight was breaded cod and chips. Happy hour was extended to eight o'clock and the tables were filling up outside. It would be a busy night and she reminded herself that this was her life right now.

She told herself not to feel too disappointed if

Jack wasn't waiting for her. He was staying in, of all places, the *Negresco*. Enough said. God knows what he had secretly thought of her crummy bedsit. Ah well, it had been good while it lasted.

And the sex had been brilliant.

CHARLOTTE 1973–1974

On her honeymoon in Cape Cod Charlotte discovered the power of sex; how it could transfix a man, making him vulnerable and defenceless, and in doing so, fill a woman with unexpected strength and love.

'You're beautiful,' Jamie whispered, holding her close in their suite overlooking the beach.

'You're much . . .' she began shyly, touching the most sensitive part of him.

'What?'

She felt him elongate in her hand. 'Much bigger than I imagined.'

'That's because of you,' he said, slipping his fingers inside her and tenderly stroking her before he entered her. The intimacy of it all was startling at first, but by the end of their honeymoon, Charlotte felt as though she'd been making love to Jamie all her life.

Then they returned home to Tamarisk.

She and Jamie started their married life in a ground-floor wing of the hotel, down beyond the kitchen area, where a self-contained apartment had been prepared for them as soon as he'd phoned home with the news of his marriage.

'This is just temporary,' Jamie said. 'We'll build our own house as soon as we're in a position to borrow enough funds.'

'It's lovely, Jamie,' she said, feeling that their first home was special and knowing that the apartment with two bedrooms, a bathroom and a kitchen-cum-living room was bigger than her parents' apartment in Chicago. She was glad to have their own space away from Teresa, his mother, and Conor, his twin brother, who had rooms at the opposite end of the building, down past Reception. Jamie's father had died of cancer two years earlier, so, between them, Jamie and Conor ran the hotel.

'Conor's the brains,' Jamie said. 'He has a fantastic grasp of the business. He's great at coming up with ideas and can work out our pre-tax profit in his sleep.'

'I'm sure you're just as talented,' she replied.

'I encourage guests to eat in our dining room and I keep the Residents' Lounge open as long as I can. Restaurant and bar receipts can go a long way.'

When Charlotte settled into their apartment, she invited Teresa and Conor for dinner.

'I'll be happy to make myself useful in the hotel,' she told them. 'I'm used to hard work and couldn't bear to be idle.' Conor and Teresa looked at her wordlessly and her face reddened as she wondered if she'd said the wrong thing.

'You're not really expected to work hard, Charlotte,' Conor said. 'You're Jamie's wife.'

'My mother always worked until she had to give

up due to ill-health,' Charlotte went on defensively, 'and I'd love to help out, in Reception, Housekeeping, Reservations, whatever.'

'Sounds great,' Jamie said cheerfully. 'Brains as well as beauty. I told you she was one in a million, didn't I, folks?'

Teresa smiled, but it didn't reach her eyes.

Jamie held her tightly in bed and told her not to worry if Conor and his mother seemed a bit awkward with her. She lay with her head on his chest, hearing the deep rumble within as he said, 'They're not used to someone as beautiful as you, with your pale-gold hair and lavender eyes.'

'They weren't expecting you to arrive home married. They're bound to be a little distrustful.'

'My mother's not the same since Dad died. They were mad about each other, the way we are. I'd hate anything to happen to you, or to us,' he said, scooping her closer to his strong frame. She pressed tightly against him, still overawed at the way he responded to her body.

Although it was a huge change from her life in New York, it didn't take Charlotte long to feel at home in Tamarisk. She felt drawn to the curving, beech-lined driveway, the way the facade seemed to hover like a pearl jewel between sweeping parklands, the elegant interior, with classy but comfortable furnishings. And Jamie had been right about the mountains. Sometimes the mist dropped silently, shrouding them in a veil; other times the sunshine slanted across, highlighting lush valleys and dales and rocky granite outcrops. Occasionally they were dark beneath a cloud-filled sky, but always, they were beautiful. She loved the clear, invigorating air and how freshly sweet it tasted after rain. She loved the community feel to the picturesque village of Glendoran and the drive up from the village through quaint and sheltered laneways.

Charlotte settled into a routine, helping out with the housekeeping and kitchen. She worked quietly and unobtrusively, as Jamie and Conor got on with the day-to-day running of the business. They catered mainly for fishing and golfing groups, hill-walking clubs, and weekenders. According to Jamie, business wasn't as good as it had been, thanks to the Troubles in Northern Ireland. But by degrees, she got the feel of the whole business, which was on a much smaller scale than Fitzgerald's, but exciting in a different way. For with its stunning location and graceful, yet homely, ambience, Charlotte felt the hotel was bursting with potential.

She met Jamie's circle of friends and their wives, and became especially friendly with Millie, who worked in the drapery shop in Glendoran. Charlotte wrote to her parents every week and phoned them each fortnight. By degrees, Teresa warmed to her, her natural reticence dropping away.

And then one evening when they were married about three months, Jamie hung back in the hotel past his usual time, and she eventually found him in the Residents' Lounge with Conor and a couple of his business friends from Wicklow town.

'I've just opened a bottle of reserve Jameson,' he said. 'Care to join us?'

Her eyes slid across the group, Jamie smiling broadly, Conor looking at her impassively and the other men regarding her with undeniable interest. 'No, thanks, I'll leave you to it,' she said, feeling four pairs of eyes on her as she turned around and went back to the apartment.

Jamie had been late coming to bed that night. She knew by his flushed pallor that he'd drank more than normal and it put her on edge. 'Don't you like Conor?' Jamie asked.

'Yes, why?'

'I just have the feeling that you pair don't get on,' he said slightly belligerently. 'Sometimes I think he resents you here. I've a good mind to tackle him about it. I want us all to be one big happy family. But you're happy?' He looked at her worriedly, his easy confidence faltering a little.

'Of course, Jamie, very happy.'

'I hope you have no regrets.'

Regrets? Her chest squeezed momentarily. Jamie was waiting, his face honest and expectant. Then she said, 'How could I when my heart is feeling things I'd never expected to feel.'

He grinned and pulled her to him. 'That's what I like to hear, woman.'

When, two months later, her pregnancy was confirmed by a doctor in Dublin, privately recommended by Millie, she was overwhelmed by the fact that she was having a baby and felt as though

130

she was the first person in the world to be carrying the miracle of life within her. She knew that Jamie would want to throw some kind of noisy party to celebrate, and open another bottle of that special whiskey of his, so she kept the news to herself for over a week to absorb it quietly and get used to the new turn her life was taking before it was broadcast all over Wicklow. Even though it was January, she went walking under chilly grey skies around the perimeter of the hotel grounds, thinking of the tiny, growing baby within her. And one afternoon she was so lost in thought that she'd bumped into Conor.

'Charlotte! What are you doing out here? It looks like snow.'

He, too, seemed to be out for a walk despite the chilly breeze. 'I'm just getting some fresh air, same as you,' she said.

'Yes, it can get stuffy in the hotel with the central heating. How are things?' he asked, falling into step beside her. 'I hope you're settling in and we're not too much of a shock to you.'

He gave her a smile that was friendly and warm, and so totally disarming that to her horror she heard herself gabbling, 'I'm fine. Actually I'm more than fine. I'm expecting a baby. And I shouldn't have told you because Jamie doesn't know yet. I'm telling him this evening.'

'A baby.' He gave her another of his thoughtful looks. Then he smiled. 'That's wonderful. And don't worry, Charlotte, you haven't told me anything.'

Jamie was thrilled with the news, almost growing in stature with pride. He threw an impromptu party and opened more bottles of special reserve. 'My mother is delighted,' he told her afterwards, 'but I thought Conor would have sounded happier.'

'He told me he was pleased,' she said.

'Yes, well he would have to say that, wouldn't he? Anyway, it's his hard cheese if he resents that I'm going to be a father before him.'

Charlotte was in labour in the busy hospital on a warm August morning before they realised she was expecting twins and rushed her into the theatre for a Caesarean section. Her baby girl was born first, and was the bigger of the twins. 'Your little boy was hiding behind her,' the gynaecologist told her. 'That's why we didn't know there were two.'

Ten days later, she brought Jack and Serena home to Tamarisk, feeling as though her whole universe had changed with the arrival of these wonderful babies. On their christening day, Jamie declared he was the happiest man in the world as he went around filling glasses.

Soon after that, Conor decided to leave.

Jamie was clearly agitated as he broke the news to her on a Sunday evening. He brought back a bottle of brandy from the hotel bar and he sloshed rather a lot of it into a crystal balloon. 'He says there's no room for him here anymore. No room! In the whole of Tamarisk! What's he on about!'

'Where's he thinking of going?' she asked. Her immediate concern was that she'd just settled the twins after a busy day and hoped Jamie's loud voice wouldn't disturb them.

'France. He has plans to develop a hotel of his own there . . . God, I never expected this. Mum is thinking of going with him. She feels Tamarisk is too full of sad memories for her. Conor wants me to buy him out. We'll have to talk to our solicitor and it might mean putting our house plans on hold for a few years.'

'That's okay,' Charlotte said, attempting to calm him down. 'This apartment will suit us fine until the twins are older.'

'Yes, but I'll really miss Conor. He's my best mate. And how will I run Tamarisk without him? Christ, Charlotte, this is a flipping disaster.'

'You have me. I'll help.'

'Are you sure about that? Are you happy here?'

'Of course I am. We'll manage. It'll be fine.'

'I wish I could believe that,' he said glumly. He stared into the amber depths of his glass before knocking its contents back. Then, he reached for the bottle again.

'Jamie, relax. I've lots of ideas for when the economy picks up,' Charlotte insisted, hating to see him despondent. 'This is a fantastic place and full of potential. I see expensive cars coming up the driveway and bedrooms filled with designer clothes and luxury cosmetics of high-spending visitors. Most of all, I see Tamarisk visitors feeling the way

I did when I first stepped into Fitzgerald's; their hearts jumping with excitement, as though they're entering a magic ground. We can make it happen. You'll see.'

CHAPTER 11

'We're not just any hotel, we're Tamarisk,' Serena said heatedly, sitting in her office on Tuesday evening. 'We'll lose half of our celebrity guests if their privacy is compromised.'

'Serena, think about it,' Brian said. 'You could stabilise your cash flow if you dropped your policy of restricting the Leisure Centre for the sole use of guests and opened it to general membership. In the next couple of years, it'll be impossible to maintain the same profit level without making difficult decisions and reducing some frills. You're still paying back the capital borrowed to renovate the Spa and install under-floor heating throughout the hotel. Interest rates have risen and we have to factor in the distinct possibility of another rise. Have a look at these figures . . .'

Serena's eyes glazed over the columns, for they were figures she preferred not to see, even though she knew she was wrong to be in certain denial. 'We were never a Celtic Tiger hotel and your suggestion goes against our principles of making the customer feel special,' she said, disgusted with the wobble in her voice. 'The last thing our guests want is sightseers gawping at them in the swimming pool or rubbing shoulders with them in the sauna. I'm not going to tarnish our image of an exclusive, pampering oasis with half measures.' She lifted her chin and said, 'I'm declaring Tamarisk a recession-free zone. I'm not doing away with the welcoming package of French sparkling wine, floral bouquets or Irish handmade chocolate. My goal is to go for five-star classification. So if things are tough out there, we have to doubly ensure that, more than ever, our guests are indulged to the most luxurious standard possible. And I have a great idea for the next marketing campaign . . .'

'Yes?' Brian looked slightly alarmed, as though he suspected Serena was going to blow the entire marketing budget.

'We can emphasise the fact that Tamarisk will never compromise the excellent level of pampering guests can expect. In fact we might even . . .' Serena hesitated before plunging on recklessly, 'I think we should publicise the fact that, far from cutting any corners, we intend to show our appreciation of their continued support by presenting guests with individually prepared gift bags of their favourite French organic spa products. Sample-sized, to take home with them as a reminder of their wonderful time in the Spa.'

Brian spluttered. 'But didn't you shoot down a suggestion to have our spa products on sale? Now you're talking about *giving* them away?'

'I thought it was slightly tacky to have them on sale, besides it spoiled the exclusivity of our products. However, if they were gifted to the guests and properly marketed . . . I'll talk to Pierre in La Mimosa and see what Jack thinks when he gets home.'

'And when will that be?' Brian asked.

'Any day now,' Serena blandly told him.

'Good. I've already tried to talk to Jack about the cash flow situation and the plunging profit margin, but he was . . . well, obviously he had other things on his mind . . .'

'Yes, obviously,' Serena said, keeping her expression neutral.

Damn Jack for not being around. He normally managed the budgets, salaries and accounts, anything with figures was his forte. Serena was the one with the ideas and she directed the other side of operations, the staffing, the marketing promotions, events and conferencing. Jack worked behind the scenes, and to routine methods and procedures. Serena knew she was the creative force, the one with the high-flying vision and ideas, sweeping her brother up in her enthusiasm and persuading him to bankroll her improvement projects. If from time to time she felt their partnership was a little unbalanced, with Jack content to number crunch and follow her lead, she ignored it.

Her meeting with Brian had been moved from Monday to Tuesday as she'd hoped that Jack would be there. When he still hadn't shown up, she'd tried to postpone again, but Brian insisted on seeing her.

Like every other player in the hospitality industry, Tamarisk had faced challenges over the past couple of years. Thankfully the high-season summer months were busy, particularly at the weekends but mid- and low-season bookings were down. Serena had introduced campaigns that rewarded loyal customers. She had, naturally, been concerned about the reduced number of high-spending corporate visitors, with the impact that had on business overall, but a lot of their celebrity clients were recession-proof and, up to now, she'd felt sure Tamarisk would ride out the storm.

'What's the bottom line, Brian?' she asked.

Brian surveyed the maze of tabulated rows of figures, pie charts and graphs spread across Serena's rosewood desk. 'Overall, if you don't have an improvement on the number of bed nights and restaurant receipts in the coming months, or reduce your operating costs, it's likely that Tamarisk will suffer a loss this year.'

After Brian had left, Serena poured a glass of spring water and sipped it slowly in an effort to calm herself. Why hadn't Jack told her that things were far from rosy? How could he have taken his eye off the ball to this extent? And why hadn't he been in contact? He seemed to have fallen off the face of the earth. Yesterday she'd phoned La Mimosa and her cousin Pierre had confirmed that Jack had left on time for his flight. That had been last *Friday*. Pierre had followed things up for her and had later phoned back to say that Jack's car hadn't been returned to the rental agency.

'Don't be imagining the worst, Serena,' Pierre had said in his accented English. 'Jack seemed fine when he left here. Maybe he's met up with friends, who knows? If there was anything wrong we would have heard by now.'

'You're right. I guess he's just being thoughtless.'

'By the way, you are still coming to the Spa and Wellness Trade Fair in Paris in September? I have to confirm all the bookings soon.'

'Of course I'll be there,' she'd said. 'I'm not going to miss that opportunity.

'Ciao, Serena. Best of luck with the naughty Jack,' Pierre had ended on a warm chuckle.

Serena had a good mind to have words with Jack when he got home, grieving widower or not. She looked through the charts and graphs Brian had left with her, trying to make sense of them.

Charlotte had offered to help out in Jack's absence, but Serena had refused. 'You've worked hard enough over the years,' she'd said to her mother. 'Besides, it'll do Jack good to know that Tamarisk needs him and he has responsibilities waiting for him. If he feels you've stepped into his shoes, he'll have less of an incentive to get his act together. That might sound harsh, but it's better that he has work to occupy himself with.'

'I agree and I've no intentions of taking back the reins. But I don't like to see you burdened with so much responsibility without Jack's support. And you have Paul and Harriet to consider too. So don't be afraid to ask for help.'

'It's only for a couple of weeks,' Serena pointed out. 'I'll be well able to cope. After all, Mum, you ran Tamarisk single-handedly for years.'

And made a huge success of it, Serena reminded herself now as she pored over figures. As fate would have it, she and Jack had taken control just before the world had been plunged into a recession – but they would survive. They *had* to.

It was all the more reason, Serena thought, to chase her goal. First step was the award. It would surely tell the world that Tamarisk was open for business. And it suited her to keep busy, and engrossed. It gave her certain satisfaction, but most important of all, it stopped her from thinking too much. She was so pre-occupied that she didn't notice Paul coming into her office until he was standing in front of her, his wedding band glinting as he rested his hands on her desk.

She looked up, feeling at a bigger disadvantage when she saw his face, set in a dark glower. 'Paul! Jesus, you startled me. What are you doing here?'

'I thought so.'

'Thought what?'

'You've forgotten. Again.'

He was wearing his white rugby shirt and navy chinos. She racked her brains as a knot formed in her stomach. 'Sorry, I've been up to my tonsils here. What have I forgotten now?'

'Harriet was hoping you'd be home so she could show off her new karate move. *I* was hoping you'd be home on time to come with me to the rugby club barbeque in Blackrock.'

The knot spread up to her chest and her head felt woolly. 'Shit. Look, I'm really sorry. I had Brian here this evening and it went on longer than I thought.'

'Why did you arrange to see him this evening? I told you about the barbeque last week.'

'Yes, but at the last minute I moved Brian from yesterday to this evening, hoping that Jack would be home. I forgot about the barbeque. Why didn't you call me?'

'I did, but your mobile is switched off. I rang Suzi and she said you were in a meeting. So I thought I'd drop by and see what exactly you were up to.'

Her face flushed. 'Why, what did you think I was doing?'

Paul shrugged.

'If I leave now and rush home to shower and change . . .' she offered. She could have used a shower in the hotel, but her navy suit and plain white top was too formal for a barbeque. She began to tidy her desk, gathering papers, scrabbling together pie charts and graphs and rows of figures, feeling almost sick to her stomach with tension as she bundled them into a pile.

Paul stood up. 'Forget it. I'm supposed to be there now and I want to get going. I can't wait for you to go home and come back. Especially through Glendoran. It's chock-a-block with tourist cars and coaches this evening. And,' he gave her a wry glance as he reached the doorway, 'at least I'll reduce the risk of being called Paul Devlin.'

In her heart of hearts, she knew it was just a throwaway remark, but it fuelled Serena's ill-temper. 'This wouldn't be happening if we'd built our house here in the grounds,' she simmered. 'As well, I'd be home earlier and able to see more of Harriet.'

She knew immediately by his darkening face that she'd struck a raw nerve. Before their marriage, a perfect site had been identified for their home on the grounds of Tamarisk, in a secluded corner on a rise over near the woods, but at the time Paul had insisted that they needed to maintain a family life independent of Tamarisk.

Now he stepped back into her office, his hands dug into the pockets of his chinos. She heard the chink of coins as his fingers played restlessly with loose change. 'Hold on a minute, I hope you're joking,' he said, looking at her steadily. 'Maple Hill is the home we planned together.'

'You said it yourself,' she went on desperately. 'Our home is over fifteen miles away, and through Glendoran which is tourist-clogged most of the time.'

'Yes, and more fool me, I assumed that it would

give us a little space away from Tamarisk and prevent you from hopping into the car during your supposed free time to make sure that the hotel was still up and running.'

'I have to be on call now and then.'

'I know that Serena, but it's happening more often than I expected and sometimes I can't help getting a little pissed off.'

'Are you still thinking of your birthday?'

Soon after Jack had left for France she'd had to cancel Paul's birthday meal in an exclusive south Dublin restaurant because she'd been delayed in the hotel when one of New York's hottest fashion designers had arrived unexpectedly, burnt out after a hectic Fashion Week and a suite had had to be kitted out to her exact criteria. Serena had made it up to him, though, and had rescheduled their dinner date for a later evening.

Paul laughed mockingly. 'I'm not that juvenile. I know things have been difficult, but I'm starting to get the impression you enjoy all these emergencies and riding to the rescue, and sometimes lately I even feel . . .' he hesitated.

Her heart hammered. 'Go on, Paul . . . you might as well spit it out . . .'

He looked her in the eye as he said, 'There are times when I feel you're far more passionate about your career than me.'

The hurt look in his eyes went straight to her heart. 'No. That's not true. You and Harriet have always come first with me. And,' her voice trembled, 'I do feel passionate about you.'

He gave her a long, steady look. Then something flickered in his dark eyes. 'So prove it. Show me how passionate you feel.'

'As soon as Jack is back we'll—'

He went over to the door and locked it. 'Forget about Jack,' he said in a silky voice. 'What's wrong with now? I'm already late. A few more minutes won't make much difference. Come on, love, show me how much I mean to you.' He pulled the end of his rugby top out of the waistband of his jeans and she caught a glimpse of the pattern of dark hairs fanning across his toned midriff.

His meaning was unmistakeable and her heart leapt into her mouth. 'Paul!'

Holding her gaze, his eyes steel-grey and liquid with desire, he began to unbuckle his belt. She stood up and came around the front of her desk, putting out a restraining hand.

'Jesus, Paul, for God's sake I'm in the office . . .'

He laughed and caught her by the shoulders. 'So?' Then, he kissed her hard. Despite her misgivings she found herself responding. 'Hey, that's good,' he said after a while, holding her in his embrace. 'You entice me, Serena. I need you. Why don't you sit on the edge of your desk and open your legs,' he nuzzled her neck as his hand slid up her skirt, 'or, better still,' he kissed the hollow of her throat as he reached her lace-trimmed panties, 'bend over the sofa . . .'

'You're messing with me,' she said, her teeth chattering as his fingers pushed inside her and his thumb began to stroke her most sensitive spot so that she felt muzzy with desire.

'I'm not. Show me how you feel about me.'

Her heart thudded but she pulled herself together. 'Not here. Someone could come looking for me . . . or the phone . . .'

His tongue flicked around the outer shell of her ear. 'So? The door is locked. Ignore the phone. Show me I mean more to you than the staff . . . or the hotel . . .' he murmured insistently.

She shut her eyes for a minute, opened them again and looked at him imploringly. 'Sorry, I can't do this.'

He released her immediately. 'Fine. Forget it.'

Guilt washed over her. 'Look, I can't . . . not here . . .'

'It's okay.' He walked across to the door, tucking his shirt back into his jeans.

'Paul, wait! Who's babysitting Harriet?'

'Ah. Harriet. You remembered. Susan is.'

Serena felt totally drained after Paul left. She sat at her desk for a while, woodenly clearing her papers, Brian's precious pie charts and graphs jumping mockingly in front of her eyes. She felt like feeding them page by page into the shredder.

What did Paul think she might have been up to? she asked herself anxiously. It was unlike him to arrive unannounced into her office like that. With shaking fingers, she pulled her handbag out of the bottom drawer, feeling like a traitor as she double checked the foil strip of contraceptive pills that were tucked away in the zipped compartment. It was the only place she could hide them, as both Charlotte and Jack had keys to her desk drawers in Tamarisk, and she felt safer keeping them close to her. At home in Maple Hill, she always removed her mobile, purse and keys before putting her bag with the others on the high shelf in her dressing room. High, in case Harriet went exploring. It was a ritual with her. She kept her supply of unopened packets in an old hat box shoved up in the uppermost corner of her dressing room.

Her efforts to keep Paul in the dark seemed so tawdry and deceitful that Serena put her head in her hands. She had a sudden image of her perfect wedding day and she felt like weeping. How much longer could she go on covering up her blatant fraud?

CHAPTER 12

Jack took a sip of airport coffee before putting his disposable cup on the table in front of him. It was bitter and too hot. He'd only bought it to kill time and give himself something to do. Across from him, a business executive was keying stuff into a laptop, his fingers urgent on the keys as though it was a matter of life or death. Some children were playing on a carousel behind him, their carefree, excited voices echoing around the concourse. He wondered idly if, in time, they'd grow up to be harried executives, filling in time before flights with pressing business matters instead of having some fun. Soon his flight would take to the skies, taking him away from Nice and Jenni.

She'd refused to come home with him.

'I know how you feel right now,' she'd said gently, 'but it wouldn't work.'

'Why not? I've never met anyone like you before. I've never felt like this either.'

'Yes, it's been great, but it was just one of those moments in time.'

'A moment? Hell, it's been almost a week. A week like nothing I've ever had.'

'You have your life to go back to and I have mine. Yours is in Ireland and mine is here, in France, and they're so different that they have nothing at all in common.'

They'd been sitting on his hotel balcony overlooking the rippling swell of the bay. It was Thursday evening, and Jenni had taken time off work so that they could spend his last night together. In a way, he'd rather have been back in her apartment where a windmill spun a riot of colour in the window frame and Jenni's washing hung suspended on a rickety clothesline that ran between her bedroom and bathroom window. So starkly removed from the luxury of La Mimosa and Tamarisk that it was laughable.

In one sense Jenni had been right. Their lives were worlds apart. She was only starting out in life. As well as being older, he'd been around, had already been married. He'd wished he could go back to the previous Friday evening and have those precious days with her all over again. He'd wished he could bring her home and have her in his life, because the thought of saying goodbye to her was killing him. He didn't know if his behaviour had been terribly foolish or utterly spoiled.

'You need more time,' she'd said. 'It's too soon after your wife . . .'

'It's not too soon. It's nearly a year. Amy and I . . . I explained all that to you, didn't I?'

'Yes, but here, where you're away from it all, it's as though your normal life has been suspended, and it's easy to ignore what happened. But when you go back home, to your family and the life you once shared with Amy, things will be different. Only then will you start to work through everything.'

'I've already sorted out my head. I wish I could just stay here. With you.'

'You're just saying that because you're nervous of returning home, facing up to things, and you want to sink your head into the sand and remain in some kind of buffer zone.'

'That's not true. You've done something to me . . . oh, feck it, I can't explain, it's great, wonderful, and I don't want to give you up.'

'You mean you've enjoyed sex without strings.'

'Jenni! Somewhere behind that friendly, carefree exterior lies a cruel streak I'd never have expected.'

'Cruel?'

'Yes. I thought you felt something for me, liked me a little . . . Hey, I was even big-headed enough to think that I gave something back to you . . .'

'You did. I've enjoyed being with you.'

'Then why can't we find some way of seeing each other again?'

'Why can't you accept we just had a holiday romance?'

'Romance? Is that what you call it?' he'd grinned.

'You know what I mean. Back in the real world, they soon fizzle out.'

'So in other words, as soon as I'm gone, you'll find someone else?'

Jenni's eyes had darkened. 'Is that what you think of me?'

Jack's heart had lurched. 'No, sorry, I'm not thinking straight because I don't want to say goodbye to you, and we should be making the most of our last night together.' He'd reached across and smoothed back a tendril of her hair, tucking it behind the jewelled headband she was wearing. She'd turned her face so that it rested in the palm of his hand. Then she'd given him an impish glance from under her lashes.

'We'll have to do something special for our last night. Let me see . . . I bet you fifty euro I can get out of my clothes a lot quicker than you.'

'Ah ha, not so fast.' He'd risen to his feet and drawn her into his arms, holding her close and resting his chin on the top of her head. Then he'd walked her backwards into his bedroom. 'I have a better idea,' he'd murmured into her hair. 'Why don't I undress you real slow and see how long I can make it last before you cry for mercy.'

As his hands had begun a leisurely journey down along the buttons of her shirt, and his fingers had grazed her warm skin beneath, Jenni's eyes had sparkled and she'd bitten her lip. He took his time undressing her, sliding off her underwear very slowly. She'd whimpered and fallen back across the bed, reaching for him with eager hands. 'Now, Jack . . .'

'Tell me it isn't over,' he'd murmured, throwing himself down beside her, gathering her close to him and letting his hand drift to the soft moistness between her thighs.

She arched her body towards him. 'Jack! You bastard! Please . . .'

'Tell me,' he'd urged, his slow fingers intimately circling.

'Okay, okay,' she'd breathed. 'We'll sort something. Please, Jack.'

'Is that a promise?' His voice had been hoarse. He'd bent down and licked her before popping open a condom and sliding on top of her.

'Promise, yes . . . now, Jack. *Now.*'

He'd pushed inside her hot softness, his head swimming with the pleasure of it. He'd been so hungry for this that he'd come almost immediately just after Jenni's body had convulsed around him.

The following morning he'd reminded her of the promise he'd extracted.

'Did I really say that?'

'Yep, you did,' he'd said, tickling her stomach. 'Would you like an action replay? So that I can remind you?'

'Uh, please.'

In the end, Jack had thought he was going to miss his flight all over again. Jenni had refused to come to the airport, so she'd said goodbye to him in his suite at the Negresco and told him she'd prefer to walk back to her apartment because she needed to clear her head.

He'd felt strangely bereft after she left the room, but he didn't dare follow her for one last kiss. Instead he'd steeled himself to check out of the hotel, drive to the airport, and leave the car back to the rental agency. Jenni had promised that if he still wanted to see her after a month, he could call her. In the meantime, he was to mark Amy's anniversary in some way. He was also to date as many women as possible. However, if he went to bed with any of them, he wasn't to contact her again.

As Jack shuffled through passport control and heard the first boarding call for his flight to Dublin, a full week after he'd missed his initial flight home, he told himself that having got through the past year, he would surely survive one month.

CHAPTER 13

Somewhere up there, there was a God, or else, Kim decided gleefully on Saturday afternoon as she stepped out of her scented bath, she had an angel looking out specially for her. She picked up a soft cream bath sheet and patted her body dry and then began to apply rose oil to her skin. Before she dressed, she stared critically at her reflection in the mirror. It was amazing that her face looked so calm and serene on the outside, when inwardly she was trembling with anticipation.

Just that morning Serena had phoned, sending Kim into a tail spin. Jack was home – and he was coming to her party. Suddenly, she was fearful as well as excited. Fearful in case she messed it all up, but excited at the thoughts of mending Jack Devlin's broken heart in the best way possible – by showing him just how much she loved him. Kim barely restrained herself from asking a flood of questions. When did he arrive? How did he look? More importantly, did Serena think he was back to himself?

'I don't know what kept him in Nice but he

finally called me to say he got home yesterday evening,' Serena said. 'He thinks your party is a good chance to say hello to everyone . . .'

Kim examined the reflection of her naked body. At thirty-five, her face needed a little help from her cosmetics to retain a dewy look. Thankfully, her figure was quite good, with long legs gracefully tapering from her shapely thighs down to her narrow ankles, and her breasts were still firm and high. She put her hands on them, closed her eyes, and imagined they were Jack's hands. She began to feel so turned on that it was an effort to get dressed.

She put on silk underwear, loving the sheer feel of it next to her skin and the way it clung to her curves. Over that she drew on a purple chiffon cocktail dress and slid her feet into a pair of kitten heels. Then she went downstairs and poured herself a stiff gin and tonic, to take the edge off the anxiety that had had her on tenterhooks since Serena's call. She went out through her sun room to the patio and the back garden, where the land-scaped flowerbeds were freshly planted and vital with life, and mingled scents of blossom and peat drifted across the air.

The early evening was beautiful. It had rained that afternoon and now the air was sweet and fresh and the sky crystal clear. She had tea lights ready in coloured glass for when the evening grew dim, and at the throw of a switch, the cleverly designed lighting system that ran around the perimeter would illuminate various garden features. In a corner, under the shade of a Japanese maple tree she had a small circular table laid out with a white linen tablecloth and a pottery vase spilling over with lavender, and two chairs drawn up. It looked like an intimate tableau, a perfect setting for lovers enjoying some time in the garden. And it was an echo of Tamarisk and the traditional way the table would be brought out and laid on the south lawn for their celebrations. She hoped it would remind Jack of this and make him feel at home. She'd even hung a few yellow balloons around the garden.

If she did everything right and surrounded him with as much love as possible, surely her dreams would become a reality.

Kim checked her watch. She had ten minutes before the caterers were due to arrive and set up food and drinks. Ten minutes to shore up her confidence, to take a few deep breaths and try and find calm within herself. She shouldn't feel this nervous: there was no need. Jack had even talked of marrying her, she reminded herself, before he met Amy, although, at the time, she'd dismissed it with a laugh.

'You're like me,' she had said to Jack, during Serena and Paul's wedding reception in Tamarisk. 'Free and single.'

Jack had tipped his champagne flute against hers. 'Yeah, we're two of a kind. Far too busy having fun to settle down, right? Although I think you rack up far more air miles than I do, tatty-head.'

'I can't help it if I'm in great demand. Are you jealous?' she'd teased.

He'd leaned in close and murmured, 'I hope you behave yourself on all those foreign jaunts.'

'Of course. I behave atrociously. You need to have fun before you settle down'.

'That's it. Hey, I once told my mother I was going to marry you.' His eyes had looked at her in merriment.

'Yeah, I think you were about ten,' she'd laughed. 'Don't worry, I'm not going to put a gun to your head.'

'Thanks, Kim. Some women I know would consider that an engagement but I'm not quite ready for the altar rails.'

'Nor me,' Kim had said with feeling, watching Serena and Paul whirl around the floor. 'Right now, I'm too busy enjoying life. I'm not ready for domestic chains.'

Funny how life could change almost overnight, Kim thought, as she strolled around her back garden and sat for a moment under the shade of the maple tree. The holy water font in Glendoran parish church was hardly the place for a eureka moment. Or perhaps there was no better spot, for the knowledge had hit Kim like some kind of miraculous rebirth. At the christening service for Harriet, about two years after Serena and Paul's wedding, she and Jack as godparents had stood together and, in between the prayers, he'd lifted the tiny, white-swaddled Harriet into his arms and she hadn't been able to stop looking at him. He'd kissed Harriet's minuscule forehead with unexpected gentleness and then he'd given Kim a soft, private smile with his blue-green eyes. It had sent a sudden jolt all through her. When they'd moved in close for a photograph, and she'd caught the drift of his expensive scent and felt his proximity, her body had suddenly become inflamed. As the rest of the afternoon had passed by, she'd felt hot, dizzy, exhilarated and alarmed in equal measure. She hadn't been able to take her eyes off Jack for any length of time. Her skin had ached for his touch and her heart had pounded when he'd laughed and joked with her. When he'd called her tatty-head, it was like a loving endearment.

How had this happened? Was it her age, the ticking of her body clock? Had seeing him holding Harriet unleashed a primeval nesting instinct? Had her love for him always been there in the background waiting to explode? Whatever it was, it felt like an explosion of sorts and she'd wanted him in a way she'd never wanted anyone before.

Over the next year, her feelings for Jack had grown, but whenever she'd run into him, she'd continued to treat him like a very dear friend. Afraid of putting him off, she'd never tried to be possessive or give him the impression that he had suddenly turned into the man she loved above all others. Even though she'd given up modelling

157

because of him, to make sure she'd have regular hours and little or no travel, she hadn't been unduly upset when a gossipy tabloid had reported that Jack and Amy Skelly seemed to be an item. Jack's social life was always media fodder and usually exaggerated. Amy had been a flirty hostess in a nightclub that boasted most of Dublin's Z list socialites in its clientele, and Kim had been sure it was nothing to worry about.

Then on a bleak January morning, Serena had dropped the bombshell.

'He said it was a whirlwind romance. And they're getting married in March. In a private ceremony in the Seychelles. But not so private that it won't be splashed all over *Heat* or *Hello!* I'll bet.' Serena's voice had been unusually scathing considering she was talking about Jack.

'I don't believe you,' Kim had felt a sharp pain in her chest.

'Neither do I believe it,' Serena had said. 'I thought that maybe you and he—'

'Me and Jack?' she'd struggled to sound normal as she got the words out.

'Yes, you're such good buddies I thought that you clicked together very well. I know he's very fond of you and you like him, don't you? I had hopes that maybe . . . never mind . . .' Serena had given a heavy sigh.

'I'm far too busy having some fun, and I don't fancy the whole white lace and promises thing,' Kim had said, instinctively shielding her battered heart. It was far too raw to take out in front of anyone, even Serena. After a silence, she'd tentatively voiced her worst fears. 'He must be in love with Amy if he can't wait to marry her.'

There was another pause, and then Serena had said, in a carefully neutral voice, as if regretting her burst of disloyalty to Jack, 'Yes, I guess he must be . . .'

Kim had partied harder than ever before over the following few months, and had begun to date Matthew O'Brien, putting on a bright face in front of both Jack and Serena, and, of course, Amy, the few times that she hadn't been able to avoid running into her. Then, overnight, life had changed again, and Amy was gone, and mingled with Kim's shock and consternation had been the realisation that Jack was free once more.

She'd joined Serena and Paul in supporting him during those first few difficult months. She'd invited him for dinner. She'd spent more time than usual in Glendoran. Little by little, although he'd never spoken of Amy, or unburdened himself, they'd talked about everything else and she'd sensed they were getting closer. Then, one evening, when they'd been dining alone, she'd been able to tell he wasn't really there.

'What's wrong, Jack?' she'd asked eventually.

He'd put down his knife and fork, looking relieved that he didn't have to continue the charade of enjoying his meal. 'Sorry, Kim, you've gone to all this trouble and I'm just not with it this evening.'

'There's no need to apologise,' she'd said. She'd gone around to his side of the table and had put her arms around his neck 'What's up? Is it Amy? Do you want to talk about it?'

He'd reached up and held her arm. 'Not really. My head is just a total fuck-up and I need to sort it out.' Then he'd told her he was going to La Mimosa to get away from it all for a while.

'Oh, Jack,' she'd been sympathetic immediately. 'I wish there was something I could do.' She'd wondered what had it been like for him to find out he was going to be a father and then weeks later having that prospect taken away from him, only to lose his wife a month after that. No wonder he needed total down time in La Mimosa. She'd looked at him for what seemed like ages, and then she'd summoned her courage and kissed his mouth. Her heart had soared and her nerve endings had quivered when he kissed her back.

He'd drawn away after a while and gently flicked her cheek. 'That was nice,' he'd said. 'You've been great. I wish my head wasn't so wrecked. Hopefully I'll get my act together in the next couple of weeks.'

'I'm sure you will,' she'd said comfortingly.

Again, in the hallway, he'd wrapped her in his arms and kissed her just before he left.

'You're special, Kim,' he'd said. 'Thanks again. I'll be back to you soon. You'll be so busy you won't even notice I'm gone.'

Now the waiting was almost over. Kim took a deep breath, inhaling the fresh scents drifting around her garden. She wondered if Jack was emotionally ready to give himself to another woman. Some of her media contacts were coming that evening, and she could almost see the photographs in the glossies' diary pages: *Kim Mulligan and Jack Devlin, at the unveiling of Kim's tranquillity garden.* Then later, her mind galloped, *Kim and Jack seem to be an item . . . Kim and Jack are delighted to announce their engagement . . .*

The doorbell chimed. It was the caterers. Suddenly, the evening was about to happen and, as she walked up the hallway to open the door, bubbles of joy fizzed up inside her.

CHAPTER 14

'I spy with my little eye something beginning with "T",' Harriet said.

'That's too easy,' Jack laughed. 'A tree.'

Harriet squealed with delight. 'I knew you'd say that, but it's wrong.'

'Wrong?'

Charlotte smiled at the reflection of Jack's nonplussed face in the rear view mirror. As she drove towards Dublin on the N11, she was conscious of feeling totally contented because everything was perfect in this moment. Serena was sitting beside her, looking fabulous in an emerald green maxi dress and gold sling-back sandals. Jack was in the back along with Harriet. She was glad she'd offered to drive them all up to Kim's party, although she was sorry that Paul most likely wouldn't make it on account of a rugby match in Galway. Charlotte always enjoyed having her family around, but this evening it was extra special, because the troubled Jack who'd left for La Mimosa had returned as her vibrant son. Whatever had happened to Jack when he was away, whatever peace he'd made with himself, he had returned a new man. He'd thrown his arms around her in a way he hadn't done in years and it had made her feel teary-eyed with gratitude.

She told herself that everything was going to be fine and that she could ignore the little anxieties playing on her mind. With Jack restored to himself, Serena would be able to ease back on her busy schedule.

'Do you give up?' Harriet asked hopefully after Jack had had several incorrect guesses.

'I give up,' Jack said with mock dismay.

'My teddy!' Harriet exclaimed with joy.

'But that's your Sulley bear!'

'No, this teddy,' Harriet giggled, her little finger pointing to the novelty Winnie the Pooh attached to her seat belt. They began all over again and there were more shrieks of excitement, to Charlotte's satisfaction.

'How's business in La Mimosa?' Charlotte asked Jack, after a while.

'They've plenty of bookings for the summer months,' he said. 'There are some exciting new wines coming on the market and I've ordered us a supply. The grounds are looking great. The huge landscaping job they did last autumn is paying dividends now.'

'Yes, they were telling me about that. How are Conor and Martine?' she asked.

'They're fine,' Jack went on. 'No sign of them retiring just yet. Although Pierre has taken over a lot of the management role from them.'

'I must pay them a visit,' Charlotte said. 'It's a while since I've been over there.'

'Yes, you should,' Jack encouraged. 'You know they'd spoil you rotten.'

'Your stay over there has certainly done the world of good for you,' she said. 'And I've just had a wonderful idea,' she went on. 'Why don't we all go over to La Mimosa for the weekend of our birthdays? We could have a party over there.'

She congratulated herself on coming up with the idea – going to La Mimosa would be a novel way of moving on and putting the past behind them.

'Sounds great,' Jack said. 'I'm up for that.'

'Serena?'

'It's a good idea, if Tamarisk can be left without us,' Serena said.

'The hotel won't fall apart because you're away for a long weekend,' Charlotte said firmly. 'Andrew should be able to manage. We'll bring some friends as well, Millie, perhaps, Kim, and if you have anyone you'd like to invite Jack . . . it would be fun. I'll fly us all over together. My treat. We'll have a barbeque on the terrace. I'll talk to Conor next week and start planning. I'm sure he'll pull out the stops.'

'Is that what happened to you, Jack?' Serena said, and something in her voice alerted Charlotte. A sliver of resentment?

'What do you mean?'

'You were spoiled rotten and indulged in all the best La Mimosa has to offer,' Serena went on.

'You look like you can't keep a satisfied grin off your face.'

Definitely a note of jealousy, Charlotte detected, deciding that Serena badly needed some down time. She was going to insist on babysitting Harriet so that she and Paul could go away for a weekend. Sooner rather than later.

Jack laughed. 'I can't keep any secrets from my twin sister. 'Because that's exactly how I feel. Only it wasn't La Mimosa.'

'What was it, then?' Serena asked.

Jack seemed to be thinking about his answer. Then he said, 'I'm still trying to figure it out myself.'

He didn't want to come right out and say it, Charlotte decided. He didn't want to baldly admit that he was finally over Amy in case he sounded a little disrespectful to her memory.

The traffic was light and they made good time in arriving at Kim's. One of her friends opened the door to them, waving a glass of wine in one hand and directing them down the hall. 'They're all in the garden, just go straight on through.'

Kim's garden was thronged with beautiful people wearing expensive clothes and sipping from crystal glasses. In spite of the milling crowd, Kim must have been alerted to their arrival by Harriet's excited squeal, for Charlotte saw her make her excuses and detach herself from the group she was talking to. She moved towards them, raising her arms in greeting. She was wearing a beautiful purple dress and she looked fantastic. Charlotte tried to dismiss the funny feeling that it was as though Kim was on stage, acting out a well-rehearsed role. She watched as Kim gave Harriet a big hug and several kisses, before embracing Serena. Charlotte was next to be welcomed and then Kim looked past her and Charlotte saw something in Kim's face and sensed an indefinable energy that radiated around her body, which struck an echo within her. She saw Kim approach Jack and fling her arms around him, and when she spotted the look of naked devotion in Kim's eyes, she felt like an intruder, trespassing in someone else's private emotions.

There was no doubt about it. Kim was in love with Jack.

Oh, Kim, my dear. When had this happened? Where was it going to end? Jack was looking at Kim as though she was his sister and Charlotte's heart ached with the knowledge that someone was going to be very hurt.

CHAPTER 15

When Jack smiled his mischievous smile, Kim felt as though she was stepping into her dream. She hugged him, allowing herself the pleasure of absorbing the clean scent of him and the heat of his skin, only letting go when she sensed his surprise at the warmth of her embrace. Take it slow and easy. No point in rushing him.

'Jack. Hi. You look great.'

'Hey, tatty-head, so do you,' he said. 'What happened to your garden? I feel like I'm on the set of Diarmuid Gavin's garden programme on the TV.'

'Before or afterwards?'

'Before, of course.'

'So you're back to taking the piss,' she said, her nerve endings jangling in delight at the wonderful nearness of him. 'Your break away has been good for you.'

'Yeah, everyone should do a bunk for a couple of months. Really sets you up.'

Did that mean what she thought it did? Had his

retreat successfully slain his demons? Could it be possible that Amy and all those unhappy memories were now in the past? Although he still bore little hallmarks of his sad year, small lines at the side of his face that hadn't been there before, he looked like a load had been taken off his mind and he was more relaxed than she'd seen him in a while. It buoyed her up and made her giddy with desire and expectation. Then she laughed. 'Why am I wasting time talking? We should be celebrating. Let's have some drinks.' She linked arms with Jack and steered him and the family over towards tables laid out with glasses and wine.

'Hey, this calls for champagne,' she said, catching the attention of one of the catering staff and asking him to open a bottle. 'And we'll have orange juice for Harriet.'

'And juice for me,' Charlotte said, smiling at her rather more affectionately than Kim would have expected. Perhaps she too was happy to have Jack home. Maybe, just maybe, she was seeing Kim as a potential daughter-in-law?

'Your garden is fabulous, Kim,' Charlotte said. 'You've come up with some great ideas. I love the water feature and the oriental grasses.'

'I didn't have too far to go for inspiration,' Kim told her. 'I just thought of the Tranquil Garden at Tamarisk and worked from there.' Charlotte looked a bit startled, and Serena gave a half smile, but Jack laughed and, to Kim, that was all that mattered.

The worst thing about being the hostess, Kim grumbled to herself, was that she couldn't take Jack off into a corner. As she mingled with her guests and was pulled in every direction, she was all the time conscious of Jack's tall figure as he mingled with the crowd, and was sent crawling with jealousy when she saw him chatting to some of the younger models who had arrived straight from a shoot, giddy and dying for a reviving drink or two. Later she thought he seemed to be spending forever chatting and laughing to Lucy O'Leary, the Galway-born model-turned-Hollywood-actress.

Then she wanted to be Harriet, who began to tire as the dusk dropped a veil across the garden, and who only had to look at Jack to be lifted easily into his arms and swung onto his shoulder.

Lucy put out her hand and stopped Kim in her tracks as she went indoors to switch on the garden lights. 'And where has that gorgeous lust-have been all my life?' she asked, her huge blue eyes staring proprietarily in Jack's direction.

'He's been married,' Kim said bluntly.

'Well, of course,' Lucy said. 'I hardly expected a ride like him to be free and single. I mean, who is he? Apart from being a relation of yours?'

'He's not a relation,' Kim said, her words feeling thin on her lips.

'Isn't he? I could have sworn he – hey, never mind. I demand all the low down. Actually I wouldn't mind going down on him,' Lucy laughed at her own joke. 'He has the sex factor for me.'

'You could have sworn he what?' Kim asked, pausing in the doorway, her breath straining in her chest.

Lucy waggled her long, manicured fingernails. 'Nothing really, I just thought he said you were practically his sister.' Her attitude was so dismissive it was obvious she didn't see Kim as any kind of rival in her pursuit of Jack.

Something dark clutched at Kim's heart but she forced a laugh. 'Is that so? I suppose it's because I've known him almost all my life. And we're very close friends.'

Lucy gave her a hard, calculating look. 'And hoping to get closer, I'd say.'

Kim frowned. 'I don't think—'

Lucy laughingly interrupted her. 'You don't think it would work because it might seem too incestuous, is that it? I'd better grab him before someone else does. Or before his wife finds out. I take it she's not here tonight?'

'Jack's wife is dead,' Kim said bluntly, finding a grain of comfort in the shock that registered on Lucy's face.

'Dead?' Lucy gripped her arm and Kim could see the comprehension burst across her face. 'Wait a minute – Jack, you said. Jack Devlin? *The* Jack Devlin? Oh, my God. Wasn't he the guy who was married to that dizzy socialite Amy? Oh, Christ. No wonder he has that look in his eyes that makes you want to ride him senseless.'

Kim's stomach lurched. Lucy's face shone with a mixture of curiosity and delight as she turned it towards Jack. She was tempted to snap that if anyone was going to kiss Jack better it would be her, but she held her tongue, sorry that she'd discussed him with Lucy at all. Kim excused herself, went upstairs to her bedroom to refresh her lip gloss and perfume, Lucy's words ringing in her ears.

Practically his sister. God.

Did Jack really see her as almost a sister? Or was Lucy confused? Maybe Jack had said he was *here* with his sister. She delayed in her bedroom, reluctant to go back down to her party and face everyone after all her high expectations had been soured. Then she realised that skulking in her bedroom wasn't going to get her anywhere. Maybe Lucy had unwittingly pointed her in the right direction. She would just have to make sure that Jack began to see the real Kim; the loving, sexy woman who was devoted to him and ready to take their relationship a big step further. She threw back her shoulders and summoned her best and brightest smile. She went back outside, helping herself to a glass of wine. She wished she could tell everyone to go home so that she could be alone with Jack. Her garden looked magical on this mild, shadowy evening, with the backdrop of twinkling lighting and flickering candles. Then she saw Jack coming towards her, and her heart stopped. It felt so right to see him here. This night was all for him, although he was totally unaware of it.

You're special, tatty-head. I'll be back to you soon.

'Kim, we have to go,' he said.

She felt a crushing disappointment. 'Already? We haven't had a proper chance to talk.'

'Harriet's tired and Serena wants to bring her home,' he said.

'Does that mean you have to leave?' she said, trying to keep the annoyance out of her voice. 'You could stay on here and enjoy the rest of the party. I've plenty of room if you want to stay over.' She tried to sound casual.

He didn't even pause to consider her suggestion and it hurt. 'Thanks, Kim, but we're all heading off together. I could do with hitting the sack myself.'

She wished he was hitting the sack with her; she had a sudden vision of the two of them collapsing on top of her bed. Kim blinked hard. There would be other opportunities. At least Jack was home and back to himself. It was a start. She followed him across the garden to the table under the maple tree where Serena was sitting down, and Charlotte sitting opposite her with Harriet on her lap.

Serena said, 'Kim, it's been a great party, and your garden is fabulous, but it's time for us to go. We're getting a bit tired.'

'I'm not tired,' Harriet objected.

'Well I am,' Jack said, ruffling his niece's hair. 'I'd a couple of late nights this week.'

His tone of voice alerted Kim and she was tempted to ask him the reason for his late nights, but the half smile on his face stopped her. He looked as though he was remembering something very pleasant and she didn't want to know.

'I'll go around and say our goodbyes,' Jack offered.

'I'll bring Harriet to the bathroom before we go,' Charlotte said.

Charlotte rose to her feet and Kim sat down in her place. Serena looked exhausted, Kim realised. She'd paid little attention to her friend all evening. Now she saw that Serena's face was pinched and there was an air of anxiety about her. 'Serena, are you okay?'

Serena gave her a big, bright smile. 'I'm fine. Everything's great, Kim, really. I don't think Paul's going to arrive now, he was probably delayed getting back from Galway. Sorry we're running off and we haven't even had a proper chance to talk, but Harriet's flagging.'

'And so is Jack, from the sound of it,' Kim looked at her enquiringly, wondering if Serena could throw any light on his remark.

'Yes, though he seems in good form and it's hard to believe the transformation.'

'We must have a get together, the four of us,' Kim said, 'You and Paul must come for dinner, and bring Jack as well. You could even stay over if Charlotte minded Harriet.'

It would be perfect. The four of them, nice and cosy in Kim's dining room. Dim lighting and soulful music. Brunch the following morning, and Jack at her breakfast table. What bliss. Why hadn't she thought of this in the first place, instead of planning her garden party? And unwittingly providing competition for herself?

Kim's attention was distracted as she saw Jack stroll across to Lucy, obviously to let her know he was going home. Once again a streak of jealously tore through her at the idea of Jack figuring Lucy was important enough for him to say goodbye to. She hardly noticed Charlotte returning with Harriet and Serena rising to her feet. In a daze, she followed them out to the hall door, Jack now carrying a sleepy Harriet. Then in a flurry of hugs and goodbyes, they were gone. She waited until their tail lights disappeared from view and then she returned to her party.

A lot of Dublin's socialites and wannabe starlets were drifting into her sun room, others were hanging out in her kitchen. Someone had changed the music to a fast rock beat and it pumped through the downstairs of her house and spilled out into the garden. Her party was a mega success, but it all felt empty now. She treated herself to a glass of champagne and was slowly sipping it in the kitchen trying to put on her bright, party face when the doorbell chimed again.

'I'll get it,' she said to no one in particular. She opened the door and Paul Taylor was waiting outside, holding a bottle of wine.

'Paul! They've just gone.'

'Just gone?' His face dropped.

For a moment she felt at a loss. Then she stepped aside, ushering him inside with a sweep of her hand. 'Come in, have a drink . . . You're here now so you might as well stay for a bit.'

He seemed reluctant, but he followed her down the hall in the direction of the thumping music while she chattered away, raising her voice to be heard. 'Harriet got tired, you see, so they all headed back.'

'All?'

'Charlotte and Jack as well. Serena wasn't expecting you to arrive. Anyway they left in rather a hurry. You're welcome to my party and I insist you have one glass of wine.'

'Just one, then.'

She watched as Paul strolled outside and was immediately surrounded by a bevy of admiring, flirtatious models. Even Lucy zoned in on him like a heat-seeking missile. Kim's sharp eyes could see she was clenching in her tummy and pulling back her shoulders to emphasise her boobs as she put a hand on his arm and moved in to give him a friendly kiss.

Not a chance. Paul wasn't the type to stray and why should he when he had the lovely Serena waiting at home? All the same, she almost choked

175

on her champagne as she saw Lucy reach out and deliberately pinch Paul's muscular bum.

God forbid Serena ever did anything to rattle her marriage. For there would be plenty of women willing to take her place and jump into bed with Paul.

CHAPTER 16

Sometimes when Paul woke up first, he found himself looking at his sleeping wife because it was the only time he found her relaxed and peaceful. When she was awake, you could almost see the sparks of energy and determination coming from her.

This Sunday morning, when he turned to look at Serena in the soft, morning light, she was unconscious to the world, blonde hair tousled and her mouth slightly open. He wanted to put his lips to that ripe mouth but he decided not to disturb her. There were faint shadows beneath her eyelashes, and her closed eyelids showed a delicate tracery of pale-mauve veins. There was something very tender and vulnerable about her that squeezed his chest and he wondered what dreams she was having in that twilight zone.

He slipped out of bed, and instead of going into the en suite, he gathered his clothes and went on down to the main bathroom, the better to leave her undisturbed. When he was dressed, he checked on Harriet. His heart melted as he looked at his sleeping daughter in her pink and white bed, her little cheeks flushed, and her teddy on the floor.

The moment of her birth had been an epiphany for him. Serena's labour had been protracted and he'd begun to think it was all some kind of a surreal dream and that there wasn't really a baby in there struggling to be born, when suddenly she'd arrived, a solid presence, in his life. He would never forget the reality of holding her in his arms, the tiny, all-knowing eyes that slid around his face with a calm expression that said, ah, yes, here is my daddy. He had the feeling she already knew every vital part of him, right to his soul. As for Serena, he had loved her more than ever, and despite her exhausted face, she had never been more beautiful to him. It had been a sacred moment, and the thoughts of being blessed with another such moment in the not too distant future and having the experience of watching a baby becoming a little person in his or her own right filled him with joy. He picked up Harriet's teddy and tucked it in beside her.

Then he let himself out the hall door to get the Sunday papers.

Up behind the house, some half a kilometre away, a forest trail led to the back of Glendoran village. It was a fifteen-minute jog for him. The trail was quiet, with little noise except for the wind in the canopy of trees, his rhythmic breathing, and his footfall on the forest floor, which was soft with fallen leaves and fern. Now and then he disturbed a sparrowhawk or a crow, who cawed noisily before fluttering away through the trees. Shimmers of iridescent light filtered through the green canopy, and in gaps between the trees he caught glimpses of the mountains. The perfect solitude gave him time alone to clear his head and he found his steady jogging and regular breathing in the natural surroundings helped to put some clarity on his jumbled thoughts.

He was, he knew, far more in love with Serena than the first time he'd seen her, when she'd swept him off his feet, her sidelong glance effortlessly knocking him for six in a way none of his rugby opponents had ever succeeded in doing.

And even though they'd been married for six years, sometimes he felt as though he was stomping on something delicate if he said the wrong thing to Serena. Lately, he seemed to be saying the wrong thing a little more often. Still, he had to admit that he'd come on a little too strong when he'd tried to have a little fun in her office. Then, last night, he'd left Kim's party after one drink and when he'd arrived home, a remark of his sent her off the deep end.

'Why didn't you text me to say you were leaving?' he'd said. 'You could have stopped me from dropping into Kim's. I nearly caused a riot with marauding women looking for sex. One of them even said she wanted my baby. Huh! But there's only one woman who's going to have my baby, isn't there?' He'd reached down and slid his hand under her shirt.

She'd pushed his hand away, which was most unusual for her. 'Jesus, Paul, I'm starting to think you have sex on the brain,' she'd snapped.

'Hey, I can't help if that's the way you make me feel.'

'Yes, but— oh, forget it,' she'd said, stalking out to the kitchen.

Afterwards, she'd said she was sorry, she was just tired, but he'd still felt miffed and wondered why she was so touchy. That was why he was afraid to ask her outright if he was imagining things or if she really was miles away at times, despite their efforts to have another baby.

That was another thing on his mind. He'd thought that Serena would have been pregnant by now. It was almost a year since they'd begun to try for that precious second child. Although Amy's death hadn't helped matters.

Paul quickened his pace and shoved a low-hanging branch out of his way.

Amy. That had been some blow. In spite of her being such a high-maintenance wife and dangling Jack like a puppet on a string, his heart had gone out to his brother-in-law. They had all been pulled up sharply by the shock of someone of their own generation meeting such an untimely end. He would never forget how upset Serena had been.

And sometimes, Paul thought, as he crested the

hill and started down the vale into the village, he could be a pig-headed eejit. Even now, Serena was bound to be out of sorts after it all. His wife might be a clever, efficient businesswoman but her heart was very soft. On top of that, she'd been busier than ever taking up the slack for Jack, not only in the months following Amy's death but in particular in the past few weeks, when he had fecked off to France. He just had to be patient a little longer. And, he decided as he jogged into the village, if Serena wasn't expecting by the end of the summer, he was going to talk to her about seeing a specialist. Though thirty-six was still a relatively fertile age; women were having babies in their forties. As he slowed his pace and turned up Main Street, an unwelcome thought flitted through his mind and took root, shattering his peace.

There could, on the other hand, be something wrong with him.

CHAPTER 17

Serena was surprised when Jack dropped into Maple Hill soon after breakfast.

'I didn't think you'd be up this early,' she joked.

'Not early enough to catch Harriet and Paul,' he said, peeking into the playroom as he came on down to the kitchen.

'They've just left to visit Paul's parents,' she explained, relieved that Paul was out of the way, especially after she'd stupidly snapped at him the night before. It had been a bad moment for her and she'd had to escape to the kitchen to get a grip on herself.

Now Jack was shifting from one foot to the other, giving the distinct impression that he was uneasy about something. She popped a capsule of cappuccino into the coffee machine. 'Well, what is it?'

'Can you do without me for another week? I've a lot to sort out at home . . . you know, Amy's stuff . . .' he gave her a rueful grin. 'I haven't touched any of it so far. Then there's a rake of red tape I've been avoiding . . .'

Despite her own problems, a wave of sadness

and regret washed over Serena. Jack clearing out Amy's clothes and belongings, in a sense getting rid of the evidence of the life they'd shared.

'I'll help,' she offered. 'You can't do all that on your own.'

'No, it's okay, I want to go through her stuff myself. And I'm in the frame of mind to tackle it now. I want to clear out everything, open the windows and let a blast of fresh air in.'

'Hang on a minute,' Serena had said, her mind filled with images of Jack in a fit of misplaced enthusiasm, haphazardly stuffing everything and anything to do with Amy's life into a pile of cheap plastic sacks. 'What about her sister? Would she like any of Amy's belongings that might be of sentimental value?'

'I've already had Karen over, before I went to La Mimosa, so that I could give her a lot of Amy's jewellery. Don't worry, I won't be crying into the wardrobe. I'll put on the loudest music I can without waking up the countryside, and I won't just fire everything into black sacks either. Most of her clothes will be sent to a charity shop. Then I have to start on all the bloody paperwork. A week should give me plenty of time. And it's her anniversary next Friday. So I want to mark that in some way.'

'I can arrange something if you like?'

'No, thanks, I'll just do my own thing.'

One more week. She'd survive, even if it seemed she'd been holding the fort for ever, but if it meant that Jack was finally freeing himself from the past, it would be worth it.

As the week went by, Serena made sure to be home as early as she could in the evenings, and when she was at home, she stayed away from her laptop and resisted the impulse to phone Tamarisk to make sure all was well. On Friday, she sent up a silent prayer for Amy and wondered what Jack was doing to get through the day. Her mother was spending the day shopping in Dublin. Neither of them could believe it was a year already since the dreadful phone call from Jack in Thailand, where he'd been on holiday with Amy.

That evening she was pleasantly surprised when Paul suggested a trip to the beach with Harriet. It was a fine summery evening, and as they walked along the golden strand tasting the salty breeze, Serena felt her cares melting away. She told Paul of Charlotte's plans to fly them all to La Mimosa for the birthday weekend. Harriet was already excited about it and she was so full of fun and mischief as she barrelled up and down the strand that Serena wanted their walk to go on for ever. Later that night, Paul turned to her in bed, his hand caressing her breasts and sliding down to the warmth between her thighs. She sat up a little so that she could pull off her silk nightdress. Then she moved into the warmth of his arms and snuggled into his chest. He lifted her face and kissed her. It was a long, deep kiss that quickened her senses and when she felt Paul's hard arousal nudging against her hips, her insides watered. Their love-making was brief but intense, as though they both wanted to come together as quickly as possible. Afterwards Paul held her close and told her not to move.

'It's best if you stay still for a few moments and let Mother Nature get to work,' he murmured, his hand on her hip.

Serena did as she was told, her mind whirling as she lay still beside him. Eventually she knew by Paul's breathing that he had fallen into a deep sleep. She tried to calm her racing heart by thinking of their walk on the beach earlier that day, her sense of freedom and the gentle shush of the waves. But the luxury of falling into a peaceful sleep eluded her, long after she had slipped away from his grasp.

On Jack's first day back in Tamarisk, Serena phoned him at half past ten.

'Come up for coffee,' she said. 'I'm sure it's strange to be back.'

'You bet,' he said. 'I don't even know where to begin getting up to speed.'

'Just give me ten minutes while I order a tray. Scones?'

'Yes, please. They don't taste quite the same in La Mimosa.'

Serena knew by his tone of voice that he was smiling. It was great to have Jack smiling over something as simple as the prospect of a freshly baked scone. 'Right. See you soon.'

After phoning down to the kitchen, she went across to her low table by the window. Outside the lawns of Tamarisk gleamed in the bright Monday morning and the oak trees slumbered in the sunlight. It was good that the day was behaving itself for Jack's return to work. She looked forward to showing him how well she'd managed everything in his absence. She angled the sofa so that it was a little closer to the table and gave them both a view of the parkland vista.

'I want to talk to you about some new promotions and an idea I have for spa goodie bags,' she said when he arrived at the same time as the coffee and scones. 'And Jack,' she went on, feeling a lift of excitement, 'the really good news is, I've just heard this morning that Tamarisk is on the shortlist for the Celebrate Ireland award – Haven of the Year. The next stage is the anonymous site visit and the ceremony will be held in Dublin in six weeks' time.'

'Brilliant! Are you my clever sister, or what?'

She filled him in on some of the details. She chatted about some of the celebrities who'd recently visited and mentioned some of the glowing endorsements they'd given. 'However, the most urgent thing right now is to set up a meeting with Brian,' she finished.

'Don't mention finances. That's one tiresome task I'm not looking forward to tackling.'

Serena was taken aback. He could have shown a little enthusiasm given the long break he'd had. 'The sooner we talk to him, the better,' she said.

'Whatever you say.' Despite his words she sensed an overall lack of interest.

'Harriet's delighted you're back,' she said, changing the subject.

'She's a great kid. Fabulous. But is everything okay between you and Paul?' Jack asked.

'Yes, why?'

'I dunno, you look a bit strained.'

'We're fine,' she said. 'What about you? You're different since you came home. Are you . . . is it . . .'

'You mean am I reconciled to Amy? Yes, I feel better about some things that were bugging me. Other things I know I can't change, but I refuse to lose any more sleep over them.'

She wondered briefly what kind of regrets Jack could have. He couldn't have done any more for Amy, or couldn't have been a more dedicated husband, but she merely said, 'Good. I'm glad to see you getting your life back. And Jack, I was glad when I saw your mug shot in one of the tabloids over the weekend. Coming out of a nightclub with Lucy O'Leary.' She'd actually smiled to herself when she'd seen the photo, pleased that Jack was out on the town again and back to his favourite haunts.

'That was nothing, just a casual date.'

'I hardly expected it was anything else. The last thing you need is any serious involvement.'

'Thing is, Serena . . .' Jack got up off the sofa, went over to her desk and fidgeted with the stationery. He lifted up a pen and put it down again. Then he perched on the edge of her desk. 'That date was part of an agreement. Hell, I might as well tell you . . .' he paused, looking as though he was considering what he was about to say.

'I met someone.'

'*Met* someone? What do you mean?' Serena was confused. Her hands smoothed down the skirt of her grey dress.

'What you usually mean by that. I met someone. In Nice. On my way home.' He pushed himself off the corner of her desk and started to pace the floor. 'She's been fantastic to me. She made me feel, oh God, just amazing. I bumped into her by chance and we got talking . . . one thing led to another. Remember I missed the flight? That's how I met her. And after that, I was spending time with her, getting to know her, having fun for the first time in years. Jeez, Serena, I still can't believe the way she gave me my life back. She really made me feel that the world was wonderful again.'

Her brother looked delighted with himself, as though he had accomplished something wonderful and was awaiting her congratulations. At first Serena thought she'd misheard. Then as his words sank in, she was gripped by a rush of anger. Jack had been dilly-dallying in Nice with a girl when he should have been home picking up the reins. As if he hadn't had enough down time. She also felt ridiculously rebuffed, thinking of the way she'd supported him, taking on additional work, reassuring him that everything was okay, even though she was putting in longer hours to compensate for his absence. All her efforts to keep the show on the road and give him some space had gone completely unnoticed.

'I don't understand,' she said, fighting hard to hide her feelings.

'Neither do I!' he laughed. 'I guess you could say I was swept off my feet.'

'How come you went out with Lucy?'

'That's the agreement I made with Jenni, the girl I met in Nice. I wanted her to come home to Tamarisk, so that we could get to know each other more, but she refused. She told me to go out and date other women and see if I still felt the same about her after a month.'

Jenni. She was called Jenni. Whatever spell she'd cast over her brother, she'd kept him in France when he should have been home.

Serena couldn't fathom why she felt so bloody annoyed. Then she realised. Despite the support both she and her mother had given him when he'd been going through a nightmare time, Jack had turned to a stranger to give him his life back. A stranger who had managed to bring about that remarkable turnaround in the space of a week and who was fantastic and amazing, unlike his reliable, dependable sister who had merely bent over back-wards for months and months to make up for his apathy and then his absence. And before all that, who had willingly excused him time after time when Amy had dragged him away from Tamarisk.

'But Jack, you barely know her.'

'I know. It's mad. But time doesn't come into it,' he said, looking so happy and satisfied that Serena was speechless. Even more so when he went on, 'It was instant attraction. We're waiting a month to see if we still feel the same way about each other and I can't wait for the month to be over.'

'You're not going back to France?' This was too much. Apart from Jack being a little crazy, no way could she cope with another absence or carry the can indefinitely.

'No, I want her to come here, to Tamarisk.'

'But, Jack . . .' Serena was silent, grappling with her thoughts. It sounded like a recipe for disaster. He was surely in lust, for it couldn't be anything else. Her gut instinct was telling her that Jack was on the rebound, and still in a vulnerable state, but he was standing there with a big, happy grin on his face fully expecting her to be happy for him, so how could she burst his bubble?

He came back across to the sofa and kissed the top of her head. 'Look, Serena, don't get all worried and big sister-ish on me.'

'I'm not your big sister.'

'Sometimes . . . look, don't make me sorry I told

you. And I'd prefer it if you kept Jenni strictly to yourself for now. I don't want word of her leaking out to the tabloids, she's too special to me. I'll tell Mum in my own good time.'

After he'd left her office, Serena sat in her chair and wondered if she'd imagined that whole conversation. He wanted to bring a girl called Jenni back to Tamarisk after a week. Was he for real? Involvement with anyone was the last thing Jack needed for a while yet.

Especially after what he'd gone through with Amy.

CHAPTER 18

'We met on the N11,' Amy had said in her breathless, little-girl voice. 'It was romantic in a different way. It was dark and wintry and I was stranded with a flat tyre. Jack was my knight in shining armour and insisted on helping me even though the AA man was on the way. He saved my life.'

It had been the third time Serena had heard the story of the drama and it was beginning to grate on her nerves, along with the sound of Amy's cutesy voice.

'Apart from an older sister I'm all alone in the world,' she'd said to Serena when they first met. 'Both my parents died in a car crash, years ago.' These words had been delivered with such mega fluttering of the eyelashes and tiny breathy gasps that any sympathy Serena may have felt vanished swiftly. So from the beginning, Serena had had reservations about this petite, baby-faced blonde with the china-blue eyes who only had to glance in Jack's direction for him to snap to attention. It hadn't just been a case of her being close to her twin and feeling no one was good enough for him.

There was something about Amy that had put her on edge.

Jack had known Amy barely three months when they'd become engaged.

'Engaged? Already?' Serena had been shocked when he told her.

Jack had looked a little uneasy. 'Thing is, sis, Amy's pregnant, but scout's honour you'll keep this to yourself.'

'That doesn't mean you have to marry her,' Serena had tried to keep a scathing note out of her voice, quite convinced that Jack was being stitched up. Though she'd known he'd have to take his share of responsibility for their baby, it was just like him to live up to his knight-in-shining-armour status and whisk Amy to the altar rails.

'Maybe I want to marry her,' Jack had said, giving her a stubborn look. 'But don't tell anyone she's pregnant. Not even Mum. Amy's determined that we'll have a wedding day just like anyone else. With no wagging tongues.'

Two months after their engagement, they'd caused a sensation in Irish social circles by marrying in a private, beachfront ceremony in the Seychelles. A wedding day just like anybody else? Yeah right, Serena had glowered when she saw their photos in *Heat*. She'd glowered even more when Amy had constantly called Jack away from Tamarisk to rescue her from one thing or another, things that most normal women in their early thirties would have taken in their stride.

'Her car won't start and she's stranded in the middle of nowhere,' he'd said, asking Serena to go ahead and have the staff meeting without him. She'd found out later that the middle of nowhere turned out to be a mile outside Glendoran.

Another time, when they were working late on their summer promotions, he'd had to leave because Amy thought she'd heard an intruder in the garden. Yet again, just before another important meeting, Jack had been called away because the washing machine was on the blink and water was streaming all over the kitchen.

'This is a bit much, Jack. Surely someone else could sort this out,' Serena had said, going down to his office to have it out face to face.

'No, Amy's in a panic and I'll have to see to it myself,' he'd said, his closed face ensuring no further argument.

It hadn't only been work that he was dragged away from. Amy had conveniently come down with the flu the very weekend Jack was to go to the UK for a premiership match with a couple of his mates. As far as Serena had been concerned, her brother was being well and truly manipulated. Amy had only had to look at a glass of wine and she was tipsy and she'd used this as an excuse to hang out of Jack or get him to take her home early.

When she and Paul had been invited to dinner with Jack and Amy, shortly after their wedding, Amy had been nervy and giggly and even though she was drinking very little, she'd managed to knock over a half-full bottle of red wine, sending the liquid coursing across the white damask table-cloth. She'd clung to Jack and burst into tears. Silently, Serena had helped Jack clear the table and bundled the stained cloth into a bag.

'This is terrible and we wanted it to be perfect, because we asked you over specially to share our wonderful news,' Amy had said, wiping her eyes and hiccupping.

Jack had shot Serena a warning glance and she'd composed a suitably innocent face.

'What news?' Serena had managed to sound terribly interested.

'I'm having a baby,' Amy had squealed. 'A honeymoon baby. My hormones are all over the place, but Jack has been very kind and understanding.'

What had upset Serena was the fact that in all of this, Jack seemed to be dealing with a helpless child and not an equal partner. Worse, not by a word or a breath had he appeared to think there was anything wrong with this. She'd asked herself how Jack had landed himself in such a mess. If Amy hadn't become pregnant, the possibility was that their relationship would have run its course and he would have soon tired of her. A month after the grand announcement, Jack had gone away to a three-night hospitality convention in New York, and Serena had wondered privately what kind of bug Amy would catch this time. But there had been a peaceful silence from Garryvale when he was away, and no one had been more shocked than Serena when Jack had told her he'd arrived home to find that Amy had lost the baby.

'She's been very brave,' he'd said, when he'd stood in her office and broken the news. 'She waited until I came home to tell me, not wanting to interrupt my weekend. It happened just after my flight took off and, luckily, she was staying with her sister while I was gone. Karen brought her to the hospital and she was discharged yesterday.'

'How is she now?' Serena had asked.

'She's very upset,' Jack had said soberly. 'I've tucked her up in bed and told her not to worry about anything. I'm taking a few days off to spoil her a little. I might bring her to La Mimosa for the weekend.'

Serena had tried to squash her annoyance. More spoiling for the girl who'd only had to crook her small, perfectly manicured nail. She'd tried to pull herself together. What kind of a monster was she? Amy had lost a baby, for God's sake. The least Serena had been able to do was show some empathy. But, after the past few months, she had been a little thin on empathy.

'How about you, Jack?' she'd asked, hating the dark shadows under his eyes and knowing the loss of the baby must have affected him equally badly. There was a touch of grey in his hair, just above his temples. Her easy-going brother, who had often driven her mad but who had always brought a smile to her face, had gone. The change in him made her feel sad.

'I'll be fine, honest sis,' he'd smiled an empty smile, wrenching her heart. 'Don't worry about me. My main concern is looking after Amy.'

And he had looked after her, taking her to La Mimosa for a weekend and, after that, continuing to arrive into work late or go home early.

'She's still depressed,' Jack had said a few weeks later. 'Losing the baby has taken a lot out of her. I'm taking more time off and bringing her somewhere warm to recuperate. Thailand might do the trick. Surely all those white-gold beaches, guaranteed sun and waving palm trees can't fail to cheer her up . . .'

CHAPTER 19

Charlotte was conscious of a knot of tension in her stomach as she dressed for lunch. Even when she'd phoned La Mimosa that morning to arrange the birthday weekend, Conor had been quick enough to pick up a thread of anxiety in her voice.

'We'd be delighted to host the birthday celebrations in La Mimosa,' he'd said. 'Martine and I always look forward to seeing you and all the family. I'll reserve enough rooms immediately, but Charlotte, it's good to think you're all moving on after last year's sadness. I know it took a lot out of Jack, as well as you and Serena. How's my little poppet, Harriet?'

'Harriet's great. Full of endless questions and she'll be tormenting you with her latest karate moves. How's Simon?' Charlotte had asked, referring to Conor's grandson.

'He's at that stage too. More to the point, Charlotte, how are you? I thought you'd sound a little more upbeat? What are you getting up to these days?'

'Nothing much.'

'Charlotte! You disappoint me. I was hoping you'd tell me you're planning to travel the world and take it by storm.'

'Oh, I will,' she'd said, lightly. 'Some day.'

Some day, she mocked herself as she dressed for lunch. When I feel I deserve a new start. Her lavender-blue eyes critically skimmed her image in the mirror. The cream silk Moschino she was wearing said safe, understated elegance. On a whim, she opened her wardrobe and took out a pair of traffic-light red Jimmy Choo pumps. Now she looked like she wasn't taking herself too seriously and was ready for fun. Just perfect for having lunch with her friends in Glendoran's renowned seafood restaurant and for announcing to herself and the world that she was ready for the next stage of her life, even if she didn't exactly feel like it or know where it was heading.

Although the lunch date was causing her a little concern.

'I'm afraid Hilary heard about our lunch and insisted on inviting herself,' her friend Millie had said on the telephone the previous day. 'Cathy let it slip and it was impossible to fob her off short of telling her out straight that we didn't feel like entertaining her or her mischievous tongue.'

Hilary. Her nemesis and a toxic acquaintance she tried to avoid if possible.

'No worries,' Charlotte had said. 'I'm a big girl and should be able to handle her.'

Now she glared at her reflection and told herself

not to be such a wuss. She picked up her car keys and left before she chickened out and changed her mind.

'Hi Charlotte, great to see you,' Millie said, when she joined her at the table. The corner table by the window facing out onto the park running behind Glendoran's Main Street was perfect. As Charlotte sat down and picked up her linen napkin, she noticed that it was set for four. She'd been half hoping that Hilary might change her mind, but obviously she hadn't.

When Charlotte first met Millie, soon after she came to Tamarisk, Millie had been a junior sales assistant in the one and only drapery shop in Glendoran. Now the same drapery shop was a very successful boutique, owned and managed by Millie. Over the years, she'd trebled its size and transformed it into a mecca for wedding and occasion wear, attracting die-hard fashionistas from all across the country. She'd also become a good friend to Charlotte, and Charlotte always enjoyed the company of her warm-hearted friend.

'Thanks for organising this,' Charlotte smiled. 'I know I've been neglecting you lately. It's a wonder you still have my number in your phone!'

'Nonsense! It's lovely to see you. Cathy and Hilary should be here soon. I hope you don't mind about Hilary,' Millie went on in an apologetic tone of voice. 'I know you and she don't always see eye to eye but you can blame Cathy for spilling the beans!'

'I won't blame anyone,' Charlotte said. 'As Harriet would say, it's cool.'

And it was, up to a point.

The condescending attitude of Hilary, the wife of a property developer, had always grated on her. It had its roots in basic jealousy, since Hilary had always considered that Charlotte had usurped her chosen station in life as Jamie Devlin's wife and mistress of Tamarisk. Years ago, when Charlotte was still a new bride, Hilary had made a deliberate play for Jamie at a dinner party, outraging Charlotte with her sexually overt behaviour. Millie had taken Charlotte aside and explained that no one had been more aghast than Hilary when Jamie had arrived home from his work experience in New York with Charlotte in tow. Since then, Charlotte had been armed and ready for Hilary and her barbs.

This lunch-time, everything seemed to be going fine, the women chatting about the slight pick-up in the economy. Cathy, whose husband was a publican, admitted he'd almost been on the brink of closure. Millie confided that she was relieved to see her business improving. 'Not that I've been hanging on by my fingernails, thankfully, like some poor unfortunates who got in over their heads on the strength of those madly successful years . . .'

Her voice trailed away just as Charlotte intercepted a warning glance that Cathy shot in Millie's direction.

Hilary drained her wine and turned to Charlotte.

'I'm sure you find it a huge relief that you don't have to worry your little head about the finances of Tamarisk.'

'I've never had to worry about that,' Charlotte said, smiling sweetly.

'Now that you've handed over the reins to Jack and Serena you must find it a huge change to have time on your hands after such a demanding career,' Hilary said. 'One of the biggest problems with retirement is how easy stagnation can set in unless you have planned in advance for those long, empty days.'

'I wouldn't know as I've no intention of stagnating.'

'Oh gosh, I didn't mean you personally, Charlotte!' Hilary's laughter tinkled. 'I was speaking hypothetically. Everyone knows that you're bound to find something worthwhile to occupy your days. I'm sure you don't feel you've come to the end of your shelf life.'

'Hilary, I'm not exactly gathering dust just yet,' Charlotte struggled to inject a note of humour into her voice. She sipped her mineral water slowly and wondered what Hilary had up her sleeve.

'An aunt of mine has told me that doing crosswords is supposed to be very effective,' Hilary went on, slugging more wine. 'It can help stave off the beginning of Alzheimer's.'

'So can plenty of sex,' Millie interjected. 'Something to do with the flow of blood during orgasm. So get yourself a lean and hungry toy boy,

Charlotte. We're still stuck with our ageing husbands. But hey, we're not in the zimmer-frame brigade, not for a long time. And if you're that worried about your brain cells, Hilary, perhaps you should stay away from the booze. An aunt of mine told me that alcohol kills off brain cells faster than anything else.'

'Charlotte won't have that problem, anyhow,' Hilary countered swiftly. 'Did you decide to give up drink on account of Jamie? I suppose it's safe enough to mention it now, he's been gone a long time, but I always thought it must have been devastating for you to see him turn into a heavy drinker. Whatever drove him to it?' she added darkly.

'Ouch, Hilary, I don't think that's any of our business,' Cathy said.

'Yeah, knock it off,' Millie threw her a dark look.

'It's fine,' Charlotte said, determined not to give Hilary the satisfaction of seeing how angry she was at the turn in the conversation. 'I think the whole of Glendoran knew that Jamie had a drink problem, so it's no secret. And as Hilary said, it was a long time ago. I have to thank your husbands for the way they often escorted him safely home at the end of a night. As for running Tamarisk, all I can say is that it gave me the greatest pleasure. I've no doubt Hilary that you appreciate what a privilege that was. After all, it was one of your own ambitions, a dream I swiped from right under your nose. So no hard feelings.'

There was a thick silence. Charlotte could almost hear her heart racing. Hilary glared at her unblinkingly. Then she picked up her bag and rose to her feet. 'You don't know the half of it,' she snapped as she tottered off to the ladies on unsteady legs.

Charlotte shook her head at Millie and Cathy. 'Sorry about that. I sounded like a child, although I'm doing them an injustice for I doubt if Harriet would ever speak like that. I feel ashamed of myself.'

'Don't be,' Millie rose to her defence. 'You're too hard on yourself. I don't know what got into Hilary, but it's the last time I'll be lunching with her.'

'I was the one who told her we were meeting up,' Cathy said. 'But there's a reason for Hilary's rotten behaviour and I should have told you before today. It seems her husband is playing away and Hilary has to decide whether to ignore it or tackle him head on. She's afraid he'll leave her and feels she's too old to start again.'

'I'm shocked he hasn't left her before now,' Charlotte snorted.

'That's not all. On top of that, Ted's business isn't viable any longer. He's one of the ones whose been clinging on by his fingernails hoping to ride out the recession, but—'

'He got caught riding someone else,' Millie quipped, her voice ringing with delicious satisfaction.

Cathy frowned and tried to hide her grin.

'Seriously girls, I heard Ted made some stupid errors of judgement and he's run out of options. Their extravagant lifestyle is history and the pension pot is empty. Hilary is scared to death.'

'I should feel sympathetic but I don't,' Charlotte said. 'Anyway, ladies, I'm going to head off before she comes back. I'm being a coward, I know, but I don't feel up to her. Tell her I have a headache or something . . .'

'Or a date with a toy boy, to stave off your Alzheimer's,' Millie laughed, giving her a hug. 'We'll get together soon and have a good chat. Without Hilary.'

'Millie!'

Cathy blew her a kiss across the table. 'You're looking great anyhow, that's another thing Hilary is probably annoyed with. She can't afford her regular Botox or facial peels anymore. Let alone her fashion trips to Milan.'

'You'll have me crying in a minute,' Charlotte shook her head, anxious to make her escape before Hilary returned. She was relieved to step out into the fresh air and cross the car park to her car without incident.

She sat behind the wheel for a moment, allowing her heartbeat to return to normal. Why had she been unable to shrug off Hilary's bitchiness? How come she'd reacted stupidly by going on the defensive and responding with silly and childish comments?

She knew, though, that her comments had been

driven by guilt. After all, it had been Charlotte's fault that Jamie had started to drink too much. Still, she was disgusted with her childish behaviour. She wondered what exactly Hilary had meant when she sneered that she didn't know the half of it.

For Charlotte, running Tamarisk had been less of a privilege and more to do with a blind instinct for survival. Thanks to her ability and hard work, she'd managed the business end successfully, but she couldn't say the same for her marriage or the way she'd raised her children. Maybe someday she'd get it all right and get her act together, she mused as she drove home.

She got her second shock of the day when she saw a tall, lean figure standing in the ditch, sticking out his hand to hitch a lift just outside the village. Then she recognised the craggy face of Claudia's minder, even though she'd only seen him once, in the Quiet Room in Tamarisk. She was surprised to see him as she'd assumed he'd gone back to America with Claudia and her cavalcade. She surprised herself further by braking hard, bringing her Saab slewing to a halt just beyond him. She watched him loping towards her in the rear-view mirror and wondered if Hilary's remarks had addled her completely.

'What on earth are you doing?' she asked as he opened the passenger door and bent his head to look in at her.

Up close, she saw that his eyes were the brightest

blue. Paul Newman eyes. She felt a flutter of disquiet in her chest as they fastened on her.

'You stopped,' he said. 'I thought you were offering me a lift.'

She didn't know how she'd expected him to sound. Kind of twangy and American, perhaps. His voice, though, was perfectly measured, warm and deep. It made her think of rich, fine wine and it unsettled her.

'I *am* offering you a lift,' she said crossly. 'Get in.'

'Sure? You don't sound too happy about it.' Although his voice was respectful, there was laughter in his eyes. He was about her age. No, younger. Mid-fifties. Probably a retired cop, supplementing his pension by following a sexy diva around the world. He must be taking a break and had decided to return to Tamarisk, as many people did when they fell for its charm. His minder duties obviously paid well.

'I'm not annoyed with you,' she said.

'Really?'

'I'm annoyed with myself. It's nothing to do with you. Now, do you want a lift or not?'

There was the blast of a car horn behind them and he nimbly folded his body into the passenger seat of the car.

'I suppose you're going back to Tamarisk,' she said.

'Yes, I was out for a walk—'

'You didn't get very far.'

'I'm on my way back,' he said. 'I walked as far as the next village.'

'Hmm, a six-mile return journey, not bad.'

'But when I recognised you coming along in your car I decided to cut short my exercise.'

He'd recognised her, in her car? On the strength of seeing her clad in a voluminous robe in the Spa. She put that piece of information away for now.

'You probably need to reserve your strength. You can't physically overtax yourself in case you fall down on the job. I'd say you need to be fully alert.'

'How did you know?' he sounded surprised.

Charlotte had to concentrate on the bends in the road but she sensed him looking at her closely. 'I'm good at figuring things out. I suppose that's why you're taking a break? To chill out for a while? Your job must be very demanding. All that travelling and looking after people . . .'

'You get used to it, believe me. Although towns and cities look much the same after a while. And what about you?'

'What about me?'

'How come you're annoyed with yourself?'

Charlotte tried to fix him with a glare, but it was difficult given that she needed to concentrate on driving along twisty laneways. 'It's complicated,' she sighed. Silence fell between them for a minute and then she went on indignantly. 'But it boils down to the fact that because I'm semi-retired from a demanding job, my arch enemy seems to think I'm on the verge of my dotage.'

'Which you're not?'

'Of *course* not.'

This time he allowed a short silence before he said, in a voice laced with humour, 'I trust you told her you were chilling out for a few weeks in your favourite retreat while you made plans to scale the Rockies and cycle across Peru, before you paraglide across Victoria Falls . . .?'

They turned in at the entrance to Tamarisk. As always, Charlotte's heart lifted as she drove up the driveway. This time she felt a bubble of mirth rise up inside her. 'Actually, right now, I believe my friends are telling her that I've gone off with my latest toy boy. In an effort to stave off dementia.'

She stopped the car in front of the hotel entrance.

'Dementia? I don't quite make the connection but I think that would beat cycling across Peru,' he said in a neutral tone of voice. 'Thanks for the lift.' Then, when she made no move to get out so that her car could be valet parked, 'Aren't you coming in?'

'No, I'm not staying in the hotel,' she said primly, some tiny bud of mischief preventing her from revealing exactly who she was.

He grinned. 'I hope I haven't dragged you out of your way.'

'No, you haven't.' She watched as he marched across the forecourt and disappeared though the entrance. Then she drove around the track that led to the back of the hotel, to where her house was carefully screened by a thick beech hedge.

He was, she realised, the first man to cause a flutter of interest in her since Jamie had died. Not that she deserved anything to come of it, given the skeletons in her cupboard.

CHARLOTTE 1979–1982

'Don't wait up, I'm popping down to Glendoran for a few pints and I'll be late,' Jamie said.

Charlotte hid her sinking heart as she sat in the office in Tamarisk after dinner that evening. She had a meeting with the bank manager scheduled for first thing the following morning to ask for an immediate increase in their overdraft and it looked like she'd have to go it alone, as Jamie wouldn't exactly imbue anyone with confidence when he had a hangover.

Jamie wasn't an alcoholic, she told herself. He had just fallen into the habit of drinking a few beers and whiskeys regularly, and a late night meant he'd roll home at around two in the morning and be unable to put his mind to any significant work the following day. She was disappointed with his way of distancing himself from their marriage, and it also meant she was working harder than ever keeping the hotel afloat, but the few times she'd tackled him about it, she'd made matters much worse.

After Jamie had stormed out following a row, she found the twins hiding under the kitchen table,

Serena clamping her chubby five-year-old hands over Jack's ears.

'Darlings! Come out, it's okay. Serena, pet, what are you doing?'

'Jack doesn't like the shouting so I stopped it from going in his ears.'

'It's fine now,' she said, feeling horrified. 'Daddy was just being noisy. Come and look at the cartoons on the television.'

After that, for the sake of peace, Charlotte remained silent whenever Jamie told her he'd be out late.

'How will you get home?' she asked, knowing there was no point in reminding him about the meeting as it would only irritate him. At least he had the sense to leave the car whenever he popped down to the village. The hilly laneway up from Glendoran was no road to take after a few pints.

'You don't need to worry about that,' he grinned in that easy-going way of his. 'Someone will give me a lift.'

Someone. One of his drinking buddies who was less inebriated than he was. Sometimes even the pub owner or one of the staff had dropped him up. Because Jamie was outgoing and popular, and was everyone's best friend. Charlotte was fairly sure it was only drink that kept him out late at night. Had there been another woman, she'd have heard of it – Glendoran was such a close-knit community. Or would she? Sometimes she had her suspicions. An attractive man like Jamie was bound to draw women like bees to a honeypot and to some of the locals she was still regarded as an outsider, a blow-in. Then there was Hilary and her naked envy.

She sighed heavily as she clicked on the lamp and opened the ledgers on her desk. She began to run through figures, getting her thoughts in order for the meeting with the bank manager. The renewed world-wide oil crisis and the bitter unrest in the north of the country meant that Tamarisk was struggling. Americans were staying away in their droves. Ireland was in the grip of a full-scale recession and there was a severe slump in the tourist industry. It was all so different from the bright, shiny future she'd envis-aged when she'd left New York, and so much had changed in those few short years that it felt very scary indeed. She was so engrossed in her figures that she hadn't heard Serena coming into the office until she'd looked up and saw her seven-year-old daughter standing in front of her desk. Serena was wearing her pink nightdress and her slippers and was clutching her favourite rag doll. Her soft blonde hair was mussed up as though she'd been tossing and turning in bed.

'Serena, darling! Can't you sleep?' As it was after nine o'clock, she'd assumed the twins were fast asleep. Heather, from the village, looked after them while Charlotte was busy in the hotel or out at a function, sometimes even putting them to bed, as she had that evening. 'Come here to me!' Charlotte held out her arms, feeling warmed as the slight body of her daughter snuggled into her embrace. She was glad her parents had lived long enough to see the twins, making the journey to Ireland and spending a month at Tamarisk when Jack and Serena had been two. Six months later, her mother had died from severe pneumonia and Charlotte's beloved Papa had lasted a year after his wife, dying peacefully in his sleep, even as Charlotte had been making plans to bring him to Tamarisk to live out the rest of his days.

'What are you doing, Mummy?'

'Just some reading.'

'Reading what?'

She dropped a kiss on the top of Serena's head as she turned the page of the ledger. 'I'm just doing the sums darling. We also need to fine tune our market strategy . . .'

She hadn't realised she'd said the words aloud until Serena asked her with the cutest mispronunciation, 'Mummy, what's stat–er-gy?'

Charlotte kissed her again. 'It's making sure the guests feel special by treating them as though they are the most valuable person to walk through the door.'

'I think you and Daddy are the most valuable.'

'And you and Jack are even more valuable. But I think you should be fast asleep. This is important stuff, darling, otherwise I wouldn't be in the office this late.'

'I was asleep. Daddy woke me when he came in to say goodnight.'

Great, Charlotte fumed. 'And Jack? Is he awake too?'

'I came to get you because he has a pain in his

tummy. Daddy brought up cake from the kitchen and he ate too much. I gave him his cars to play with but he still has a pain.'

Charlotte tore her eyes away from the debit column. It would have to wait until she settled the twins again. Damn and blast Jamie. On bad days, he hardly noticed the twins. On good days, he went to ridiculous lengths to show his love for them. She lifted Serena into her arms and her small daughter clung like a monkey to her while she carried her down the corridor, into their apartment and into the twins' bedroom. Jack was fast asleep, upside down on top of his bed with his thumb in his mouth. The bed covers were askew and cake crumbs were scattered on top and mashed into his collection of matchbox cars.

'Silly Jack,' Serena said, one arm around her doll as she picked up his cars, shook off the crumbs and put them carefully in his toy box.

'Hush, darling, he's not really silly, he's just not as sensible as you.'

'Daddy's not as sensible as you,' Serena said in a matter-of-fact voice. 'You do all the important work and Daddy goes out.'

'Hush, pet, into bed with you. Daddy loves you.'

'Mummy?' Serena's huge eyes fastened on her as Charlotte tucked her in.

'Yes, pet?'

'Me and Jack want *you* to come to the Sports Day in school tomorrow instead of Heather.'

Charlotte's heart ached. 'I want to come too, but I

can't. Not tomorrow. You're going have a great day. Maybe next time.' For a moment, she thought of asking Jamie to go, but she just as quickly dismissed it. He'd surely disrupt the events with boisterous behaviour of his own.

Serena's eyes dulled with disappointment.

Sometimes Charlotte was still there in that moment, feeling the echo of that ache in her heart.

CHAPTER 20

'Kim! Got you to myself at last!'

Kim put a bright smile on her face when Matthew O'Brien finally managed to corner her, looking sexy, attractive and extremely beddable in his white shirt and dark trousers.

All night, she'd felt his eyes darting in her direction from the other end of the table. They were part of a group of twelve in Dublin's Town Bar and Grill to celebrate the engagement of Andrea and Gordon, mutual friends. Andrea was a friend from Kim's modelling days. Kim had forgotten that Matthew played golf with Gordon and hadn't realised he'd be there. Neither had she known that Lucy would be there; it had been nerve-wracking to sit across from her, fresh from her date with Jack.

The tabloid photograph of Jack and Lucy outside a nightclub still rankled like a coiled snake in her belly. She'd been horribly enraged when she'd spotted it and only slightly relieved when she saw a photograph of Jack with an up-and-coming DJ a few days later. And then, the following weekend, he'd been snapped with the ex-fiancée of a rock star. They'd all been at her party, she'd realised in a clutch of futile anger. How had she allowed this to happen?

So between Matthew and Lucy, she wasn't surprised to find that she'd barely tasted her food, drunk too much champagne and tossed back quite a lot of Chianti. And then she'd had to go to the ladies and when she emerged she found Matthew waiting between her and the table.

'Why do I get the feeling you're avoiding me?' he asked.

'Because I am,' she laughed, as though she was cracking a huge joke. 'No, seriously, I gave up sex for Lent.'

'Lent?' He lifted a rakish eyebrow. 'That's long gone.'

'Yeah, I decided to keep it up and I think it's best if I'm not tempted.'

'So you find me irresistible? And from what you're saying, you were only using me for sex?'

'Of course,' Kim answered coyly.

'But you must be crawling the walls by now.' He looked at her with a gleam in his eye.

'Maybe so.' She fluttered her eyelashes at him, realising too late that she was flirting with him and sending out all the wrong signals.

'We'll have to do something about that. Although Kim,' he hesitated, fixing her with his navy eyes, 'great and all as it has been, I'd like to think I mean more to you than a sex fix.'

Kim was hugely relieved when they were

interrupted by a chat-show host who had spotted Matthew. She was terribly sorry for interrupting them, she gushed, but was very keen to have Matthew guest on her show. Watching Matthew smile bashfully at her comments and wink at Kim to include her in the conversation, she wished there was an easy way of letting him down.

'Talk later,' he mouthed to her when Kim excused herself and escaped back to the table.

She'd known Matthew for about four years, and had fallen into an easy friendship with him. His father owned a chain of leisure clubs which Matthew managed and his business interests took him abroad quite a lot, but he often caught up with Kim on his trips back to Dublin, and they frequently found themselves mixing in the same social circle. Just after Jack and Amy had got engaged, she'd bumped into him at a party and gone back to his apartment, falling into bed with him in an attempt to take the edge off the long, lonely night.

Kim had been pleasantly surprised, for as well as being clever and kind he'd been great in bed, and they'd spent many a night together enjoying brilliant sex all over his penthouse apartment.

She saw Lucy looking appreciatively at Matthew as he turned on his charm with the chat-show host. So far, Lucy hadn't mentioned her date with Jack, as though she sensed that Kim was itching to find out what had happened. Had they gone to bed? Were they seeing each other again?

Maybe she should go out with Matthew. Especially if it meant they might be snapped coming out of a nightclub at three in the morning, looking intimate together, and that a certain someone, Jack, for instance, might see this, get jealous, and realise that he was missing something. As well as that it seemed a long time since she'd felt wanted and desired, a long time since she'd enjoyed the satisfying bliss of good, raunchy sex. She missed it, from the affection of an all-embracing hug to the pleasurable intensity of orgasm. But it wouldn't be fair to use Matthew that way, no matter how needy she felt or how much she wanted to shake up Jack. She smiled at the waiter as he topped up her wine and then tried not to guzzle it too quickly.

She was glad when the meal came to an end. There was talk of going on to a nightclub, but as the group of them emerged up the steps onto Kildare Street, and began to walk around by the Shelbourne Hotel, Kim hung back, realising that she'd had too much to drink and was likely to say something stupid to Matthew or Lucy. She thanked Andrea for a wonderful night, and felt a little guilty as she watched Matthew stroll ahead unsuspectingly, not realising she was jumping into a taxi.

Her house was in darkness. She was beginning to hate coming home in the dark, alone.

After she switched on the lights, she slid her feet out of her glittery heels and padded down to the kitchen in her bare feet. She opened the fridge, rattling the contents, and pulled out a bottle of wine. Just one small nightcap, she promised herself, sloshing a generous amount into a glass. It was well after midnight; she switched on the outdoor lighting, opened the door to the cool night air and stepped out onto her illuminated deck. Even though it was quiet and peaceful, with the silhouette of neighbours' trees etched against the inky sky, and the air pleasantly fresh on her face, she felt low and depressed – a feeling she hated.

She checked her mobile but, this time, Matthew hadn't bothered to leave a message. There was just an earlier voicemail from Serena, who'd been phoning for a chat. Kim drained her wine and shivered a little under her thin wrap as she listened to the voicemail and realised that Serena sounded a little down in herself as well. She hadn't been in good form the night of the party either. And the day she'd met her for Sunday lunch, Serena had been edgy and emotional and quite unlike her usual self.

Anyone else might have felt jealous of Serena's great lifestyle, Kim knew. Between her glittering image and career, her sexy husband and cute daughter, her friend appeared to have it all. But she knew Serena well enough to realise there were times when her friend's life had been fantastic on the outside, but troubled on the inside. She'd seen her pale face and strained eyes in the months after Harriet's birth, but not by a whisper did Serena admit she was feeling anything but perfectly happy. Occasionally, growing up, Kim had found herself comparing her parents unfavourably with Serena's; there was Jamie, her father, so tall and influential-looking in his suits, always very jolly, and her slim, glamorous mother with the American voice, who wore beautiful clothes and expensive perfume and who was very busy in her important, flower-scented office in the beautiful hotel. But when Serena had come to Kim's house to play, her dazzling friend had been quite happy to watch her mother at her sewing machine and her father out in the shed, and she'd always enjoyed the freshly baked cakes and apple tarts that Margaret Mulligan had whipped out of the oven in between making bedspreads and curtains. Years later, Kim had finally cottoned on to the fact that Charlotte hadn't been around much when Serena and Jack had been growing up. Also, it had been well known in Glendoran that behind his jovial front, her father was an alcoholic. It was something that Serena had never talked about, even to her best friend.

Kim stared out into her garden, and saw a deflated yellow balloon caught on a tree branch, and she thought of the parties in Tamarisk. Looking back, they hadn't always been what they were cracked up to be either. There'd been the time when Serena had disappeared during a particularly lavish party, where everybody who was anybody had been invited, including the relations from La Mimosa.

It was Jack who'd first noticed that Serena wasn't

around. 'She's missing all this, so let's go find her,' he'd said to Kim.

Having walked as far as the woods, they'd retraced their steps and found Serena sitting on a bank down by the river, hugging her knees.

'What's wrong?' Kim had asked, taken aback, knowing that Jack had also spotted her tears, but had seemed to be feeling at a loss.

'Hey, what's up, sis?' he'd asked eventually.

She'd lifted her chin and had given them both a determined smile, as if daring them to challenge her. 'Nothing. It's fine. The sun was hurting my eyes. That's all.' It clearly wasn't fine, but Kim had known by the resolve in her glittery eyes that Serena wasn't about to admit anything was wrong.

'Come on, you're missing the fun,' Jack had said. 'If we don't hurry back all the champagne will be gone.'

Serena had never spoken to Kim about whatever had upset her. By then, Kim had known that even though they were the best of friends, at times Serena preferred to put on a good show rather than admit anything was wrong. But didn't they all keep secrets from each other? It was a fact of life that no one truly knew everything that went on in the private depths of another's heart. For starters, Serena still hadn't a clue how she really felt about Jack.

The gossip pages were making a big fuss about him being back in circulation. And for someone who was usually savvy enough to evade the press,

Jack seemed to be behaving like a kid in a sweet shop. Having fun. Playing the field as well as playing to the press. She wondered how he was really feeling behind this new playboy front and where he was tonight. Maybe he wanted to get the last year out of his system and get back in the groove of life. He couldn't have come through this last year unscathed. He needed a woman who'd be tender and patient, loving and caring.

Someone like her, Kim thought.

There was no point in wallowing in her low feelings, Kim decided, as she padded back into the kitchen and put her empty glass in the dishwasher. Why sit and wait until Jack found her? Kim opened a drawer and riffled through some post. She picked up a cream invitation card and smiled.

The next morning, before she lost her nerve, she phoned Jack.

'I've two tickets for a fashion event in Dundrum,' she told him. 'Champagne, sushi and mingling around rubbing glamorous shoulders. Are you up for it?'

'Hey, tatty-head, a fashion thing doesn't sound like my scene,' Jack said, sounding upbeat, 'but it would be nice to catch up with you.'

Kim's heart lifted. 'It's not my scene anymore but the launch of a new label is useful to see whatever trends are emerging,' she said. 'It should be fun.'

'I'm all up for some fun,' he said. 'So I guess you're on. Six o'clock you said?'

'Yes, it should be over by nine.' She was tempted to ask him to stay over but she stopped herself. One step at a time.

Her heart thumped when she saw him waiting for her in the bar at Harvey Nicks in Dundrum Town Centre two evenings later. Having gone through every item in her wardrobe, her svelte figure was encased in a silvery green Chloé cocktail dress with a plunging neckline that barely covered her curves. Practically his sister? We'll see about that. She walked towards him, knowing she was drawing admiring looks from the crowd, and she had the conviction that her life was about to change completely.

'Jack! Thanks for coming! I know it was rather short notice . . .' her voice dried up in her throat. He looked sexy in a dark grey suit and white shirt, cufflinks gleaming at his wrists, and she felt a throb of desire as he leaned forward to kiss her cheek. She sat on the stool beside him, her skin hot with the awareness of him as he ordered a white wine for her.

'You know I'd do anything for you,' he grinned.

'You're having a drink?' she asked, noticing the gin and tonic in front of him. A drink meant he wasn't driving home tonight. As the launch would be over by nine o'clock, she'd secretly hoped that they might go back to Terenure afterwards. He could easily stay over and drive home in the morning. Now it looked as though he'd had the same idea and her heart soared.

'Yes, I'm not going back to Wicklow tonight,' he said, crushing her hopes. 'I'm staying with Tom and Anita. They live in Mount Merrion and have been tormenting me to drop in and say hello since I got back. Between Amy and everything else, I've lost touch with him over the past couple of years so it's a chance to catch up.' He looked at her a little worriedly as though sensing her disappointment. 'Is that okay with you?'

She smiled brightly. 'Of course, Jack. It's great that you're seeing your mates again.'

'They have a baby now,' Jack went on, 'a little girl.'

'Oh.' Kim's mind raced as she wondered how to deal with this obviously painful subject for Jack. But what could she say, her thoughts raced. How could she offer some comfort without being patronising or reminding him of what he'd lost? If things had been different, he'd have a son or daughter by now. She glanced sideways at him, trying to gauge his mood, words failing her.

He touched her bare arm, sending a hot spark through her. 'Relax, don't look so worried. I can handle it.' The warm depths of his eyes were easy and unconcerned.

'Good for you,' she said. 'I'm glad to hear it.' She leaned towards him, put her hand on his hard thigh, and continued in an intimate tone of voice, 'I know how difficult it all must have been. I'm happy to think you're coming out at the other end. If there's anything I can do . . . or say . . .'

His face gave nothing away. 'Thanks, tatty-head, you've already been great.' He didn't take her hand away, but neither did he cover it with his. After a while she removed it and picked up her drink. She thought of his kiss and what he'd said to her in the hallway before he'd gone away, but tonight there was no trace whatsoever of the vulnerable Jack who'd held her close and told her he'd be back soon. Although this was scarcely the place for a heart to heart.

Just as she had expected, the fashion event in Dundrum was thronged with models, television personalities and the usual wannabe celebrities who saw it as a full-time job to play the social circuit. Noise levels prevented normal conversation, and most were only interested in downing as much free champagne as possible and being seen with the right person. Unfortunately that included Jack. Time and time again, he was pulled away from her side and the only good thing to come out of the evening was that his eyes continually met hers across the room, sometimes in hilarity as he tried to get away from scantily dressed females. Occasionally he looked bored and his eyes asked to be rescued, but she revelled in the warmth of knowing those private looks were all for her, carrying tacit messages only she was sharing.

And she did manage to get their picture taken together. When she spotted a photographer bearing down on Jack, she hastily made a bee line for him, arriving by his side as the photographer began to snap. This one's for you, Lucy, she thought, thrusting out her cleavage and clinging to Jack as they posed for the volley of flash bulbs.

Eventually the crowds began to drift away, they began to dismantle the stage and all the lighting, and the waiters went around collecting empty glasses, squashed up napkins and the remains of food. She watched Jack kiss goodbye to a couple of young, giggling models. One of them ran back to whisper something in his ear and he threw back his head and laughed. Kim felt jealousy curdle her stomach and told herself to get a grip. Then he sauntered over to her, a grin still plastered to his face.

'Well, that was . . . an experience to say the least. Thanks, Kim.'

'No bother. Anytime.'

'Is this how you spend your free time? Circulating at events like these?'

'I have better things to do but now and again I have to show my professional face. Sometimes I look around and wonder what it's all about,' she admitted in a burst of honesty, hoping it might encourage him to open up to her. 'It's scarcely deep and meaningful, is it?'

'If you're starting to go all philosophical on me, we've spent too long here. Next time out we'll try the local pub, although I haven't forgotten that I owe you dinner.' He grinned.

He remembered! Her heart glowed.

It was half past nine when they strolled out to

the waiting line of taxis. He suggested seeing her home and she forced herself to sound cheerful. 'There's no point in dragging you out to Terenure when Mount Merrion is in the other direction.'

Then he said, as though he had only just thought of it, 'Why don't you come with me to Tom and Anita's? I'm sure they'd love to see you . . .'

It was very tempting. She almost said yes. But Jack had waited until the last minute to invite her and she wasn't going to be anyone's afterthought or turn up unannounced at this hour on a couple with a new baby. And she wanted to give Jack space to see his friends, without feeling that Kim had to tag along.

She heard herself say smoothly, 'No thanks, Jack. Another time. You must come out to Terenure soon. Maybe with Serena and Paul,' she added, suddenly nervous of picking up where they had left off the last time he'd come for a meal.

'Sounds good.'

'I'll arrange something with Serena.'

A taxi drew up in front of them and suddenly he stalled her just as she was about to step into it, and the whole night took on a different complexion. 'Actually, Kim, I'd like to have a chat with you about a few things, personal stuff, though it's probably a bit soon yet . . .' he looked at her closely, and there was something very warm in his eyes that made her heart jump.

'Sure, Jack, any time.' She kissed him goodbye. Then all the way home she felt like kicking herself. Lucy O'Leary would have jumped at the chance of accompanying Jack to his friend's house, even if the invitation was an afterthought. Why was she hiding her feelings away instead of letting Jack know how special he was to her? What was she afraid of? Rejection?

Yet he wanted to talk to her. *Personal stuff . . . it was a bit soon yet.* That had to mean something. Surely, she prayed, it meant that the precious nugget of hope she'd clung to and cherished over the last year would finally be realised.

CHAPTER 21

On Sunday evening, the new restaurant overlooking the sea was busy. There were floor to ceiling windows, semi-circular booths for small, intimate parties and long comfortable banquettes. Modern and ultra cool, Serena thought, and not in the same league as the gracious elegance of the Oakwood restaurant in Tamarisk. She sat with Paul at a table for two alongside the window, where they had a view of the rippling bay beyond the sand dunes. The horizon was already hazy, so that to Serena's eyes, sea and sky seemed to blend together into a soft grey veil. On any other occasion, the tranquillity would have calmed her spirits. Susan was babysitting Harriet and Paul had arranged to leave the car at home and get a taxi to the restaurant. He'd booked it all as a surprise for Serena, bringing her to the restaurant she'd talked about checking out rather than his favourite Indian in Wicklow town.

Paul summoned the waiter and ordered a bottle of Moët. 'It's good to have you all to myself without fear of interruption,' he said.

'Thanks for this. I feel as though I'm on a date.'

'So you should. You did say Jack was on call in case of any emergencies at Tamarisk?'

'He is.'

'Good. I want to see you relaxing completely and now that life is getting back to normal, I think this calls for champagne.'

Serena flicked a strand of blonde hair back behind her ears and licked her lips. How was she going to stay happy and relaxed for the next couple of hours? Her period arrived earlier that week and she knew he'd been a little disappointed. And she had only one more packet of pills left, which meant another trip to the family planning clinic to renew her prescription. It was something she had to plan carefully in advance in order to cover herself for an absence of almost three hours, but the round trip to Dublin where she was an anonymous file number was unavoidable. A wave of anxiety spiked inside her, causing her to feel nauseous. She resolutely pushed it to one side. She'd deal with all that when the time came. Otherwise she'd make herself ill. Right now, she was out with Paul, who'd gone to trouble to arrange tonight. She was glad she'd dressed up, selecting a cream Grecian-style dress that draped softly around her curves, and sky-high gold sandals.

'What do you think of the choice of food?'

'It's not bad,' Serena said, studying the menu. 'It's not in the same league as the Oakwood, although they're busy enough for Sunday night.' She glanced around at the diners, some of whom she recognised, who nodded back to her. She hoped that she and Paul would be left to enjoy their meal in peace and not be bothered by anyone who might be curious to find out what she thought of the restaurant, or the wine list, or, worse, wanted their photo for the local press, and might end up calling them Mr and Mrs Devlin. But they were left undisturbed to chat about the upcoming weekend in La Mimosa and projects coming up in Paul's job and she enjoyed her dish of tender duck breast, while Paul had cooked sea bream. They shared a bottle of South African Glen Carlou, and split a tiramisu between them, while the evening dimmed outside and the garden lights came on.

'That's the end of the bubbly,' Paul said, draining the last of the Moët into her flute. He clinked his flute to hers, his dark eyes smiling. 'Who knows, Serena, maybe we'll have something else to celebrate soon.' She ignored the knife-like stab in her stomach and smiled at her husband. 'Yes, indeed.'

'But the last thing I want is you feeling under pressure,' he went on. 'And with Harriet starting primary school in September, it's probably just as well she'll be settled in before there's any sign of another baby, in case her little nose is out of joint.'

Serena breathed out slowly. 'I can't imagine Harriet feeling like that.'

'Probably not, but it'll be a big change for her, moving from the crèche into school.'

Serena shook her head. 'She'll be fine. She's used

to being out there, mixing with other children and the crèche will collect her straight after school and hold on to her until one of us picks her up. It's all arranged.'

'But I presume you'll be around to collect her for the first week or so? To make sure she's okay with the change?' Paul looked at her questioningly.

'The first week?' Serena gave an embarrassed laugh and tried to avoid his gaze. To her acute shame, she hadn't even thought about it. Months ago, Harriet had been enrolled in Glendoran primary school along with her friend Sophie, and as far as Serena had been concerned, it was just a natural progression and not that big of a deal. Her daughter was sociable and outgoing and was used to being with other children, and, come September, Serena had assumed, there wouldn't be all that much difference between Harriet spending her mornings in the classroom instead of the crèche.

'Anyhow,' she went on lightly, 'it's not as if Harriet's been wrapped up in cotton wool all these years.'

Paul looked uncomfortable. She knew that look. It meant he was very politely, and very carefully, holding back his annoyance. 'I thought it was one of those things that normal mums did for the first few days . . .' he said, his dark eyes inscrutable as they flickered across her face.

Normal mums? Serena thought.

'Some of the women in the lab are taking that

week off work and I plan to be late into the office those mornings so I can see her off . . .' he went on. 'I thought you'd be taking some time off yourself to meet Harriet after school and make sure she's happy and settled.'

'Harriet will be fine.' Serena gave a half-laugh. 'I'll be there for the first day, but that's all,' she said, trying to defend herself against his unspoken criticism and, worse, her own self-reproach at not giving any thought to this change in her daughter's life. Even if she hadn't needed further proof that she wasn't a normal mum, she didn't want to spoil Paul's illusions. She took a deep breath, anxious to get the next bit over with, and said with a casual tone, 'Besides, I've already arranged to go to a trade fair in Paris later that week.'

Paul looked at her as though she had dropped a bomb. 'I don't believe this. So you're abandoning her again,' he said, tight-lipped.

She felt hot and cold. 'What do you mean "again"?'

'Like after Harriet was born. You couldn't wait to get back to the office and then high tail it off to some exotic location.'

'Paul, that was work,' she said faintly. 'And I didn't go back to the office until Harriet was two months old.'

He was right in one sense. When Serena had returned to work, she had thrown her energy into the upgrade of the Spa. Paul hadn't been happy when she'd taken business trips to Switzerland and

235

Koh Samui, researching the best and most exclusive spa facilities when Harriet had only been four months old, even though Serena had satisfied herself that her little daughter was well settled into the crèche routine.

He had refused to accompany her.

Thankfully for Serena her research had more than paid off so her trips had been worth it. Now her inner voice urged caution in the face of Paul's burst of resentment. The last thing she wanted was any kind of a scene with him, never mind in a public restaurant. Her skin prickled with anxiety and she forced herself to sound pleasant, 'I'm surprised you're bringing this up now, it was years ago. And I've gone away since to trade fairs,' she pointed out evenly, 'and you didn't object.'

'I agree,' he said, his voice as even as hers, although his eyes were cold. 'But don't you think the timing of this one is off?'

When she didn't answer, silenced by guilt, he went on, 'I brought you out tonight hoping we were making a fresh start after the last bloody awful year. Now I find out you've overlooked a big milestone in our daughter's life in favour of your job. I know you have to go to trade fairs now and then, but I can't believe you've arranged to swan off to Paris the very week Harriet starts school.' He shook his head. 'When I look back, so much of our marriage has revolved around you and your career. No wonder I'm beginning to ask myself why you married me in the first place.'

She felt her face draining of colour. 'Paul, let's not have this conversation here. If it means that much to you, I'll cancel Paris.'

'You're missing the point. I don't care if you cancel on account of me. You should be cancelling on account of Harriet. What I don't understand is why you arranged it in the first place or how you conveniently forgot that it was such an important week for our daughter.'

'I'm truly sorry about that,' she said, consumed with self-condemnation. She hadn't thought for a minute that Harriet would need her support during those first few days in school. Not when the girls in the crèche were more like a mother to her than Serena. She nailed a fake smile to her face as they left the restaurant shortly afterwards. When they reached Maple Hill, Paul arranged for the taxi driver to take Susan home and, for the first time in years, they went to bed without resolving the anger between them.

Serena didn't sleep a wink. How could she, when she had the feeling that everything she was struggling to hold together was beginning to fall apart?

CHAPTER 22

Amy Winehouse crooned seductively in the background as Jenni loaded up her tray with beers and cocktails. 'Back to Black' was one of her favourite songs. She couldn't hear it very well though, because The Anchor was noisy and packed. Outside, in the warm evening air, the pavement tables were spilling over with people, and everywhere she looked there were customers clamouring for attention. She'd lost count of the number of chicken curries, steak and kidney pies and supreme of salmons she'd served, never mind the bottles of Heineken and Corona, and glasses of Smirnoff and cranberry she'd balanced on her tray and ferried out to satisfy the thirsty masses.

Pub grub. Home from home. Surely part of the whole holiday experience should be trying different food. Although she'd be out of a job if visitors decided to desert pub grub in favour of the quaint, delicious restaurants that peppered Vieux Nice.

Early July in Nice, and the weather was hotting up, the sultry nights holding a ribbon of light above the western hills and casting a pink flush across the sky until late. The season had also

238

hotted up; the city was busy with tourists, the hotels were full, the promenade was swarming with visitors and the Cours Saleya was full of bustling crowds from morning until night. She'd been given extra shifts, which meant she was earning more money and had less time to spend it. She supposed that was good, although some of her friends were annoyed when she said she was too tired to stay out late on her night off, whenever she had a night off.

'Hey, Jenni, table ten are screaming for their sweet and sour pork and cod and chips. They said they've been waiting for ever.'

'Coming up, Colin,' she said to the fresh-faced student from Ireland with the anxious look, who was coming in from the pavement tables with a tray loaded with used crockery. He'd been working in the bar just a week and still took the customers' demands very seriously. It would take him about another week to learn to relax and go with the flow. If he was one of the few who couldn't rise above the constant barrage of needs, he'd never survive the busy summer season. She put on a big smile, and brought her loaded tray out to table number eight. Then she went over to table ten and asked if they wanted more drinks. She didn't tell them the kitchen was mega-busy as one of the chefs had taken the night off to go to Monaco with his girlfriend. Their food would be along in a minute so they might as well get their drinks in now, she suggested brightly. They were on holiday after all, so they needed to relax and push the boat out a little. Where were they from? Scotland, how lovely. Were they enjoying Nice? Had they been up to the Parc du Château? Having placated them a little with some bright chit-chat, she took the order for a glass of sweet white wine and a Guinness, and entered it on the touch screen over the register.

Over beyond the serving area inside the bar, Colin was conscientiously scraping every morsel of food off the plates into a bin and carefully placing the used cutlery into a small basin. He looked as though he was quite happy to be hiding away from the general melee. He still hadn't copped on to the fact that it was important to speed up this part of the operation so that he'd have more time to spend taking customers' orders.

'Busy tonight,' she smiled.

'Jeez, it's hectic. Is it always like this?'

'It gets worse. But you'll be fine. You Irish guys can charm the birds off the trees. If I were you, though, I wouldn't worry too much about making the plates look as though they haven't been used. The dishwasher will take care of all that. Save your energy for the customers. That way you'll get more tips.' And there's less chance you'll be fired, she silently thought.

'Oh, right.'

She'd shown Colin the ropes on his first night, happy to take him under her wing. She liked the sound of his voice, his Irish accent, his slight air of vulnerability. In some ways he reminded her of Jack. Although only a very pale imitation, she'd never met anyone quite like Jack.

And probably wouldn't again.

It was just four weeks since the morning she'd left him in the Hotel Negresco. She'd felt slightly aimless as she'd given him a last smile before walking out of his hotel bedroom. Everything between them had been so intense and full on that in the moment of leaving him, she'd felt cut adrift, and almost unsteady on her feet. She'd crossed the road to the promenade and walked in the direction of the Old Town, staring out at the rippling sea. When she'd seen an aeroplane banking in the sky after takeoff, its wings gleaming silver in the sun, her heart had given a jolt. Sounds around her had lulled temporarily. She'd stopped in her tracks and stared back at the famous domed roof of the hotel. It had been enough to remind her that they were worlds apart.

She came from a council estate in London and, much to her parents' annoyance, had dossed through her local comprehensive school, finding it grim and boring. She'd done a basic computer course after she left school and had found that boring as well. She'd gone from job to job and thought she had landed on her feet when she got a job in Selfridges on Oxford Street. Then her father had died and things had gone wrong at home, and Jenni had walked out and come to France. She didn't intend staying in Nice for ever.

She had other plans and quite a few options. Some of the mates she hung around with were talking about a year in Australia, travelling out through Cambodia and Vietnam. She was toying with the idea of joining them. Someone else had a sister in Boston who could help arrange a temporary visa and a job. Or she could travel across the border and work her way down through Spain.

She didn't intend to return home to London for a very long time. If ever.

As for Jack, given what he'd told her when he'd opened his heart to her, he'd been in a very vulnerable place. She knew what it was like to feel vulnerable and cut up. She'd felt like that after her father had died. She'd come to Jack's rescue and offered him everything she had. Hopefully she'd helped him make peace with his demons.

So the morning he'd left she'd continued down the promenade, dragging deep breaths of the warm air into her tight chest as things righted themselves again; the lap of the waves, children's high, excited squeals, the whirr of roller blades from skaters hurtling along the track. She'd told herself she'd never hear from him again. All that stuff about her going home with him had been ridiculous. The reality was that he'd go back to his life and forget all about her.

Yet she'd begun to find herself struggling at work to keep up a bright, breezy front. She wondered if Michael had guessed that she'd had a fling with

Jack. He'd said nothing at all to her. She could imagine him blowing a gasket if he suspected what she'd been up to. He seemed to have taken the place of the father she no longer had. Her mates didn't know either. They would have said she was mad to be crashing out with someone who was so much older than her. But all of this didn't stop her from thinking about Jack, or remembering the way it had been between them. Compared to him, other guys seemed immature and selfish. She'd never experienced anything like the hot passion that had swept her away, even the fun they'd had, but most of all the way he had made her feel – wonderful and amazing, all woman, sexy and alluring, as though she was giving him a wonderful gift and was really special to him.

As though she was important.

And it hadn't just been sex.

He'd brought her out to lunch, spinning up the coast as far as Cannes and into restaurants where Jenni was afraid to even look at the prices on the menu, encouraging her to order whatever she wanted and smiling affectionately at her when she insisted that ice cream was her favourite dessert. He'd brought her to Villefranche, and they'd slowly driven past outdoor cafés flanking the quayside, where diners had looked at the sleek black with the top down and Jenni had felt as though she was playing a part in a glamorous movie.

On their last afternoon, he'd brought her up to Antibes and, once again, her jaw had dropped at the size of the yachts and boats moored along the quay, before he'd surprised her by parking the car and taking her out into the blue infinity of sky and sea in one of those fabulous yachts. She'd sat on the deck, feeling the sun on her body, sipping pink champagne and had pinched herself and wondered what had happened to Jenni Anderson from Primrose Hill.

But the problem was, even though she'd told herself it had only been a holiday fling, nothing in her life was the same after he left.

On the surface she'd tried to be the same happy-go-lucky Jenni who chatted to her customers and breezed through her work in the bar, but going out with her mates into hot stuffy clubs, where Jäger Bombs and Kamikazes were lined up against the bar ready to be knocked back and get you drunk as swiftly as possible, had begun to seem like a total waste of time. And when she pushed through the crowds out onto the packed and even stuffier dance floor and moved around to the loud, pulsating beat, she thought of the way she'd danced with Jack under the stars in the Place Masséna, as music floated across the warm evening air.

So when he did phone her, on a Sunday morning, she didn't know what to think.

'It's been a month, Jenni,' he said, the sound of his voice bringing it all tumbling back to her like a tidal wave. The scent of him, the way his eyes rested on her, as though she was someone very special, the warmth of his arms around her, the raw honesty in his face, and the hot, hard feel of him inside her. The look in his eyes when they were locked together.

God.

'Jack! How are you doing?' She'd just got out of bed and was standing in her tiny kitchen alcove wearing a white T-shirt and a thong.

'Missing you.'

Missing her? Missing Jenni Anderson? She didn't think it was possible for someone to miss her. 'Yeah, sure.' She gave a half-laugh from sheer nervousness.

'You don't believe me?' He sounded hurt.

'Jack, hang on a minute,' she softened her voice. She walked over to her unmade bed and sank down onto a corner of the mattress. 'You're back in your life now and I thought you would have forgotten all about me. I wasn't really expecting you to call.'

'Weren't you?' He sounded even more hurt.

'What about . . .' she paused, her free hand fidgeting with the bed sheet, scrunching it into a ball. 'I told you to go out on dates, to see other women . . .'

'I followed your instructions, to the letter,' he said. 'I even have proof.'

An unexpected streak of jealousy. 'Proof?'

'Yeah, photos of me out with some of Dublin's best-looking chicks. I went to a lot of effort just so you'd know I was serious about this and so you'd know that when I called you, I knew exactly what I was doing and it wasn't just temporary between us. I went back to my normal life, Jenni. And guess what? I need you in it. I want you in it.'

There was the sound of her toaster popping and the aroma of freshly toasted bread, but she ignored it. Instead she fell back across the bed and stared at a spot on the ceiling, the phone clamped to her ear. It was strange to be listening to his voice like this. She could picture him right beside her. She was lost for words for, in spite of everything they'd shared, she'd never expected this. It would never work. He was crazy, wasn't he?

'Jenni? You still there?'

'Yes . . . look, honestly, I think you're still caught up in our holiday romance.'

'How soon can you get here?' he asked as though she hadn't spoken.

'Are you for real?' She was half laughing now, trying to take the sting out of her words. 'Look, I can't just walk out of my ultra-important, high-profile career, or leave my luxury apartment . . .' her head felt scattered, her thoughts slewing around, and she tried to muster her arguments. 'I have a life here, you know, I have friends . . . other plans.'

'You're going back on your word.'

'What?'

'You promised? Remember?'

'I said you could call me,' she said in a small voice, hardly able to believe he really wanted her. 'But I thought it was a nice way to say goodbye.

I didn't expect you to contact me. I thought you'd soon forget about us.'

'Dammit, I wish you weren't at the end of a phone. I want to see your face, look into your eyes, hold you tight . . . I want to be back in your room with you.'

He sounded, she thought, as though he meant every word. She squeezed her eyes shut to blot out visions of him in her room. He shouldn't be saying these things to her. It was too overwhelming to take in.

'Jack, it was only a week, just a few days out of normal life . . . special days, okay, but like all these things if you saw me again you'd probably run for cover and ask yourself where your head had been.'

There was a long silence and this time she thought he'd put his phone down.

'Okay,' he said, 'maybe you need more time. Maybe it's selfish of me to expect you to drop everything and come to me. How about I give you another week to think about it? Come for a visit. Tell your boss it's an emergency. Let someone else cover you for a while. Come for a week, two weeks, and we'll see how it goes . . .'

The next few days went by in a blur. Jenni accepted every invitation she could, relaxing on the beach with friends during time off between shifts, partying out late after her night's work, filling every hour of every day. It was the best way to make sure she had no time to think about Jack or his phone call.

She decided that all she had to do was refuse to answer Jack's calls and he'd soon get the message. The whole idea of her going home to his place in Ireland was crazy. He'd only ever seen the happy-go-lucky Jenni who hadn't a care in the world. He hadn't seen the side of her that had been hurt and rejected when she'd lived in London and that had lashed out angry and confused. He knew very little of the details of her background, and didn't fully appreciate the gulf between them.

But there was something else happening to her. Something she preferred to ignore, something so enormous she pretended it wasn't happening. She put her unusual tiredness down to her hectic socialising. And when she threw up after a night out, she decided she'd had some dodgy food. Then it happened again. She went home straight after work on Friday night as her exhaustion finally floored her and she still had an upset tummy.

She woke at five o'clock on Saturday morning. Sunrise was about an hour away. She knew this by the muted grey light rimming the edge of her curtains. As she lay there in that quiet and peaceful zone before she fully connected with the day, things came together in her head; her tiredness, her upset tummy and the sudden tenderness of her breasts. There was no ignoring it, no denying the truth staring her in the face.

She was pregnant.

She sat up in the bed and wrapped her arms around her knees. She wondered what her mother would say if she could see her now. Or her dad for that matter. She wondered what Jack would say, after everything he'd been through with Amy. Was it fair to land him with this? Even though he'd said he wanted her in his life. Funnily enough, she didn't feel scared. Considering the way her life was about to change so completely, she was amazed that in the moment before it all began to shift, she felt so perfectly centred and calm.

CHAPTER 23

For the first few days after their heated words in the restaurant, Paul had been very cool towards Serena, even though she'd told him quietly that she'd cancelled her trip to Paris. She'd been relieved to see that he was as anxious as she was to avoid a strained atmosphere in front of Harriet, and he'd been careful to mask his chilliness towards her whenever Harriet had been around. And in a way it was Harriet who'd brought them back together.

When Paul had brought her home from the crèche, where she'd learned a new song, her excitement had been so contagious and she'd been at such pains to show off to her parents that they'd found themselves standing together in the playroom, smiling in unison at their daughter's singing. When they'd caught each other's eye, Serena hadn't been able to look away. She'd put everything she could into that look – her hopes that the coolness between them would be resolved, her fears that it might not be, her regret for allowing it to happen in the first place.

Paul had given her a long, silent glance in return.

There'd been no sudden harmony between them, but a thaw had set in and after they'd both read Harriet a bedtime story and tucked her up in bed, they were on speaking terms again. By the time a week had passed, the incident had been put behind them, but the tension it had unleashed in Serena made her even more on edge as she planned her next trip to the family planning centre in Dublin.

Her previous visit had been just before Christmas, so the guise of spending a day in Dublin for Christmas shopping had been perfect. Now she needed to come up with something that would satisfy not only Paul, but Jack and Charlotte, in case they came looking for her, and any friends who might spot her car in the city-centre car park.

There was nothing like a little subterfuge to really complicate life, she thought desperately as she arrived home to Maple Hill on Monday evening with her excuses ready. For once, Paul was on the internet in the study, absorbed in the screen. She stood in the doorway for several moments, and watched him silently. He was sitting with his back to her, and he seemed all at once terribly innocent and vulnerable.

Why couldn't she tell him what was going on in her head? He was her husband and he deserved the truth. So what if he discovered his wife was far from the positive, can-do person he'd fallen in love with and a hopeless mother to Harriet? Why couldn't she admit what was in her heart of hearts? She hesitated at the door while everything ran through her head, and just as she was weighing up the full repercussions of baring her soul, he turned around as if sensing her presence, and his smile was so warm and unguarded that she pushed all her misgivings to one side. She came up behind him, looped her arms around his shoulders and, leaning forward, dropped a kiss on the side of his face. And she felt she had already taken the first step into her planned subterfuge.

'Hi darling,' she said. 'What are you up to?'

He smiled at her, 'Just reading an article on a new wonder drug. Harriet's out in the sand pit. She's had her tea, but I'm going to eat shortly. Maria left some beef stir fry ready in the fridge.'

'Sounds nice, I'll have some of that.' Over the past week, she'd deliberately waited until she got home to have her evening meal, rather than grabbing something in Tamarisk, so that she and Paul could sit down together.

He reached up and clasped her arm. 'Great. I'll open some wine.'

'And just so you know, I'm taking a couple of hours off in the morning.'

'Oh? Good for you.'

She was relieved when he looked back at the screen, his right hand on the mouse as he scrolled through the document, his left hand holding onto Serena's arm. She hoped he wouldn't feel her trembling as she went on, 'Yes, I've an appointment in a city-centre beauty clinic. I've heard marvellous reports about a new organic facial and

I want to sample it for myself before we decide to bring it to Tamarisk.'

'So it's work,' he turned in his seat and grinned up at her. 'I was hoping you were taking some time for yourself. Still, a facial will be relaxing, although from where I'm sitting, your skin is so perfect that you don't really need it.'

It took a monumental effort for her to get through the rest of the evening, and the following morning she drove up the N11 with a very heavy heart. Paul had kissed her goodbye and told her to enjoy herself. Charlotte had thought it was a great idea and Serena had had a worrying moment when she'd said she'd come with her, only she was seeing Millie.

Jack had been non-committal. 'I thought we were meeting Brian,' he'd said.

'Jack! Do you even look at your diary?' she'd found herself snapping at him. 'That's first thing in the afternoon. I'll be well back by then and you'd better be there. There's stuff to discuss. Important stuff.'

'Okay, sis. Relax.'

Serena was back in Tamarisk before lunch-time, her six months' supply of pills concealed in a paper bag at the bottom of her bag, which she stowed safely into her desk drawer. She'd be even more relieved when all but her current month were out of harm's way in the hat box in her dressing room. She left her office and went downstairs to satisfy herself that everything was running smoothly and was coming through the Tamarisk foyer, glad to be back in her groove and feeling that the anxiety of the morning was finally behind her, when Andrew came out of the reservations office.

'Ah, Serena, I've had a phone call I need to discuss with you,' he said.

'Yes?'

'It's Marilyn Moore.'

The rising star of one of Ireland's most popular soap operas had booked out almost a third of the rooms in Tamarisk for her forthcoming hen's weekend. 'I can't think of anywhere else that my wide circle of friends and I would be better pampered on my special weekend,' Marilyn had gushed.

'What does Marilyn want now?' Serena asked, deciding she'd better deal with this instead of heading on down to Jack's office to discuss their forthcoming meeting.

Andrew gave her a half smile. 'She called Reservations this morning and made anonymous enquires about our rates. Then she called your office but when you didn't pick up, the call was routed to me. She feels she's not getting a special enough deal given the number of rooms she's booked and has talked about cancelling . . .'

'Thanks, Andrew, I'll deal with this,' she said. She was so not going to get rattled about this, Serena decided immediately, going up to her office. She needed to stay calm. Marilyn had been in contact with Serena several times with her list of demands growing by the minute and still her hen-party weekend was a full month away. Serena didn't dare ask how her wedding plans were coming along, but felt very sympathetic towards the poor unfortunate wedding planner, whoever he or she was. She brought the soap star's details up on her laptop and dialled her number.

'Serena! Thank you for calling me back so swiftly,' Marilyn's modulated voice rang in her ear.

Serena's mobile bleeped indicating a text message and she glared at it. It was Jack, texting to postpone their afternoon meeting with Brian. What the hell was he thinking? She had to put her annoyance to one side as she flung down her mobile and focused on the soap actress and her outrageous demands. Not that she was going to give in to her over the accommodation rates, which were already very favourable. She didn't intend to send the message out from Tamarisk that blackmail was acceptable. A complimentary spa treatment and a bottle of the finest French wine for the bride-to-be was about as far as she was going to go. As she expected, Marilyn eventually accepted her offer and backed down.

She was no sooner finished talking to Marilyn when her mobile buzzed. This time it was Emma, Sophie's mum, on the line.

'Emma. Is everything all right?'

'Yes, Serena, I just wanted to remind you that my niece is having her birthday party this evening and you said it was okay for me to bring Harriet along with Sophie? I'm off work early and I'll go straight to the crèche to collect them. They'll enjoy it, there's a bouncy castle and a magician, a slide show and face painting . . .'

'Yes, that sounds good. I really appreciate that you're bringing Harriet . . .' especially when it was the kind of favour that Serena couldn't reciprocate.

'Don't be daft,' Emma said cheerfully. 'I'll enjoy it too. My sister has four kids and I think about six more are coming to the party. It'll be supervised bedlam. It's my sister in Dublin, so I'll have Harriet home just after eight o'clock.'

'Thanks, that's fine.'

Serena felt a momentary pang that Harriet was going to have an evening of great fun courtesy of Sophie and her family, and not thanks to her mother. Maple Hill would seem quiet and boring to her after all that excitement. She switched off that train of thought very quickly and phoned through to Jack. She'd assumed when he'd postponed that he needed more time to gather together reports and figures in advance of meeting Brian. He knew that decisions had to be made regarding their financial future and the discussion had been held up long enough as Jack had no sooner settled back into work when Brian had gone on holidays.

But there was no answer from his office, or his mobile.

★   ★   ★

256

Dublin airport was far busier than Jack had expected.

For some crazy reason, he'd assumed that Tuesday afternoon would be peaceful enough. All the way up the motorway, he'd pictured himself waiting quietly while he calmed his nerves. But the arrivals area was bedlam. There was a large extended family taking up loads of space as though they owned the joint, complete with banners and balloons and loud excitement, and children running around shrieking and laughing, getting in his way and blocking his view of the flow of passengers spilling through the gap in the opaque glass doors. Sometimes, there were interminable moments when the doors remained firmly closed. Then a gaggle of travellers would arrive together, pulling suitcases and pushing trolleys. He shifted from foot to foot, amazed at how nervous he felt, and he wished he could tell everyone to get lost and get the hell out of his way so that he caught the first sight of Jenni coming through.

If indeed she did come through and hadn't changed her mind. From the time of her surprise phone call to him on Saturday and her text earlier that day, confirming her afternoon flight, he had been afraid to believe it was really happening.

He checked the monitor again. Now it was thirty minutes since the flight from Nice had landed. Did it take that long for the luggage to be unloaded? What the hell were the baggage handlers up to? Or was there a delay in Customs? When the doors whooshed open again disgorging passengers, including the impeccably uniformed airline staff, he felt like grabbing them and asking if there was any sign of a fun-loving girl with dark, choppy hair.

The noisy family let out a loud cheer and wildly waved their banners and balloons as two twenty-somethings came through pushing trolleys with what looked like dilapidated backpacks in the last throes of existence. Bright young things, they looked like they were around the same age as Jenni. To judge by the state of the luggage and the warmly enthusiastic welcome they received, they must have been coming back from some kind of a worldwide adventure, the kind of thing that Jenni would surely expect to experience, and far more exciting than anything he had to offer. He had a moment of sheer terror. He'd been kidding himself. What if Jenni had been right all along? What if it had just been a bubble in time, a week suspended out of normal existence? How come a room with a single bed where noisy trains glided by outside and a windmill whirred in the window, somewhere so removed from his normal life, could have filled him with such peace and made him feel safe?

As well as all that, he might be the co-director of a multi-million euro family business, with a lifestyle to match, but when he lay sleepless at four in the morning, or stared at his face in the mirror last thing at night, he was a haggard-looking widower of almost thirty-six who had been through the wars and then some.

He wasn't even supposed to be here. He was supposed to be at a meeting in Tamarisk. Serena had said it was important but, what the heck, it couldn't be so urgent that another day or two would matter. He'd taken the easy way out by texting both Serena and Brian asking for a postponement. Already that afternoon, he'd ignored two calls from Serena. Why couldn't his sister just accept that he was busy without needing to know his every movement? He'd told nobody of his whereabouts, just in case Jenni changed her mind.

But she didn't.

It was momentarily quiet when she finally came through the doors. There was a kind of hiatus in the afternoon before another wave of greeting relatives and friends descended upon the waiting area. He saw her straight away. She was clutching a shoulder bag with one hand and pulling a medium-sized case with the other, the kind you'd use for a decent length of holiday, and this filled him with satisfaction. It seemed to take forever for her to get to the end of the barrier, but it was less than five seconds.

'Jack.' She tilted her face to him. The smile she gave him was full of assurance. His heart thumped painfully, and then flowed over with a mixture of emotions. She put her face against his shoulder and stayed absolutely still. Her hair tickled his nose, and he breathed in the fresh, clean scent of her and felt the solid warmth of her body against his. He knew immediately that it hadn't just been a once-off bubble of time. It was something that was very much real. And here and now, it was everything he'd ever wanted.

After she'd talked to Brian to reschedule, and had phoned Jack twice only to get voicemail, Serena went down to his office. She pushed open the door and looked around the spacious room with panelled walls, original landscape paintings, a huge antique desk and splendid views of the Wicklow mountains. It had once been Charlotte's office and the hub of the hotel when she was in charge.

Not only was it empty, to Serena's dismay, but the desk was far too neat and tidy for someone whom she'd hoped to be busy at work. Jack knew how important this meeting was. Where the hell had he got to? She felt exasperated as she stalked back upstairs to her office and with difficulty she turned her attention to a report from the Spa detailing a breakdown of the previous month's bookings. It was only as she prepared to go home and she tried Jack's mobile again to find it was still switched off that Serena felt gripped by unease.

Jack had been very down in himself before he'd left for La Mimosa. Maybe his cheeriness on his return had been a front, designed to reassure Serena and his mother that he was okay. When she thought of it now, the turnaround in him had been amazing. Perhaps too amazing, for in spite of appearing to pick up his life again he might still be riddled with anxiety and blaming himself for what had happened with Amy.

Amy! A melange of images flashed in front of her, deepening her uneasiness.

The phone call from Thailand in the early hours of the morning had been shocking. Through her brother's almost incoherent voice, it took a long time for Serena to figure out that Jack and Amy were just into the fourth day of their holiday when he'd woken to find her pale and lifeless in bed beside him.

'She'd been on anti-depressants since losing the baby,' he'd explained in a tearful, broken voice. 'We were out last night . . . I didn't think she'd had too much to drink, but it must have been enough to confuse her as she obviously took an accidental overdose . . .' his voice had thinned and trailed away.

'Jack! I don't believe you! This is dreadful.' In the dark of the early morning, she'd been cold with shock and didn't know what to say to ease his horror. 'Paul and I will be there as soon as we can.'

'No, definitely not Paul,' Jack had insisted. 'Please, Serena, just you. The less fuss the better.'

'I'll be with you as soon as I can,' Serena had told him, wishing she was there already.

She'd flown out immediately. Amy's sister Karen had remained at home, far too upset to leave the four walls of her house. And it had been grim. Everything about it had been ghastly and shocking.

261

Jack's ravaged face had cut Serena to the bone. Her earlier dislike of Amy had taunted her constantly. Jack's hopes to keep it as quiet as possible and avoid a media circus had been dashed when word of the tragedy leaked out and made front-page news. There had been pictures of Jack and Serena arriving back at Dublin airport, their faces hidden behind dark glasses. Amy's funeral had been thronged, her grave covered with flowers and flickering candlelight. But all too soon the media had found another scandal to devour and Amy became yesterday's news. Her Facebook page had been flooded with tributes at first, but then they too dwindled to a trickle and then a halt, like the candles on her grave. Now, just over a year on, Serena realised sadly, it was as though she'd never existed.

Except in Jack's heart.

What was she doing wallowing in memories, Serena suddenly thought, when Jack was probably hurting somewhere. Since he'd come home from France, she couldn't recall a time that her brother had been off the radar. Neither was it like him to disappear just before an important meeting. She powered off her laptop, her impatience spilling over as it slowly shut down. She grabbed her bag and car keys. She would run by Garryvale, just in case.

In case of what she didn't know, but just to reassure herself that he was okay.

* * *

Since Jenni met Jack in the airport, it seemed as though she'd stepped into some kind of magical world that bore little resemblance to life as she had known it so far. Jack's car was huge, with soft squashy seats, and it rolled smoothly down a motorway that took them in a surprisingly short space of time from the airport and surrounding suburbs into the glens and mountains of the countryside.

They chatted lightly about her journey and her replacement in the bar, and she sensed that they were both feeling their way around the conversation, making chit-chat for the sake of it, while getting used to each other all over again. The real questions could wait: is it still the same between us? What do you think of me now? Was I right to come? Jack seemed more self-assured now that he was on his home territory, and a far cry from the vulnerable Jack who'd clung to her and wept that very first night they'd been together. The night she figured it must have happened. From time to time, her eyes drifted to the countryside around her. Green folding into green, right through the spectrum of shades from yellow-green gorse to the dark velvety smudge of a forest glade, big skies with high-flying, white puffy clouds, a line of trees marching across the top of a rolling hill. Sheep grazing in fields. The rocky, barren summit of a mountain top. Blackbirds rising from a field and wheeling into the air.

Ireland. Her first ever visit. She liked it.

She'd told him on the phone the previous Saturday that she would spend a month with him to see how they got on. She'd get a leave of absence from her job. There were so many students looking for summer work that it would be easy enough to find a temporary replacement. At first Michael had been stupefied. What did she think she was doing? Had she taken leave of her senses? But in the course of arguing with her, he'd soon backed down. He'd sighed and told her to come back anytime, he'd even organise a flight for her.

But when Jack eventually turned into a driveway and through wooden gates that silently opened for them, the sight of his luxury home stunned her into silence. Then Jack showed her around. She found her voice as they came back downstairs and she stood in his magnificent hall with the vaulted roof, soaring windows and wrought iron wall decor. 'Jack! You never told me you were this wealthy! I don't know what I'm doing here,' she admitted.

'You're with me,' he said, wrapping his arms around her. 'That's all you have to think about. Nothing else really matters.'

She didn't know what to say so she leaned into his chest, surprised at the warm rush of familiarity.

He cooked omelettes that they ate at the kitchen table along with fresh bread rolls. He started to take her clothes off in the kitchen. She felt shy at first but as soon as he touched her, she melted. After that, he brought her upstairs to his plush bedroom with the vast bed. When she closed her eyes, they might have been clinging together on her tiny single bed, so well did she know the lines of his hard, muscular body, the feel of his touch, the scent of his skin, and the mind-blowing pleasure he gave her that left her breathless.

So it was all brilliant.

Until his sister arrived.

CHAPTER 24

By the time she was accelerating sharply down the beech-lined avenue away from Tamarisk, Serena's anxiety was mounting. She shouldn't have felt annoyed with Jack earlier on. He was obviously upset and having a bad day. He deserved some breathing space and understanding, and if his twin sister couldn't give him that, well who could? She was glad of the power in her car as she tore up the lane towards Jack's house. She arrived at Garryvale, jabbed her remote control to open the electronic gates and sent up a scatter of stones as she drove up the gravelled driveway. She felt a moment of relief when she saw his car parked at the side of the house. Then she realised it didn't automatically mean he was home or that he was okay. She came to a halt and, grabbing her bag, jumped out of her car and marched to the porch. She pressed the doorbell and heard it chime inside the hall.

There was no answer.

She waited several moments and stabbed at the bell again, her nerves on edge when there was no sign of her brother through the glass in the hall door. A little desperate, she peered through the front window into his reception room. She was just about to walk around to the back of the house when the hall door finally opened and Jack poked his head out.

'Serena! What's up?'

Her immediate relief was superseded by curiosity. 'Nothing. I just . . .' her voice trailed away. Jack was wearing a pair of jeans and nothing else. His chest and feet were bare. His dark-red hair was sticking up as though he had been raking his fingers through it. Or, the thought crystallised, someone else had been raking fingers through it. He grinned at her, looking abashed, reminding her of the ten-year-old Jack who'd been caught raiding the orchard. He certainly didn't look as though he was upset or having a bad day. On the contrary, he looked as though he'd been having an excellent day until Serena had rudely interrupted him.

So much for her sisterly concern.

'You'd better come in,' he said, throwing the hall door wide open.

'It's okay, I don't want to intrude,' Serena said evenly. This was not the time and place to have a go at him. Tomorrow, back in the office, she would tell him exactly what she thought of his skiving off. And this afternoon of all times, when it had been crucial to talk to Brian.

'Don't be silly, come on.' He disappeared back inside, leaving her little choice but to follow him into the reception room.

'I don't think I should be here,' she said, biting back her annoyance, wondering if his latest squeeze was still in the house, or, to be exact, in the bedroom.

'It's fine, Serena. Sit down. It's about time you two met anyway.'

Her legs suddenly weak, she sank down onto the edge of his sofa as the full meaning of his words hit her between the eyes. She barely had time to absorb them before he hurried out into the hall and she heard him calling for her.

'Jenni! Come here! Come down to meet my sister. Don't be shy.'

Jenni wasn't the least bit shy, to judge by the way she came into the room wearing an oversized T-shirt which was so big on her that it must have belonged to Jack. Beneath it – *good God* – unless Serena was seeing things, she was wearing boxer shorts, again they could only belong to Jack. *Sweet Jesus*. Her tanned legs were bare. They were slender and shapely. Jack threw his arm around her and held her tightly to him. Jenni snaked an arm around his waist and in her bare feet, the top of her head barely reached his chin.

If Amy had been a pussy cat, feline and clingy but with sharp teeth and hidden claws, Jenni was like an affectionate dog, her face open and guileless, her big eyes the shade of soft caramel toffee. Her short black hair was mussed up, her mouth swollen. As though she felt Serena's close scrutiny, she clenched the front of the T-shirt tighter against the swell of her breasts, inadvertently revealing the outline of her curves complete with hardened nipples. She seemed incredibly young, unsophisticated and carelessly sexy.

Serena felt dizzy with shock. She'd forgotten totally about Jenni. Jack had only spoken of her once. Then when she'd seen photos of him in the press out with other women, three or four, at least, after Lucy, she'd assumed it had been merely a holiday romance that had temporarily swept him away.

'She arrived this afternoon, didn't you, Jenni?' Jack said with pride in his voice. 'Until she walked through arrivals I wasn't even sure she'd come.'

So Jack had been hanging out in the airport that afternoon. While she'd been looking for him, worrying about him, convincing herself that something was wrong, he'd been enjoying the drama of the airport wait for his girlfriend. Correction, lover. For he'd obviously brought Jenni home and taken her straight to bed.

'Hi, Serena, pleased to meet you,' Jenni said, as though it was the most normal thing in the world for her to be standing half-naked in Jack's house while he introduced her to his sister. At first, Serena was too bemused to place her accent, then she realised that it was English, possibly London.

'Hello, Jenni,' she said. She didn't say she was pleased to meet her. She couldn't. She felt sick to her stomach but she didn't quite know why. She picked up her bag and rose to her feet. 'This is obviously a bad time,' she said. 'I've disturbed you. Anyway I have to get home to Harriet,' she went on, forgetting for the moment that Harriet was at a party. 'I'll see you tomorrow, Jack,' she said, giving him a meaningful look.

'You will indeed,' he said cheerfully. 'Not sure what time I'll get in at. It all depends . . .' he winked at her and left the rest of his sentence unfinished.

'I'll see myself out,' Serena said, conscious of a red mist in front of her eyes as she went out into the hall.

Jack followed her out. 'Hey, sis, what do you think? She's great isn't she?' His face was one big happy grin that filled her with unease. 'I might bring her up to Tamarisk later in the week and introduce her around,' he went on. 'I might even find a job for her to do, in time, of course, after she's settled in.'

Settled in? A job in Tamarisk? She's great?

'I'll talk to you tomorrow,' Serena said, barely trusting herself to speak. She stalked through the door and closed it behind her, resisting the impulse to slam it.

Jenni was relieved when Serena left. While Jack went out to see his sister out, she padded into the kitchen to get a glass of water. She stared around, freshly amazed at the spaciousness and the high spec of it all; the acres of glass-fronted presses, a gleaming double oven that looked practically unused and a row of copper pots and pans, all perfectly co-ordinated and shiny with newness. There was a long, pale oak table and six leather chairs arranged in front of a large picture window framing a garden filled with plants and shrubs and a fabulous mountain view. In another corner there was a seating area, with a bookcase and a magazine basket and a squashy sofa facing a plasma screen on the wall. The perfect comfy nook to relax in, she thought, compared to his ultra-chic reception rooms to the front of the house.

And littering this wonderful kitchen, the trail of her abandoned clothes and underwear.

'I don't think your sister likes me,' Jenni said, when Jack followed her into the kitchen. She turned around and stood with her back against the counter as she sipped some water. It was cool and refreshing. Jack had already told her it was directly piped from a natural source.

'Of course she likes you,' Jack said. He put his hands down on the counter top on either side of her body, trapping her there. He bent down and kissed her on the forehead.

'Nah. She's looking out for you. She's nervous in case I upset you, like Amy.'

'Don't be silly, you and Amy are chalk and cheese. When I called you down though, I forgot most of your clothes were in the kitchen,' he said, grinning happily. 'You look very sexy in my T-shirt.' He took her glass out of her hand and put it down.

271

Then he lifted the T-shirt over her head. She felt cool air on her breasts and her ripened nipples.

'Hey, what's this?' he stood back and looked at his boxer shorts.

She grinned. 'All I could find in a hurry.'

'Mmm. Tempting.' He dipped his fingers into the open fly and she felt a jolt of pleasure.

'Jack. I need to ask you something,' she said, trying to keep a clear head for the moment.

'Ask away.' He bent and licked her nipple.

'Are you quite sure it's all behind you? Amy and all that . . .?'

He raised his head and looked at her, his smile warm and carefree. He didn't answer immediately. Then he said, 'Quite, quite sure.' He lifted her up onto the counter. He scooped her to him so that their noses touched. She wrapped her legs around his waist and nuzzled her head into the warm cleft between his shoulder and chin. It felt good. She was glad she'd come. Nothing mattered but being here with him now. It was as though everything in her life before Jack had ceased to exist.

CHAPTER 25

As Serena marched through the hall door in Maple Hill slamming it behind her, Paul came out of the front room and looked at her in surprise. Dammit. She needed some time alone to calm down and get her head together. He must have seen the way she'd screeched to a halt outside the house and slammed the car door, and even though she was wearing expensive shoes, had given the near-side tyre a kick for good measure.

'Serena? What's up?'

'Nothing,' she retorted, dropping her bag on the table in the hall and stalking down to the kitchen. She opened a press and took out a bottle of gin, pouring some into a glass. From the fridge, she took out a bottle of tonic, filling the rest of her glass. She didn't wait to add crushed ice or a slice of lime. Standing in the kitchen she took a large gulp, and then another.

'I need this,' she said.

'You'd better tell me what's the matter,' he said. She noticed that his hair was still damp-slicked from the shower and he had a clean, spicy smell.

He had changed from his work suit into blue denim jeans and a short-sleeved black top. She took another gulp of her gin and tonic. Thankfully, she'd remembered in the nick of time that Harriet was out at a party.

'There's nothing wrong,' she said. 'Nothing beyond darling Jack moving his latest girlfriend into his house.'

'I see,' Paul said. 'No, on second thoughts, I don't see. So what if he has? Why should that have you in a temper?'

Why indeed? That was the big question that had annoyed the hell out of her as she drove home. Why should she care?

'Jack's hopeless when it comes to women,' she said, trying to make sense of her rage. 'He hardly knows this girl and he's totally infatuated with her. He's too much of a soft touch. Look what happened with Amy. I know we shouldn't speak ill, etcetera, but anytime she crooked her little finger he was off. And then I ended up holding the fort in Tamarisk many a time when he was called away.'

Paul appeared to be considering her words and then he said, 'That's more to do with you than him.'

She was taken aback. 'What do you mean?'

'He knew he could depend on you, so he'd no worries skiving off whenever. Maybe if you'd been less prepared to fill in for him from time to time, he would have put his foot down with Amy.'

'Thanks a bunch,' Serena glared at him, recalling the ease with which Jack had taken himself off that afternoon and his casual text. What could she have done to prevent that?

'Jack is still in a vulnerable place,' she said. 'I don't want to see him hurt anymore.'

'Ah, poor Jack. Come on, Serena, he's a grown man,' Paul said irritably. 'He's well able to take care of himself. He doesn't need you to mother him.'

'Mother him? How dare you!'

'It's the truth,' Paul said mildly.

She watched him, speechless, as he took a glass out of the press and poured himself some tonic. 'I'm not taking away from what happened with Amy,' he said calmly. 'It was dreadful, no one deserves that kind of crap in their lives, but you need to step away from him and let him get his own act together. From the sound of it, he's moving on quite nicely.'

'Can't you see, he's got mixed up with this Jenni girl on the rebound?'

'No, I don't see that at all. I don't even know why we're discussing it.'

'Oh God, you're so—'

'What?'

'Infuriating.'

'Infuriating? Me? Because I'm spelling out a few home truths?' he said evenly. 'If you ask me, Serena, you're the one who's making life difficult for yourself. You're the soft touch where your

275

brother is concerned. Most of the time Jack does what he damn well pleases.'

Serena was indignant. 'Not always. He was rightly led up the garden path by Amy.'

'I thought he went into marriage with his eyes open. It wasn't as if he was a love-struck teenager.'

'He was struck with something all right because Amy was pregnant before they got married, and that was the reason he whisked her up the aisle, or rather, up the beach,' Serena said, the words slipping out heedlessly.

Paul's eyes glinted. 'Oh, I see. I didn't realise she was already pregnant. You kept that close to your chest, didn't you?'

'Amy didn't want any tongues wagging when she married one of Ireland's hottest bachelors. She wanted a perfect wedding day, without rumours or innuendoes. Jack told me, but he asked me to keep it to myself.' Serena saw his face darken from annoyance to resentment and realised too late how Paul would react to this.

'Why couldn't you at least have shared that with me?' he sounded hurt. 'I'm your *husband*. How come I didn't know, along with the rest of the world? Why did you lump me in with the wagging tongues? Oh, sorry, I'm not a Devlin. I'm out of the golden circle.'

'That's not true.'

'Yes it is.'

'Paul, look—'

'Don't patronise me.'

To her horror, all her knife-edge emotions came together; anger at Jack, frustration with herself and helplessness in the face of Paul's resentment, and Serena felt like lashing out. She took a step in his direction and, as though he read her mind, Paul took a step towards her and put a restraining hand on her arm.

'Don't,' he said.

'Don't what?' She jerked her arm to remove it from his grasp but his grip was as tight as steel. Incensed, Serena lifted her other arm but Paul clamped onto that also.

'Let me go,' she said through gritted teeth.

'I will when you apologise.'

'You're the one who should apologise.' She struggled to free herself, flashing him a furious glance.

'Me?' Paul laughed. 'Hey, I'm only pointing out a few home truths. This is good. I like it when you're in a temper. We might get some more things out in the open. Some more family skeletons. Is there anything else you want to tell me? Anything hidden in the Devlin closet?'

Serena tussled with him, trying to disengage herself. She looked down at his arms, strong, masculine, and covered with a pattern of dark hairs. She realised that her silk blouse had freed itself from the waistband of her skirt and that Paul was standing very close; so close that she could inhale his scent and when her eyes flicked over his face she could see the iris of his dark eyes, the curve of his thick eyelashes, his mouth, just inches away. Her skin flashed where he touched it, and something flickered inside her.

The atmosphere was charged.

Paul let go of her arms. She didn't move. She couldn't. A wave of pure lust washed over her as she stared at his eyes, which were now full of naked longing, and he stared back at her, hiding nothing. She couldn't remember the last time she'd felt so dizzy with desire.

'Christ, Serena, I love it when you're all fired up,' he muttered.

They came together, their mouths clashing and grinding against each other. Hungry for each other. After a while, Paul drew back and steadied her head with his hands. 'God, you're incredible.'

He began to kiss her again; slow, deep, unhurried kisses that fired all her nerve endings and sparked into her liquefying core. Any traces of coolness that had lingered between them over the past week melted away. He pulled at her silk blouse, slipping his hands underneath and she felt his warm fingers stroking her bare skin. She shivered. He started to undo the buttons, but Serena forestalled him before he went any further.

'The bedroom . . .' she murmured. Although their rear gardens stretched considerably away from the house, she didn't feel entirely comfortable making love in the kitchen.

'Chicken,' he grinned at her, his eyes heavy with desire.

He picked her up as though she was Harriet,

and half-ran, half-walked her into their bedroom, where evening sunlight flooded through large picture windows. He pressed a switch in the wall that shut down the blinds. Sunlight glowed softly through the closed blinds and painted the room with a warm luminosity.

'Where were we?'

'Here,' Serena said, swiftly unbuttoning her shirt and her trousers and letting them flutter to the floor.

'God, you're beautiful.' His voice made her heart flip, and made her feel wanton and sexy, and she fell into the part, lying back across the wide bed in her diaphanous La Perla lingerie, hungry for this, hungry for him and striking a raunchy pose while he pulled off his clothes. Already fully aroused, he flung himself down on the bed beside her.

'Your skin is like pearl in this light,' he said. He ran his hand up and down the curves of her body. Serena's senses hummed. God how she needed this, needed him, right now. This was the best sex they'd had in a long time. Passionate, impulsive, wild.

'I can't say quite the same of yours,' she teased, her hand enclosing the thick, rigid strength of his erection.

'I'll make you pay for that!' he muttered, sinking his face into her lace-covered breasts, and then using his teeth to pull down the frilly cups. When he began to swirl his tongue around her swollen nipples,

Serena gratefully fell back against the thick cream pillows and lost herself in the splinters of desire shooting through her. Just when she felt she could no longer bear the waiting, Paul slid off her white lace panties and Serena bit down sharp on her bottom lip as he spread her legs.

'Aaah.' She heard herself moan. His fingers were gentle and then firm as they dipped inside her and he circled her sensitive, tingling hotness. She felt the taut heat building up inside her but wanted to share it with him. She wanted to feel the hard length of him buried inside her when she finally came.

'Please,' she gasped, twisting and turning, 'I can't wait . . . much longer . . .' She pushed his hand away and turned towards him, ready to slide on top of him, reaching for his erection and already anticipating the raw pleasure it would bring.

Then from the hallway, there was the unmistakeable sound of her mobile.

Serena automatically tensed. Harriet? Tamarisk?

'Leave it,' Paul muttered hoarsely, throwing his arm across her body.

'I can't,' Serena shifted under his hold.

'I said forget it.'

'It might be important.'

'Stay where you are.'

'It could be Harriet,' Serena said, attempting to sit up.

'I'll go,' he growled, getting off the bed and striding naked towards the door. She watched the play of powerful muscles across the proud set of his shoulders, the long, perfect indentation of his back bone and the pale gleam of his bare buttocks as he left the room.

Afterwards, that was the last imprint she held in her mind of the way their lives had been. Afterwards, she was amazed that her whole existence could alter from the beat of one minute to the next. That one moment, everything could be okay, at least on the surface, the next, that surface torn away and her life in splinters around her.

Her phone stopped ringing, and she heard Paul's voice, but he didn't come back to the bedroom. She listened, trying to gauge if he was still talking to someone. But then there was silence, and it was a long silence that even from the hallway seemed to carry a tense quality. Then she remembered – she'd left her mobile in her bag. Which Paul had obviously had to rummage through.

Her mobile. In her bag. On the table in the hall. *Shit.*

An icy thread of fear propelled her up off the bed. She picked her silk shirt up off the floor and slid her arms into it. It barely covered her hips. She sensed it was important not to delay to pull on her trousers, so she wrapped her shirt around herself, hugging herself for comfort as, heart pounding, she hurried through the bedroom door and out into the hallway.

Too late. Paul was staring into space. He was oblivious to the fact that he was totally naked.

Her phone was clenched in his hands and items from her handbag were scattered across the table. They had obviously spilled out as he delved for her phone. Her car keys. Her lip gloss. Her hotel pass.

Her six-month supply of contraceptive pills.

Serena froze. There was no way to undo that moment. There was a long, painful silence, a moment of disconnection, a rearrangement of everything they'd ever been to each other and Serena's heart plummeted. She noticed, oddly, that flower petals had drifted to the floor, probably dislodged by Paul as he reached for her bag to get to her phone.

Then his broken voice stabbed into her head. 'What the actual fuck . . . do you . . . were you . . . are you telling me that every time we – *oh, God!* I can't believe this!'

'Paul, I can explain—' she couldn't bear to look at his devastated face. Then it changed, as anger exploded across it.

'Who is he? Who are you screwing?'

Serena recoiled. '*No!* There isn't anyone else! Let me explain . . .'

'You must be screwing someone else if you're still on the pill. Is that why you work late so often? And what about Paris? No wonder you were so keen to go? I'm the biggest bloody fool. But fuck you. It's over.' His voice was raw with hurt.

'Over?' her voice quavered. In vain, she tried to pull down the edges of her shirt in order to cover her nakedness.

Paul was far too angry to notice her feeble attempts to cover herself. 'Our joke of a marriage. Don't you know how much you've betrayed me? Never mind Harriet? Jesus! Is that where you were this morning? Some fucking beauty clinic! I've been a stupid fool. How could you have done this to us? How *could* you?'

'I swear to you there isn't anyone else. We can talk . . . I can explain.' Her voice trembled. She was clutching at straws. It was obvious to Paul that she'd deceived him big time and he wasn't in the mood to listen to anything she might say.

'Talk? Go to hell, Serena. And fuck your lover, whoever the bastard is.' He strode past her, grim determination in the hard angle of his jaw. He flung her phone down in the direction of the table. It missed and skittered across the floor.

'Please, listen to me . . .'

'Bollocks. We're over.'

She hurried after him into the bedroom. The duvet was crumpled and she saw an image of them writhing on it, moments earlier. Damn Jack. If it hadn't been for him, she'd have come home as normal, put her mobile on the table and put her bag safely in her dressing room. But she couldn't blame Jack for this. She'd caused it herself. She watched in frozen horror as Paul flung on his clothes.

'I didn't mean to deceive you . . . but you have it all wrong—'

'Go screw yourself.' His voice was hoarse with anger and it sliced into her chest. She was in the grip of a nightmare as she watched her husband shove his feet into his shoes and stride out into the hall.

'Please,' she cried out through thick sobs. 'Let me explain . . .' she ran after him as he marched to the door. He ignored her outstretched hands. He strode out the door and slammed it behind him. She heard the screech of tyres as her husband accelerated out onto the laneway.

Then, silence.

CHAPTER 26

Kim lined up a row of scented candles and put the finishing touches to her dining table, giving it a rueful smile. She'd phoned Serena at the beginning of the week, inviting her and Paul for dinner, along with Jack. But now the table was set for two instead of four. The cosy night she'd fondly anticipated, with Jack sitting across the table, and Paul and Serena joining in the laughter, wasn't happening after all. Serena had texted her earlier that day to say she was coming alone. Despite her disappointment, she had a succulent beef and Guinness pie simmering in the oven, a light pavlova for dessert and a choice of wine ready.

Maybe it was time to admit her feelings to Serena. Up to now, she'd been too nervous, but telling Serena made perfect sense after all. Serena had said many times that she thought they'd make a great couple. Kim felt suddenly energised as she went upstairs to shower and change, as though everything was clearer and lighter in her mind. She put on a soft lilac dress and silvery sandals. She was just spraying her perfume when the phone rang. It was her mother, phoning from Spain.

'Hi, Kim, glad I caught you at home on a Saturday night.'

'I'm having a night in with Serena.'

'Great,' her mother sounded upbeat. 'Tell Serena I was asking for her. And darling Harriet. They should come out to visit. I know we usually talk on Sundays but your father and I won't be around tomorrow as we're off to a fair in Seville . . .'

'Sounds good.' Kim chatted away, filling her mother in on her week's work, and listening to what her parents had been up to. She still felt touched after the warm and welcoming birthday celebration they'd arranged for her. Given the way she'd sometimes dismissed them growing up, she felt she didn't deserve such unconditional love.

Soon afterwards, Serena arrived with a bottle of Moët and a black leather Mulberry overnighter, her Gucci sunglasses pushed up on her head. She was casually dressed in denim jeans and a pink chiffon top. Her hair was tied back in a ponytail and she was wearing very little makeup. She looked vulnerable and almost ethereal in the delicate air of fragility that surrounded her. She was working far too hard, Kim decided, as she hugged her and kissed her on the cheek.

Serena walked down to the kitchen and dropped her bag on the floor, putting the Moët on the counter. She went over to the French doors and stared out at the bright evening.

'Would you like to sit outside for a while?' Kim suggested, opening the door. 'Food will be ready in thirty minutes or so.'

'I said no trouble.' Serena frowned. 'I'm not all that hungry.'

'It was no trouble, and of course you'll eat, even if it's just to soak up the drink,' Kim insisted. She fetched stripy cushions for the garden chairs and led Serena outside, returning to her kitchen to open the champagne. She filled two flutes, realising that it would be easier to talk outside and unburden herself in the peacefulness of the evening. She'd feel a bit calmer out in the fresh air. But Serena wasn't in a hurry to sit down. She fidgeted around, champagne in her hand, admiring her garden again.

'How's the family?' Kim eventually got Serena's attention.

'Fine, fine,' Serena said with a brittle air. 'Charlotte was asking for you, and said to say she enjoyed her evening here.'

'And Jack?'

Kim had wondered as to how she might best put it to Serena. *You'd never guess, but I really, really, love your brother. It means so much to me that I was afraid to tell you before now.* Or maybe something a little lighter, less emotionally charged: *That brother of yours has a lot to answer for. I haven't been able to even look at another man because I'm thinking about him so much.* Now she hesitated and took a gulp of champagne. She'd decided to just speak simply and from the heart when Serena spoke first.

'Don't mention Jack.' Serena sounded scathing.

'Why not?' Kim was bemused. Now that she'd decided to open her heart it was all she wanted to do, but Serena's next words shattered it into tiny pieces.

'Jack thinks he's in love again, already!' Serena said dismissively. 'I know he's my brother, but he's crazy.'

Kim laughed. She could feel a big grin stuck to her face, but it was a nervous reaction. 'You're joking.'

'I wish I was.' Serena gave a heavy sigh and finally sat down under the striped umbrella with a sombre look on her face. 'He's met someone,' she said flatly.

'Met someone? What does that mean?' Kim's voice sounded high and tinny.

'The usual. Boy meets girl,' Serena laughed hollowly. 'That's how he was delayed coming home from Nice. He stayed there for another week, just to be with her.'

Kim was terribly still. It didn't make sense to her. They were just words that Serena was saying and she heard them bouncing around some space inside her head, without forming any connection with her brain or her feelings. The catch in her chest was paining her but she tried to breathe through it, taking little breaths, in and out, telling herself there was no real need to feel like this.

There was some kind of mistake. Serena was talking a load of rubbish. Jack had come to her garden party as soon as he'd got home. He'd flirted with Lucy and even gone out with her afterwards. He'd been playing the field for the past couple of weeks and, funnily enough, Kim hadn't minded any of this, for she'd felt it was part of Jack's return to normality and she knew his casual dating didn't mean anything.

Then he'd come to the fashion event with her and even said he wanted to talk to her. What kind of personal stuff had he meant?

'I feel furious with him,' Serena went on in a dull voice. 'I don't know if he's just bringing more trouble down on his head. And I don't know anything about this Jenni person—'

'Who?'

'Jenni.'

So she had a name. It wasn't just a figment of Serena's imagination. Someone called Jenni had kept Jack in France. And not just for one or two nights, but for a whole *week*. It must have been a hell of a week. The words jabbed painfully through Kim's head. Anything that she had prepared to say about her love for Jack, any confidences she'd imagined exchanging with Serena, all the unburdening she'd fondly pictured dissolved into the void, and she felt incredibly sad.

Jenni. Kim hated the sound of the name. Somehow, though, she roused herself from shocked immobility to put a whole sentence together, the words comforting her as she said them aloud and heard them being uttered, as though that somehow gave them credence. 'It can't mean anything. He's been dating a long list of women since he came home. He even came out with me last week.'

Serena slowly shook her head. 'He's been doing that on purpose. Under Jenni's orders.'

'What?'

'He'd wanted to bring her home before. After just a week. She told him to go out and date other women, just to make sure he knew his own mind. Now, she's landed over to visit him. But from what I've seen of her, it can only be a fling and it won't last. I saw how cut up he was after Amy. No one could have taken her place so soon. I think he's crazy not to give himself more space, but that's Jack for you, heedless as ever. Only I didn't come here to talk about him, although you might as well know what he's been up to. You're good friends, after all . . .'

Good friends! Kim's heart bled. She closed her mind to the fact that Jack's new girlfriend was here in Ireland and that she'd told Jack to see other women as a kind of test. Was that why Jack had gone out with her? No. It couldn't be. After all, he'd said he wanted to talk to her about personal stuff. The most important thing to remember was Serena's conviction that it was a ridiculous fling that wouldn't last. And if anyone knew Jack, Serena did.

'I have . . . I have something else to tell you, and that's why I wanted to see you.' Serena was still talking, as though she hadn't carved up Kim's heart into tiny pieces.

Once again, Kim noted how delicate Serena seemed. Could she be pregnant? Was that why she'd called? To share her good news, little realising that she'd just dealt Kim a hammer blow? She couldn't take this. Serena might be her best friend, but she couldn't bear to listen to her good fortune while her own life was suspended in misery. A wave of frustration washed over Kim. Then she realised that Serena had dropped her head into her hands and was crying like a baby.

'Oh God, Kim . . . Paul and I . . . we've split,' she babbled. 'That's why I'm on my own tonight. I think our marriage is over.'

The rest of the evening, the evening she'd fondly anticipated opening her heart to her friend and unburdening herself, turned out to be a nightmare for Kim. She found herself putting her own heartache to one side as she tried to console Serena. She wasn't sure what had happened, or what exactly had gone wrong. Serena just sniffed and cried, going through a box of tissues that Kim had hastily grabbed out of a press when she'd run inside to lower down the thermostat on the oven. She said she'd behaved very badly and couldn't forgive herself, let alone expect Paul to forgive her. He'd walked out of the house and she didn't think they'd ever get back together again.

'He didn't come back until this afternoon, to take Harriet out for a couple of hours,' Serena said raggedly. 'He was wearing different clothes, so he must have gone shopping. He wouldn't talk to me. He just looked right through me. Harriet thinks her dad is working on some kind of secret experiment. That's he's staying very late in work and leaving really early in the mornings. And it's all my fault. Oh, God, I've been a terrible fool . . .'

'It's okay, Serena,' Kim soothed, inwardly mocking herself as she poured more champagne and watched it fizz in her crystal flutes. You'd think they were celebrating something instead of drowning their sorrows. At least it was mind-numbing alcohol. 'Does Paul know you're here tonight?'

'Yes, I had to tell him that Charlotte was minding Harriet. I thought he might have said he'd babysit, but I think he's staying in a hotel. I pretended to Mum that Paul and I were coming here together rather than face any questions. Now I've just real-ised that Harriet might let something out of the bag. It's all such a mess . . .'

Serena wept afresh and talked through her tears. What would happen to Harriet? To her? Why had she wrecked her marriage? Kim had never seen her confident, successful friend in such a state. Serena's face, blotchy with tears, was unrecognis-able. In spite of her own dejection, she felt a rush of sympathy for her friend. She bet that Paul wasn't crying into his beer somewhere and just managed to stop herself from saying this out loud.

They ended up finishing the champagne and drinking a bottle of wine. By now it was dark and Kim had to persuade Serena to come in to the kitchen and have something to eat.

'I've hardly eaten since Tuesday night,' she said as she shook her head.

'Is that when—'

'Yes, that's when Paul walked.' Serena plucked another tissue and pressed it to her tear-ravaged eyes.

'Not eating won't do you any good. You must keep your strength up,' Kim urged, taking her by the hand into the kitchen. Serena obediently allowed herself to be led to the table, as though all the fight had gone out of her. She picked at some food and they went through another bottle of wine. Afterwards, Kim had to help Serena up the stairs to bed. She came back down and tidied up before taking out the carefully prepared Pavlova from the fridge. She opened the bin, angled the serving dish, gave the meringue base a nudge with her finger, and watched as the entire confection slowly slid down and crumpled into the bin.

She'd knocked back far too much booze, so she was surprised that she felt totally sober. Or maybe she just couldn't feel anything at all. Maybe she was still in frozen shock at the thoughts of someone called Jenni butting in on her dream in a matter of days. As she got ready for bed, she kept reminding herself of Serena's words, repeating them in her mind over and over like a comforting mantra: 'it was only a fling and it wouldn't last'.

CHAPTER 27

Charlotte felt shocked and dismayed when Serena called to collect Harriet on Sunday and blurted out that there were problems between her and Paul.

'What do you mean, problems?' Charlotte asked, her hand shaking as she pushed away the Busy Lizzie plant she'd been repotting. Her daughter's anguished face said it all. She ran her peat-dusted hands under the tap, automatically checked for Harriet but she was safely in the living room, watching the end of a cartoon show.

'Problems, as in he's temporarily walked out.'

'Oh, Serena, so it's more than just a row,' Charlotte said, the depth of her sadness taking her by surprise. 'Is it serious? Although that's a stupid question. It must be if he's walked out.'

'He says he'll never trust me again.'

'Trust?' Charlotte recoiled. Surely that didn't mean what she thought it did?

Serena shook her head. 'There isn't anybody else, but I can't . . . talk about it . . .'

'Oh, love, I wouldn't expect you to,' Charlotte hugged her. 'That's your private business. I'm shocked and upset, for both of you, and Harriet. If there's anything I can do . . .'

'We're trying to keep it from Harriet,' Serena said in a hopeless kind of voice that tore at Charlotte's heart. 'She thinks her daddy is working on a special experiment. She's bound to sense that something is wrong soon.'

'I'll help with Harriet in any way I can.'

'Thank you. I don't know how I'll explain when . . . if . . . it's over for good.'

'Darling! Don't even go there! Every good marriage hits a few bumps along the way. You have to work through them. Do you think your father and I sailed through our marriage without a few ups and downs?' Charlotte made a face. 'Although forget that! We had more than our fair share, and I'd never dream of comparing Paul with your father.'

'No,' Serena smiled sadly.

'But you're not unlike me, and that's what worries me,' Charlotte went on. Before Serena could protest, she went on. 'You spend too many hours in the hotel when you should be delegating to your staff. Late nights, and weekends, family time. In other words, all the mistakes I made.'

'Mum, what happened between me and Paul has absolutely nothing to do with Tamarisk,' Serena said, her face white. 'And you can't talk like that. If it had been left to Dad, the hotel would have run downhill years ago. You did a fantastic job.'

'Yes, but at what expense?' Charlotte gave her a half-smile. 'Darling, I just hope you can sort things out with Paul. Talk to him. Make him listen. Do whatever you have to do. He and Harriet are precious to you and I don't want you to have any regrets . . .'

Regrets. Charlotte tried to clear her head and was silent for a long moment. She laid a hand on Serena's arm and was tempted to unburden herself, and then Harriet came flying into the room in her roller boots and a Batman cape and the moment passed. Charlotte later realised this was a relief. Serena was in no fit state to hear her mother's confession. What had she been thinking of?

After they left, she found it impossible to settle to anything. She watered her plants half-heartedly. She picked up her book and put it down. She grimaced to herself at the way Serena thought she had done a great job of running Tamarisk. Little did her daughter know that in those early years, it had been a matter of survival in more ways than one.

Tamarisk weathered the downturn of the eighties, thanks to Charlotte never taking her diligent eye off the finances and being innovative with her marketing strategies. Jamie's common touch and indulgent personality were an advantage when it came to guest relations, particularly the female visitors. Although her marriage was a far cry from the devotion her parents had to each other, down through the years she and Jamie had adopted a compromise. She tolerated his drinking so long as he didn't go overboard and he never questioned the business decisions she made, giving her free rein to run the hotel.

Then the nineties brought a new era of prosperity and Charlotte began to realise her vision for Tamarisk. The ground-floor wing that the family lived in before moving to the renovated coach house was demolished to make way for a leisure complex. They became twinned with La Mimosa when Charlotte and Jamie went over to see the improvements Conor had introduced. In the mid-nineties, Jack and Serena finished college and, between slotting into roles in Tamarisk, they travelled to get experience in other world-class hotels. But nobody could have predicted the way the publicity of Serena's marriage to Paul would bring the fortunes of Tamarisk to a new and more exciting level, just as celebrity culture became a national past-time and the Celtic Tiger reached its peak years, transforming Ireland into one of Europe's wealthiest countries.

Charlotte occasionally wondered what her parents would have made of her affluent lifestyle. Other times the whole celebrity fad seemed empty and meaningless to her. Then on the morning of her fifty-sixth birthday, which would also have been her thirty-fifth wedding anniversary, she found herself in floods of tears and full of unresolved grief when she thought of Jamie. It was more than time, she'd decided, to hand over the reins, take a much-needed break and get on with the rest of her life.

But her timing couldn't have been worse, she now thought ruefully. For, shortly afterwards, a global recession had taken Ireland and the world by surprise. Jack became embroiled with Amy and additional responsibility fell on Serena.

And now Serena's marriage to Paul was in trouble. Charlotte sighed unhappily. She wondered what could have gone wrong and fervently hoped that history wasn't repeating itself.

But it couldn't be. For her daughter had assured her there was no one else.

Something different about her house rang a warning bell the minute Serena stepped through the door on Sunday afternoon.

'Where's Daddy?' Harriet demanded. She was still wearing the roller boots and the Batman cape she'd had on when Serena collected her and now she whizzed down the hall and into the kitchen, obviously sensing the same emptiness as Serena. She knew the ground rules about no skating in the house, but she was taking full advantage of Serena's low mood.

Another reminder that she was a hopeless mother. As if she needed any.

'I told you, darling, he's busy at work.'

'I'm sick of him at work and doing spearmints,' Harriet pouted. She clanked out of the kitchen and into the playroom, stomping her boots on the floor.

Serena wanted to scream across her empty kitchen. I want him home. Here. Now. She couldn't believe how much she missed him. Another thing she hadn't realised until he'd walked out was the amount of time he'd actually spent looking after Harriet on account of the long hours she worked. He wouldn't talk to her or take her calls. Even when he'd called to take Harriet to her karate class, and out on Saturday afternoon, he'd refused point blank to talk to Serena other than exchange polite greetings in front of Harriet.

She had to summon every last trace of patience until Harriet was settled in front of a DVD. Then she checked around the house and already knew by the feel of everything that Paul had taken a lot of his clothes. She stepped into his dressing room and felt nauseous when she saw the empty spaces where his suits, shirts and shoes had been. Two pieces of luggage were missing from the storage area under the shelves. By the time she looked into the en suite and saw almost all of his toiletries gone, the physical pain was so bad that she doubled over with it and collapsed, dry retching, on the bed.

He'd come home when she was getting sloshed in Kim's, knowing the house would be empty and Harriet safely out of the way. He'd packed enough clothes to keep him going for weeks. It was too late for her mother's advice. She'd already stamped all over Paul's hopes and dreams, pounding them into dust. She closed her eyes and tried to block out the pain but it came at her in relentless waves.

CHAPTER 28

On Wednesday morning, Charlotte accompanied Millie to the city centre to check out emerging fashion designers who were showcasing in the Powerscourt Design Centre. They spent a fruitful couple of hours admiring some fabulous creations and Millie placed quite a number of orders. Now they were sitting in a booth in the wood-panelled Saddle Room of the Shelbourne Hotel, having just enjoyed lunch.

'That was a good morning's work,' Millie sighed with satisfaction after their coffees arrived. 'I was impressed with some of those young designers and they're very competitively priced.'

'These days it's more important than ever to support home-grown talent,' Charlotte said.

'Definitely. It was good to have you with me, and I trust,' Millie had a wicked gleam in her eyes, 'that it stopped you from stagnating at home.'

'You haven't heard anything from Hilary since our lunch?' Charlotte asked.

'No. Not a word,' Millie's face broke into a broad grin. 'I thought you would have lost about a week's sleep after that incident.'

There was a silence, then Charlotte said quietly, 'I've other things to keep me awake at night besides Hilary.' She stirred her cappuccino and absently put a spoonful of froth into her mouth, grateful that Millie remained silent. 'Serena and Paul have had some kind of serious bust-up.'

'Oh, Charlotte.' Millie's face was full of empathy. She reached across the table and patted Charlotte's arm.

'I feel so totally helpless,' Charlotte went on, voicing thoughts that had plagued her during the last couple of nights. 'I don't know what's happened. Serena hasn't confided in me, and I wouldn't expect her to, but I can't help wondering if there was anything in her upbringing, or anything lacking on my part that could have contributed to whatever bad patch she's in right now.'

'Charlotte, stop right now. You're torturing yourself with the question that parents the world over ask when something goes wrong in their child's life and the answer is a resounding "no, of course not". I won't sit here and let you wallow in some kind of misplaced guilt. Serena and Paul's marriage is their business. More than anyone else, with the exception of Jamie, possibly, I know how much you were both mother and father to those children and worked so hard for them.'

'That's it, you see,' Charlotte said slowly. 'I wasn't always there. A lot of the time I was busy running a business. Sometimes I wonder how much of that Serena absorbed, and helped to turn her into the focused, hard-working, career person she is today.'

'And what has that got to do with her marriage?'

'A lot. For all this equality stuff, which is something I heartily agree with, the reality is that it's bloody hard for women to have everything once they have a family. Serena is missing out on so much with Harriet, like the way I missed out on stuff with the twins when they were growing up, and I suspect, although I could be wrong, I'd say that her long working hours and her drive and determination for her career are finally coming home to roost.'

'You don't know that for sure. And you're forgetting something else . . .'

'What's that?'

'Your family have been through a very rough year after Amy. That's bound to have had an effect.'

'Yes, if anything, Serena's had to work even harder to compensate for Jack. Something like the way I had to compensate for Jamie.'

'Oh, Charlotte, you mustn't think like that.'

Jamie's drinking had never been a secret between the friends. The only thing that remained a secret from everyone was exactly why her husband had turned into an alcoholic.

Charlotte said, 'When Jack was away, Serena wouldn't accept help from me. You know how stubborn she can be. And I didn't want to interfere in what was now her and Jack's business. Maybe I should have insisted though.'

'Charlotte, shut up,' Millie said good-naturedly. 'Stop making a stick to beat yourself with. I'm glad we've had this chat because I'm going to keep a closer eye on you to make sure you don't wallow in a load of crapology. Relationships are complex. None of us know what really goes on behind closed doors, so until Serena actually tells you, you have no idea as to what's gone wrong in her marriage. All you can do is be there for her. Tell me about Jack,' Millie went on. 'I see from the newspapers that he's back from France and out gadding about, no doubt breaking hearts all over again.'

'That's yesterday's news,' Charlotte said. 'His new girlfriend has followed him over from France and is now living with him.'

'No!'

'Yes. Her name is Jenni and she's from London,' Charlotte said. 'I met her last week. She's just twenty-four, young and cute, and I've no idea what he's thinking . . .'

Charlotte fell silent. Serena told her about Jenni the previous week, sounding very scathing on the phone. According to Serena, he made a right fool out of her and missed an important meeting in Tamarisk.

Then, Jack brought Jenni to meet her. She didn't know what she expected – some blonde, Amy lookalike, much like one of the many legions of girls that Jack had befriended over the years – but she didn't expect someone so young and yet possessed with so much calm assurance. Jenni

305

wasn't wearing any makeup. She didn't need to, not with that dewy, translucent skin and huge brown eyes, fringed with enviously thick dark lashes.

'Isn't she fantastic?' Jack said, following her out to her kitchen when she went to make tea. 'God, Mum, I feel she's given me my life back again . . .'

'Jack! Really?' she said, nonplussed, her hands painfully gripping the kettle. Jack seemed full of a barely suppressed excitement that set her on edge. She couldn't believe he'd be so impulsive as to invite a girl he barely knew into his home. Jack's heart had taken a big hammering over the past year. She found herself agreeing with Serena that his relationship with Jenni, if you could call it that, seemed to be on the rebound. Then there was Kim, whose love for Jack had been obvious to Charlotte. This would surely break her heart. Why was love so complicated? So painful?

'According to Jack, Jenni has turned his life around,' Charlotte confided in her friend, knowing it wouldn't go any further.

'Sounds like he's having all the fun.'

'Yes, Millie, he certainly is, and he's quite oblivious to me watching with bated breath. I don't want Jack's heart mangled all over again.'

'Maybe Jenni will be good for him. Families, though . . .' Millie shook her head. 'They'd drive you crackers if you let them.'

Millie was right. And she'd taken up enough of

her time with her family problems. 'Let's talk about something more cheerful,' Charlotte suggested. 'The wedding. Is everything falling into place for you?' Millie's daughter Lorna was getting married the following week. The ceremony in the local church would be followed by a lavish reception in a marquee in the grounds of Millie's spacious country home.

Millie grimaced. 'Did you say cheerful? Anything but. I'm at the tearing-my-hair-out stage with guest lists and seating plans. The wedding planner has gone on holiday and Lorna is having a nervous breakdown. And Patrick is driving me mad practising his father-of-the-bride speech.'

'It'll all come together on the day, you'll see.'

'I won't have the energy left to enjoy it.'

Charlotte didn't respond at first because her attention was caught by a couple who passed their table and were shown to a booth further up the restaurant. He was tall and craggy faced, and casually dressed, and his arm was slung around his companion who was equally tall and blonde, but half his age, and looked as though she had just stepped off a glamorous Dolce & Gabbana photo shoot. They settled into their booth and, as if sensing her interest, his eyes slowly travelled the distance between them. She held her breath as they fastened on hers. Deep-blue, Paul Newman eyes. Charlotte flinched but met his gaze steadily. He waved at her and his companion looked curiously at her before turning her attention to the menu.

Charlotte felt a flash of disappointment. Somehow she hadn't expected the Bodyguard to be involved with someone much younger. It was obvious from their relaxed body language and the way they talked about the menu that they were very comfortable with each other.

'Hello, Charlotte? Are you with me?' Millie asked.

'Sorry, just distracted by one of our customers who's come in with his girlfriend,' Charlotte said, secretly appalled at how deflated she felt.

The waiter interrupted them by saying that the gentleman at table ten would like to buy them a cocktail. Charlotte forced herself not to make eye contact with the Bodyguard. She smiled fixedly at the waiter. 'That won't be necessary,' she said. 'We'd like the bill as we're leaving.'

'He mustn't be one of your favourite customers, if you're doing me out of a free cocktail,' Millie drily observed. She turned around and gave the Bodyguard an interested stare. 'Not bad. Quite sexy, actually. Charlotte, are you sure—'

'Millie! I hardly know him,' Charlotte said. 'If you'd like a drink, I'll get you one.'

'Not at all, I've to get back to the boutique. But, seriously, it's quite a while since Jamie. You're more than entitled to have some fun.'

'Fun? Yeah.'

She hardly knew him at all, Charlotte reminded herself crossly as they left the hotel and turned down towards the car park. Why did she feel like a spurned sixteen year old? She should be far more concerned about her family instead of indulging herself with silly notions. And how could she think of having fun with another man when Jamie was dead? It didn't matter how many years he was gone, sometimes it still felt like yesterday.

Afterwards, at home, her mind flew back to that bright September evening, when like most of the world, Charlotte was glued to the television, tears streaming down her face as the full extent of the horrific fate of the Twin Towers in the New York she knew and loved unfolded and struck terror and sadness in her heart. Life would never be the same. New York would carry the scars for ever. A shocked Serena had already phoned from the Canaries, where she was on holiday with Kim. Jamie was in Dublin that afternoon visiting his tailor, but he phoned from Glendoran to see how she was coping with the dreadful news.

'I've just stopped for a quick pint,' he said, 'but I know you must be feeling sad, so I'll be home soon.'

That was Jamie all over. He had the best of intentions, but didn't always follow them through. When her phone rang again, Charlotte assumed it was Jack, calling to commiserate from Rome where he was working.

But it was Patrick, Millie's husband, phoning from the village. He was having a pint in the pub with Jamie, also watching the terrible events on the television, when Jamie had collapsed. He was being rushed to hospital.

'We're not sure what's wrong. Millie and I are calling to bring you to the hospital, Charlotte. Stay put until we get to you.'

Stay put? Funny, she, who usually had boundless energy, found herself frozen, immobile, incapable of even picking up the remote control to switch off the television, while something icy cold ran through her veins. She knew instinctively that Jamie wouldn't survive.

And now, even though it was years later, there were times when she was still there in that frozen spot, gripped with remorse.

CHAPTER 29

'Serena, you're not going to like this, but . . .' Andrew's voice on the phone sounded apologetic.

Serena was on the alert immediately. 'But what?'

Andrew continued hurriedly, as if by speaking fast he'd reduce the impact of the bad news. 'I'm afraid there's been a double booking for next weekend—'

'A *what*?'

'Somehow or other our Presidential Suite has been reserved for two parties this weekend.'

'Somehow?' Serena snapped. 'You mean one of the reservation staff was careless. Whoever it was, they're fired. Right now.'

'It was Amanda. She's been having some personal problems,' Andrew said, his voice sober.

'Now she has an even bigger problem, hasn't she?' Serena said curtly. 'Send me through the booking details immediately and I'll see what I can do. In the meantime, you'd better talk to your incompetent staff.'

She slammed down the phone and felt ashamed of herself. She'd never lost her temper like that with her trusted staff. Typically, Jack wasn't around. Although this time he'd flagged his absence in advance, explaining to Serena that he had an appointment that afternoon with a Dublin solicitor to go through Amy's affairs and was going to bring Jenni with him to show her some of the sights. But today of all days, Serena did not want a problem. She'd already told Andrew she was busy and didn't want to be disturbed unless it was an emergency. She'd been sitting at her desk when his call came through, staring vacantly at a document outlining the requirements for the coveted five-star classification.

She needed a stress-free day because Paul was calling for Harriet that evening, to bring her to her karate class. He'd sent her a bland text to remind her. But without telling Paul, she'd arranged for Charlotte to bring Harriet to her class. It meant she would have some time alone with him. Time to talk. Time to argue, but hopefully time to explain her behaviour and tell him how sorry she was. He'd probably be furious with the way she'd engineered it, but by now she was desperate to try and get through to him. Glancing at the clock, she saw that she'd just a couple of hours left to try and work out what she might say to her husband and her stomach churned. She had to take several calming breaths before she steadied herself enough to check out the booking details that Andrew had mailed through.

David Clarke had booked the Presidential Suite

two months earlier for himself and his wife Ali. David was an up-and-coming television presenter and, possessing a winning combination of charisma and decisiveness, he was hotly tipped to have a dazzling career ahead of him. His special requests had included three dozen red roses, a magnum of chilled Bollinger and private spa treatments. It was their fifth wedding anniversary and in his email he'd admitted that he wanted to spend some mega quality time with his wife to make up for his long working hours.

Unfortunately, his details had not been entered correctly on the system.

Then, a couple of weeks earlier, the Presidential Suite had also been booked for Jessica Stevens, the Oscar-winning Hollywood actress. Her PA, in a personal call to Serena, had emphasised that she needed peace and quiet in luxury surroundings. Serena had read that Jessica was recovering after cancer surgery, so she'd been proud of the fact that Tamarisk had been chosen as a suitable bolt-hole for her.

It wasn't just Amanda's fault, Serena realised. It was also her failure, as she usually double-checked bookings for the important suites at the start of each week. Only this week her head had been elsewhere. Both parties were equally deserving of their ultra-luxury weekend. This was a part of the job she hated – someone was going to be disappointed and would remember for ever the incompetent reservation staff at Tamarisk and it would be the subject of damning dinner party gossip. She felt like getting back to Andrew and telling him to sort it out, but the habits of a lifetime kicked in and she stared outside at the bright July afternoon, trying to gauge how they could get out of this mess with the least amount of damage to their reputation and the minimum amount of stress to herself. She'd no time or energy to spend on this. The idea came to her and it was a long shot, but it was the only solution. Serena swivelled around on her chair, and then she picked up the phone.

When she'd finished the call, she sat and tried to work out how she might best get through to Paul.

Paul changed gears as he drove up the incline outside Glendoran and towards Maple Hill. He wondered, and not for the first time, if he had been a little hasty in walking out of the house when he'd discovered Serena's betrayal. Looking back, it had seemed so childish and immature, the behaviour of someone who simply gave in to their most basic urges rather than behaving as an adult. But he'd been terribly hurt and beside himself with anger, and he'd felt he couldn't bear to be near Serena for a minute longer. Besides, he had been so consumed with fury that he knew he needed to distance himself from Harriet until he calmed a little. The last thing he wanted was to frighten his daughter with his incandescent rage when she came home from her party.

It had all seemed so demoralising when he'd checked into a south Dublin hotel. After a couple of days, he'd called back to the house to see Harriet, his heart hammering as he rang the doorbell. The sight of Serena at the door had inflamed him again, and fear of what he might blurt in anger in front of Harriet had stunned him into a bitter silence.

Then on Saturday evening, when he knew Serena and Harriet were safely away from Maple Hill, and the adrenaline of his heightened emotions had subsided a little, he'd called in to the empty house. It was the worst thing he could have done, for the house rang with memories. He'd picked up Harriet's pillow and breathed in his daughter's scent. He'd stood in her playroom, remembering the evening she'd shown off her karate and his heart had squeezed. But worst of all, of course, was standing in the bedroom he'd shared with Serena.

She must never have stopped taking the pill, he'd realised. Right from the time, over a year ago, when he'd thought they were . . . God. He turned away and closed his eyes, but this was worse for his thoughts ran around and around in a painful circle as images of them making love rose up to taunt him, and the sound of Serena's cries of pleasure echoed tortuously in his ears. How much of it had been fake? Why had she spoiled it all? There had to be someone else. He couldn't think of any other reason for her to need contraception.

Then, all those times she was late home from work, the times she went away to trade fairs and publicity events . . . her planned trip to Paris without a second thought for Harriet . . . It was easy enough for Serena to have an affair. One of his deepest fears, even after they were married, had been that she'd start to find him dull and boring, compared with the glamour and excitement of her busy career and the lifestyle it gave her. Now it seemed the worst had happened.

Enough. Overcome with loss, he'd sat down on the side of the bed and sobbed.

After a while he'd pulled himself together and before he realised the implications of what he was doing, he'd gone into his dressing room and pulled a case from under the shelf, filling it haphazardly.

Now, of course, as he turned in at the gate of Maple Hill to collect Harriet for her karate, it felt as though the breach between them was irreparable. He rang the doorbell, unwilling to walk in unannounced.

'Hello, Paul.'

She still looked beautiful to him, classy and elegant, even though her face was pale and her eyes were shadowed. And why was he thinking like this? He was the biggest fool in the world. 'Where's Harriet?'

'She had to leave early for her karate,' Serena told him. 'Mum brought her and she's expecting you to follow her on down. I thought it might give us a few minutes to talk.' She stood aside, obviously hoping he'd come in. He sensed something desperate about her, but, bloody hell, he wasn't about to make anything easy for her.

'No thanks.'

'When are we going to work this out between us?' she blurted.

'There's nothing to work out. I told you, it's over, we're over. Finished, done and dusted.'

'But we can't go on like this . . .' she said.

We can't go on? He felt his anger bubbling. She was the one who had caused it. He thought of her sleeping with someone else and his stomach turned. He thought of the way she'd pretended to try for a baby, all those time they'd made love and, deep inside, he wept. Did she seriously think they could sort out their problems that easily?

'I don't see why we can't go on exactly as we are? I've moved into an apartment near the job.' He had just decided it on the spur of the moment and the look of fear on her face gave him a sour sense of revenge. For an apartment was scarcely an arrangement you made for just a couple of weeks.

'I'll have to talk to my lawyer and formalise certain arrangements for Harriet and our finances,' he went on, scarcely knowing where the words were coming from, 'but I doubt if your life has changed one iota.'

'I'm going into work, if that's what you mean. What else can I do? Sitting moping at home isn't going to bring you back, is it? Or change anything that's already happened. So although it might look like I'm doing okay, that's only on the surface. Underneath – God, Paul . . . please . . . you've no idea how much I regret what has happened.'

'It's a bit late in the day for that,' he said. 'I don't know why you married me in the first place. My head is wrecked trying to figure it out. Who else are you screwing? How long has it been going on? You must have been still on the pill to make sure you wouldn't become pregnant by the bastard, whoever he is.'

He saw the blood draining from her face.

'Jesus, Paul, no way. I swear to you, there's no one else.'

For a moment he almost believed her. She looked like she was speaking the truth but then self-doubt kicked in. How could he be sure? Could he ever trust her again? 'How can I believe anything you say when you've been lying to me for the guts of a year?' he hissed. 'I was beginning to think there was something wrong with my sperm count.'

She hung her head and shook it silently.

'I think you would have let me go to a fertility clinic rather than tell me the truth,' he went on harshly. 'You didn't want another child, yet you pretended we were trying hard to make a brother or sister for Harriet. *Why* Serena? It has to be someone else.'

'There isn't anyone else. You must believe me. Yes, I made sure I didn't get pregnant. Yes, I went along with pretending we were trying for a baby. It was terribly wrong of me, and it made me feel bad about myself, but it had nothing to do with another man. It had everything to do with being afraid.' She lifted her head and caught his eye. There was something very forlorn about her that hit him in the chest, but he ignored it.

'Being afraid? You? What shite are you coming out with now?'

'I was afraid. Of the whole baby thing. From the time Harriet was born. I couldn't handle the thought of another baby. It could even have been twins – they run in the family. I'm a coward and a failure. But how could I admit that? Mothers all over the world have three, four and more children. Look at your sisters, with their families, how capable they are. How could I tell anyone that I didn't feel I could cope with a small baby?'

'Christ, Serena, you've got to be kidding. You're one of the most successful people I know. I can't accept that.'

'It's true. You loved Harriet to bits. You were mad about her and were delighted to think we were one big happy family. How could I spoil all that on you by admitting I didn't feel the same? I hated the feeling that I was falling short and unable to cope. It made me feel ill. Then when I went back to work and Harriet went into the crèche, I was so relieved. I figured Harriet would be looked after properly and that the trained nannies in the crèche would do a better job than me. For the first time since she was born, I felt more like myself, back in control of my life again.'

Paul's heart sank. He might have known it all came back to Tamarisk. He still couldn't make sense of most of Serena's words, they didn't add up. She was Harriet's mother, she'd given birth to her, so what the hell was she on about? He still didn't know for sure if there was another man involved.

The one thing he did know, and it hit him right between the eyes, was that even if she had half a dozen lovers on the side, his biggest rival was always going to be Serena's career. 'I should have realised that your soul is welded to Tamarisk even to the exclusion of Harriet, never mind me,' he said. 'For that's what this is really about. Another pregnancy would have meant time off work, visits to clinics, hospitals, maybe not feeling up to full par for a while. Then when the baby arrived, more demands, less time for your precious hotel, perhaps less energy. Your only purpose and satisfaction in life comes from that hotel. Not me, nor Harriet. Did you ever love me? Don't bother to answer that when it's quite obvious you only used me. I was nothing better than a convenient fuck twice or three times a week.'

He threw her a furious glance before turning on his heel and heading back to his car.

Serena watched in dismay as Paul's car skidded down the gravel driveway and tore out onto the lane. She'd no one to blame but herself, for no one knew about the dark days after Harriet had been born, the days she'd never spoken about, the time in her life that was sealed tight and well and truly concealed from everyone, even Paul.

It should have been so different, she thought.

CHAPTER 30

As soon as she reached the motorway, Kim pressed her foot to the floor and her SUV shot forward. She increased the volume of the music and let the sound of Lily Allen flood the interior of her car, feeling an unexpected lift in her heart as she sang out of tune to snatches of the lyrics. There was nothing better, she decided, than driving through the south Dublin countryside on a sunny summer's morning, with the motorway relatively clear of traffic and the Wicklow mountains a blue-grey smudge growing on the horizon. Particularly when she was en route to Tamarisk.

She hadn't seen Serena since the Saturday night when she'd got sloshed in her kitchen. She'd phoned her a few times to see how she was, and was upset to hear that things still weren't resolved with Paul. It was obviously more serious than a tiff. She had deliberately not enquired about Jack. Or Jenni. For afterwards, in the clear light of day, Kim told herself that it was still early days after Amy so Jack was bound to be acting silly. As Serena had pointed out, it was crazy behaviour to ask someone to come home with you after just a week.

Jack would come to his senses soon enough. If Serena's predictions were correct, Jenni had already gone back to wherever she came from.

Then Serena had left a message on her mobile yesterday afternoon while she was busy with a client. 'Kim . . . I know you're probably up to your gills, but I'm calling on the off-chance in case you can do me a huge favour . . . Ring me back when you get a chance.'

When she phoned Serena back, her friend explained that she had a double booking for her Presidential Suite and rather than let either party down, she was hoping that one of the Premier Suites could be upgraded. Like, within the next forty-eight hours.

'I have until late afternoon on Friday to turn this around,' Serena said. 'Hang the expense. If you've any ideas, contacts or pull that would help me to put this together . . . We can do without adverse publicity. I have an award to win and I need to get this problem fixed without losing face. You're the only person I can think of,' Serena continued. 'I know it's absurdly short notice, Kim, but it's a bit of a crisis and if there's anything you can do . . .'

'I'll just check my appointments,' Kim said, swiftly deciding that whatever was on her schedule would be put back. Occasional delays were inevitable in her line of work. Sometimes materials weren't up to the high standard required or a consignment of furniture was late. On Thursday afternoon, she was supposed to be meeting a television actress who wanted to source some original farmhouse furniture for her country residence in Westmeath. On Friday, she was meeting the new owners of a high-class Dublin restaurant to talk about concept and design ideas for a complete refurbishment. Depending on what Serena wanted she could reschedule for late Friday and Saturday perhaps. Nothing was more important than Tamarisk and the opportunity to show Jack the talents she could bring to the business.

'I can postpone some stuff and go down to you tomorrow morning,' she told Serena.

'Are you sure? I don't want you to mess your clients about . . .'

'Not at all, I don't have any urgent deadlines and I can facilitate them another time. No sweat. What are friends for after all? If I can't help you out . . .'

'You're a star,' Serena sounded relieved. 'Naturally I'll double your usual fee and pay all expenses.'

'You don't have to do that,' Kim insisted. She didn't admit that she would do it for nothing, free gratis, if it meant earning brownie points with Jack.

She'd risen extra early that morning and taken utmost care with her appearance, bearing in mind that Jack would be seeing Kim, the interior stylist, in action. Cleavage was out of the question. Likewise too much makeup, jewellery or perfume. She had to strike a balance between looking businesslike and professional, yet attractive and sexy.

Feminine yet strong was the way to go. Her Karen Millen navy tunic dress was perfect.

Tamarisk looked beautiful in the morning light. Her heart swelled as she pulled up at the entrance porch and began to unload her laptop and material samples. The porter was out immediately to give her a hand and, in no time, Kim was whisked into the lobby, along with her equipment, with her SUV safely parked.

'I'll let Serena know you're here,' the receptionist said, pressing a button on her phone.

But Serena had obviously seen Kim's arrival, for she glided down the stairs, immaculately dressed as usual, a bright smile plastered on her face. Up close, Kim saw the taut lines on her friend's forehead and the unhappy flicker in her eyes that reminded her all was not well with Serena's marriage.

'Serena, hi,' she gave her a warm hug.

'Kim, thank you, you're a darling for coming at such short notice. You're really helping me out of a tight spot. I'll go through a few details with you first and then we'll have a look at the room.' Serena gave instructions for Kim's stuff to be taken to her office and for some coffee to be sent up. Finally, she told the receptionist to route her calls to Andrew for the next hour, before leading Kim upstairs to her office.

Kim noted with a tiny pang of disappointment that Jack wasn't joining them.

* * *

'Well, what do you think?' Jack asked, throwing open the door to the vast bedroom, and replacing his master key card in his pocket.

He watched Jenni walk through from the dining room and stroll around the bedroom, looking at the luxury furnishings in wonder. 'Wow. This is some space. I was never in anything like this before.'

He smiled at her childlike pleasure. He'd woken up late that morning, feeling re-energised. The meeting with the Dublin solicitor had gone well the previous afternoon, as he started the ball rolling tying up the red tape around Amy's affairs. Afterwards, he'd had a fun couple of hours showing Jenni around the city and that morning he'd been suddenly reluctant to leave her in Garryvale for the day while he went into work. On impulse he'd asked her to accompany him. 'I'll show you around the hotel and find something for you to do,' he'd said.

'Once your sister doesn't mind.'

'Why should she?'

'I told you, she doesn't like me.'

'She will, as soon as she gets to know you. I'll bring you up to her office first, if that makes you feel better.'

But the door to Serena's office had been closed, which meant she was with someone and didn't want to be disturbed, so he passed it by and went up the stairs and brought Jenni along the corridor to the Presidential Suite.

Jenni flicked the tasselled curtains and grasped a pole of the king-sized, four-poster bed, swinging out of it. 'I've only ever seen something like this in an upper-crust magazine in the dentist's surgery. What did you say it was called again?'

'The Presidential Suite. And stop messing with that pole. It's giving me all sorts of ideas.'

'Like what?' she swung out of the pole again and gave him a look that was innocent and provocative all at once.

Jack grinned. 'Like I'm not sure if we should be here at all.'

She gave him a mischievous grin and murmured, 'You did say you'd find something for me to do . . .'

'We don't have time for a major overhaul,' Kim said, 'but we should be able to accessorise one of your suites to add a few touches of ultra-luxury as soon as you decide who to put in there. You could even change the name to something like the Royal Suite to set it apart from the Presidential and the rest of the Premier suites.'

'I knew I could rely on you, Kim. I just can't think straight at the moment.' Serena looked gutted.

'God, I'm sorry. Besides all this, how are you coping?' Kim asked, gently now, mindful of Serena's pale face and shadowed eyes.

'I'm not. I'm finding it hellish, but we'll talk later,' Serena said, replacing her empty coffee cup on the tray and rising to her feet. She took a master key card out of her bag. 'I want to get this problem sorted. At least it's taking my mind of Paul. The clock is already ticking and both parties expect to be here around five o'clock tomorrow. I'll show you one of the suites . . .'

In Kim's opinion the Premier suites at Tamarisk were the epitome of indulgent relaxation. 'I don't know how I can improve on perfection,' she said, looking around and taking in the sumptuous decor.

'Yes, well we have five suites along this corridor, all similarly styled,' Serena said, adjusting a cushion on an already perfectly dressed bed.

'That's something you could change,' Kim said, strolling around. 'Why don't you have them reflecting different themes? If you wanted to take these suites and turn them around, the possibilities are huge. But that's for another day.'

'It is. But for now, how would you add some luxury to this suite?'

'You could upgrade some of the soft furnishings in a matter of hours, if I make a few phone calls. How about silk wallpaper behind the bed, and a matching canopy, pillows, and cushions? I know the perfect shade of gold and mulberry that would add an element of luxury. You could have matching lamps and rugs throughout the suite. Think faux fur rugs and a mulberry throw. Vintage lamps and a couple of antique mirrors. I know exactly where to put my hands on them. And it would be perfect for Jessica.'

Kim could feel the new look of the suite taking

shape and it was exciting to be working with Serena in Tamarisk, even if it was just for a couple of days. She kept expecting Jack to drop in any minute. If this was a crisis situation, surely he'd be involved, even if it was just from a budgetary point of view?

'How about the bathroom?' Serena asked.

Kim walked over to the bathroom and looked around, admiring the bales of thick towels and robes with the Spa logo, and the walk-in mosaic tiled shower cubicle as well as the deep Jacuzzi bath. 'It's already quite superb. I'd suggest more candles; Max Benjamin or Jo Malone, with scents that would complement your range of toiletries from Provence . . .' she came back out into the bedroom. 'Posies of summer flowers in vintage jugs throughout the suite. Books and music. A complimentary private therapist to drop in for a couple of hours on both Friday evening and Saturday?' Kim had to stop as Serena was shaking her head and smiling.

'This is great, Kim, I really appreciate it.'

'I'd like to have a look at this Presidential Suite if it's free,' Kim said. 'Just in case there's anything I might have overlooked.'

'Sure. It's unoccupied right now. This way.'

Serena led the way down the carpeted corridor, unlocking the door to the suite at the end. They walked across the thickly carpeted living room and just as Serena opened the bedroom door, they both heard laughter floating out of it.

The laughter stopped abruptly. There was a long, agonising moment of silence. Kim knew the scene in front of her would be seared into her brain for the rest of her life. Through the open doorway she saw a dark mop of sexy, bed-head hair and a pair of brown eyes staring at her from the middle of the four-poster bed. The girl looked as though she had made a hurried dive under the duvet and her bare legs were sticking out. Jack was standing by the side of the bed. He was totally naked and clutching a pink T-shirt in front of his groin. Clothes were scattered on the floor.

'Hey, sis – oh, Kim . . . Hi, you guys . . .' he began. Behind his bravado grin, he looked embarrassed.

'Jack. What the fuck?' Serena said in a barely controlled voice.

Kim wanted to laugh hysterically in spite of her icy, numbing shock, because Serena's expletive was so out of character and yet such an unintentional pun. To her acute mortification, she found it difficult to take her eyes off the pink T-shirt Jack was using to cover what was clearly a slowly subsiding erection. She forced her gaze upwards to his bare torso, which was lightly smudged with dark-red hair. It didn't help that it was the kind of broad chest you wanted to nuzzle into. Then, she dared to look at his face.

'I was showing Jenni around our number one suite, and well . . .' Jack's blue-green eyes glinted irrepressibly, all traces of embarrassment had melted away.

Just as the name seared into her brain, she heard Serena say in an icy voice, 'Hello, Jenni. My brother has clearly broken the rules. Our number one suite boasts lots of luxury extras but that doesn't include sex on tap. Anyway, Kim,' she turned away from the couple by the bed and walked back to Kim, touching her arm briefly, 'I think you've seen more than enough to work out a plan.'

'What plan?' Jack asked, as Serena began to close the bedroom door.

'You wouldn't know,' Serena said over her shoulder, her voice dripping with sarcasm. 'You weren't around yesterday to realise that we have a crisis on our hands. Kim has kindly agreed to come down to help sort it out.'

'Thanks, Kim,' Jack smiled at her and she felt it was the smile of a traitor. 'I'll talk to you later and introduce Jenni properly to you. This is scarcely the right time . . . hope we haven't embarrassed you.'

Kim didn't even attempt to smile as it was beyond her capabilities. She followed Serena out of the suite wondering how she managed to move as her legs seemed totally numb.

'This is the second time I've almost caught Jack getting his rocks off,' Serena said tightly as they stepped down the staircase to the first floor. 'It's gone beyond a joke. And don't tell me he's making up for lost time.'

Kim was light-headed. Had that really happened? It was like a bad dream. She'd never be able to look at a pink T-shirt again without feeling sick. She'd never be able to look at Jack again without feeling cut in two. A little voice whispered that she should salvage what was left of her self-respect, make some excuse to Serena and leave straight away. But she was in no fit state to drive anywhere and she needed to find out more about Jack's new girlfriend so she knew exactly what she was up against.

'I'm really sorry you had to witness that, Kim,' Serena said when they were seated in her office and she had ordered fresh coffee. 'Just wait till I get Jack to myself.'

'Forget it, Serena.' Kim sought to control herself as the initial numbness began to recede so that she felt every inch of the deep blade of envy that was embedded in her stomach. She tried to blot out images of Jack and Jenni and what they might be doing. Somehow, she managed to go through the details of the revamp with Serena, explaining that she could show her some samples on her laptop, then she had calls to make, people to track down and shopping to do. Anything to keep herself busy and stop her from crying her heart out.

'If all goes well, I can have the suite turned around by lunch-time tomorrow.' Her mouth felt as though it was full of shards of glass as she spoke.

'I can't thank you enough, Kim. My head is elsewhere these days.'

Kim waited.

Serena looked haunted as she elaborated. 'Paul and I . . . It's crazy. I can't believe it. I never thought he'd walk out like that . . . I tried to talk to him yesterday evening and I just made things worse. God, it's mad. And it's all my fault.' Her voice caught and tears glimmered in her eyes.

Kim was gripped with sudden frustration. Serena had had the world at her feet, the fantastic career, the fabulous husband and lovely child – precious things that were eluding Kim and now seemed farther out of her reach than ever. How could Serena have been so careless? And why was Kim the one who had to listen to Serena and all her woes when she had to keep silent about her own heartbreak?

'I'm going around trying to pretend it hasn't happened,' Serena continued. 'What a sad, self-deluded case I am. Then I'm trying hard to keep Harriet happy as well. Now she thinks Paul is sleeping on the job because he's so busy. It's impossible to see how we'll get out of this nightmare.' Serena pulled a tissue from a box and dabbed her teary eyes. 'And it doesn't help that when I need his support, Jack starts acting like a randy teenager who's just discovered sex.'

Kim felt faint, wondering if she could possibly take any more. If anyone was a sad, self-deluded case, it was Kim and not Serena. She was thirty-five years of age. She was an intelligent, mature woman, who had built up her business, even in these troubled times. Why, oh why, was she chasing a dream when it came to Jack? The thing was, she realised bitterly, that it was very difficult to give up a cherished desire or face the fact that it might never happen. Not while there was even the tiniest glimmer of hope to cling to.

'Are you still on for La Mimosa?' Serena asked, breaking into her thoughts.

La Mimosa? Kim tried to focus her thoughts. Charlotte had invited her for the big birthday weekend. 'It was good of Charlotte to invite me, but I don't want to intrude on family stuff.'

'Kim, hello, you're practically family. And you've always been at our birthday parties. It's just two weeks away but I can't see Paul and me back together by then,' Serena sighed and more tears rolled down her cheeks. 'I don't want to go but Harriet's all excited and I don't want to ruin that on her.'

'What about Jenni?' Kim was nearly afraid to ask.

'Jenni? Nah,' Serena scoffed. 'It'll be all over by then. If anything, what you saw today just shows he's still not thinking straight. Sooner or later, he'll cop on to himself and realise it. Right now, Jenni's a novelty. *And* a bad influence, I've never known him to mess around in any of our hotel rooms before. That's a first and it shows he's really lost the run of himself, big time.'

★   ★   ★

Kim didn't see Jack again until the following day when she was putting the finishing touches to the Royal Suite. She was alone in the suite, adjusting the flower arrangements, when he walked in, wearing a beautiful suit and pale-grey shirt. Her heart almost stopped.

'Jack! Hi,' she said, blushing as she remembered what had happened the previous day.

He didn't seem to notice her discomfort. He looked around the room and gave a low whistle. 'Wow. This is superb, Kim, well done. Serena told me you dropped everything and got us out of an awkward situation.' He crossed the floor to her as he was speaking and when he was right beside her, so close that she caught the scent of his aftershave, he put a casual arm around her shoulders and gave her a friendly squeeze. She looked at his face, the cleft in his chin, his generous and very kissable mouth, his blue-green eyes crinkled humorously at the corners as they regarded her fondly and felt like weeping. So near and yet so far away.

'I'm glad to help. I enjoyed it.' Her voice was husky and almost betrayed her.

'By the way, I'm really sorry if I embarrassed you yesterday. I didn't mean for that to happen . . . It's certainly not the way I wanted to introduce you to Jenni.'

He looked apologetic, she had to concede, but her gaze slid away from his eyes when a stark image of his bare chest and what lay in wait behind the pink T-shirt clouded her vision.

'Don't worry, I've seen worse,' she said, forcing a light tone. 'I'm not sure if Serena mentioned it,' she gabbled, hurriedly changing the subject in case he went into a torrid explanation, 'but we were talking about a revamp of all the suites? Individually redesigned so as to reflect different themes.'

'Hey, that's a brilliant idea,' he said warmly, obviously pleased to be on safe ground again, 'however it's not something we'd be looking at in the short term. We need to consolidate our finances and get back on track. I took my eye off the ball in recent months. I just didn't have the interest or enthusiasm.'

'That's understandable,' she said, wondering why the heck she was being so bloody understanding and realising it was simply because she loved him.

'But I'm glad to say that things have finally turned. Thanks to Jenni,' Jack said. 'She's amazing. She's made my life worth living again. You must come for dinner. Stay the night and have a few drinks. I want her to get to know all my friends. And we go back a long way, don't we, tatty-head? You're almost family.'

Almost family. Kim felt gutted. Why couldn't she be the one to make Jack's life worth living again?

CHAPTER 31

Just after dawn on Saturday morning, Charlotte slipped out of bed and peeped out through a gap in the blinds at the fresh, almost silvery morning. A glimmer of sunshine was cresting the horizon and shimmering across the curving mountain folds. The light reflected off the windows of homes scattered around the lower slopes of the hills so that they gleamed like tiny jewels. There wasn't a cloud in the flawless, milky-blue sky. She turned back and looked at her rumpled bed, testament to the restless night she'd just had, and decided that she was far better up and about.

In the brand-new morning, all was quiet and peaceful in the Tranquil Garden, save for the call of the larks and the sparrows. Wearing her swimsuit under her robe, Charlotte walked along the path lining the dew-drizzled grass, inhaling the scents rising from the rose bed and the herbaceous border. Silently, she let herself in through the side door to the Leisure Centre. She was looking forward to having the pool to herself at this early hour, diving into the smooth, silky surface like someone walking on silent, virgin snow. As she passed by the empty reception desk, something caught her eye and she looked through the glass to the pool.

She wouldn't be alone.

At first she wasn't sure who it was. The rising sun was dappling the side walls and shimmying off the surface of the water. Then she realised that there were two of them, moving slowly together through the silvered surface, so close and so much in perfect symmetry with each other that they appeared to be one. Down at the far end of the pool, they came up for air and tread water while they held onto the bar, their dark, wet-slicked heads close as they spoke to each other.

It was Jack. And Jenni.

After a short while, they got out of the pool and, holding hands, they took a running jump into the deep end, sending up an iridescent spray. Then Jack rolled onto his back, scooped Jenni into his arms and they glided down the pool together one more time.

Charlotte shrank back behind the reception desk and watched them, unobserved.

Like her, Jack and Jenni must have driven up to Tamarisk in the breaking dawn. Even that, of itself, astounded her, given that Jack, unlike Serena, had never been a morning person. And no matter what Serena might say about Jack's scary impetuousness, or what misgivings she might have had herself, she could see that her son was totally alive to the moment and totally in tune with Jenni. Even from a distance, she could see it in the tender way he held her and in the way his whole body was leaning attentively towards her. And although there was nothing overtly sexy about them – Jenni's swimsuit was black and strictly functional – she sensed a unity so profound between them that she found it oddly moving.

'She's like a breath of fresh air in my life,' Jack had said to her, when he'd called in one evening.

'In what way?' she'd asked.

'I dunno. But it's the only way I can explain how she lifts me up; a breath of clear, sparkling air that goes all the way through me, refreshing and inspiring. It's like nothing I've ever had before.'

She'd listened to what he'd said, she'd seen the enthusiasm lighting up his face and the warmth in his eyes, but she told herself he was just grasping something novel and different in an attempt to distance himself from the heartbreak that Amy had caused. Jenni was, she was convinced, nothing but a temporary distraction. But if she helped her son to sever the past, what harm could it do? She'd just hoped he wouldn't become so involved that his heart was on the line all over again.

This morning, however, she wasn't so sure of her convictions. Watching him now, she had the unnerving feeling that her son was in love. Possibly for the first time in his life. For she had never seen him quite like this with Amy or with any other girlfriend. Happy, relaxed and totally absorbed. She thought of the incident in the Presidential

Suite in Tamarisk, which Serena had reported back with outrage, and suppressed a sudden smile. At least this morning he was wearing his swimming trunks, and she supposed she should be grateful that he'd spared her blushes. Although taking a running jump into the pool was forbidden and neither of them had bothered to wear the compulsory swimming hat, something Serena would take a very dim view of. Not that she was going to know. Charlotte had no intentions of telling her daughter of this early-morning tryst. There was no way to put it into words, to explain what she'd just witnessed. Serena would scoff at the idea of Jack being in love so soon after Amy's death, in a misguided yet loyal attempt to protect her brother from the possibility of inflicting himself with more heartbreak. And in desperate trouble with her own marriage, she was bound to be cynical.

'A breath of sparkling air that goes all the way through me,' Jack had said. Right now, Serena wouldn't empathise, but Charlotte appreciated the meaning of his words only too well, for watching Jenni and Jack, she remembered – God, she remembered – how love and passion could sweep you off your feet, changing your life when you least expected it.

She was gripped with nostalgia and regret. For unlike her son, who could follow his heart and lavish his love on Jenni, she'd been caught between duty and passion. Feeling as though she was a trespasser, Charlotte waited until Jack and Jenni glided down to the far end of the pool before she stole away, taking a circuitous route around the pathway outside, as far away from the windows of the swimming pool as possible.

'Who was that?' Jenni asked as she caught a movement out of the corner of her eye.

'Where?'

Jenni stared outside at the sparkling morning. The floor-to-ceiling windows of the swimming pool looked out onto the back lawns at Tamarisk and, beyond that, the woods. The swathe of emerald lawn was calm and serene and, even though she'd never considered herself much of a nature lover, she couldn't deny that the scene outside was full of peaceful beauty that filled her with pleasure. 'I thought I saw someone out there, an early-morning stroller, but whoever it was they're gone.'

She and Jack were sitting on the edge of the pool, dabbling their feet in the water. Their wet-slicked bodies were touching shoulders, arms and hips, and she found it strangely comforting to feel the proximity of Jack's physical presence.

She'd seen a different side to him that morning.

She'd been surprised the previous evening when he'd suggested a trip to the pool, feeling sure that he had an ulterior motive. 'Will this be like the day you showed me around Tamarisk? And we ended up embarrassing the hell out of your sister and her friend? I know it was partly my fault, but Serena and Kim will never talk to me again.'

'Of course they will. I mean a real swim, as in swimsuits, front crawl, breast stroke. Unless . . .' he'd quirked a rakish eyebrow.

'No thanks,' she'd said firmly. 'A real swim is fine. I don't want to run the risk of embarrassing your guests.'

'We could go very early, before the pool is open.'

'Is this all you want me for?' She'd challenged him, half serious, half in earnest. 'Fun and games? To play living on the edge with?'

He'd shaken his head. He'd caught her and held her fast against him so that she could hear his heartbeat. 'I can't get enough of you, you must know that,' he'd murmured. Then he drew back, held her at arm's length, and looked at her steadily. 'But we – us – it's more, it's bigger, it's everything, and far, far better than anything I've ever had before.'

She'd stared at him for a long moment, unable to fathom his look. She'd felt something intangible pass between them, something that made her a little unsteady on her legs. Then she'd laughed, the carefree Jenni laugh she'd always used when she was unsure. 'Right so, you're on. Proper swimming with swimsuits, and early, before the pool is open. Although be warned. I don't venture near the deep end.'

'Trust me. I'll look after you.'

She thought he'd change his mind, but he woke her just after dawn, kissing her awake, drawing her close in the bed against his hot skin, making hushed, early-morning love that filled her with delight – so that there was less chance he'd be tempted to ravish her in the pool, he'd whispered.

He was a good swimmer, and better than she had expected. And he'd kept his word, surprising her with his mixture of strength and tenderness as they'd swum and floated and drifted in the sunlit, cocooning water. Surprising her even more with the funny kind of emotions he was causing inside her. What was happening to her? Normally afraid to go out of her depth, she'd trusted him implicitly, giving herself up to the security of his hands and body much in the way she gave of herself when they made love. Now as they sat with their bodies touching, she felt something shift and loosen inside her, and her heart swelled.

She wondered if she was falling in love. She, Jenni Anderson, in *love*?

Or was it something else entirely, perhaps an intrinsic need to feel deeply connected to this man because of the tiny life inside her?

Jack stood up and held out his hand, lifting her to her feet, dropping a kiss on her damp head. 'Come on, time to dry off, get dressed and go home for breakfast.'

They drove back down the avenue of beech trees, Jenni still amazed at the way huge parts of her life seemed to be shifting out of focus, as though she was shedding an old skin.

'It's really beautiful here,' she said, looking around

at the rolling parklands, set against the backdrop of mountain folds, hazy now in the morning light.

'Yes, I told you it was, didn't I?' Jack grinned.

'I was too overawed the first couple of times you brought me up the avenue to really appreciate it.'

Overawed? She'd been shocked into silence the first time she'd seen Tamarisk. She should have known to expect something special, if Jack's house was anything to go by, but for all his talk about Tamarisk, she'd never expected the luxury of the hotel and natural beauty of the surroundings. Once again, her calm composure had deserted her and she'd felt like a total interloper.

Then, when he'd shown her the sumptuous Presidential Suite, she'd felt more like an intruder than ever, and so she'd teased him with the bed pole, feeling the need to connect with him, and had ended up being mortified in front of Jack's sister and her friend. Jack had tried to reassure her, but Jenni had been totally embarrassed. Afterwards, she'd wondered what on earth she was doing there. The whole dynamic of Jack's background and life was so much at odds with her own; a background and life he knew very little of. Surely she was better off returning to her job on the Cours Saleya, or even heading home to London, no matter how difficult that would be, and making the best of things for the sake of her own sanity and the tiny life within her?

But this morning, she felt different again; startled and panicky with the deeper emotions Jack was causing her to feel, yet a little stronger in spite of the scariness of it all. And, her thoughts crystallised, it wasn't just a vague blob of life inside her. In time, it would be a baby. Jack's baby. A son or daughter who could be part of his life, part of his future, and, she realised, looking back at the panorama as they reached the entrance gates, part of all this.

If Jack wanted it, of course.

CHAPTER 32

No matter how dazzling it was, a party could be the loneliest place on the planet, Kim decided, as she pushed her way to the bar through the crowd of minor celebrities and wannabe models. She ordered a double vodka.

At eleven o'clock on a Saturday night, the Silver Club, situated on the top floor of one of Dublin's glitzy hotels, was heaving with designer-clad and designer-scented bodies. She'd almost given it a miss, feeling stressed out after her visit to Tamarisk and the whole Jenni thing. She still couldn't get over the fickle twist of fate that had made Jack miss his flight home and bump into Jenni outside a bar in Nice. But instead of sitting home alone, nursing her envy or driving herself insane wondering what Jack might be doing at that moment, she'd made a huge effort to shower and dress, ploughing through her wardrobe for last year's Stella McCartney shift dress and arriving at the party alone.

She was sick of arriving at parties alone.

Smiling and greeting acquaintances, Kim tried to look as though she was having fantastic fun.

The music beat thumped and lights flashed frenetically, and you had to shout at the top of your voice to be heard. It was the kind of atmosphere that used to energise her. Two scantily clad twenty-somethings were moving to the music, dancing in a way that they probably thought was as provocative as their thigh-high minis, but that, in reality, looked silly. The kind of abandoned way she would have danced ten years ago, feeling the world was at her feet and life was full of glittering excitement.

Where had those ten years gone? It seemed as though a huge chunk of her life had fast-forwarded itself, without her noticing it. As well as that glum fact, the excitement that life had promised back then had totally evaporated. Apparently, Lucy O'Leary felt much the same way, and that was why she was having a bash for her thirty-fifth birthday.

'I was in shock when I reached thirty, so I let that pass,' she'd admitted to Kim in a rare burst of confidence. 'And I'm not going to celebrate the big four-oh unless I have a ring on my finger and at least one baby. I'll be hiding under the duvet otherwise.'

'I know how you feel,' Kim had told her.

'So I'm having an in-between-the-milestone birthday,' Lucy had said. 'Thirty-five is still young enough to have some hope of marriage with the expectation of motherhood. I don't want thirty-five bumps, but I'm inviting thirty-five sexy eligibles.'

'Are there that many left in Dublin?'

'I doubt it. That's why my trawl is stretching out to London, Paris and New York, and encompassing everyone from twenty-five to forty. I'm restricting the number of voracious females but you can come, on one condition.'

'I think I can guess what that is . . .'

'No going home with anyone unless I give my permission.'

'Don't worry, I won't.'

The barman passed across her glass and she twirled her plastic straw around, mixing the ice cubes and a slice of lemon through her drink before she took a deep slug. She was reluctant to move away from the relative safety net of the bar, keenly feeling the fact that she was alone in spite of being in a crowd, and she felt gripped with a sickening hunger for Jack. Deep down, she felt more inadequate and insecure than ever when she thought about the young twenty-four-year-old with the bed-head hair and the big appealing eyes who'd distracted him enough to be invited to share his home on such a short acquaintance And had then encouraged him to be so spontaneous within the refined walls of Tamarisk.

The music changed to the Lily Allen tune she'd been singing en route to Wicklow and sudden tears pricked the back of her eyes. Feeling stupid she moved away, out towards the roof garden, hardly seeing where she was going.

'Hey, Kim!' Someone touched her arm.

Paul Taylor. He was standing by the glass door that led to the rooftop garden with two other guys, but when he attracted Kim's attention he excused himself.

'What are you doing here?' she asked, raising her voice against the music and conversation. Apart from the time he'd dropped in late to her party, she was used to only seeing him when he was with Serena so it was strange bumping into him like this. He was wearing a pair of jeans that hugged his powerful thighs and ass. His casual shirt, open at the neck, showed off the breadth of his muscular chest. There was no doubt that Paul Taylor exuded full-on masculinity. In a moment of panic, she realised that if she hadn't known who he was, Serena's husband would definitely have snagged her interest.

Jesus.

In the next breath, she realised that he had probably snagged the attention of quite a few of the predatory women.

'Don't stare at me like that,' he said.

'Like what?'

'As though I've just crawled out from under a stone.'

Kim stared at him without blinking. 'I thought this party was restricted to sexy eligibles. You happen to be married to my best friend, and you're out on the pull while she's sitting at home broken-hearted.'

He held her arm and leaned in close to her while

he spoke, holding her gaze with his thick-lashed, dark, steely eyes. God. The man was pure sex. 'Number one, I am not on the pull. I came here with friends from work because I'm sick of spending most nights alone pacing the floor of a poxy apartment. Number two, I doubt if Serena is crying into her silk handkerchief. More than likely she's devising her next plot to make Tamarisk a world-class hotel.'

'Wow!' Kim stepped back, surprised by the anger in his voice. Serena was right. From his tone of voice and the implacable look in his dark eyes he was a long way off resolving things with her. 'You haven't got a chip on your shoulder – it's more like a meteorite.'

He looked at her as though she was stating the obvious. 'How did you expect me to be? Jumping for joy? I have feelings too, you know. Feelings that have been trampled all over. Has Serena told you why we broke up?'

'Well, no. She's finding it too difficult to talk about.'

'That doesn't surprise me. She can't bring herself to admit the fool she made of me.'

'I don't want to hear this. Serena is my best friend.'

'Unfortunately, and you won't like this, neither you nor I are Serena's best friend. From where I'm at, her main priority is that goddamned hotel, next is picking up the slack for her brother, then comes Harriet, and maybe at that point, either one of us gets a look in.'

'Paul!'

He gave her a rueful grin. 'I told you you wouldn't like it.'

'I think . . .' she paused. 'Can I get you another drink?' In spite of herself, she was curious about why Serena and Paul had split, considering all they seemed to have going for them. How had Serena reached a situation where her hunky husband was out prowling amid a gaggle of preying women?

'I'll get them,' he offered. 'I'll be quicker getting through that manic crowd at the bar. What's your poison? Vodka?'

Kim nodded.

'Why don't you grab a seat outside on the deck and I'll be back in a mo.'

Kim sat in an aluminium seat and tipped back her head. One side of the roof garden had a sloping canvas awning that was edged with strands of twinkling fairy lights. The other side was open to the dark, velvety sky. Below the roof garden, the shadowy night-time was pinpricked with lights from other buildings and sounds of Dublin streets drifted up, blending into the background. It was warm enough to sit outside on this July evening and the night air was refreshing after the heat of the club. This was her friend's husband. She wasn't doing anything wrong. She was going to see if there was anything she could do to help get their marriage back on track. Nonetheless, it was nice to have a man looking after you, pushing his way to the bar to get her a drink, even if she'd only borrowed him for a while. It also meant she wasn't alone at the party anymore.

Kim watched as Paul came out with the drinks, weaving through the crowd. She remembered the night, long ago, when he'd first met Serena. He'd been younger then and more unsophisticated. Now, years later, his body had filled out and marriage and fatherhood had left an indelible stamp. The stamp of responsible maturity and an innate gravitas.

'Cheers,' he tipped his glass against hers. 'What are you doing here anyway? Are you out on the pull?'

'No way,' Kim said. 'I had a gap in my diary. Does Serena know you're here?'

He didn't answer at first and let the silence stretch between them. 'So when was the last time you saw her?' he asked.

'Look, Paul, she really is in bits,' Kim began. 'She told me your split was all her fault. I wish you guys would sort out your differences. I hate to see her cut up and both of you unhappy.'

'When was the last time you saw her?' Paul repeated.

'Well, yesterday, actually,' Kim told him.

'And what was the occasion? Was she crying on your shoulder? Or by chance asking you to babysit Harriet?'

'I was doing some work, in the hotel.'

He looked at her quietly, clearly waiting for her

to elaborate. She spread her hands in a conciliatory gesture. 'I was restyling one of the suites, as there was a bit of a crisis.'

'A bit of a crisis?' He raised an eyebrow. 'With one of the hotel suites?'

'Yes, and Serena asked for my help.'

'A crisis.' He shook his head. 'Did one of the customers object to the colour of the bedspread? Or the scent of the shower gel? Or the way the bog roll was folded? You see, I think Serena would find that more of a crisis than a breakdown in her marriage. But I'm relieved to see that it hasn't interfered with her job.'

'God, you really have it bad, don't you? That's not fair. Serena asked for my help because she didn't have the energy to sort out the problem herself, which is not like her. Of course she's been crying on my shoulder. You should have seen her face the night she told me about you guys. Do you really expect her to spend the whole day in bed in a torrent of weeping? She's going around trying to put in a normal day's work, okay, but it's an act. Underneath she feels as though her world has come to an end.'

'Problem is, Kim, a lot of our marriage has been an act. I really feel I don't know Serena at all. She's played me like a right fool.'

'I can't accept that,' Kim said stoutly, feeling out of her depth and wondering if she'd bitten off more than she could chew in talking to Paul like this. She searched for a lifeline. 'Serena loves you,' she went on, feeling as though she was grasping at straws to judge by the unimpressed look he was giving her. 'Harriett and you mean everything to her. You're a huge part of her life. Okay she works hard at her job, but she'd never treat anyone like a fool. Least of all you. She has far too much respect for you.'

'Kim, darling,' Paul gave her a crooked smile and slowly shook his head. 'From what I can see, the hotel is the only thing that gives Serena total satisfaction and makes her feel useful. I'm trying to figure out if her ambition knows no bounds or if she's still trying to prove something. Maybe it goes back to her alcoholic father not giving her enough attention . . . who knows? And as for Jack . . .' Paul paused.

'What about Jack?' Kim's voice cracked painfully.

'There are times when Serena is more like a controlling mother to him than his sister.'

'Don't be ridiculous. You're way out of line.'

'Am I? Jack has always let Serena take the lead. He was always far too busy enjoying his life and playing the role of the eternal playboy to be serious about anything.'

'He married Amy, didn't he? They were going to start a family. I call that serious.'

Paul looked at her speculatively. 'Didn't you know that he only married Amy because he felt he had to? She was pregnant.'

Something cracked apart inside Kim. 'What are

you saying? Amy didn't become pregnant until after the wedding . . .'

'That's what I thought too,' Paul said. 'I only found out recently that Amy didn't want any fingers pointing. God knows what she intended to say when the baby arrived but she wanted her perfect wedding day untarnished with gossip or the media insinuating that she had coerced Jack into marrying her. Serena was furious that Jack had allowed himself to be snared.'

Kim was silent. At the time, as she'd tortured herself looking at photos of their wedding day in *Heat*, Kim had asked herself just what exactly Amy had that she hadn't, to make Jack love her enough to marry her. Now she knew. Jack had fallen for the oldest trick in the book. Serena had known all along and hadn't told her. Although there would have been no reason for Serena to break Jack's confidence and tell her as she didn't know how Kim felt about Jack.

'All of that ended in rather a disaster. Why are you raking it up? What has any of it got to do with you and Serena?' she asked, conscious that her voice was trembling slightly with the surprising news.

'I was upset that Serena felt she couldn't trust me enough to tell me. We were supposed to be married. When Amy died and the phone call came through, Serena dropped everything to rush to Jack's side. I'd wanted to go with her, but she refused. I know what happened was a terrible tragedy and Jack had my sympathies, and it sounds childish and selfish in the context of Amy's tragic death, but I had the feeling that I was being excluded.'

Kim bit her lip. She could empathise with Paul because Jack and Serena were so close that sometimes she'd felt excluded. 'I suppose in the circumstances . . . It must have been very upsetting for them both.'

'It was upsetting for everyone. Since then, Serena has been working her butt off to make up for Jack's inability to pull his weight, often pushing me and Harriet aside.'

'Yes, but how on earth could Jack have pulled his weight this year?' Kim pointed out.

Paul folded his arms and sighed. 'You're right, Kim. It's been difficult and I'm just thinking of myself, but lately I couldn't help getting pissed off with Serena's preoccupation with her job. And now, unfortunately, there are other, far more serious problems between us . . . Look, sorry about all this,' he said finally. 'You've come to a party and the last thing you want is to be listening to an old sourpuss like me. You should be back inside,' he smiled, 'mingling with the sexy eligibles.'

'You're not an old sourpuss,' Kim said pleasantly. 'Your feelings are perfectly normal. Everyone has been under a strain in the past few months. However, I think Serena's mad to be setting you loose among a horde of man-hungry women. Anyway, I'm going home. I didn't particularly want to be at this party and I'm pretty shattered as it's been a busy couple of days,' she said. Busy and emotionally draining, before she'd even bumped into Paul with his surprising revelations.

'I hope Serena appreciated your work,' he said.

'She did, of course. Look, I don't want to interfere,' she risked putting a hand on his arm. It felt taut and muscular. 'But you guys have a lot of talking to do.'

His dark eyes were shuttered. 'We should have talked a long time ago. It's too late now.'

'Paul, don't be ridiculous. It's never too late for anything.'

To her surprise, he insisted on seeing her home.

'Where are you staying?' she asked.

'I have an apartment in Cherrywood,' he said.

'Then I'd be dragging you out of your way,' Kim told him, a similar conversation not so long ago echoing in her ears.

'I don't want to be at this party either and a gentleman always sees a lady home.'

She found it unnerving to sit beside him in the back of the taxi, aware of his masculinity as she never had been before. She had to remind herself that he was her friend's husband, and Harriet's father, and that any dangerous thoughts she might have skittering around the back of her head had to firmly stay there. It was just such a long time since she'd had sex. And seeing Jack practically seducing Jenni hadn't helped matters. Even Matthew

O'Brien seemed an attractive proposition. When they reached her house in Terenure, Paul jumped out of the taxi and came around to her side to open the door. A true gentleman. She recalled Serena telling her with satisfaction that, thankfully, it didn't stop him from letting rip in bed.

'Thanks for listening to me,' he said. 'Sorry if I sounded like a pain in the ass.' Then he leaned over and kissed her on the cheek.

She had the sense that he was as lonely as she was. She put out her hand and let it rest on the front of his jacket. She thought of the empty apartment he was returning to, and the dark, equally empty house, silently waiting for her, with sleepless hours ahead of her filled with a kaleidoscope of chaotic images: Serena, seeing Paul for the first time; she, dancing with Jack at their wedding; the shock of Amy thrusting out her engagement ring, the picture of their wedding day in *Heat*. Jack carefully cradling Amy in his arms when she'd had too much to drink at a party. Most cruel of all though, just yesterday, when Jack told her that someone called Jenni had made his life worth living again.

'Paul . . . do you fancy a coffee? Or a drink for the road?'

He looked at her in the yellow wash of the street light. 'Yeah, why not?'

She waited on the pavement while he went back to the taxi and paid the driver. It was good to have company as she unlocked the door and stepped into the dark hall. She brought him into her front room, switching on lamps.

'Wine, beer or coffee?'

'A bottle of beer would be good, thanks.'

She kicked off her heels and went into her kitchen to fetch the beer, leaving the main light off. She opened the fridge for ice, the oblong of white light washing harshly across her face like a spotlight. It was just a drink for the road, she felt like telling it. Nothing else. She poured a glass of wine for herself then brought the drinks through.

Paul was standing in front of the mantelpiece, admiring her oil painting of the Wicklow mountains that had pride of place on the wall.

She handed him the beer. 'I was lucky to come across that one Sunday on Merrion Square,' she said. She didn't dare tell him that it was, for her, a reminder of the wild, primitive beauty of the glens and hills surrounding Tamarisk.

'It's very beautiful and soothing,' he said.

'Yes, it is.'

They stared at the painting in silence. Then Paul said, 'In a way it's not unlike you.'

She waited, her breath in her throat.

'You're beautiful, Kim. And there was something very soothing about the way you listened to me tonight.' His words fell into the dimly lit room, changing the feel of it for her and sweeping away the lonely evenings she'd spent there.

Her voice was gentle as she said, 'I don't know

what happened between you and Serena, but I know it's very hard to live with any kind of rejection.'

'The voice of experience. You understand because you've been hurt too, haven't you?'

Kim couldn't talk. She merely bit her lip and nodded her head.

'Whoever he was, he was a fool. And I shouldn't really be here.' He gave her a half-grin.

'No, probably not.'

He drank some beer. Then he put the bottle down and picked up his jacket, slinging it over his shoulder. 'It's best if I go.'

'Okay.'

He hesitated at the door, turned to face her; a split-second moment that gave Kim time to reach his side, so that it seemed perfectly natural to kiss goodnight. And after that butterfly brush of his lips on her cheek, it seemed perfectly natural to turn her mouth so that their lips met; to lean into him so that his kiss intensified, reaching into her emptiness with a tenderness that ran like a warm river right through her. It seemed right to lift her hands and twine them in his dark, wavy hair and kiss him back, pressing her body towards him. When his hand shimmied across her curves, she loved it for the pleasure it brought and the way it comforted her ragged emotions.

Locked tight in Paul's embrace, the kiss seemed to go on for ever. It would have been so easy to take his hand and lead him upstairs in the semi-darkness, into her room and onto her bed. For he was a man who had told her he found her beautiful and soothing, and it dripped like soft honey onto her sore heart. She thought she was going to explode soon if she didn't have sex. It would have been so easy to cling to this man in the darkness, to wrap her legs tightly around him, letting him fill her aching void.

But this man was, a warning voice whispered, her best friend's husband.

Paul must have come to his own senses for he sprang away, tucked his hands into his jeans pockets and said, 'We didn't . . .'

'No. It wasn't us. Not really.' Kim hugged herself to contain her trembling body.

'Just two people caught up in something . . . mad.'

'Yes, exactly.'

'You're very desirable, Kim, but . . .'

'I'm Serena's friend and I love her,' she gabbled. 'I kind of love you too, as an extension of Serena, if that doesn't sound too crazy. I was there the night you met. I'd never seen Serena look at a man the way she looked at you, and she raved about you afterwards. You must talk to her to find out what's in her head. It's the only way.'

'I dunno,' he shrugged. Then he smiled and said, 'You're a good kid, Kim. One of life's givers, I suspect. You deserve the best. Sorry if I made a fool of myself.'

'You didn't. It wasn't us. Just two strangers sharing a moment of comfort.'

'Thank you. For everything.'

'Serena is gutted you know,' Kim said, stalling him in an effort to make some good, secretly horrified that she'd almost dragged her best friend's husband up the stairs and into her bed. 'I've known her since I was five and you were never second best with her, you were always The One. I've never seen her so broken-hearted.'

'I feel broken-hearted too. Even though I was the one who walked.'

'Why did you walk out?'

'I was so angry that I couldn't stay under the same roof and I was afraid of what I might say or do in front of Harriet. I remember my parents having rows and it's not very pleasant.'

'Serena's parents had rows too, from what I gathered, not that she talked much about it. You said it yourself, their father was an alcoholic and their mother wasn't around much. I wouldn't go so far as to say she's like a mother to Jack, but she's always looked out for him. Growing up, they were left to their own devices a lot. I suppose they're even closer than most twins.'

'I still can't understand why she hides things from me.' His face looked bleak and Kim wished she could fix it for both of them.

'Serena has always put on a good face. She's very conscious of family loyalty and I'd no idea her father was an alcoholic for years. I'd no idea that Amy was pregnant either and I'm her closest friend. She likes to keep up a front and put the best side out. Even yesterday in Tamarisk, she put on a good face in front of the staff although I knew she was crumbling up inside.'

'Why does she do that? Is she too proud to admit to a failing?'

Kim sighed. 'I dunno. The older I get, the more complicated I realise life is.'

Paul lifted an eyebrow in wry amusement. 'Complicated?' And on that note he left.

Afterwards Kim went up to bed and slipped alone between her cotton sheets.

CHAPTER 33

Paul was late collecting Harriet from Maple Hill and it was after two o'clock on Sunday by the time Serena heard his car tyres scrunching on the gravel outside. It was a dull, cloudy afternoon with spats of rain and a gusty breeze, a perfect reflection of her edgy mood.

'Harriet, Dad's here,' she called, testing the sound of her voice, wondering if she'd be able to talk to him without it cracking.

Harriet flew out of the playroom into the hall before the doorbell even chimed. '*Goodie!* We're going to the movies today!'

'Bathroom first, and don't forget to wash your hands.'

'Aw, *Mum.*'

'Harriet!' Serena was insistent. She was buying herself a few precious moments alone with Paul. She'd gone over and over everything she'd said to him the last time he'd called, wondering how she could explain herself properly. But he wouldn't even come in. He stood in the porch, his face set and drawn.

'Are you okay?' she asked. It was obvious from

the dark circles under his eyes that he was far from okay. The strain of it all was getting to him.

'How could I be okay?' he snapped. 'Where's Harriet?'

'She'll be here in a minute. Look, you got it all wrong the other day . . .'

'I thought I understood it very well. Your main satisfaction in life comes from your job,' he fumed. 'Even now, with our marriage in serious shit, you haven't lost the ability to sort out whatever crisis comes your way quite magnificently.'

'What are you talking about?'

'I bumped into Kim last night at a party. I thought the grapevine would have got to you by now.'

A party. She tried to fish through her frozen brain cells to recall where Kim had been going the previous evening. Some glitzy event with a guaranteed high ratio of eligible men to women, she dimly recalled. Paul had been there, surrounded by plenty of preying females, interested in getting a man between the sheets and securing another notch on their bedpost. For all she knew, he'd been at plenty of such parties since he'd left. He'd only told her about this one because he knew Kim would be reporting back. Maybe he'd even been enticed to sleep with some of those women. Was that why he looked as though he hadn't slept last night? Nausea rose in her chest.

'No, I haven't been talking to her. Why?'

'You needn't look so worried. We left the party early and I saw her home.'

A ridiculous spark of jealously pierced her at the idea of Paul and Kim together in the back of a taxi, talking and chatting as they spun through the dark, night-time streets. It was Kim, she reminded herself. She should be relieved that it had been her friend and not someone who might have enticed Paul into bed.

'She told me she'd been helping you sort out a crisis in Tamarisk,' Paul went on. 'Obviously what's happened between us hasn't stopped you from giving your time and energy to your job.'

'You're wrong,' she said, her hands fluttering helplessly. Tears pricked her eyes and she swallowed hard. 'We ran into a problem. The reason I called on Kim was because I hadn't the energy to sort it out myself.'

Then Harriet tore up the hall, shrieking with delight as she ran out to the porch and flung herself on Paul. 'Daddy!' she squealed. 'I'm ready now. Let's go.'

Paul ignored Serena as he lifted Harriet into his arms and carried her to his car.

Her legs were trembling as she walked into her home office and sank down dispiritedly at the table, putting her head into her hands. When the phone rang she grabbed the cordless extension, filled with the ridiculous hope that it might be Paul, phoning from the laneway outside, asking her to join him and Harriet. Instead it was Jack, inviting her for dinner.

'Dinner?' Serena echoed, dragging her focus back to her brother.

'I'll collect you and bring you home afterwards so you can relax and have a couple of glasses of wine,' Jack said. 'I'd like Jenni to meet you properly. You two didn't exactly get off to a good start.'

'I wonder why.'

'I've already told you I take full blame for the episode in the hotel,' Jack said, sounding remarkably upbeat and not in the least apologetic. 'But come on, it wasn't a crime. We were just having some fun.'

'Yeah. Fun.' Serena snorted. 'Good job I was with Kim and not a prospective customer. For all you know the visitor for the Celebrate Ireland awards could have been in the hotel, looking around.'

'I know, I know. We've already been over this. I guess I'll never hear the end of it.'

'Don't forget we have the award ceremony next weekend.' Award ceremony? It was the last thing she wanted to attend.

'I won't forget. How about this evening?'

'You mean Jenni can cook?'

'Darling, sis, if I didn't know you better, I'd swear you're being sarcastic. I hope you'll come. It'll give you a chance to get to know Jenni.'

'I'm not being sarcastic. I'm just being your concerned sister, and trusting that your heart won't get another bruising.'

'All the more reason to come. You'll see for

yourself that there's no danger of history repeating itself.'

'I should hope not,' Serena said sharply.

'Speaking from the viewpoint of a concerned brother, how are things between you and Paul?'

'Not good,' Serena admitted.

'Jeez. How long is it now?'

'One week, five days.'

'And you're worried about my heart taking a bruising?' Jack's tone softened. 'Hey, you must be finding it pretty difficult.'

'I am,' she admitted, finding it impossible to pretend. 'He's just collected Harriet and they've gone off to the movies. He'll have her back here by six. She still thinks her Dad is working on an experiment, but the test trials mean he has to sleep in the office. I had to tell Maria, the housekeeper, that there were problems, as it's obvious to her that he's left me. We can't go on like this for much longer. It's so awful that I can't believe it's actually happening.'

'I always thought Paul was as reliable as they come. Scarcely the type to walk out on you and Harriet.'

'I drove him to it. '

'Come on, I find that hard to believe.'

'No mention of it this evening, please. Not in front of Harriet. Or Jenni.'

'No, of course not. So you'll come then?'

She hesitated. What was she doing, accepting a dinner invitation to Jack's to get to know his girlfriend while her marriage was in smithereens? Some days as she went through the motions, trying to hold herself together, she found it surreal, as though her broken marriage was suspended under a layer of frozen ice. She was afraid that she'd slip through a hole in the ice and never find her way back to the surface again. Why wasn't she doing something more constructive to fix the deadlock between her and Paul? But that seemed to be an impossible mountain to climb. 'Maybe it's not a good idea, Jack . . .'

'Look, it'll do you good to get out of the house for a couple of hours – and Jenni *can* cook.'

Jack sounded like a big kid, dying to impress. Growing up, it had always been her he'd turn to when he wanted to show off. His collection of chestnuts, gleaned from the trees in Tamarisk, his new skateboarding techniques as he whizzed down a pathway to the woods, his first time to swim underwater the full length of the pool. Their father had never been there in any real sense of the word.

Neither, for that matter, had their mother.

'Okay. You can pick us up at six thirty,' she said.

'Great, see you then.'

Serena put down the phone. She was just about to speed dial Kim, when the phone rang again.

Kim's first thought on waking that Sunday had been one of fervent gratitude. Thank God she hadn't slept with Paul. Thank God they'd both had the sense to step back from the brink. Was she really so dejected with her life that she'd considered the ultimate betrayal? Sleeping with her friend's husband, coming on to him when he was obviously hurting? Or was she just so desperate for sex that her principles had temporarily gone out the window? Thankfully she'd gone to bed alone, yet she waited until she had showered and dressed, had her breakfast and a fortifying coffee before she phoned Serena.

'Hi, Serena, hope I'm not disturbing you.'

'Kim! I was just about to phone you. You saw Paul at the party last night? You talked to him?' Serena's voice had an edge of hysteria.

Nothing happened, nothing happened, nothing happened, Kim reminded herself. 'Yeah, Paul was there.'

'And? Come on, Kim, was he with anyone? Tell me please. I'd rather know the worst.'

'Relax, he was with a couple of guys from work. We had a chat and left in a taxi. He insisted on seeing me home.'

'Did he?'

'Serena? You still there?'

'Just about.'

'Look, Paul still loves you. He seemed as lonely as I was, going home to his empty apartment. So he's not out celebrating his freedom or anything like that. Or looking for other women.'

'What do you mean, as lonely as you?'

Kim laughed hollowly. 'You probably don't

realise this, but sometimes it's a real drag to be going home time and time again to an empty house. I guess we were like two ships passing in the night. Both of us going home alone.'

'Could be something I might have to get used to. Was there anything in what Paul said that would give me some hope?'

Kim didn't know what to say. 'He might need more time to come around,' she replied eventually.

'More time? What made you think that?'

'Whatever happened between you guys, he still seems angry.'

'Angry. That's putting it mildly.'

'Would you like me to drop down to you this evening?' Kim offered. 'I could be there in just over an hour and we could watch some comedy movies, as far from a love story or romantic weepie as you can get. I'll even bring some chocolate and vino. Better than sitting home worrying and brooding.'

'Thanks, but I'm sure you've more exciting things to do on a Sunday evening besides keep me company. Anyway, I've been invited to Jack's, so that I can get to know Jenni better. Jack is concerned that we didn't hit it off. Can you believe that? I hope he's not asking for trouble because the night Amy had us over for dinner just after they were married, it was a disaster.'

'Was it? You never told me that.'

There was a short silence. 'Yes, well, Amy wasn't a great cook, so it'll be interesting to see what Jenni's like.'

'Whatever she serves up, she certainly seems to have her hooks into him,' Kim said evenly, sensing there was more to the story but Serena wasn't telling her. Family loyalty again.

'I still think Jack is just with her on the rebound.'

'They looked very cosy to me the other day.'

'Course they did. He was just about to jump on her. But it's just sex. I can't think of any other reason why he's so taken with her. And Jenni must have realised that she was on to a good thing straight way. Why else would she have followed him home? On the strength of knowing him a week? Although he scarcely knew Amy a wet week when she dragged him up the aisle.'

'Dragged him? So Paul was right?'

'Why? What did he say?'

'He told me that Amy was already pregnant when she married Jack . . . I guess I wasn't supposed to know.'

'Oh, Kim, I was sworn to secrecy. Mum didn't even know.'

'It does explain the hurried wedding, the media being told they were so much in love that they didn't see the point in waiting. And even, I suppose, why Jack married her in the first place . . . I often wondered what the great attraction was, not that I suppose any of this matters now,' Kim sighed.

After the call, Kim felt hollow. She was sorry she'd had to listen to talk of Jenni and Jack in the same sentence and it didn't help to know that they'd invited Serena to dinner as though they were a proper couple. But she would be forever grateful that she hadn't slept with Paul. He was a sexy guy, and but for the fact that she was Serena's friend, anything could have happened between them. There had been any number of women there last night who might have lured him between the sheets, given his vulnerable mood. She hoped for both their sakes that Serena and he would make up their differences before things got worse.

And she was staying in herself tonight, and opening that bottle of Spanish red she'd been keeping for a special occasion. If anyone deserved it, she did.

CHAPTER 34

Charlotte was wearing a check shirt and Levi jeans when she strolled out of the house on Sunday evening to enjoy some fresh air. Her target was a wooden bench in a small clearing at the back of the Tranquil Garden, set against the west-facing boundary wall. You reached it via a small track that veered off the pathways meandering around the main garden and, although slightly concealed, you still had a pleasant view of flowering hydrangea, spears of lavender and the water feature, as well as the western sky on the horizon.

She was almost adjacent to the bench when she realised it was already occupied. She only had to see the long, outstretched legs to guess who it was, before she saw the granite face, eyes closed, as his head tilted back and rested against the boundary wall. She stopped in her tracks. Then she saw the plugs in his ears and tell-tale wire that snaked down to his waist. He was hooked up to his iPod and lost to the world. But in true bodyguard fashion, not so lost that he didn't sense her presence. Before she had a chance to tip-toe back the way she'd come, his eyes flew open, blue as a deep summer's sky and, in that first, defenceless moment, they were full of vulnerable and genuine warmth. He sat up straight and pulled the plugs from his ears. She wondered what he'd been listening to.

'Hi.'

'Hi,' she said, deciding in that split second to continue on walking as though she had merely passed this way by chance. Silly, really, when it was obvious that the bench had been her target.

'I'm sitting in your seat,' he said, sizing up the situation immediately.

'Not at all,' she recovered herself enough to sound crisp. 'It's scarcely my personal property.' Even though in a sense it was, for everything around here was her property, albeit held in trust for Jack and Serena. 'I'm sorry if I've disturbed you.'

'There's plenty of room for two,' he said, sliding along the bench as if to prove this. 'I'm just finished listening to some music so you haven't disturbed me.' He looked at her with a slight challenge in his eyes as though daring her to accept his invitation.

She wavered fractionally. She had a sudden vision of Jack and Jenni holding hands and jumping into the swimming pool together with a joyful abandon that was enviable, as well as utterly contagious, and suddenly she wanted some of that for herself and it prompted her enough to smile back at him and sit down.

'What were you listening to?' she hazarded. It was a bit nosy after all, finding out what was on his iPod. Serena had had to answer that question last year for a magazine article, she recalled, and she'd had to make most of it up as she never had much time to listen to music.

'Pink Floyd,' he said. 'Reminders of my misspent youth.'

He didn't look like someone who could have had a misspent youth. His level-headed expression spoke of someone who had always kept his act together. She wondered what he would say if she told him that she'd had, in many respects, a misspent life. Instead she fell silent.

'Nice spot, isn't it?' he said.

'Yes, it is,' she said, not sure if he meant that particular location or Tamarisk in general.

'This is my third time here,' he said conversationally. 'I discovered it this year. The perfect place to relax and recharge the batteries.'

'It certainly is,' she said. 'It takes you away from all the daily stresses and strains.'

'During my career, I've been in many a hotel room and they're almost all the same, bland, soulless, even down to the furnishings but here . . .' he hesitated. 'I dunno, it's different. More homely and relaxed. The facilities are top class yet still carry a personal touch which is a difficult balance to strike. It seems miles removed from anything resembling a cosmopolitan jungle, yet Dublin is so close. About as perfect a haven as you can get.'

She filed his words away and made a mental note to tell Serena. She tried to place his accent but it was impossible. A hint of New York overlaid with London, with lots of Irish brogue thrown in. 'Sometimes you can get jaded with travel,' she said, steering the conversation away from Tamarisk as she felt a bit underhand about discussing the merits of it when he didn't know who she was. She should have told him straight away. Now the moment was gone, for it would sound as though she was boasting if she admitted her identity.

'Tell me about it! It can be exhausting flying to different cities in as many days. It's okay if you want to go shopping, then a night or two in New York and Boston goes down very well, particularly with the female members of the crew.'

'Yes, I can imagine your job is very demanding. All that travel and responsibility. Filling in time in strange cities. Then you have to be very fit. If anything goes wrong, you must carry the ultimate can.'

He gave her a long, appreciative look, and he seemed surprised that she was au fait with the finer demands of his job. 'Yes, I would,' he nodded his head. 'And things do go wrong, but thankfully not very often.'

'I suppose that nowadays, with communication so instant and technology almost having a mind of its own, security matters are easier in some ways, yet more difficult in others.'

'We always have to be ahead of ourselves and

ready to respond. Technology has made the job easier and a lot safer, but, yes, more difficult in other ways.'

'Do you have much trouble with the fans?'

He looked at her, puzzled. 'Sorry, I don't understand?'

'The fans, at a gig, probably trying to get on stage?'

'What fans?'

'Fans, as in supporters, at a concert, gig, event?'

There was genuine confusion on his face. 'Sorry, what has that got to do with my job?'

Charlotte's brain raced. She went back over their conversation right from the beginning, in case she had missed something. 'Claudia, the 02?'

'Who's Claudia?'

Who's Claudia? Her mind furiously backtracked. Somewhere she'd goofed, and quite spectacularly.

'Oh, never mind. I've obviously confused you with someone else. I think we should just forget all about our conversation and start at the beginning.'

He grinned disarmingly. 'Only after you tell me what you thought I did for a living.'

'I can't. I feel far too embarrassed.'

He was very kind. He could have played it out, made more of her discomfort, perhaps taunted her a little until she came clean. Instead, he held out his hand and said, 'Hi, my name is Laurence and I'm an airline pilot. Commercial, mainly long haul.'

She stared at him, aghast, as this information filtered through her brain, and everything she'd thought about this man turned upside down. Laurence. Not Doug, or Clint, or Hal, as she'd half expected.

Laurence. A lovely name. It held the promise of good, intelligent conversation, of books and music, of solid reliability and genuine friendship. It spoke of uncompromising attention to detail. Passengers would feel safe in his hands.

An airline pilot? She felt laughter tremble inside her as she thought back to their conversation. She took his proffered hand and shook it. He had a warm, firm handshake. She mentally discarded her picture of him standing guard in front of a crash barrier at a gig, earpiece and walkie talkie, vigilant eyes keenly scrutinising the crowds. Instead she saw him in a pilot's uniform, marching through the arrivals hall of an exotic airport, along with his cabin staff, having safely landed his 747 or whatever.

God.

'And you?' his eyebrows rose.

'Me? Nothing exciting, I'm afraid. I'm Charlotte and I've kind of retired.'

He looked at her as though he was waiting for her to enlarge further, but she simply shrugged and said, 'Long story.'

They talked a little about the weather and the need to make the most of the fine summer evenings, then to her disappointment, he checked his watch and told her that although he'd love to hear more, he'd already delayed long enough and he had to be somewhere else in about ten minutes' time. 'A dinner reservation,' he explained, 'and I'd rather not be late.'

She watched his tall, lean figure striding off in the direction of the hotel and wondered who was waiting for him. But the answer to that came as no surprise, when a short while later, curiosity brought her around by the side of the hotel and caused her to glance in through the windows of the restaurant. Thankfully he didn't see her, as he had his back to her. He was sitting at a table for two with his blonde girlfriend, who was laughing at something he'd just said. He had obviously brought her to Tamarisk for the weekend to enjoy the delights with him. He'd probably sat in the Tranquil Garden to pass the time while she was indulged and pampered in the Spa. She wondered what her name was. She wondered if he'd reserved one of the suites, and knew that a quick chat with the girls on Reception would tell her everything she wanted to know, but she wasn't about to go there.

She should be laughing at herself, Charlotte thought crossly, strolling back along the path. For some of the flirtatious notions she'd had about this man – Laurence – were so ridiculous they were simply hilarious. And she should have learned her lesson after all these years.

Passion wasn't for her, apart from the fervour she'd lavished on Tamarisk when she'd found out her marriage was empty of hot-blooded excitement.

And she'd made her choice a long time ago. She stopped for a moment, staring out across the shadowed lawn, remembering . . .

Another party. Another celebration. Another gathering on the south lawn at Tamarisk.

This time pink and blue balloons are drifting from the trees. They run into each other on the terrace and instead of joining the family out on the lawn, they stall for a bit.

'You seem to be happy,' he says.

'I am. Mostly.' She bites her lip. He's caught her off-guard. She's no time to put up a front and there is a wealth of meaning in her words.

'Mostly?' He gives her a long, thoughtful glance.

'Well Tamarisk keeps me busy,' she says. 'It doesn't give me much time to think . . .' *of what might have been*, she almost adds. It's as though she says it aloud, for their eyes connect in a long moment of understanding.

He says, his voice unexpectedly intimate, 'Tell me you felt something and I wasn't just imagining it.'

What was always unspoken between them suddenly blooms into life. 'You felt it too?' she murmurs.

'Of course. From the first time I saw you. Out there, on the lawn.'

Another silence. Even though she's a little older and wiser her pulse skitters and she puts her hand to her sleek, bobbed hair and smoothes the skirt of her cream chiffon dress with restless hands. She wants this moment to go on for ever.

She wants him to always look at her with those loving eyes.

'Sometimes . . .' she looks at him from under her lashes, 'Sometimes I wonder . . .' her courage falters . . . *what it would have been like with you.*

'I wondered too, what it would have been like between us.' Again, he seems to know what she's afraid to utter. 'It's not too late for us to be together,' he says.

He takes her hand and she allows herself this moment of bliss. 'It was always too late for us. With the twins there was never an option.'

'The twins are wonderful. I'd never separate you from them.'

'It wouldn't be fair on them. Their lives are here, in Tamarisk, with both their parents. I love them, and far more than I thought I could ever love anyone.'

'Even me?' He's joking. Kind of. She sees it in his eyes.

'That's different.'

'But not different enough for you to leave here.'

'No. I can't mess up the twins, or divide their loyalties. Or ruin Jamie's life. He loves Tamarisk and he loves the twins in his own way.'

'It's a funny kind of loving that has its head stuck in a glass a lot of the time. I think he's already messed up his life.'

'It's nothing I can't handle. And maybe I'm partly to blame.'

'Why?'

'He senses I don't feel the same about him as when we were first married.'

'There. You see? It should be us, together.'

'It can't be. Go back to your girlfriend. Be happy and don't look back.'

'That's poor consolation.'

'That's the way it has to be. I'll be happy here with the twins, and,' she smiles and gently extricates her hand from his, feeling bereft, 'I guess Tamarisk will be my consolation.'

'Hush.' He puts a warning finger to his lips, silencing her. 'I thought I heard someone.'

Suddenly alarmed, she looks around and listens attentively. After a moment she says, 'Relax. There's no one there. Everyone's out on the lawn. Come on, it's almost time to open the champagne and then we'll gather the children and light the candles.'

They stroll across the lawn towards the tables under the trees. On the big square birthday cake there are ten pink and ten blue candles. One for every year.

CHAPTER 35

'**M**ore wine?' Jenni lifted the bottle out of the cooler and angled it towards Serena's glass. It was, Serena noted, an expensive white from Jack's cellar, one that he had imported from Languedoc in France. She wondered if Jack had chosen the wine or allowed Jenni to run amok in his cellar and select whatever took her fancy. In either case Jenni probably hadn't a clue how much the bottle of wine was worth, considering the way she was sloshing it into Serena's glass. She ignored the need to guzzle it as quickly as possible and soothe the ball of tension that was cramping her stomach.

There had been a terrible scene when Paul had returned with Harriet earlier that evening. Harriet had refused to let go of him, lying on the ground and clutching his ankles, crying for her daddy to stay at home and not go off to his horrible job. Eventually Serena had calmed her down with the promise of a great time in Jack's house and a chance to play his Wii, but not before Paul's accusatory eyes had blamed her for the debacle. She'd felt like calling Jack and telling him to forget the meal, only Harriet would have had another tantrum, and Serena felt totally shaken by it all.

Jenni looked great. She wore a soft, white blouse over a blue T-shirt, blue cotton trousers and flip flops. Primark or Top Shop, Serena guessed. Her tousled dark hair was pinned back with decorative hair slides in a haphazard way that made it seem all the more sexily attractive. A thin silver chain glittered around her neck. It was expensive and at odds with her high-street look and Serena fleetingly wondered if Jack had bought it for her. She wore very little makeup and she looked sparkly clean and fresh, casually sexy, and about eighteen years of age. She already knew her way around Jack's kitchen, and added a dash of seasoning and a twist of herbs to an aromatic chicken casserole dish like a professional, proffering a spoonful for Jack to taste and laughing at his look of approval. She had no problem with Serena sitting on a high stool at the island worktop and watching while she prepared a dish of fluffy basmati rice and sliced crusty, wholegrain bread. But none of this endeared her to Serena any further. Compared with Jenni, she was decidedly overdressed in her pencil slim skirt, waterfall silk blouse and glittery heels. And as she watched her brother, and his happy-go-lucky demeanour, she felt more and more convinced that Jack had simply been swept off his feet by lust for someone who was the very antithesis of Amy.

'Help yourself to wine, Serena, don't wait for

me to pour it,' Jenni chatted. 'Is Harriet allowed some lemonade?' she asked in a quieter voice, glancing at Harriet who was engrossed in showing off her new karate moves to Jack on the rug in front of the sofa.

'Yes, I'll let her have a glass.' Serena said. Anything to keep Harriet happy.

'Hey, Jenni, watch this,' Jack called, play-fighting with Harriet. He tumbled across the rug with his niece, then to Serena's surprise he lunged at Jenni so that the three of them were rolling across the floor, giggling and laughing together. In between their tumbles, when Harriet was looking the other way, Jack grabbed Jenni around the waist and kissed her soundly on the mouth. All they needed was a big friendly dog bounding between them and pots of paint or toilet rolls to complete the picture of the perfect TV commercial family.

A mixture of envy and sadness swept across Serena. When was the last time that she and Paul had played like that with Harriet? She'd often seen Paul on his hands and knees with Harriet, but rarely, if ever, had it been the three of them in a messy tumble. She drank more wine, feeling ridiculously weepy and distinctly out of it all.

Dinner was a relaxed affair at the kitchen table. In recent days, Serena's appetite had all but vanished but she enjoyed the delicious chicken casserole. Even Harriet cleared her plate.

'What's the verdict?' Jack asked her, smiling triumphantly. 'Do you think Jenni passed the culinary test?' He slid his arm around Jenni's waist and hugged her to him. Infatuated wasn't the word, Serena decided. It was more like besotted, beguiled and bewitched. Jenni responded by resting her head momentarily in the hollow of his neck. Serena had no option but to smile through the lump of envy and exasperation that stuck in her throat.

'Yes, it's lovely,' she said. 'I don't know where you learned to cook, Jenni, but it's quite delicious. And don't mind Jack. It wasn't a test,' she felt compelled to say as if to dispel the image that she'd come here like a diligent headmistress to give Jenni marks out of ten.

Jenni gave her a composed smile. Jack's eyes gleamed with I-told-you-so satisfaction.

Over an equally delicious dessert of summer fruit flan Harriet surprised everyone by announcing that she thought Jenni's hair slides were awesome. Harriet, who had shrugged ribbons and hair slides and anything pink or girly from the age of two. And where had she learned the term 'awesome'?

'Do you really like them, darling?' Serena asked, managing to keep the surprise out of her voice.

'Yes, and I like Jenni,' Harriet said with childish candour.

'Here.' Jenni pulled a slide from her hair and, lifting a tendril of Harriet's hair, she secured it at an angle. Harriet sat perfectly still, beaming with delight while this took place, a Harriet who normally only let Serena go near her dark, wavy hair under protest.

Harriet reverently patted the slide, as if reassuring herself that it was in place. 'Thank you. I like that.'

'Aren't you having some wine, Jenni?' Serena asked, when she eventually shook off some of her low spirits and noticed that Jenni seemed to be sticking to water.

Jenni held her gaze unwaveringly. 'I'm fine for now. I'll have a drink with Jack later.' She smiled softly at Jack as if to confirm that they would be enjoying a cosy tête-à-tête over a bottle of wine after the guests were safely dispatched home.

'Good,' Jack smiled back at her. Turning to Serena he went on, 'Jenni told me she was at such a blast of a party before she left Nice that she's hardly been able to look at wine since.'

Something sparked at the back of Serena's mind but it was far too unthinkable to contemplate. Even for a millisecond.

Then Harriet chirped up. 'Is your house in Nice, Jenni? Where are your mum and dad? Are they in Nice?'

Serena listened closely, her interest aroused by the sad flicker that slid across Jenni's face before she resumed her normal, carefree expression.

'No, my mum lives in London but my father is dead.'

'That's sad,' Harriet said. 'It's like Amy. Amy's

dead too and Jack was sad for a while. Can we be friends?'

'If you'd like to be.'

'Hey, awesome!'

It wasn't only Jack, it was also Harriet who was now besotted, Serena fretted sourly. After the meal, Jack hooked up the Wii and proceeded to play a boisterous game of bowling with Jenni and Harriet.

'We were practising this last night,' Jack said, 'so I hope that Jenni learned something. Although she spent too much time laughing to take in my advice. Even though the loser had to pay a forfeit. Lots of forfeits.' He shot her a meaningful glance.

Jenni frowned and darted a look at Harriet. 'Jack!'

Serena's mind was filled with a picture of her brother and his girlfriend having sexy fun with a silly game and a bottle of wine, turning the kitchen of his designer house into a playground. Paul had suggested they get a Wii the previous Christmas but she had refused. She tried to recall exactly why she'd been against the idea, but it escaped her for now.

'Mummy, you should play too,' Harriet beseeched.

'Yes, come on, Serena,' Jack said.

'No, you go ahead, I'll sit this out,' she said, unwilling to be drawn into the general uproar. She sat on the sofa, sipping yet another glass of Jack's good wine, and as she watched the horseplay, she wondered why she had always been the focused and organised one, whereas Jack was full of devil-may-care, often responding heedlessly to life. She couldn't fathom it right now, not when the tension in her stomach seemed to be tightening even further. And not when Harriet was screaming with delight as she scored the highest points, assisted no doubt by Jack and Jenni deliberately making a botch of their own games.

She didn't have to worry about being silent as Jack drove them home. The sun was setting and the sky was stained with puffy marmalade clouds. From the back seat, Harriet chatted non-stop as they cruised through the village and swept up the incline to Maple Hill. She *loved* Jenni. When she grew up she was going to have hair like hers. Jenni was going to bring her to the movies soon, and they were going to go swimming together in Tamarisk. Was Jack going to marry her? Like he had Amy? She was awful sorry that Amy had died, but at least Jack now had Jenni. She couldn't wait to go to the movies and McDonald's in Dundrum with her.

'You can't expect Jenni to bring you up to Dundrum,' Serena said.

'But, Mum, she's been there already with Jack so she knows where it is,' Harriet piped up.

'McDonald's?' Serena said quietly to Jack.

He threw her a grin. 'Yeah, so?'

Dusk had settled a smoky glow around the countryside, and pin pricks of light could be seen dotted about on the lower slopes of the adjacent hills when Jack pulled up in front of Maple Hill.

'Thanks, Jack,' she said.

'I'll bring Harriet in,' he said, opening the back door of the car and unbuckling her seatbelt.

Serena opened the hall door, switched off the alarm and turned on the porch light so that a column of brightness sprang out. Harriet scampered out of Jack's arms and ran into her playroom. 'I'll see you in the morning,' Serena said, unwilling to invite him in. She'd had just about enough of Jack's smug, self-satisfied delight.

Jack kissed her cheek. 'See you.'

'Don't forget we're meeting Brian at ten o'clock to go over the finances,' she said.

Jack rolled his eyes like a teenager being reminded of his school homework by a stern parent. 'Don't worry, I'll be there.'

'Enjoy the rest of your evening,' Serena said.

Jack ruffled the top of her head 'You take care, won't you? Will you be talking to Paul later?'

'I doubt it.'

'I hate to see you guys like this.'

'Me too,' Serena gave him a sad smile.

He went across to his car. There was the sound of his powerful engine starting up and then his headlights swept across the front garden, out onto the lane until they were swallowed up by the encroaching dusk and all was quiet again. Before her, the countryside stretched out, quietly watchful as it settled for the night. Behind her, the house, empty without Paul, waited like a cavern and Serena felt like screaming. Kim's words came back to her, about how much of a drag it was to be going home alone. She wondered how Paul was coping with his empty apartment, or if he was, indeed, home alone, or out somewhere in the palpating sexual energy of a city-centre nightclub.

She closed the door and rested her head against it for a long moment, too drained to even cry.

CHAPTER 36

Jack felt a stab of regret as he gunned the BMW down the laneway away from Maple Hill. At the T-junction, he halted briefly before he took the turn for Glendoran village and home. He switched on some music, keeping the volume low. There was a lingering ribbon of scarlet on the western horizon, his car cruising comfortably along, the window open to a thin stream of air, while the sound of Alicia Keys wafted around. Best of all, Jenni was waiting at home.

It could have been perfect, except for the image of his sister standing alone in the light of the porch. There was no doubt that Serena was a workaholic. She'd always had a focused energy which, luckily for him, she'd been more than happy to pour into the running of Tamarisk, coming up with sparkling innovations, and making his life a lot easier than it might have been. Knowing this, he felt a little ashamed that he hadn't always shown his appreciation. And when he'd needed her help last year, with Amy and all that tragedy, she'd come up trumps.

He couldn't imagine what had caused Paul to

walk out on her and darling Harriet, anymore than Serena knew the deep, dark truth of what had really happened between himself and Amy. Had Paul been unfaithful? He didn't seem the type. Whatever had happened, his classy, hard-working sister didn't deserve to be in this situation. He had a good mind to lock the pair of them up in the Presidential Suite at Tamarisk and throw away the key until they came to their senses.

Jack slowed down as he passed the speed limit sign on the outskirts of Glendoran and as he cruised by the end of the road where Kim had grown up, he wondered why such a kind, beautiful woman was still unattached. He'd joked with her on and off about marriage, but, naturally enough, neither of them had meant it as they were practically brother and sister. He hoped she'd find someone just as caring as she was and not a silly rascal like him.

He passed by shops and restaurants decorated with hanging baskets and window boxes, the small supermarket, and the prettily landscaped roundabout in the centre of the crossroads. He drove past the laneway that led to the entrance to Tamarisk, and along the narrow country road until he reached his own home. He forgot about Serena and her problems and enjoyed the rush of happiness that washed over him at the thought of Jenni waiting for him. They would have a glass of wine as they chatted about the evening and then he would take her to bed. He wondered, briefly, what he had done to deserve such an unexpected second chance.

He sprang out of the car, locked it, and hurried in through the porch and down the hallway, thankful to see Jenni in the kitchen, sitting on the sofa, with a lamp softly burning and scented candles flickering warmly. He tossed his keys down on the table. 'Come here to me, you fantastic, sexy lady. I've been dying to kiss you properly all night.'

She got up from the sofa and came into his arms, her perfume smelling of fresh flowers, and he kissed her warm mouth, a long, deep kiss that neither of them wanted to end. He held her tightly, welding the soft contours of her body to his, and he forgot everything else as a flame of desire shot through him, almost stunning him in its intensity. They stood, wrapped together for long moments in the quiet, semi-darkness of the kitchen.

'Jenni?' he breathed, his hands pressing her hips into his.

'Yes,' she sighed. Her fingers were already on the buckle of his jeans but he stalled them. Instead, he brought her back to the sofa and pulled her onto his lap. He peeled back her white blouse, lifted her T-shirt over her head and flung it aside. Then he unhooked her bra and buried his face in her breasts, nuzzling and licking and teasing her ripe nipples with his teeth and tongue until she arched her back and cried out.

'Please, Jack.'

He drew back and smiled at her. 'Please what?'

'You know . . .' she said. 'I want you. Now.'

'Now? Here?' he said, finding it hard to inject his voice with mock horror when he felt as though he was going to burst with need himself.

'Shit, yes, now, anywhere, I don't care . . .' She slid off his lap and opened the button at the waistband of her trousers, dragging them off along with her panties. He eased his jeans down over his straining erection. Jenni smiled at him, a big, sultry, girl-woman smile, and climbed onto the sofa, lowering her tight moistness down the length of his silky hard erection and rocking to and fro until his head was swimming and he reached the point of no return. Grabbing her buttocks, he held her fast against him and his breath stalled while he tipped over into a powerful climax.

'God,' he whispered against her cheek when he had recovered his breath, 'what just happened?'

'We happened. You and me,' she whispered back, wrapping her arms around his neck and nuzzling into him.

Later, they made love one more time, Jenni surprising him with her frenzied passion as she writhed and twisted around him, scratching his shoulders with her nails, sliding her body against his as though she couldn't get close enough to him. He didn't recall falling asleep, but obviously he had, for when he woke he was lying on his back with the duvet up to his waist. The bedroom was dark, only the grey light from the uncurtained window telling him that shortly it would be dawn.

The previous evening came back to him in a rush of warm, remembered pleasure. He stretched luxuriously and turned around. Beside him, Jenni was sitting up in the bed, her knees drawn up to her chin, her arms wrapped around them, her dressing gown over her shoulders.

'Good morning, you beautiful lady.' She didn't reply immediately and there was something in the quality of her stillness that alerted him and made him sit up. 'Jenni?'

At last, she looked at him. But her smile, forced and nervous, stopped his hand from reaching out towards her.

'What's up?'

Jenni looked away, avoiding his eyes. 'I've just been sick, it's nothing really.'

'Nothing?' he frowned. 'But the lovely food—' He sat up straighter and clicked on the lamp. Her face was pale and sweaty. The door to the en suite was slightly ajar.

She continued to stare into space and there was a tense silence that sent a flutter of panic through him. Was she ill? Had it all been too good to be true?

'It wasn't the food,' she said.

'Then what?'

'I wasn't going to tell you just yet,' she said in a low murmur, 'I wanted to wait and see how things were between us . . . how we got on . . .' her voice trailed away. In spite of her soft, uncertain tone, there was something determined in the upright way she sat, something indomitable in her eyes when she at last turned her gaze to his.

'Tell me what?' The question was superfluous for he knew, already, and his racing brain tried to get a grip on the full meaning of what she was about to say, as once more his life turned on its axis.

'I'm expecting our baby, Jack.'

For a moment Jack felt blank. 'I don't know what to say,' he admitted.

'You don't have to say anything,' she said. 'You don't have to do anything just yet. I know it's a shock. I understand if you're dazed. I've had time to get used to it.'

'How long have you known?'

'Three weeks. I'm almost two months gone. I think it must have happened that first night . . . Remember?'

'Two months . . . God . . . Yes, I remember.' The condom had slipped one of the times they'd made love during that night. But caught in the first, exciting flush of passion they'd made light of it, neither of them wanting to think for a minute that anything could come of it or spoil the headiness of that night. He took her hand and held it. 'Is that the reason why you came? Would you have followed me home otherwise?'

'Honestly? I don't know.' She took her hand away.

'How do you feel about it?' he asked.

'Nervous, excited, happy . . . Jack?'

'Yes?'

'This is not the same as Amy. I want you to be very sure of that.'

'Of course it's not the same. How could it be? Jenni. God. This is more than I can take in . . .' he didn't know what to say, terrified of uttering the wrong thing or upsetting her in any way. He felt the need to reorient his life and come to grips with this whole new trajectory. Right now, though, Jenni needed his attention. She'd been sick. He recalled something about tea and toast being good for that. 'Would you like some tea?' he asked, glad to focus on the ordinary.

'Yes, please.'

'Stay there. I'll make us some tea and toast and bring it up.' He took his pillow and stuck it behind her, and when he had tucked the duvet around her, as though she was a child like Harriet, he left the room and padded downstairs.

When he looked around the kitchen it seemed different; a stranger's kitchen. He knew the reason for this was because he was the stranger in his own life. A stranger because he'd never really known what he'd wanted – Tamarisk had always just been there, encapsulating everything and swallowing them all up. Serena had always been so sure of herself and where she fitted in. There was no doubt that their forceful and dynamic mother had been her role model. He'd known from early on that he wasn't as confident as Serena so he hadn't even tried to compete. Following in his sister's wake, he'd never had her self-assurance, or a sense of his own identity. Their father had been a shadowy figure on the edge of their lives, more of an onlooker who had decided early on to take a back seat. Growing up, Jack had sometimes felt that the Devlin family could easily be divided into two; on the one hand, the strong, focused women, blazing a trail, foiled on the other side by the easy-going men, himself and Jamie Devlin. Occasionally, he'd wondered about his father's fondness for alcohol. Surely he'd wanted for nothing?

Now, for him, fatherhood was waiting in the wings. He'd thought he'd been about to embrace it before, but that time and those circumstances had been so very different as to bear no resemblance to this present reality.

'I'm pregnant, Jack,' Amy had said in her little-girl voice, twisting her fingers as her blue eyes had pinned his. On hearing those words, he'd felt as though a door was slamming shut. Her timing had been perfect because he'd been about to tell her that it was over between them.

The sky in the east was brightening and while the kettle was coming to the boil he stepped outside to the fragrant, new morning. He looked across at the brow of the age-old hills, covered in rocky scree and heather, and in the far distance, the folds of wooded valleys, pine forests and the rising peaks. Soon they would be touched with morning sunshine. He realised that he was looking at valleys and peaks that had been there for thousands of years, and that during those years countless people had come and moved through the stage of life before passing on to make way for another generation. He had a strong sense of fate playing out and of this being his moment of awareness of himself, as he made his contribution to the grand cycle of life. Peace and certainty wrapped around him.

His father had passed on, but like seasons coming around again, he was going to be a father. Where was it written that he would automatically follow in the laid-back footprints of Jamie Devlin? Where, for that matter, did it say that he had to imitate the gritty determination of Charlotte and Serena? Or that he was falling short if he couldn't? There was nothing to stop him from making his own footprints.

All he needed was a little more self-belief.

He went back into the kitchen and organised tea and popped bread in the toaster. He took butter out of the fridge. Jenni loved the taste of creamy Irish butter on her toast.

Jenni.

'I'm expecting our baby, Jack.'

This time he felt as though a door was opening.

CHAPTER 37

Brian passed around hard copies of several Excel spreadsheets. 'Following last week's initial discussion, I've gone through these again and the bottom line is that you have to take some form of remedial action as soon as possible.'

Serena was filled with a slow-burning anger. In the past two weeks, they'd already had a couple of briefing sessions with Brian. Now, this morning, when effective decisions had to be made to safeguard the future success of Tamarisk, Jack, far from being back in action, seemed to be a million miles away. His eyes glanced over the rows of figures and his expression never wavered. He might as well have been checking out the television guide, Serena fumed. If anyone, she was the one who should have been excused from making a contribution. Surely it was Jack's turn to carry her for a while? She was the one with a broken marriage to sort out, for God's sake. What was she doing here anyway, trying to talk figures with a disinterested Jack when Paul was somewhere out there? And would she ever get rid of this awful pain in her chest?

'You mean we're in deep shit,' she said caustically. 'Jack, what do you think?' She faced him directly as they sat around the antique table in his office. 'Have you any views on how we can turn this around by the end of the next quarter? Or failing that, at least by the end of the year?'

'Is it that bad?' he asked.

'That bad?' Serena snapped. 'Have you been listening to anything this morning? Or during the last couple of weeks? These figures are bordering on disaster.'

'Hey, hang on to your hat, there's no need to fly off the handle,' Jack said, looking faintly perturbed.

'I'm quite entitled to fly off the handle,' Serena said, heedless of Brian staring circumspectly out the window. 'All the effort and work I've put into Tamarisk and this is where we are now? Looking at a plunging profit line? This isn't good enough. And it didn't just happen overnight, you know.' She glared at Jack, tempted to say that if, on his return from La Mimosa, he'd taken up the financial reins with half the enthusiasm he'd shown for the arrival of Jenni into his life, he might have effected some damage limitation. She must have got through to him, finally, because he gave her a long, considered look and began to nibble on his pen before asking Brian for his opinion.

Serena listened impatiently as Brian outlined one more time, for Jack's benefit, the changing business model of the entire hospitality industry.

'Corporate business has fallen through the floor.

People are more careful about parting with their cash on luxury items such as an exclusive weekend away,' Brian said. 'They're reducing the number of nights they stay. They're eating in the bar rather than the restaurant. It will be a long time before we're back to the free and easy spending of the noughties, if ever. And I know some of your clientele are virtually recession proof but you can't depend on them to rescue you.'

'So what do we do?' Jack said.

It was the kind of information that Jack should have had at his fingertips, Serena fumed.

'In a nutshell, you must cut back your cost base, renegotiate with your suppliers and introduce incentives to encourage visitors. Not so long ago, your unspoilt scenery, friendliness of the welcome and excellent hospitality was a major selling point. Now visitors demand excellent value for money, while still enjoying the benefit of top-class service.'

'I've already said I'm not prepared to compromise our luxury status,' Serena said.

'You might have no option,' Brian said.

'In other words we need to reposition Tamarisk into a more affordable bracket,' Jack said.

'Affordable?' Serena's heart sank. 'That smacks of bargain beds. It goes against our whole culture.'

Jack shrugged. 'Maybe we need to rethink that culture, effect a little rebranding.'

'Rebranding?' The word stuck in her throat. 'We have an award ceremony coming up on Friday night, in case you had forgotten. We're on the short list because of our exclusive Tamarisk tradition. I'm not going to sell us short.'

'I think we should forget about going for five-star status and concentrate on being the best possible four-star,' Jack said.

Something heavy settled in Serena's heart. Everything Jack was saying went totally against all they had worked for. Correction, all *she* had worked for. What had got into him? Why was he so prepared to give up without a fight? Effect a little rebranding? Forget about striving for better, for the covetable five-star classification, just like that?

'And maybe we should be on Twitter and Facebook,' Jack went on. 'Jenni wanted to become a fan of Tamarisk but she couldn't find us.'

'*Face*book?' Serena said scathingly. 'Don't be ridiculous. Anyway I hate all that cyber-acquaintance stuff.'

'You shouldn't underestimate the power of social networking,' Jack said, quite unperturbed.

'Brian, I think it's clear that Jack and I have a lot to discuss, before we come to any decisions,' she said, biting back her rage.

After Brian had left and they were alone in his office, Jack sat back, his arms folded in front of him and asked. 'What was all that about?'

'All what about?' she retorted. 'Where are you coming from? Are you trying to wreck everything we've built up in recent years?'

'I'm not trying to wreck anything at all,' he said

neutrally. 'I'm trying to apply some common sense to our situation.'

'Common sense? Jack, winning Haven of the Year would give us some good publicity, and push Tamarisk even further up the honours list. That would make the best of sense to me.'

'We can't afford to waste time chasing awards when we need to consolidate what we already have. Why do you feel the need anyway to compete with the likes of Ashford Castle or the Ritz-Carlton?'

'I wouldn't dream of competing with them. Tamarisk is in a league of its own.'

'Next it'll be a question of out-doing the Burj Al Arab and the Emirates Palace,' he muttered.

'Don't be facetious.'

'Look, I know I took my eye off the ball in the past couple of years. Maybe if I'd paid closer attention to our balance sheet, we wouldn't be in this situation now. It won't happen again. I've already told Brian that I want us to meet every week so that our costs can be fully scrutinised.'

'I don't want any cutbacks. How will that look in the media? Everyone will think we're in trouble and customers will stay away.'

'If we're careful with our marketing campaign, pitching Tamarisk favourably won't be an issue. If you don't feel up to the job we could enlist outside help.'

'What do you mean, feel up to the job?'

Jack shrugged. 'I know you're in a bad place

right now and your personal life is going through the wringer—'

'My personal life never has and never will interfere with the way I do my job. Get it?' Serena's face felt stiff with rage. 'How dare you be so condescending.'

'Oh, come on, sis, get off your high horse. You don't have to put up an act in front of me or pretend to be superwoman. I know you're hurting. I know your brains are scrambled right now. But for once in your life let down your guard. It's okay to be a messy human being now and again.'

'I must be hearing things,' Serena gabbled. 'I can't believe what you just said.'

'Sorry if I upset you, but I'm trying to help in a roundabout way. I've been thinking recently—'

'Don't tell me. I can imagine. Jenni has made you see everything differently. Why bother striving for excellence or awards? What's the point in working hard or having ambitions? Life should be full of fun. Let's have a quickie in the Presidential Suite. Forget about that meeting you were supposed to attend. And when you're finally collared by your wicked witch sister, don't bother paying attention.'

'Now you're being ridiculous.'

'About as ridiculous as you are, becoming so shagged-up with someone that you forget to come home, then when you manage to get home you can't keep your trousers on—'

'Shut the fuck up, Serena. Cut it out.'

Jack's white, set face sent a warning signal that she ignored as his uncharacteristic words fuelled her own temper. 'How dare you talk to me like that. I'm fed up walking on eggshells around you, picking up the slack and letting you away with murder. When I think of all the sacrifices I've made . . .' her voice broke and she was furious. She made an effort to control herself. 'I thought when you finally came home, you'd be back to normal. Instead, you've lost the run of yourself.'

'Serena, I really appreciate all your support, and the hard work you put into the hotel, I think you're extremely talented, but I never asked you to make any sacrifices on my behalf. You should be very clear about that. Secondly, you mean you thought I'd be back to the Jack you could boss around once more and have under your thumb.'

'What?'

'You never liked Amy, did you?' his eyes glittered as he suddenly changed tack. 'And you never liked her because I put my relationship with her before my job.' Serena sensed something different about him, something steadfast in the way he was looking at her, as though deep down he really didn't give a shit about what she thought. She wasn't used to that look from Jack and it unsettled her even more.

'I never liked Amy because she took advantage of you and she was the most helpless, insecure, clingy female to ever walk the earth. I never knew what you saw in her.'

'Maybe I thought I needed someone insecure

and clingy to make me feel strong. Believe it or not, she made me feel indispensible when I began to date her. As a matter of fact Amy never liked you either. You intimidated her with your perfectionist streak. She knew she could never measure up to the high standards both you and Charlotte expected of the wife of Jack Devlin. And I bet you don't like Jenni either.'

Her brother had a strangely triumphant gleam in his eyes that Serena recklessly ignored. 'How did you guess? How could I be a fan of someone who encourages you to forget your responsibilities and get stark naked at every opportunity?'

'Jenni has shown me that life can be good again, and that I don't need to depend on someone vulnerable to shore up my own self-respect. And yes, she's helped me look at my life in a whole new light. Believe it or not, I no longer feel as suffocated by Tamarisk as I used to. And from now on, I won't be under anyone's thumb or feel smothered by expectations that I can't or don't want to meet.'

'I can't believe you're talking about our heritage like that. She must have rightly screwed up your head, never mind your dick, this – this girl you picked up. What would she know about Tamarisk and our traditions? She's just a bar girl from nowhere.'

There was silence in the room. Even Serena was taken aback by the words that had tumbled from her mouth. Worse, though, was the derisory look

Jack gave her. His tone of voice was very cool when he said, 'Guess what, Serena, I could almost swear that you're jealous. Or else you're an even bigger fucked-up bitch than I thought.'

Serena wheeled around and succeeded in getting through the doorway, even though she couldn't see it properly through her mist of anger. Somehow, she found the strength to go up the staircase to her office. Then she locked the door behind her and collapsed on to the sofa. Jack's words reverberated around her head, and his look of contempt blazed in front of her eyes. But the biggest problem of all, she realised painfully, was that he had been perfectly right in everything he had said.

She *was* jealous of Jack and his new happiness.

And she *was* a big, fucked-up bitch.

CHAPTER 38

On Tuesday afternoon, just as she hurried out of House of Fraser in Dundrum, Kim bumped into Lucy, dressed to perfection in white jeans and an emerald top, clutching a fabulous Pauric Sweeney bag.

'Kim! What's this I've heard? Why didn't you tell me!' She pushed her long dark hair back from her face and glared anxiously at Kim.

'Tell you what?' Kim asked.

'Jack Devlin. It's all over town that he has a new girlfriend. *And* she's years younger than him. He's supposed to be besotted with her. How did she manage to slip under my radar? After all the high hopes I had . . . No wonder he didn't come to my party. What I'd like to know is how she managed to get her claws into him and snatch him from right under our noses. Especially yours, Kim,' she went on a little maliciously. 'You must be wondering where you went wrong. Especially with your advantage of inside information.'

Kim felt like laughing. Inside information, yeah, right. 'I don't know anything other than it's just a harmless flirtation.'

'You mean you hope that's all it is. Can I quote you on that?' Lucy asked, her eyes gleaming.

'No, you can't.'

'I can't believe another sexy ride has bitten the dust.' She turned to go, then at the last minute she turned back to Kim. 'Although I see you're already eyeing up the fresh talent. You don't waste any time.'

'What do you mean?'

'I saw you slinking off with Serena's ex after my party. Don't worry, I won't tell on you!'

Kim was relieved that she'd nothing to feel guilty about and no tell-tale blush on her face. 'Don't be ridiculous. Serena's my friend and Paul was just seeing me home. And he's not her ex-husband, by any stretch of the imagination.'

'Really? I'd say it's only a matter of time. You looked quite good together. I could have sworn you were ready to offer him the very best of your consolation skills?' Lucy paused, looking closely at Kim.

'No thanks,' Kim laughed. 'Besides, I've better things on my mind.'

'Like?'

'Like going to the opening of that new wine bar tonight. With Matthew O'Brien,' Kim said pointedly. He'd phoned her on Sunday evening and Kim had finally agreed to go out with him again. She'd been so shocked at her near escape with Paul that she'd decided a night of rampant sex in Matthew's apartment might take the edge off her need. Her vow of celibacy could take a hike for one night.

'I've an invite as well so I'll probably see you there,' Lucy said. 'I feel sorry for Serena, even though her loss is Dublin's gain. Wonder what she did to chuck Paul out of the marital bed. From what I heard, he felt he was left with no option.'

'Who told you that?'

'I bumped into one of his sisters at a party on Sunday night. Small world, isn't it? That's why I've decided to forget I saw you two looking so cosy. You know what they say about shooting the messenger and neither you nor I want to upset the Devlin apple cart, just in case Jack gets bored and comes out to play again. Mind you, if I had the chance of getting off on Paul, I wouldn't say no.'

Kim watched as Lucy finally weaved away into the crowd, having delivered her ridiculous parting shot. She, too, was obviously smarting that Jack was off the market, for now.

So Kim was sure she was having a mirage when she walked out to the underground car park just in time to see the back of Jack's car gliding by before it turned up one of the aisles and glided into a vacant slot halfway up the aisle. Her heart thumped as she went over to greet him, trying to look nonchalant, even though her fingers were almost crushed with her tense grip on her carrier bag. Then to her total shock, Jenni stepped out of the driver's seat and opened the rear door for Harriet. There was no sign of Jack.

Her first impulse was to run, but Harriet

413

scrambled out of the car and spotted Kim straight away. 'Kim! Guess where we're going?' Her excited shriek echoed around the car park. She danced up to Kim, wearing pink clips in her hair. Jenni went around to the boot, opened it, and lifted her bag out of it, hoisting it onto her shoulder looking as though she'd been driving Jack's car all her life. She turned around and smiled at Kim.

Kim felt sick. 'Hi Harriet, Jenni,' it was an effort to speak.

Harriet was almost tripping over herself in delight. 'We're going to the movies *and* McDonald's.'

Kim was on the point of asking Harriet if her mum knew she was here when she realised how ridiculous she'd sound. Of course Serena knew she was here, and Jack for that matter, as he had obviously entrusted the keys of his BMW to Jenni. She was really worming her way in, Kim thought savagely.

Jenni proffered her hand. She was wearing a delicate silver bracelet and a matching chain around her neck. 'Hi, Kim. I guess you know I'm Jenni,' she said, her smile not in the least self-conscious. 'We weren't properly introduced. I hope we didn't embarrass you too much that time in Tamarisk.' Her London accent, including the way she pronounced Tamarisk, was attractive. Everything about her was attractive.

'Not at all,' Kim managed to say.

'I could have killed Jack, he's far too bold,' Jenni went on, using his name with a familiarity and confidence that seared like a knife in Kim's heart.

'Don't worry about it,' Kim forced a laugh. She lowered her voice so that Harriet wouldn't overhear. 'I'm well used to Jack by now and his devilment. It's not the first time he was caught with his trousers down and, knowing his playboy reputation, it won't be the last. I'm glad to see he's having some fun and getting back into circulation. Serena and I thought he'd never get over Amy.'

Jenni's hands began to fidget with the chain around her neck. Kim itched to know if Jack had bought it for her.

'That's fabulous, it has a beautiful cut. Is it new?'

'I have had it a couple of years. My mother bought it for my twenty-first,' Jenni admitted.

'You're so young, Jenni! A word of caution, though.'

Jenni gave her a level glance. 'Yes?'

Kim was shaking inside as she went on, 'I wouldn't expect too much of Jack if I were you. It's still very soon after Amy and he was really in bits, so he's bound to be acting a little weird. Don't take him too seriously and, above all, don't let him mess you around.'

'Jenni, come on,' Harriet urged, pulling her by the hand. 'We'll miss the movie.'

Jenni's smile was very cool. 'Yes, we'd better go. Nice to meet you, Kim.'

The two of them headed into the shopping centre and the movies, Harriet's excited chatter receding in the distance. Kim stalled where she was, still trembling. So what if she'd sounded bitchy? At least she'd put down a marker, even if her words were leaving a bad taste in her mouth. She looked at Jack's car. It wouldn't take a minute to bend down and let the air out of his back tyre. She could just imagine Jenni phoning Jack to explain her predicament and the echoes it would bring of Amy. It might make Jack think twice about a girl he'd met and brought home after just a week. For a long moment, Kim wavered. Then before her imagination ran away with her, she headed to her car as quickly as possible.

The event to celebrate the opening of Dublin's newest wine bar was swarming with media and glamorous socialites. It had sounded like harmless fun to Kim, along with the promise of a night in bed with Matthew, but she found it a huge effort to mingle and chat and look as though everything was great. She was relieved that the event was so thronged that meaningful conversation with Matthew was almost impossible. But eventually the crowd thinned out, and he found her sitting alone for a moment.

'You looked as though you're miles away,' Matthew said, smiling at her a little awkwardly and slipping into the empty seat beside her. 'I thought I might be more welcome if I brought you over a drink.'

'Thanks, Matthew,' she said, accepting the cocktail.

'It seems a long time since we've been out together,' he said, the tentative expression on his face replacing his normal confident manner and telling her that he was feeling his way very carefully. 'I think you and I should have a good chat, sometime soon.'

He could only mean one thing. Cheesed off with her, he wanted to wind up their on–off relationship. Kim laughed mockingly. He couldn't have picked a worse time, considering she was still shaken after her encounter with Jenni.

'There's nothing wrong with now,' she said, wanting to get it over with.

'What I'd like to know, Kim, is if there's any hope for me?'

She was so surprised by his question that she pretended to misunderstand. 'Oh there's plenty of hope for you. I haven't read your tarot cards but I'm sure you can look forward to a long and prosperous life.'

'I meant as in us being more committed and I suppose you've given me your answer,' he said quietly.

She was mortified with the flippant way she'd treated his question. Matthew didn't deserve that. 'Sorry, I didn't mean to be frivolous. You took me by surprise, that's all.'

'Surprise? Surely you realise how I feel about you? Or has it all been a waste of time?' He looked at her for a long moment, his face open and honest, and she quailed inside. 'I'm mad about you, Kim.

I was hoping we'd have a future together. I don't know if you've been deliberately avoiding me or if I'm just paranoid. And this is not quite how I pictured having this conversation, by the way. I'd hoped we'd be out somewhere for a cosy meal.'

She caught the glint in his eye, hurt mixed with regret, a dollop of injured pride, and realised how difficult it must have been for him to broach the subject. She saw her own desire for Jack mirrored in the way Matthew was looking at her and felt a pang. Six months ago she might have been insensitive enough to duck the issue, to laugh and kiss his cheek, and tell him to stick around and see where it led, but now she was only too aware of how desperate it was to hang on to crumbs of hope, the way it eroded your sense of self-worth, as well as the wretched unhappiness it brought. Why couldn't she feel for Matthew what he felt for her? It would have been so easy, so neatly sorted. But life wasn't easy, and solutions were rarely parcelled up tidily. Whoever thought they were was a fool. On the other hand, she enjoyed Matthew's company, he was intelligent and kind, and the sex was great between them. She was thirty-five and there were few men like Matthew left in her social network. If Jack's marriage had continued, she probably would have made a go of it with Matthew. Why couldn't she do that now? Was it better, at her stage in life, to cut her losses, settle for mister second best and forget about her dreams?

'Look, I can see I've caught you on the hop,' he said, placing his hand on her arm. 'This isn't the place or time for a talk. You might need more time to think . . .'

He was clutching at straws and she didn't want to demean him any further. She didn't need more time to think, not when her heart was telling her what to say. She saw Lucy over by the bar, wearing a see-through top and chatting to a young guy about half her age. Lucy threw Matthew an appreciative look. No doubt she thought they were having a cosy tête-à-tête and would consider Kim a right eejit for what she was about to do.

She took a gulp of her Cosmopolitan, her fingers shaking on the stem of her glass, grabbed her courage in both hands, and silently said goodbye to him as she began to speak. 'Matthew, of course I'm thankful for having you in my life, and I have feelings for you too. I enjoy going out with you, we've had some fun . . .' she hesitated.

'But? I know there's a 'but' in there somewhere.'

'There's no easy way to say this,' she looked at him, willing this moment to evaporate.

He smiled at her, a lopsided, sad kind of smile and she could have kicked herself.

'There's no point in pretending or stringing you along,' she said, hoping he'd understand and not get too cut up about it, 'I'm very fond of you, you're kind and intelligent, and I'll probably regret saying this, but if you're asking me if we could have an exclusive relationship, I'm afraid I have to say no.'

His smile vanished and the look on his face was almost unbearable. Without saying a word, he rose to his feet and walked away.

CHAPTER 39

Although Charlotte knew that the wedding of Millie's daughter would be a glittering social occasion, she had mixed feelings about going. For, at the last minute, Serena had cried off.

'I don't really know Lorna all that well, she's years younger than me,' she'd told Charlotte. 'You'll be with your friends and if I know Millie and Cathy at all, you'll have so much fun you won't even miss me.'

Charlotte's heart was bleeding for her daughter and she knew it was only a flimsy excuse. The wedding could have been a networking opportunity for her, the kind she would usually jump at, chatting to everyone with effortless ease. But with her marriage in crisis, Charlotte wasn't surprised her daughter wanted to stay away. She felt like giving it a miss herself, only Millie would never have spoken to her again.

'No worries, Serena,' she had said gently.

She'd arranged to pamper herself from head to toe, in her determination to appear head held high, and go out all guns blazing on behalf of her daughter as well as herself. She booked a rejuven-ating facial and an invigorating body wrap in the Spa in advance of the day, and had her hair and makeup done on the morning of the wedding. She put on her royal blue Helen McAlinden taffeta and her silver Jimmy Choos and knew she looked younger than her years.

'Bring it on,' she silently mouthed, in an imita-tion of Harriet, as she posed in front of her bedroom mirror. Bring on what exactly she didn't know, other than she felt fully armed and ready for anything.

On a bright Wednesday afternoon, she joined over two hundred guests who watched as Lorna exchanged vows with Dermot. Then they flocked to the reception, which was held in a lavishly appointed marquee erected in the grounds of Millie and Patrick's country home. Kim would have loved an eyeful of this, Charlotte thought as she glanced around the marquee, momentarily cross that she hadn't thought to invite her as her guest. Kim was somebody else who needed a pick-me-up with lots of TLC. She had to give herself a mental shake and make an effort to forget her negative thoughts before they took hold. She was here now, at her best friend's daughter's wedding. Serena's and Kim's prob-lems were for another day. After the six-course meal, she felt upbeat and happy, thanks to Cathy's chirpy company and Millie's occasional droll comment that charted the varying degrees of her mother-of-the-bride nerves whenever she managed to escape for a while from yet another over-enthusiastic guest or family member.

Ready for anything, Charlotte had announced to her image in the mirror, but not quite ready to face Hilary and her husband Ted, even though Millie had warned her she'd had no choice but to invite them to the evening celebrations.

'I couldn't leave them out,' she'd told Charlotte, 'I was hoping they'd refuse to come on the basis that an invite to the afters wasn't good enough. But there was no keeping Hilary away.'

Charlotte watched them circulating, yet steering clear of her table as they chatted to friends and neighbours, and she was relieved when they settled down beside some colleagues of Ted's. Hopefully they'd stay there for the night, and leave her in peace.

If she'd been prepared for Hilary and Ted, she was not prepared for the sight of Laurence appearing at the edge of the marquee and surveying the gathering, just as the dancing got under way. By now it was evening and Ireland's latest up-and-coming boy band was in full swing. She watched his eyes move around the crowded marquee and knew that he hadn't seen her yet, but it was only a matter of time. He seemed to be alone, and was wearing a sharply cut dark suit, with a white dress-shirt open at the neck.

Sexy.

'What's he doing here?' Charlotte asked Millie,

who had just sat down beside her to take a short break from her mother-of-the-bride duties.

'Who?' Millie feigned ignorance.

'You know,' Charlotte said sharply.

'You mean Laurence?' Millie grinned. 'He kind of invited himself. He happened to be in my shop last Saturday and we had a bit of a chat.'

'I suppose he was buying silky underwear for his girlfriend.'

'Not quite, she—' Millie didn't get a chance to talk further as Laurence arrived beside them. She stood up immediately, welcoming her guest and encouraging him to avail of the champagne and canapés being served by an army of waiters. Then she excused herself, saying that she needed to rescue her husband from the clutches of great aunt Agatha.

'Charlotte.'

'Laurence.'

They spoke simultaneously.

He said, 'Am I interrupting you?'

By now Millie was already on the far side of the marquee, getting as far away from Charlotte as she could in the shortest time possible, and Cathy was up on the floor dancing with her husband, so Charlotte was alone.

'You're not interrupting anything,' she said politely, her manners automatically rescuing her.

'Sorry I had to rush off the last time,' he said.

Don't forget that this man is already spoken for, Charlotte reminded herself. What did he think he was doing here, lowering himself onto the seat beside her, looking, her heart jumped, far too strong and masculine for the frothy chair covers held in place with yards of flouncy ribbon.

'Have I said something wrong?' he asked, shooting her an amused glance, a smile hovering on his lips.

She composed her face. 'No, I'm fine.'

'I enjoyed talking to you last week, and I'd love to hear the rest of your story. I was sorry I had to rush off just when things were getting interesting.'

'Is that why you wangled an invite to the wedding?'

'Wangled? You make it sound as though I schemed my way here.' He fell silent for a moment. Then, with a gleam in his fabulous blue eyes, said, 'Actually, I did.'

'You might find it a complete waste of time.'

'I'd say your life story is uniquely interesting.'

He was flirting with her. He held her glance a little longer than he needed to, his smile was attentive, and his arm had just managed to sneak itself around the back of her chair. Charlotte felt a mixture of outrage and delight, yet she couldn't help feeling that she wanted to relax into his arm and sit there for the rest of the night.

'It's far too long to bore you with,' Charlotte said.

'I think it would be fascinating,' he said, looking as though he had all evening to listen to her. A waiter carrying a tray of brimming champagne flutes paused by their table and Laurence plucked off two glasses and handed one to Charlotte.

'No thanks, I don't drink alcohol,' she said, waiting for the inevitable reaction.

'Can I get you something else?' he asked.

'I'll have some water, thanks.'

'So, where were we?' Laurence asked, when Charlotte had been handed a glass of chilled spring water.

Unfortunately we weren't anywhere, she thought crossly. Aloud she said, 'What's it like, being an airline pilot? Did you always want to be one?'

'Yes, it's in the family, so it seemed a natural progression for me.'

'So it wasn't one of your passionate growing up things?'

'No, afraid not. My father and his brother were both pilots. As a job it's much like any other; busy days, some not so busy, days when you don't feel like going to work, except in my case you can't afford to make a mistake. It's not as glamorous as you might think, and involves a lot of time spent in painstaking safety checks, and a lot of time in hotels, which begin to look the same after a while. That's why I enjoyed my visit to Tamarisk so much. It felt like home from home, but in very splendid surroundings.'

'Good.'

'I went there to chill out,' he said, 'it was recommended to me by one of my—'

'Girlfriends?' she hazarded.

He shot her a look of surprise. 'No, it was a psychiatrist friend of mine. You see, I'll let you into a secret, Charlotte. You probably think I have a romantic career, jetting all around the world, but I won't be employed as a commercial pilot for much longer. As of now, I'm kind of staring down the gun barrel of compulsory lay off, redundancy . . . Whatever you want to call it, or whatever terminology you use to fudge it, it boils down to the fact that I'll soon be out of a job.'

She was taken aback by his honesty. She cast an eye across the floor, checking that Cathy and her husband were still chatting to friends, glad that she and Laurence were being left to their own devices.

'I'm finding it an even bigger challenge than making sure I don't compromise the safety of my passengers,' he went on. 'Silly of me, as I thought I'd go on full steam ahead, but thanks to global cutbacks in the industry, it looks like I'll be bowing out a few years before I expected to. My first trip to Tamarisk was an attempt to get my head around it. I've been back twice since.'

So that was it. The prospect of redundancy had obviously turned his head, sending him into a midlife crisis and the arms of a woman half his age.

'It's not silly to find that challenging,' she said. 'It's a major life change. But there's no reason why you can't go full steam ahead in another direction.' Although clearly you already have, she thought to herself.

'Like the way you have?' he said. 'Staving off any

427

prospect of dementia with a succession of toy boys? Although I feel I'm missing a significant link there . . .'

Charlotte smiled.

'I know you told me you'd retired in theory, but how could you ever really retire from Tamarisk?' He gave her a quirky smile.

'So you know.' She felt caught out.

'Yes, since the day you gave me a lift. I was nosy enough to ask the porter who you were, thinking you must be local. I know I put you in an awkward spot the other evening, enthusing about the delights of your hotel. I thought you might have been only too pleased to boast about your success, but you're obviously a very modest person.' The gleam in his eye was telling her something else. He was teasing her, and enjoying it.

'I've nothing much to boast about,' she admitted. 'My success is the result of hard work and luck. But seeing as we're being honest, there are other parts of my life where I fall far short of what I would have expected of myself.'

Charlotte couldn't believe she'd admitted that to a virtual stranger, but she felt okay with it. The tempo of the music quickened as the boy band got into their stride and began to belt out a disco classic, and the crowd on the dance floor grew more riotous.

'Shall we find somewhere outside where we can talk?' Laurence asked. 'Or am I dragging you away from your friends?'

She hesitated. 'I need to go to the ladies,' she

said, hoping it might give her time to think. This was where she should say forget about going outside, yes you are dragging me away from my friends, and why, oh why are you here, because although I'm in very good nick, I can't compete with twenty-somethings with radiant skin and sylph-like figures.

But Charlotte forgot about all that as he rose to his feet and she asked herself how come she hadn't noticed how tall he was? Then again, she'd never actually stood beside him to appreciate that he was a good six inches taller than her. Just nice for fitting her head into the groove between his neck and shoulder. She forgot she was supposed to be all grown up and allowed herself to feel a flutter somewhere she'd never expected to feel a flutter again. She folded her silk wrap around her shoulders and, plucking her bag off the table, followed Laurence through the maze of chairs and tables, through the arched, fairy-lit entrance of the marquee out to the dusky July evening.

'I'll be back in a minute,' she said.

'I'll be here,' he told her.

Charlotte slipped inside the house, through the dining room, and up the wide staircase to the bathroom. The door was locked and she was just about to slip along to Millie's en suite when it opened and Hilary stepped out.

'Why, Charlotte! Fancy meeting you here.' She gave her a glance of cool superiority, and looked, Charlotte realised, delighted to have her to herself.

She stood in the doorway, blocking Charlotte's entrance. 'Did you come on your own? You probably hadn't much choice. I hear all is not well in the Devlin dynasty, between Serena's marriage hitting the rocks and Jack finding a little French filly to amuse him.'

Charlotte held her face in check, determined to reveal nothing. 'Excuse me, Hilary,' she said, indicating that she wanted to use the bathroom.

'Oh, I'm not finished with you yet,' Hilary said bitchily. 'You ran off so fast the day we had lunch that I didn't have an opportunity to finish our conversation. I have to applaud your loyalty to your husband. I'm glad you found it the greatest pleasure to be mistress of Tamarisk. I found it an equally great pleasure to be mistress of the man you neglected in favour of running the damn show. It was my privilege to look after Jamie's most intimate needs.'

'You mean you were one of his shags,' Charlotte said coolly, even though her heart was hammering.

'What do you mean 'one of'? Jamie had no one else except me.' Hilary's poking finger jabbed her in the shoulder and incensed Charlotte.

'Sorry to disillusion you, but Jamie had a circle of fuck-buddies as big as your overdraft,' she lied blatantly, feeling a wave of nausea rise within her. She knew she was behaving disgracefully, but this was no time for her usual restraint. 'I'm sorry you fell for the neglect story, the oldest trick in the book. The important thing is that he always returned to spend the night with me after his quick shags because they never satisfied him enough. Now if you'll excuse me,' she smiled sweetly, 'I really have to use the bathroom. I don't want to pee all over my ultra-expensive, bespoke Jimmy Choos. And then I have to get back to my toy boy.'

Hilary's jaw dropped as she soundlessly moved aside.

The terrace was lit with low-level lighting and Charlotte and Laurence had a view of the long marquee, with its row of windows affording them views of the guests moving around the dance floor. Charlotte took slow, deep breaths of the scented night-time air, in and out, as though ridding her stomach of Hilary's venom.

'So tell me,' Laurence asked, 'what was the tipping point that made you step back from running such a successful show?'

'Guess what, Laurence?' she said, trying out the sound of his name and liking it. 'My own children never even asked me that question. They accepted it at face value when I said I'd had enough after thirty-five years.'

'That's normal,' he chuckled. 'Children, no matter how mature they are, find it hard to see their parents as people with separate, independent lives. But you're getting away from the question.'

'The answer is simple, and I could have told you that without dragging you along to the wedding. I felt I'd had enough.'

'Yes, but did you wake up one morning and feel that life was passing you by? What was it like to step back from such a power base?'

There was a long pause. Charlotte looked out into the dusky night and hugged her wrap more securely around her shoulders. It was all too easy to talk to this man. 'Anyone looking at me would think that I had a very successful life. In some respects, yes, but in others, definitely not. My marriage, for example. Jamie, my husband, is dead almost nine years,' she went on, speaking honestly. 'There were issues . . . Our marriage fell short of what he expected and most of that was my fault. I felt very remorseful after he died but I buried it and kept busy. I woke up one morning and realised that I hadn't really come to terms with it. That's one of the reasons. Silly me, I thought some time out would resolve things and give me a new lease of life, but so far it hasn't happened.'

'I'm separated a number of years, and my wife is living in Germany,' Laurence said. 'But there's no such thing as coming to terms with a loved one's death.'

'Unless, like me, you're living with a mountain of regret.'

'What kind of regret?'

'My husband was an alcoholic. I ignored it for a long time because it was my fault. Early in our marriage, I lost my passion for him. Jamie's drinking affected us all. I had to work hard to

432

keep the business going, particularly in the early years when the children were young. Serena grew up constantly seeking her father's approval, which he was never capable of showing unless he was drunk and then it seemed insincere. Jack was denied a strong, male guiding hand and grew up full of insecurities that he hid underneath a devil-may-care attitude. Insecurities that caused him to become embroiled in an unsuitable marriage. But that's a story for another day . . .'

After a while he said, 'Is that why you don't drink yourself?'

'I gave up alcohol when I found out I was pregnant and I stayed off it because one of us had to have a clear head, and to redeem myself a little,' Charlotte laughed wryly. 'Are you happy now that I dragged you along to this wedding?'

'You didn't drag me along. I had an ulterior motive.'

Amusement bubbled in his voice and she was glad he had lightened the atmosphere. 'An ulterior motive?'

'What did you think I did for a living?' Laurence asked. 'We talked about a demanding job, with travel and responsibility and there was mention of security matters. But you really threw me when you talked about fans, at a concert. Did you mistake me for a singer, or some type of rock star? Some people say I'm a dead ringer for the bass player from U2.'

'You're slightly warm but—' she laughed.

'Come on, you can't leave me high and dry.'

'I thought you were some kind of minder or bodyguard.'

'*Bodyguard?*'

'Yes, you were in Tamarisk the same weekend as an American singer, who was there with her stylists and steel ring of security, and I jumped to the wrong conclusion, I'm sorry.'

There was silence. She had put her foot in it. It would be best to slink away quietly. Then she realised that Laurence was laughing. He gave a full-bodied laugh that set her off so that both of them were laughing.

'That's the best I heard in a long time. A bodyguard! Just wait until I tell Juliet. She'll crack up.'

Charlotte crashed to earth. 'Juliet? That lovely girl I saw you with?'

'Yes, she's beautiful, isn't she?'

'Good. I'm sure she'll help you come to terms with changing your life around.'

'She already has. I don't know where I'd be without her.'

Charlotte felt chilly in spite of the balmy evening. What kind of a fool was she, allowing herself to be attracted to someone who was clearly in a relationship, and with someone much younger? 'You could always bring her scaling across the Rockies or paragliding across Niagara Falls,' she said sharply.

'Oops. What brought that on?'

'I forgot you were with someone,' she admitted. She thought of all the trouble she'd gone to, preparing for the wedding. She remembered that as she'd left the house she'd felt she was ready for anything, as though something good was just around the corner. She didn't feel like that now.

'*With* someone? You mean Juliet? You think I'm with Juliet and it has annoyed you?'

Charlotte bit her lip.

'Juliet is a fitness instructor in a busy London gym. She's been home on holiday. She's my daughter, my only child.'

'Your *daughter*?'

His daughter. Something lifted inside her. Images of them in the Shelbourne Hotel, then dining in Tamarisk altered completely. Not the cosy tête-à-tête she'd assumed, but a father and daughter being totally comfortable with each other.

'I'm glad you were annoyed, perhaps even a bit jealous,' Laurence went on. 'I returned to Tamarisk not for the service or to sort out my head, but because of you. I think it was the sound of your voice that first attracted me, before I saw you in that muffling bathrobe, clutching it close to you in case I ravished you. If I told you what I'd been thinking right then, you'd call the police. And there's really only one reason why I'm here tonight . . .'

He fell silent. Sounds of music and conversation filtered across the lawn. On the eastern horizon, the moon was just coming up in the dark blue sky, wider than a crescent, yet not full, and right under it, as though it had tripped off the edge of the moon, a solitary star gleamed like a jewel. She fastened on this like a talisman. She thought of Jamie's drinking, and his late nights, and knew deep down that she'd long ago suspected he was seeing Hilary. Not that it mattered anymore. In a funny way, she hoped it had helped him a little. Then she thought of the way she'd stuck by him, and chosen duty before passion, and worked hard to give them all a good life. She was finished with looking back as of now. It had served its purpose. 'The future is what counts, Charlotte,' she heard her beloved Papa say. '*Your* future.' The most important people in her life were Jack, Serena and Harriet. Yet why was it always children first? What about her? And what about this man sitting quietly beside her?

Laurence's eyes were full of warmth as he looked at her and something flared inside Charlotte. He reached out and cupped the side of her face with the palm of his hand. She felt a leap of pleasure as she moved into his arms.

CHAPTER 40

Sitting on the sofa in the kitchen, Jenni took a deep breath and put her nerves aside. Maybe this wasn't the best time and place, they'd just had the most marvellous sex, and she was about to spoil the lovely sparks between them, but she couldn't put it off any longer. She'd already booked her flight that afternoon, her anxiety levels swirling as she'd clicked the mouse and confirmed her payment details.

She said, 'Jack, I need to go home. Back to London.'

His face darkened. 'London? I thought you were happy here.'

She had told herself to stay cool, that he was bound to be annoyed, but it didn't make it any easier. 'I am, but it's Wendy, my mum. I never told her I was coming to Ireland. She thinks I'm still in France.'

'What? Why doesn't she know?' She watched him running an agitated hand through his thick hair and cursed herself.

'See, Jack, there's stuff you still don't know about me, like how I ended up in Nice.'

'What kind of stuff?'

'Look, I never told you, but I was kind of running away from home.'

The long stare he gave her made her feel shaky inside. 'Go on,' he said.

'Thing is, I'd a big row with Mum last year. Dad had only been dead two years when she started seeing someone else, a guy called Pete. Then she told me they were getting married. She said she'd loved Dad so much that she was willing to put her trust in finding love again. It's what he would have wanted, she said and, at forty-five, she was too young to think of living the rest of her life on her own. I was angry and hurt. I thought she was being disloyal to Dad. Anyway, we had a blazing row and I left my job and jumped on the Eurostar to France. I've hardly been in touch with her since, beyond sending her a couple of postcards telling her where I was and where I was working.'

'Why didn't you tell me this before now?' Jack asked.

'You'd enough things going on in your own head,' she said. 'I just wanted to be happy, cheerful Jenni for you, and not the Jenni who had baggage and who said terrible things to her mother.' His annoyance vanished and she should have been relieved but instead she was dismayed to feel tears in her eyes. This wasn't her. Was she over-emotional of account of the baby? Whatever it was, it ran deep in her blood and made her want to have things right with her mum. She needed her now. She wanted to share her happiness at expecting a baby, to tell her all about Jack. She wanted to tell her she was glad she'd found Pete and was happy again. They all missed her father, but now that she had Jack, she could imagine how empty her life would be without him, so how could she expect her mother to go through the rest of her life without love and companionship?

'I'm coming with you,' Jack said.

'No, I need to do this on my own. I've a lot of making up to do. And I want to talk to Mum about Pete. I never really gave him a chance. I was pretty horrible to him. I can do a very mean Jenni, you know.'

Jack grinned at her. 'Really? I better stay on your good side! I'm sure your mother and Pete will understand how you felt. Your mother loves you.'

'That's the thing. You see, if she feels even one tenth for me what I feel for our tiny baby, I must have hurt her a lot . . . I didn't realise . . . I want to see her but I can't help feeling nervous and upset. I was never like this.' She started to blubber like a child. She was mortified. She'd never cried in front of Jack before. He was beside her in an instant, giving her a big hug.

'It'll be fine,' he said. 'She'll welcome you with open arms. And as soon as you've made your peace with your mother and Pete, I want you to come straight back here.'

'Do you still want me in your life?'

'What kind of question is that? Of course I do.

You and the baby. But I don't like this idea of you going to London. When are you thinking of going?'

'I'm flying out early on Saturday morning,' she said.

'Saturday? That gives us very little time. Just a couple of nights.'

'You're going out Friday night, aren't you? To that award ceremony with Serena?'

'I'm not going anywhere if it's our last night together, for now at least.'

'It will be because I expect I'll need a week or so to sort out a few things in London. See some friends, that sort of stuff. I left in a hurry when I went to France.'

'A week? I know how much can happen in a week. How do I know you won't forget about me when you catch up with your friends? They'll probably think you're mad for hooking up with an old guy like me and persuade you to stay in London.'

She shook her head. 'You're not an old guy. But I'll miss the weekend in La Mimosa and your birthday.'

'Don't worry about La Mimosa. We can go another time, all by ourselves. All I want is for you to come back here to me after you've talked to your mum and your friends and Pete. And I'm going to do my best between now and Saturday morning to make sure you do.'

When Jack stepped into her office on Thursday morning, Serena thought he'd come to apologise and bury the hatchet before they presented a united front at the award ceremony on Friday night. She'd hardly spoken to him since Monday. She'd bumped into him in the hotel foyer a couple of times, but had put on a neutral face in front of the staff and guests. Jack had done likewise. It was silly and stupid behaviour. They were supposed to be successful adults running a successful business. They had problems that needed solving. They had Friday night with all its publicity and full media glare coming up. Then the following weekend, La Mimosa.

'Jack! Hi—'

'I'm sorry about the other day,' he began pleasantly, not looking very contrite. 'I shouldn't have spoken to you like that.'

'I said things I shouldn't have said either,' she admitted.

'Thing is, I got really thick when you slagged off Jenni.'

'I know, I'm sorry. I just felt concerned for you.'

'Don't be. We're very happy. And we have some news.'

'News?'

'I've just been around to tell Mum and I want you to know that Jenni's expecting a baby. I'm going to be a daddy.'

She stared at him for a long time. The gaunt-faced Jack of a few months ago had well and truly vanished. She should be happy for him. Instead she felt a rush of irritation. And something else she couldn't believe.

Envy.

How was this happening? Why was she feeling like this? And why now, when it was far too late?

'You're very quiet,' Jack said, watching her closely.

'Oh, Jack, how did this happen?' she blurted, swallowing her astonishment at herself. 'Were you so gutted over Amy that you needed to rush out and get another girlfriend pregnant to make up for the loss?'

He gave her a funny kind of look before saying, 'Look, we didn't set out to have a baby. And I know it's early days in our relationship. But I'm crazy about Jenni. These things happen and we're pleased, if a little overawed and nervous.'

She pounced on the word. 'Nervous? Why?'

'Wonderful as it will be, it'll be a huge change in our lives. I've known since Monday morning but I needed time to get used to it.'

Monday morning? No wonder he'd been miles away at the meeting with Brian. She recalled the words she'd flung at him and felt ashamed of herself.

'Aren't you happy for us?' he said.

'I'm just concerned that it's a bit like Amy all over again,' she said.

'And I'm trying very hard to tell myself that you're concerned for my welfare, but, believe me, Serena, this is as about as different from Amy as you can get. I hoped you'd be happy for us. The other thing I need to tell you is that unfortunately I can't make tomorrow night.'

She must have misunderstood. 'Tomorrow night is the award ceremony,' she said, speaking very slowly.

'I know and I'm really sorry but I won't be able to make it. Jenni's going back to London first thing Saturday because she needs to talk to her mother and sort out a few things. She feels overwhelmed by it all, and a little fragile right now. That's why I want us to have a quiet night in on Friday. It'll be our last night together for a while and I don't want to leave her on her own.'

'I don't believe this.' Serena shook her head slowly. 'You won't be around on one of the most crucial nights of the year for us just because Jenni's going home to London?'

'It's not as simple as that. I'm half afraid she mightn't come back and I want to do everything in my power to make sure she will.'

She could hardly find the words. 'Jack, this is important for me, for *us*. You can't do this to me. You have to be there.'

'Nonsense. You're the face of Tamarisk, not me. You're the one people will want to see. And I bet, if Tamarisk wins the award – which I hope we do, you deserve it if anyone does – it'll be your name they call out, not mine. So it's no big deal if I'm not there. I'm sure Charlotte will go with you.'

'I've already asked her to mind Harriet.'

She'd asked Paul to mind Harriet, but he'd surprised her with a blunt refusal. 'If it's anything to do with work forget it,' he'd said. So she'd turned to Charlotte, who'd instantly agreed and promised to drop her back late on Saturday morning so that Serena could have a lie-in. A lie-in? Serena had mocked herself. She hadn't had a proper sleep in weeks.

'Why don't you ask Kim to go with you?' Jack suggested. 'I'm sure she'd enjoy it. You could stay with her and make a night of it. It's not compulsory that I must be in Dublin, holding your hand. You'll be well able to manage without me.'

'Maybe *I* need you there. Maybe I'm not so able to hold the fort.'

'You're the most capable person I know. The night will be a doddle for you.'

'It's happening all over again,' Serena's voice shook. 'Your girlfriend just has to crook her little finger and you down tools. Or cry in your arms and you conveniently forget that you have a business to run. I really wish you'd wise up.'

Jack's eyes mocked her. 'I'm sorry you have such a bad opinion of both of us. I thought you'd be a little more gracious. But Jenni won't be coming to La Mimosa either, so at least she won't spoil your birthday.'

'Not coming to La Mimosa? Sounds to me like she is doing a bunk,' Serena knew she shouldn't taunt Jack like this but she couldn't help it. 'Maybe

444

Jenni has more sense than I realised. I'd a feeling it wouldn't last, so go on, make the most of your last night together!'

'I'm not even going to answer that,' he said.

CHAPTER 41

Charlotte knew she was taking far too long to get ready. She had dithered between wearing a Chanel dress that Millie had snapped up for her at a Paris fashion event, or a smart Paul Costelloe jacket and trousers, and then decided to wear the dress. She remembered the time she'd dated Jamie and had had to scour Macy's for bargain-basement clothes.

So much had happened in between.

She took lots of care putting on her makeup and she sprayed her favourite scent, an expensive bottle of Dior that Jack had brought back from France. Then she went downstairs into her living room, sat down and waited. It wasn't long before she heard the click-clack of high heels coming up the path. Charlotte had already had a visit from Jack that morning, and she'd guessed that shortly after he'd left, she could expect to hear from Serena.

'You're all dressed up?' Serena frowned, her forehead creasing, making her look agitated and unattractive as she stepped into the hall and went into the living room.

'Yes, I'm on my way out shortly.'

'You know, don't you? About Jack?'

Charlotte nodded her head.

'I find this hard to believe,' Serena said. 'What is it with Jack? Is my brother a sucker for punishment, or what? Did you know he can't come with me to the ceremony tomorrow night because he wants to stay home and babysit Jenni? He's half afraid she's leaving for good. And if she does happen to come back from London, I guarantee he'll be missing from Tamarisk again, running off to hospitals and clinics. I'm fed up having to carry the can for him . . .' Serena suddenly ran out of breath.

'Serena, darling! Where has all this come from?'

For a moment, her daughter seemed dazed. She looked around as though she was trying to figure out where she was and what she was doing. 'I don't know. I just know I feel angry and upset. What has Jack been thinking of? After everything he went through with Amy you'd think he'd have learned his lesson.'

'Serena,' Charlotte said gently, perturbed with her pale face. 'Don't you think this is Jack's business? He's a grown man. Why are you so fired up? So angry? Is it that much of a disaster that Jack's girlfriend in expecting his baby? He's almost thirty-six years of age. Surely he can organise his own life?'

'Of course it's a disaster. This has all happened on the rebound from Amy and it'll only end in tears.'

'Whose tears? I've watched them together. Jack seems to be happy, and more contented than he's been in a long time. This could be the making of him. He's had a very tough time. A miscarriage can be deeply upsetting, almost as much for a man, never mind losing his wife so soon afterwards . . .'

'Are you always going to use that as an excuse for his rash behaviour?'

'I'm going to say something to you now and I don't mean to hurt you but I hope you'll think very carefully about this. Why are you spending time and energy fretting over your brother's life? Surely you should be putting that time and energy into sorting out your own marriage? I've kept my silence because I don't like to interfere, but I can't stand by anymore and watch while your life falls down around you. For the sake of your health and happiness, never mind Harriet's, you and Paul have to sit down and talk this thing – whatever it is between you – through. And if Paul was here now I'd tell him exactly the same thing.'

Serena stared at her, unsmiling. Inside, Charlotte was shaking. She hated talking to her daughter like this, but she'd no option. There was no time for Serena to respond, for just then she heard her doorbell chime. God, what awkward timing. She couldn't have chosen a worse moment to introduce Serena to Laurence. For a moment she hesitated, torn in two. It was her first real date with Laurence, but how could she leave Serena like this?

'Who's that?' Serena asked.

'It's Laurence, a friend of mine.'

'Laurence?'

'Yes, he's asked me out for a meal and the theatre in Dublin.'

'You have a *date*?'

Charlotte felt flustered. 'Well, yes. But look, I'll cancel if you don't want me to.' What was she saying, she asked herself? What more could she do for Serena? She couldn't solve her problems. Serena had to do that for herself.

'Don't let me stop you, I've been telling you for ages to go out more,' Serena said with a tight smile.

'Only if you're sure,' Charlotte said, her heart heavy.

'Don't be ridiculous, Mum. You don't need my permission.'

Charlotte put her hand on Serena's arm. 'Listen, darling, I'm here to talk, anytime, that's if you want me. And I'll take care of Harriet tomorrow night and keep her for as long as you want.'

'So where did you meet him?' Serena asked.

'I met him here, in Tamarisk, and we talked more at Lorna's wedding. He's separated, with a daughter. I don't know much else, yet. I'm half thinking of inviting him to La Mimosa next weekend as Millie can't make it.'

'Really, Mum?'

Charlotte moved towards the door as the bell chimed again. 'I can hardly believe it myself,' she said, smiling at her daughter. 'I suppose you'll think I've lost the run of myself, much like Jack. Yes, that just about sums it up. I think I've taken a leaf out of his book.'

Serena barely registered the warm handshake and smiling face of Laurence and the fact that he reminded her of someone. The sight of her mother stepping into Laurence's car and waving goodbye, all dressed up, at a time when Serena felt vulnerable and afraid of her feelings unlocked a reel of memories that were so powerful they made her dizzy. Instead of walking back around to the side entrance of Tamarisk, Serena stepped into the Tranquil Garden, a place she rarely had time to enjoy. Now, she sat back on one of the secluded benches and, taking a few deep breaths, she listened to the birdsong and the tinkling wind chimes as long-buried images tumbled through her head;

'I'm late for the staff meeting, quick kiss now before I go . . .'

'I'm needed in the foyer and I could be delayed, so you might be asleep when I come up to kiss you goodnight . . .'

'Sorry, darling, I can't bring you to the party, I'm off to a business function in Dublin . . .'

Age eight, ten, twelve – it had always been the same. Her mother's perfect face, the whisper of silk, a crisp, starched shirt, the click of her high heels. Then the drift of perfume hanging in the empty space where she'd just been. The empty space in Serena's heart. Charlotte always in a hurry, moving beyond her reach, going somewhere more important. More important than attending a school play or tucking her up in bed.

On the one hand, Serena had been terribly proud of her glamorous mother as she flitted off to various functions or important appointments. But there had been many times when she would have preferred Charlotte to be an ordinary mum, like Kim's. A mum whose hands were dusted with flour and whose face was rosy from the oven. Who queued to get a front-row seat for the school concert and who wouldn't allow you out to play until all your homework was done.

Serena sat back and closed her eyes, full of the overpowering feeling that the pillars of her life were crumbling around her. Jack was scarcely talking to her. Charlotte was gone on her first date since Jamie died, and the Tamarisk business model needed an overhaul. Then there had been the startling moment when she'd felt envious of Jack as she'd pictured him with a baby, the moment she'd been too terrified to revisit. As for Paul . . .

By now, missing him went beyond hungering for the brush of his fingertips against her skin, or the comfort of his calm, attentive presence when she arrived home in the evenings. It was a sharp, physical pain that she carried in her heart wherever she went.

And there was no sign of it letting up.

CHAPTER 42

Kim thought that Serena looked perfect for the glitzy ceremony in Dublin's Burlington Hotel. She was wearing a Synan O'Mahony sequinned cocktail dress, had had her hair done so that it flowed like a sheet of pale silk, and her Tiffany jewellery sparkled. But behind the smiling face Serena presented to everyone, as they milled around the pre-dinner drinks reception, sipping cocktails and tasting tiny canapé slivers, Kim sensed the panic radiating from her friend.

She sensed it because she recognised it all too well. She was caught in a panic of her own. Ever since Serena had phoned her on Thursday afternoon.

'Apart from the award itself, it's an important industry networking night, just what Jack needs to get back into circulation,' Serena had said. 'I can't believe he's cried off on account of Jenni.'

'Cried off?' Kim had prompted, suspecting immediately why Serena had phoned her. Kim to the rescue again? No way. She'd already been making up her mind to refuse – she'd decided for the sake of her sanity to pull back from Jack Devlin and everything to do with him. And then Serena uttered the magic words that changed everything.

'Yes, Jenni's going back to London on Saturday. So Friday night will be their last night and he wants them to spend it together.'

'Going home? How come?' *Their last night.*

'Don't ask. You wouldn't believe me,' Serena had said, sounding upset. 'Besides, I had a row with Jack and I don't want to talk about him. I've enough problems of my own. So there's a free seat tomorrow night if you'd like to come. It's black tie. But I know it's short notice, and I've already looked for favours off you. So feel free to tell me to take a running jump.'

'No, I've nothing on tomorrow night,' Kim heard herself say. 'I'm not sure how good I'll be in the networking department for you—'

'It would be a chance for you to network for yourself. Bring some business cards. I can always say you've worked for Tamarisk and I'd be more than happy to recommend you . . .'

She hardly heard the rest of Serena's words. To hell with her networking opportunities. All that mattered was that Jenni was going home. Back to London. The reasons didn't matter all that much. Who cared whether she'd broken it off with Jack, or he with her? Something had obviously gone wrong. She'd heard Serena mention La Mimosa and tried to focus on the words.

'. . . that's next weekend. We're flying out early on Friday morning. Are you still coming with us?'

'How about Jenni? Will she be there?' Kim had wondered if this was all a dream, half-expecting Serena to say that of course she'd be there to celebrate Jack's birthday.

'No, she's not coming to La Mimosa,' Serena had said.

Into Kim's heart fell a tiny prism of hope. Minuscule, but still something to grasp.

'Believe it or not, Mum's bringing a boyfriend, Laurence somebody or other,' Serena had continued.

'Really?'

'Yeah. I've met him and he seems nice enough, but I got a bit of a shock at first. My mother on a date! And bringing him to La Mimosa. She's turning over a new leaf, she says. I don't know what's happening to us all, between Jack, Mum and me. We're flying out on Friday by private jet – Mum's big treat – then we're coming home by scheduled flight on Monday while Mum stays on for a few days with Laurence.'

'Would you like to stay over here, tomorrow night?' Kim had asked, trying to keep a lift of excitement out of her voice. They could talk about La Mimosa, and what to expect, what clothes to bring, for the dinner, for the barbeque. She could find out from Serena what kind of mood Jack was in.

'No thanks, Kim. I'm arranging for a car to bring me up to Dublin and collect me afterwards. Paul's calling for Harriet on Saturday morning and I want to be here. I have to try and talk to him. I hate going away to La Mimosa with this hanging over us.'

She'd temporarily forgotten about the split between Serena and Paul. So carried away with the knowledge that Jenni was abandoning Jack, she hadn't spared a thought for her friend. 'I'm sorry, are you still . . .'

''Fraid so.'

But none of Serena's despondency showed in her face at the ceremony. You'd think her world was ultra-perfect, Kim acknowledged, watching with silent misgivings as her friend circulated around the star-studded gathering, smiling too widely at respected hoteliers and captains of industry and talking rather animatedly as they moved into the splendid dining room. Over a five-course meal, where wine liberally flowed, the main topic on everyone's lips was the necessity to be creative and innovative in these difficult times.

'We must respond to the changing market,' Seamus, a midlands hotelier with bright blue eyes said. 'Otherwise we're just fooling ourselves.'

'Or shutting up shop,' Eithne Daly said dryly. 'In Castle Michael we've introduced another range of recessionary rates across our accommodation options and it's working well for us.' Her eyes flicked around the table. 'I'm sure quite a lot of you have done the same.'

'We in Tamarisk are taking a different approach,' Serena said. All eyes turned to her. Even Kim was taken aback by the determination in her face. 'We're going out there with all-guns-blazing-luxury. It's more important than ever to retain our essential character and unique atmosphere,' she went on, seemingly oblivious to the surprised looks from everyone else.

'Relax, Serena,' Seamus laughed. 'You're not filling in the application form for Haven of the Century. I think it's fair to say that the recent economic woes have compromised many a standard, never mind a balance sheet. How's Charlotte these days? I'd say she could teach us a thing or two, having successfully survived the eighties.'

'Charlotte's vision was all about enhancing visitor experiences, no matter the economic circumstances,' Serena smiled. 'And the Tamarisk ethos was built around that. I'm happy to say I'm carrying on her tradition.'

Looking at the steely glint in her friend's face, Kim felt that Charlotte might have been a lot more flexible in her approach. She was glad when the conversation turned to more general topics, although her heart wasn't really in it. Serena's undercurrents of anxiety were off-putting. Her own nerves were jangling at the thought of where she'd be the following Friday night. In her mind's eye she was already there, in the heat, sunshine and luxurious surroundings of La Mimosa. She'd visited the French hotel a few times with Serena and Harriet and had enjoyed it immensely. There would be breakfast followed by sunbathing on the patio and swimming in the infinity pool overlooking the terraces; she'd have to buy new bikinis and a couple of kaftans. There would be warm, aromatic evenings out on the terraces, sipping champagne cocktails with the sparkling Mediterranean in the near distance.

Best of all Jack in close vicinity and no sign of Jenni.

Kim had almost forgotten she was at an award ceremony until there was a flurry of activity on the stage and the main event of the evening began. The Minister for Tourism opened proceedings before the director of Celebrate Ireland made the announcements. Beside her, Serena was rigid in her chair.

Jack should be here with her, Kim realised, feeling an unusual surge of annoyance towards him. Too bad if Jenni was flying out in the morning. His place tonight was here, supporting Serena. First up was Country House of the Year, won by a hotel in Westmeath. Next was Irish Castle of the Year, and the table they were sitting at erupted when a shocked and surprised Eithne Daly won the award for Castle Michael.

Kim felt a huge pang of anxiety as she watched a flushed Eithne being photographed on the stage brandishing her trophy. Their table would hardly be lucky enough to claim two awards on the night, would they? She sensed Serena holding her breath as the director went through his speech, explaining the criteria with which the Haven of the Year award had been decided, both in response to the detailed submission document and the anonymous site visit.

'There were a record number of entries in this category, which was very heartening in view of the recent contractions the industry has faced. Or perhaps we're all realising that more than ever we need time and space for indulging in a relaxing, hospitable refuge to take us away from it all. I'm happy to say that while the shortlist is comprised of many such excellent establishments, the overall winner was chosen on the basis that it offers excellent food and genuine commitment to guests, a detail-focused approach to customer care and, most important of all in these times, real value for money. And I'm delighted to announce that the winner of the Exceptional Haven of the Year is . . .'

Kim held her breath, but already she could see Serena slumping slightly in her chair as though by some dreadful instinct she realised the award wasn't going to Tamarisk.

It didn't. A hotel in the north-west of Ireland won the award and a flurry of excitement broke out at a nearby table. Kim reached out and grasped Serena's hand as music swelled to a crescendo and a triumphant-looking woman in her early forties accompanied by an equally pleased-looking man stepped up to the stage and claimed the crystal award and prestigious accolade.

Serena gave a tiny shake of the head. 'It doesn't matter. Not really.'

'Are you okay?'

'Sure, of course.' Serena took her hand away, gave Kim a smile and, lifting her chin, she joined in the applause.

For a selfish moment, Kim was relieved her friend wasn't staying over for the night and that she wouldn't have to spend time soothing her ache of disappointment. She could, instead, go home and soak in a relaxing bath, and luxuriate in thinking of the upcoming weekend in La Mimosa.

So what if she was nurturing a fantasy? It was the best fantasy in the world and, for all she knew, it might come right this time.

Serena lay awake until the early hours, her mind racing.

She thought of how she'd felt the moment she'd discovered Tamarisk had lost the award, then the car journey back to Wicklow minus the trophy, and the texts to Charlotte and Jack. They'd both called her back. Charlotte's voice had been warm and concerned and Serena had gratefully let it wash over her as she was driven home through the shadowy night.

Jack had said, 'Chin up, Serena. Don't be upset. There's always next year and I'll be around to give you more help. I know you've been shouldering a lot lately but from now on, I won't have my head stuck somewhere it shouldn't be. Promise.' He'd sounded happy and relaxed and Serena had been forced to acknowledge that it was a big change from the strained way he used to sound when Amy was on the scene.

She remembered what Seamus had said at the table, about her mother steering Tamarisk single-handedly though the recession of the eighties, and she told herself she was lucky to have such a strong, indomitable mother. Okay, it had been tough luck in one sense that Charlotte had had to devote so much time to the business. But if her mother had neglected Tamarisk in favour of spending more time looking after Jack and Serena, she didn't like to think where they'd be today. Deep down, she'd always known this, even when she'd felt an occa-sional spark of envy at the way Kim's mother had been around for her.

Most of all though, what kept her tossing and turning was her thinking about the mixture of emotions she'd felt when Jack had told her he was going to be a father. And the realisation, at about three in the morning, that she was feeling jealous because she could already see in her mind's eye the added dimension a baby would bring to Jack and Jenni's lives as they marvelled over each new milestone; the first smile, the first tooth, the first words, and those shaky new footsteps, the fun they would have with a little boy or girl . . . all those things she had enjoyed with Harriet after the initial months were over.

All those things she could enjoy again . . . if she had the guts to try for another baby.

Where had this come from? Was it something that had quietly burgeoned deep inside her since Amy's death? A realisation that, in spite of everything the family had been through, or maybe because of everything they'd been through, life was precious? And that all those fears of not being a good enough mother, coupled with the sense of exhaustion and loss of control, were nothing really compared to the huge, life-affirming happiness and joy that a child could bring.

Or maybe it had everything to do with Paul's devastated face when he'd found her contraceptive pills. Could it be that she loved him so much she was prepared to face her fears to make him happy?

She loved him so much . . . Surely that mattered far more than anything else?

For a long time, Serena thought of her husband, her mind going over everything they'd been to each other, before she eventually fell asleep just as dawn arrived. In the distance there was the sound of the doorbell. It was so far away that Serena thought she'd dreamt it. She sat up in bed but everything had been so silent that she snuggled back into the pillows and pulled the duvet over her head. She was startled by the sound of footsteps coming down the hall and the bedroom door opening. When she sat up in a panic and saw Paul standing in the doorway, she thought she was still dreaming until he stepped into the room.

'Christ, Paul, you gave me a fright.'

'You gave me a fright when you didn't answer the bell. I thought there was something wrong.' Sitting up in bed, Serena yanked the duvet up to her chin and anchored it there by hugging her knees.

He scrutinised her tousled hair and unmade-up face. 'What's up? Where's Harriet?'

'She stayed with Mum last night. She's not home yet.' Serena glanced at the bedside clock. 'She should be home any minute.'

'So Charlotte looked after her when you went off to your work event.'

'It wasn't an event. It was an award ceremony and before you ask, no, we didn't win.'

His eyes were flinty. 'That must be a first. No wonder you lost sleep.'

'For God's sake, Paul,' her voice shook. 'It had nothing to do with the award. I haven't slept properly since you walked out. If you must know, I sensed just before they made the announcement that we weren't going to win. And in that split second, I realised that I didn't give a toss. It didn't matter. And I hope you get a great laugh out of that. I'm sure you'll find it very funny.'

'I don't find anything remotely funny about the mess our lives are in,' he said, surprising her by stepping further into the room and, hands in his pockets, he walked across to the window, staring out.

'Mess? Paul, this is nothing short of a nightmare. You've no idea how sorry I am,' she said desperately. 'Right now I'm in bits. About us, about everything.'

'Knowing you, you won't have that problem for long.'

'What do you mean?'

He wheeled around to face her. 'What will happen when the next crisis raises its head? When some celebrity throws a wobbly over the linen sheets or decides she doesn't like the flowers in her suite? Or when some movie actor is freaking out because you haven't got his reserve whiskey? I know what will happen. It'll be Serena to the rescue as usual. The only one who's capable in a crisis. You'll get caught up in the soap opera drama, you'll forget to come home for Harriet, or you'll have to get to work earlier than usual.'

'Please stop. I've tortured myself enough with all that stuff. But you're wrong about one thing. I was afraid to have another baby and it was nothing at all to do with Tamarisk, but everything to do with me. You see, I felt I was never good enough when it came to the people I love.'

'What?'

'I know I've been dishonest, to you, and to Harriet. I didn't love you the way you deserve. And you're right, I should have had enough respect for you and our marriage to look beyond my stupid pride and tell you exactly how I felt after Harriet was born. I tried to tell you last week, but you wouldn't listen to me.'

To her surprise, he leaned back against the window frame and crossed his arms. 'Okay. Tell me now. Exactly how you felt.'

Even though he was looking at her with hostility, he was prepared to listen. She grasped at that, grateful that he hadn't just stalked out. She hooked strands of her blonde hair behind her ear, and then she clutched her arms tighter around her knees, conscious that she was shaking.

'Having Harriet – it was a huge shock to my system,' she said. 'I thought it was going to be different. I'd read too many baby books showing perfect mothers and doting babies. I was sure that confident and successful Serena would manage a baby as perfectly well as she did everything else. But I found Harriet's birth terribly traumatic. After she was born – God, I can't explain how helpless I felt. She was like a stranger to me . . .' Serena paused. Baring her innermost soul like this wasn't easy. She swallowed the lump in her throat and went on. 'I wanted to be the best mother possible but I was totally overcome by the huge responsibility. I didn't know what to do when she cried or when she had colic. I never knew if she'd had enough food. Even giving her a bath, her tiny body – I was half scared I was going to drown her. I might have been in charge of a multimillion euro business, but the tiny size of Harriet filled me with fear. I felt swamped by her, and couldn't bear to listen to her crying.'

'But you were her mother. Surely that meant something?'

'That's what I'm trying to explain,' Serena said in a quavering voice. She felt tears pooling in her eyes and grabbed a handful of tissues from the box beside her bed. 'I was the mother of this tiny baby and I felt so helpless and so incompetent that it made me feel afraid and it overshadowed everything. All my life I was used to getting everything right and I was far too embarrassed to admit I couldn't cope. I felt such a failure. I didn't trust myself to be a proper mother to your daughter. I thought that the crèche would do a far better job of looking after her than me and I was so relieved to leave Harriet in their care and go back to work.' She began to laugh through her tears, but it was a sound that was almost hysterical. 'We were up for Haven of the Year last night.'

'What's so funny about that?'

'Nothing,' she sniffed. 'You see Tamarisk was a haven for me after Harriet was born. It kept me busy and made me feel useful. Even now, I sometimes feel I'm useless when it comes to her.'

For a long time, Paul said nothing. His voice was subdued when he finally spoke. 'You're not useless when it comes to Harriet. She's a fantastic kid. She's confident, strong and happy. But I really wish you had told me all this at the time. I could have helped out more.'

'I was too proud to admit that I couldn't handle it. I saw your face when Harriet was born. You were so happy with Harriet that I didn't want to burst your bubble. When you started to talk about another baby, I just felt I couldn't go back there, to that awful nightmare place. It seemed far easier to say nothing and just continue taking the pills. I was terrified of you finding out so I always made sure to keep them hidden in my bag. As time went on, it became harder and harder to find the courage to confront it. I found it easier to help sort out Jack's life instead of my own. I felt my own problem was insurmountable and I was terribly ashamed of the way I was deceiving you. It seemed easier to ignore it all and brush it under the carpet. I know I was wrong not to trust you but I was too afraid of letting you see the terrible mother I was.' She paused for a moment, her voice hoarse by now.

'And how do you feel about Harriet now?'

Harriet! She might have made a mess of the early days and there were times when she felt she was the worst mother in the world, but she was so thankful to have her and couldn't imagine life without her now. In spite of her heartache, Serena smiled. 'Of course I love her. When I look beyond the terror of those early days and think of how much she means to me now, I know my life would be empty without her.' She gave Paul a meaningful glance. 'I was glad we didn't win the award last night. I couldn't have stood up there and accepted it when I know that I'm nothing but a big, fat failure. Or a "fucked-up bitch", as Jack called me.'

'He *what?*'

'We had a row,' Serena said wretchedly.

'A row? You and Jack?'

'Don't ask me what it was about, I can't even remember.'

There was a long, tense silence. From outside there came the sound of a car coming up the lane and slowing down as it approached Maple Hill. Charlotte and Harriet.

'Here's Harriet,' she said. 'Don't forget we're off to La Mimosa next Friday.'

'Of course. The time-honoured Devlin birthday celebration goes ahead,' he said wryly. 'Whatever you do, don't break the family tradition.'

She ignored his barb. 'Harriet can't wait to go, so I suppose I'm good for something.'

There was the sound of car tyres crunching on the gravel.

'Paul. What about us?' she said hurriedly, conscious that Harriet would burst in shortly.

His face was despondent as he moved away from the window. 'I don't know, Serena. I can't believe you felt that bad and kept it all to yourself. I'm shocked that you didn't have any faith in me or our marriage. Why didn't you think I'd be supportive of you? But I don't agree with Jack. I can think of many things I'd call you, but Jack was off the mark.'

'What would you call me?' she asked.

'You're an extremely difficult person to get through to. You can be exciting and passionate, tough but soft, far too ambitious, and at times I find you impossible. Why do you always have to get it right? Why couldn't you trust me?'

Outside, a car door slammed. She heard Harriet's raised voice. Paul began to walk towards the door.

'Paul,' Serena said hoarsely, 'I'm willing to try.'

Her words stopped him in his tracks. 'Try what?'

'Try for a baby. Start afresh. I'd make sure to be better prepared this time and I'd take as much help as I could get.'

The doorbell sounded.

He looked at her with a mixture of sadness and disappointment. 'I don't know, Serena. How can I trust you again? How can I be sure you mean it and that these aren't just empty words? Why did you have to mess it all up? From what you've been telling me I think it would be very foolish of you to try for another baby just because *I* wanted it. You have to really want it for yourself. For both of us.'

'I do really want it for both of us, and Harriet. Okay, I'll probably be nervous, but I'd be more realistic this time about what to expect in the weeks after the birth. See, Paul,' she said brokenly, 'I've realised that us having another child is far more important to me than the chaos of those early baby days. So what if life was upside down? I'd manage somehow. I want us to be together and have a family, just as we planned at the start. Remember? On our honeymoon? Those plans we made for two or three children?'

The doorbell rang again.

'Paul, don't go yet.' She lifted her chin, forced herself to meet his gaze. 'The past few weeks have been the worst nightmare. I never thought I could feel so much emptiness. I love you. I love Harriet. You both mean the world to me.'

He shook his head. 'Right now, Serena, I'm not convinced you mean that.' Then he walked out into the hallway to open the door.

Serena dropped her head onto her hands. How on earth could she convince him? What more could she possibly say?

CHAPTER 43

Kim pushed back the organza curtains, opened the balcony door, and stepped onto the sun-warmed tiles. Her balcony faced the back of La Mimosa and below, the gardens fell away in graduated terraces towards the sapphire-blue sea. Full of flowering shrubs, the pink and magenta of the exotic bougainvillea, eucalyptus bushes, rose-laurel and verdant lawns, the gardens themselves were a joy to discover, carefully landscaped to surprise and delight as you strolled around. A place for romance and love.

She heard splashing sounds coming from the side of La Mimosa and Harriet's excited voice. True to her word, the little girl had got to the pool before anyone else. She heard Conor Devlin talking to her. He was obviously keeping an eye on her, although even at four, Harriet could swim. Kim felt suddenly shy at the thoughts of donning her new minuscule bikini and appearing by the pool, even though Jack had bet her she'd be the last one down.

'I'll be first,' Harriet had declared, full of excitement as they boarded the private jet Charlotte had booked to take them all to the south of France. In an effort to keep her still while they'd taxied along the runway, Jack had asked her to close her eyes and think of what part of La Mimosa she was looking forward to the most.

'The pool,' she'd squealed. 'Cos it's out in the sun, not like Tamarisk. And I can splash as much as I like. Conor will let me.'

'Conor won't let you make too much noise if there are other visitors around,' Serena had said.

'Let's see who'll be very first to jump into the pool,' Jack had said.

'Me first,' Harriet had shouted. 'Then you, Jack,' she went on, pointing at him. 'Then Laurence, um, and Charlotte. And after that . . .' she hesitated and looked from Kim to Serena.

'I bet it'll be your mum next, then Kim,' Jack had said.

'How come I'm paddy last?' Kim had joked, feeling every bit as excited as Harriet at the prospects of this weekend.

Jack had thrown her an amused smile. He'd seemed happy enough, not too upset that Jenni wasn't around. Serena hadn't discussed it with her beyond confirming that Jenni had departed for London as planned. Serena had been in a difficult mood the couple of times Kim had phoned her that week and their conversations had been brief. Disappointment over losing out on the award, Kim guessed, but also the fight with Paul was taking its toll.

Just as well they had Harriet with them, for the little girl was bursting with so much excitement that it provided an easy distraction for the adults. And if Serena and Jack were minus partners, the same couldn't be said for Charlotte. Kim thought that Laurence was lovely. Charlotte had introduced them in the airport lounge as their paperwork had cleared.

'This is Laurence, a friend of mine who's joining us for the weekend,' she'd smiled, as though it was a normal enough occurrence. Kim had been momentarily surprised as she shook hands with the solid, reliable-looking man, for she'd never known Charlotte to have a date in all the years since Jamie had died. From the conversation in the airport lounge, it was clear that Serena and Jack had only met him a couple of times and that even Charlotte was only getting to know him herself. Hats off to Charlotte, she'd decided. The man was decidedly sexy and they looked good together.

When they'd landed in Nice, two limousines had been ready to whisk the group to La Mimosa.

Kim had joined Serena and Jack in one car, catching her breath at the beauty of the Riviera coast and feeling as though she'd been suspended in a fairytale as they'd sped along in luxurious comfort. Her luggage was full of floaty chiffon outfits, tiny bikinis, and she'd carried a dress bag with a new YSL cocktail dress, carefully chosen for the gala dinner planned for Saturday night. A

French love song had been playing low on the car radio and Jack was sitting in front chatting now and again to the driver, so behind her Gucci shades, she'd been able to feast her eyes on him. Occasionally, he'd thrown a laughing glance to the women sitting in the back seat as he cracked a joke. Neither he nor Serena had mentioned Jenni. Or Paul. Kim had wanted this journey to go on for ever but, all too soon, they'd crested the hill and were gliding through the entrance gates to La Mimosa, where the elegant building with the white stuccoed walls set amid landscaped gardens was basking in warm sunshine.

By the time Kim had unpacked, lathered on high-factor sun screen and made her way to the pool, Harriet had obviously got fed up, because there was no sign of her. Charlotte and Laurence were sitting in a shaded spot of the rose garden, deep in conversation with Conor; Charlotte had changed into a soft buttery yellow cotton dress with a wide-brimmed hat and she looked, Kim thought, extremely happy and youthful. The pool area was quiet, most guests having enough sense to keep out of the sun and enjoy a siesta at this time. Kim decided she would just stay for a short while. She dropped her white kaftan on to a sun lounger and suddenly she felt more sexy than shy in her cherry-red bikini as she stepped across the warm patio and into the shimmering pool. Her heart swelled as a door opened and Jack emerged from the shade of La Mimosa, saw her in the pool and called a greeting before he dived straight in with a clean, economic movement and swam under the water until he surfaced beside her.

'Guess you won the bet, tatty-head.' He laughed and shook his wet-slicked hair so that sparkling droplets flew through the air.

She could have been sixteen years of age in the pool at Tamarisk.

The barbeque that evening floated by, filling all her senses so that they spilled over.

Kim knew she would never forget this night. The group of them on the terrace as the bright evening fell into a soft violet evening; music playing softly; the clink of cocktail glasses; aromatic food prepared and served by an efficient, white-coated team from the hotel with the minimum of fuss. The way the patio was lit, rows of flickering candlelight and tiny jewelled fairy lights strung in lacy strands. In the distance, the indigo swell of the sea. Serena in a blue dress, moving around talking and chatting, her blonde hair gleaming, Harriet giggling and showing off her karate moves, Jack relaxed and devastatingly good-looking in a steel-grey shirt, the clean scent of his aftershave lingering in her nostrils long after he'd kissed her warmly on both cheeks. She'd found it hard to keep her eyes off him and felt ever so thankful to be here with him. And all of this silhouetted against the soft glow of lights coming from the windows in La Mimosa. She felt good in her white Karen Millen dress, clinched with a silver belt and glittery heels. It was a perfect foil for her tumble of russety hair. The party was joined by Conor and his wife, Martine, and his son Pierre with his wife Diane. Friends of Conor and Martine dropped in, who seemed to know Charlotte quite well from her visits to France. And Laurence, of course, always by Charlotte's side, being introduced to everyone. Conor was a genial, generous host, but calmer and more reserved, and so different to Jamie.

And this was only Friday night, Kim silently rejoiced. There was all day Saturday, and the gala dinner in a private dining room on Saturday night, and then Sunday, with a birthday party on the lawn. Kim lifted her face to the warm, scented breeze, let it all wrap around her senses and wished she could fix this moment for ever.

CHAPTER 44

Charlotte woke early the following morning. She slipped out of bed, padded across the marbled floor and pulled back the drapes. Already the morning was sparkling in the blaze of the sun, the endless sky a bright cerulean blue, the deep sapphire sea a glittering expanse of silk. La Mimosa, in the summer, was breathtakingly beautiful and instantly calming. Laurence and she were in separate rooms.

'Are you sure about this? He seems very nice,' Conor had said to her soon after they had arrived.

'He *is* very nice,' Charlotte had smiled, 'but we're just getting to know each other. So separate rooms. For now.'

'I was surprised when I heard you were bringing a man with you,' he'd teased.

'So was I. I think I've been swept a little off my feet. Or maybe I've decided to plunge right in and go for it and see where it takes me.'

'Are you looking for my blessing as your brother-in-law?'

'It would be nice if you approved but I won't lose sleep if you don't.'

Charlotte turned from the window and wondered if the men had left for their game of golf. Conor and Pierre had arranged to bring Jack and Laurence to a course further up the coast towards Juan-Les-Pins so that they could practise their swing against a backdrop of the Mediterranean. After that, they were heading to one of the vineyards to order some wine. They would be gone until the late afternoon.

'We hope you ladies won't feel neglected,' Conor had said.

'Nonsense,' Charlotte had scoffed. 'We'll have a good chance to relax and put our feet up. I'm looking forward to indulging in a La Prairie gold radiance treatment.'

'You look radiant enough to me,' Conor had told her.

'Thank you.'

Charlotte went into the shower and as she stood under the gentle spill of spray, random images of the previous evening flitted through her head. She saw the group of them moving about, laughing and chatting, mingling with each other, and she mentally ticked them off.

Jack, handsome and gregarious as ever, looking very pleased with life; Serena, a little too thin and fragile-looking for her liking; Kim, with eyes for one person only, unfortunately; and Harriet, most uncomplicated and joyful of all. Laurence had enjoyed himself as she knew he would.

'I'm glad you're here,' she'd told him when they had a quiet moment together.

'I'm glad too. It's nice to get to know your family. Jack and Serena are great people, and they've been very welcoming to me. I hope you're very proud of them and not too tied up in those futile regrets you've talked of.'

'I'm learning to let go of them,' she'd said. 'You know I planned this weekend to help us all move on from Amy's death?'

'Yes,' he'd said, aware of what had happened in Thailand.

'But having you here is turning out to be a sort of closure for me.'

'I'm glad to hear that,' he'd said, dropping a quick kiss on her cheek.

It had been her private moving on, Charlotte realised as she stepped out of the shower. And if she wanted to test her growing feelings for Laurence, well La Mimosa was the best place for that. But not bed. Not here. It would have to be somewhere new for both of them, she thought, feeling a bubble of excitement at the prospect of that. She would have a peaceful breakfast on her private balcony, and after that, she was going to invite Kim to sit in the shade with her for a while.

'Where are Serena and Harriet?' Kim asked her.

They were sitting back in big creamy loungers under a shady canopy around the side overlooking the vineyard-covered hills. Occasionally, a far-off

479

car glinted in the sunshine as it wound around a thin ribbon of roadway en route to a sleepy, hilltop village.

'Serena's taken Harriet to a water park, along with Pierre's son. They'll be gone for the morning.' It had been very convenient, Charlotte thought, and an opportunity too good to miss. And here in the unparalleled beauty of this landscape, what she had to say might come easier.

'So it's just you and me,' Kim smiled.

'That's it, Kim. I hope you didn't mind me asking you to keep me company. Maybe you'd prefer to be relaxing in the Spa.'

'No, this is lovely. Although you'd probably prefer to be here with Laurence?' Kim threw her an inquisitive glance.

'No, it's better for Laurence to have a chance to get to know Jack and Conor. Golf is perfect. Plenty of time to chit-chat. So long as Laurence doesn't have a wildly competitive streak. And then wine tasting can be a very bonding experience, if they haven't fallen out over golf, of course.'

'I can't imagine Laurence would fall out over a game. He's a lovely man.'

'Yes, I can't believe how lucky I am.'

'You deserve it, Charlotte. How long has it been since Jamie?'

'Nine years, just about. Problem was, Kim, I didn't really feel I deserved another chance. Not after the mess I made of my marriage to Jamie.'

'What mess?' Kim looked at her curiously.

'It's not something I really talk about, and certainly not to Jack or Serena. Sometimes family is a little too close to appreciate your full confession. For, you see, I didn't really love Jamie. Not in a proper, passionate way.'

'Then why did you marry him?'

'Oh, I thought I did. When I met him first he was fun and exciting. We were married in New York, we had a short honeymoon on Cape Cod, and then Jamie brought me to Tamarisk as a new bride . . .'

The years fell away from Charlotte as she spoke to Kim. 'I went straight to bed the morning we arrived in Tamarisk as I was tired after the long, overnight flight. Later that afternoon, Jamie brought me out to the lawns where they were having a welcome party for us. It gave me a chance to meet family and friends and some staff. And then Conor came out and strolled across the lawn and everything changed. He looked so similar to Jamie, but there was a world of difference between the way they were. Different personalities and characters, Conor's calm reserve at odds with his brother's outgoing and sociable nature.'

'*Conor*?' Kim asked, looking at Charlotte in surprise.

Charlotte gave her a rueful smile. 'Yes, I thought I loved Jamie, and I did in a way, but it was nothing compared to how I felt about Conor.'

'Did he know? Hold on, Charlotte, why did you stay married? This is mad.'

'It's not really. Life is messy. I was instantly attracted to Conor. There was nothing I could do to prevent it from happening. It was a powerful need, a constant longing. I'd see him in the hotel, around Jamie, at family things. I thought I was going to die if I didn't have him. At first I wasn't sure how he felt about me, and then as the weeks went on, I began to guess that he might feel the same, I sensed something between us, always, a tension, an edginess, but we never spoke of it.'

'If you both felt that strongly about each other, why didn't you give into it?'

Charlotte smiled. 'I found out I was pregnant. So that was that. As soon as the twins were christened Conor decided to come and live in France. I knew he was doing that to give us both a chance to get on with our lives. And it did in a way, except damage had already been done to my marriage. I tried hard with Jamie, but he must have sensed deep down that I'd lost the depth of my passion for him. The only time Conor and I briefly spoke about our feelings was at one of the twins' birthday parties. So perhaps Jamie knew all along that I'd fallen in love with his brother, but I'm not sure. He said nothing about it, and I said very little about his drinking and we just muddled through the rest.'

'Charlotte! I'm totally lost for words . . . I had no idea.'

'I should hope not,' Charlotte smiled. 'I've never spoken to anyone about it. When Conor came to France he put his energy into establishing La

Mimosa. Then he met and married Martine. They're very happy together, I'm glad to say. You see, Kim, gradually over the years, with nothing to fan the flames, the passion burnt itself out. I found out I wasn't going to die after all if I didn't get to be with Conor. Time passed and we both got caught up in our lives, and touched base regularly with family things and swopped advice on the running of our respective hotels, but generally we moved on. We're great friends now, but nothing more.'

'And Jack and Serena don't know.'

'No. I'm not sure if there's much point in telling them now. I'd like them to know, though, that I was responsible for their father's drinking. I sometimes fear they carry a little guilt about that, as though they'd failed him somehow, which of course they hadn't. Serena in particular, in her efforts to make Tamarisk the success it is. Still trying to prove to the ghost of her father that she's his wonderful daughter.'

Silence fell and stretched. Then Kim said, 'I'm glad you're finding happiness with Laurence. I still think you deserve it, and you did your best with everyone over the years. At the end of the day it was Jamie's decision to turn to drink, so it was his responsibility, not yours. But, Charlotte,' she turned and stared at her, clearly mystified, 'I don't understand why you've told me all this.'

Charlotte felt anxiety leap in her stomach. It had been one thing to open her heart to Kim, but it was entirely another thing for Kim to find out that Charlotte knew what was in her heart. She held the younger woman's eyes for a long time, until Kim finally wrenched hers away and stared out across the valley with a stony expression on her face.

'You know,' she stated in a hard voice.

'I know you love my son,' Charlotte said gently.

Kim darted her a furious look and shook her head in dismay. 'Who else have you told? Serena? Laurence? Jack himself? Anyway how did you find out?'

Charlotte's heart melted when she saw the glitter of tears in Kim's eyes. 'Oh, Kim, my dear, of course I've not told anyone. Your secret is safe with me. I know because I see the way you look at him. Because I recognised that look. It was mirrored in my own face once upon a time. I told you my story because I feel partly responsible as Jack is my son, and you're a very good friend of my daughter but more so because I'm very fond of you and I hoped it might help you to move on, and not be stuck in a lonely, loveless life. You can make a life, you know, without Jack. It's in your power.'

Kim looked at her hopefully. 'But Jack's here on his own . . .'

Charlotte sighed quietly. It was going to be more difficult than she had thought, taking away Kim's dreams. 'Not for long. He is serious about Jenni, my dear. She went to London to talk to her mother because she's—Charlotte halted, unable to pass on this crucial piece of information, but knowing that Kim had to be told.

'She's what?' Kim glared. 'Don't tell me she's pregnant. I couldn't bear that.'

'She is. And of course you can bear it. Kim, you're one of Jack's great friends,' Charlotte swiftly went on, upset by Kim's devastated face. 'Don't you think that if anything was going to happen between you it would have happened by now? I'm really sorry if I'm being brutal, but I urge you not to waste your life hankering after something you can't have. I've had to let the ghost of Jamie go, the ghost of guilt that kept me stuck in the past. Believe it or not, it was only when I saw Jack moving on with a new lease of life that I realised I was letting my own life fritter away. You must have the courage to let Jack go.'

Kim's shoulders were heaving softly. Charlotte heard her sniff and felt like crying herself, but she kept on talking, trying to get through to Kim.

'You can do this. You can let him go. You're a strong, capable woman. Make room for new things in your life. You'll always have a soft spot for Jack, but you will find love with someone else if you allow yourself to be open to that possibility.'

Charlotte gently put an arm around Kim, half afraid that she might pull away. Instead Kim fell against her, and allowed herself to be hugged. Charlotte passed her some tissues.

'Sorry,' Kim gulped, 'I just—'

'You don't have to say anything,' Charlotte soothed. 'You certainly don't have to apologise. I'm the one who's sorry that I had to talk to you like this.'

'It's better than me continuing on like a fool in fantasy land,' Kim said.

'Loving someone is never foolish, Kim. It's what makes the world go around. But we do need to temper it with a dose of reality.'

'I need to go to my room. I'll talk to you later. I have to have a big think. Is there any chance Jenni might turn up here?' Kim stood up, her face red and blotchy, her eyes still brimming with tears.

Charlotte hesitated. More bad news for Kim. 'She didn't intend to, but from what Jack said to me last night, she might have changed her mind.'

'I suppose that's why he looked so happy,' Kim gulped. 'I thought it was because he was celebrating his freedom, but that was me only seeing what I was hoping to see. The same as when Serena told me Jenni was going back to London. I assumed she was finished with Jack. God, how stupid I was.'

Charlotte stood up and hugged Kim again. 'Don't think that. I know it's not easy but you will get there. One day, all this will be a memory. It's up to you what kind of memory it is. Please don't let it be a bitter one. Although it's poor consolation, I promise I won't breathe a word about this conversation to anyone.'

'Neither will I,' Kim said. 'You can be sure of that.'

After she had gone, Charlotte sat back and

looked out over the valley and out at the mountains in the hinterland. She felt the heat of the sun penetrating through the canopy and the slight breeze refreshing on her face and limbs. She tried to recapture a sense of peace. She thought about Jamie and that day long ago when she'd come to Tamarisk as a bride. She thought about Conor and the way the passion between them had mellowed to deep friendship.

She'd planned the weekend in La Mimosa to help her family move on. Jack would be fine, she sensed. And in bringing Laurence here, it had helped her to make a start on the rest of her own life.

All she needed to do was to help Serena see sense. Then she was definitely letting go.

CHAPTER 45

Eyes closed, Serena stood under the refreshing waterfall shower and wished all her sins could be washed away along with the rivulets of soapy water cascading down her body. She'd had wild hopes that Paul might have changed his mind about coming to La Mimosa. In the airport on Friday morning, her heart had plummeted further and further the nearer they'd come to the departure time with no sign of him. And as their jet had taken off, Serena's stomach had lurched with longing for him.

Paul had been in a sober mood on Wednesday when he'd called to bring Harriet to her karate lesson. But after he'd dropped her home, he'd even come in to see the big pink bag she was packing for La Mimosa. Harriet had been so excited about her holiday that, far from throwing a tantrum, she'd barely noticed her father leaving. She'd called his mobile to let Harriet speak to him after they'd arrived, too afraid to talk to him herself. But it was all so wrong. He should have been with them yesterday morning, sharing Harriet's delight. He should have been at the barbeque last night, sharing the musky evening with Serena. Then this morning, he should have been with them in the aqua park, taking pride in Harriet's determination to conquer a waterslide.

Serena decided it was better to spend some of the afternoon relaxing in the shade rather than fretting away in her room. As she walked across the foyer, making for the door out to the rose garden, someone at the reception desk caught her eye.

Jenni? It *was* her, casually dressed in a white mini-skirt and a yellow T-shirt that looked fabulous with her dark choppy hair. She was deep in conversation with the receptionist, and Serena tried to catch up with her rapid stream of French, grasping that there was some kind of problem but Jenni was getting nowhere. When she turned around and saw Serena approaching her, her face flooded with relief.

'Oh, Serena, I'm glad I saw you.'

'Jenni? Is everything all right? Is Jack expecting you?'

'I told him last night I might come over for his birthday, but I thought I'd surprise him by arriving unannounced and being here for dinner tonight. However, the hotel is full and the receptionist isn't keen on letting me into Jack's room.'

No surprises there, Serena thought. The receptionist was following hotel policy; besides, Jenni looked so young, it seemed crazy to associate her with Jack.

And she was pregnant, for God's sake, Serena blackly reminded herself, darting a glance at Jenni's tummy. It was starting to thicken already. 'Jack's been out all day, golf followed by wine tasting,' she said. 'He'll be back in an hour or so, but I'll sort this out.' She smiled at Nadine, the receptionist, and explained that Jenni was a close friend of Jack's, and it was fine to give her a key card. Nadine burst into a flood of apology and handed the card over straight away.

The concierge led the way to the bank of elevators, wheeling Jenni's case.

'I'll come with you,' Serena said. 'Just to make sure you get settled in and to tell you where everything is.'

'Great, thanks. Where's Harriet?'

'She's watching some cartoons with Simon, my cousin's son. We spent the morning in the aqua park, so she's happy having a bit of a rest for now.'

They got out of the lift on the second floor.

'Gosh, it's fabulous here, isn't it?' Jenni said. 'I only saw hotels like this from the outside when I worked in Nice. Except for when Jack brought me to the Negresco. He talked about La Mimosa but I'd no idea it was this luxurious.'

'Yes, it is rather special,' Serena agreed.

She was half-exasperated and half-amused by Jenni's reaction.

'Wow this puts the Negresco in the shade,' she gasped, moving around Jack's bedroom with the four-poster bed and silk-padded walls. She checked out the huge bathroom with the free-standing bath, deep vanity basins, spacious walk-in shower and velvet robes. Then the large balcony outside, over-looking the gardens. Serena joined her on the balcony and pointed out some landmarks. Then she went through the facilities on offer and said they were all meeting in a private dining room at seven thirty that evening for cocktails.

Jenni held up her hand, stalling her. 'Serena, sorry, but you're making me feel like an anony-mous guest. I understand if you find it hard to accept me, and I guess this is because you love your brother and are afraid he's going to get hurt again. Well he won't. Not by me. Please believe me when I say that I'd never do anything to hurt him.'

For twenty-four years of age, she was remarkably assured, Serena thought. 'Seeing as we're being perfectly honest, yes I do think it's too soon after Amy and that Jack has hooked up with you on the rebound. So I am a little concerned.'

'There's no need. I'm not like Amy, I promise you.'

Serena said as lightly as she could, 'But Jenni, you're pregnant. Already. I think it's good about the baby and I hope it all works out for you both. But to me, it's Amy all over again.'

There was a puzzled glint in Jenni's eyes. She sat down on the bed and looked up at Serena.

'I think you'd better have a talk with your

brother,' Jenni said. 'Ask him the truth about Amy. Ask him what really happened. Then see if it's history repeating itself.'

Serena felt a prickle of unease. 'What do you mean, the truth?'

'I can't tell you. It's not up to me. You'll have to speak to Jack.'

There was something in her face that shook Serena. 'I will talk to Jack. Sorry if I'm behaving like the ugly step-sister, but I can't bear to see Jack unhappy all over again.'

'I won't mess Jack about. I'm hoping to be part of his life for a long time, and I'm on the same side as you where he's concerned. I really value your closeness. It's very special. He's lucky to have you for a sister and such a supportive family around him. He told me he'd never have come through the last year only for you.' Jenni smiled and, despite herself, Serena smiled back.

She kept her anxiety in check as she left the room. The truth about Amy? What the hell did that mean? She cast her mind back, right to the beginning when Jack had first brought her to Maple Hill, then fast-forwarded to the last couple of months of her rather sad life. Was there something she'd overlooked? No, Jenni must be mistaken. Jack would never have kept anything important from her, would he?

And if he had, incredulous though that might be, he'd scarcely have told Jenni.

★　★　★

Left to herself, Jenni went back out onto the balcony and marvelled at the fact that she was here now, in this piece of heaven, waiting for Jack to come home. Then she unpacked, had a shower and got into bed. She felt a little tired and it sounded like it might be a long night, but sleep eluded her.

Her visit home couldn't have gone any better. Her mum had been thrilled to see her, likewise Pete. She'd waited until Tuesday, when she'd been home a couple of days, before she'd told them about the baby, and Jack. Her mother was very concerned – funnily enough Serena had reminded her of her in a way with her concern for Jack – and had said she hoped that Jenni knew what she was doing. A baby was a very special gift, but needed buckets of love and security, as well as money.

'I have all that with Jack,' she'd explained, knowing they found it hard to accept that she had met someone and was now expecting his baby in such a short space of time. Even she was still finding it hard to believe.

'I can see by your face that you're very happy,' Pete had said.

'I'd rather meet this Jack guy before I give my opinion,' her mum had said, silencing Pete for a moment.

'I think that Dad would have liked him,' Jenni had said softly.

Her mum's face had crumpled a little. 'I guess that would be good enough for me.'

'Jack wants you to come over to visit us so you'll see where I'm living.'

The three of them had gone out for a meal that night and, over the next couple of days, Jenni had tidied up loose ends, clearing some of her stuff into the attic, pruning her wardrobe and sorting out her bank account. It was as though she was clearing the decks, ready to begin a new life. She'd caught up with her friends, meeting some for lunch, emailing the rest of the gang to bring them up to date and explain everything.

Then when all of that was done by Friday, it had seemed silly not to fly to the south of France, and La Mimosa. She couldn't wait to see Jack and tell him how well everything had gone. She'd also wanted to drop in to see Michael in The Anchor. Beyond a couple of texts to tell him she was fine, she hadn't been in touch.

And most especially, she wanted to be with Jack for his birthday. She put her hand on her tummy, still finding it hard to believe there was a baby in there. Whatever happened, she knew she could trust Jack. He hadn't yet told her he loved her. But even if the worst happened and he tired of her, she knew he'd look after their baby.

She must have fallen asleep, for the next thing she knew he was kissing her awake, in between laughing and cuddling her to him.

'Hey, how did you get here? This is a lovely surprise!'

It had been a long week without him and she'd

missed him. Any last, tiny doubts she might have had about what she was doing there vanished in the way she turned her face to his and felt as though she was turning towards the sun.

CHAPTER 46

No one would miss her. They would all carry on partying quite happily without her. Even that thought filled her with fresh misery. But as Kim packed her case, shoving in her colourful bikinis, she was determined not to launch into fresh tears. She'd already cried enough since her chat with Charlotte. Cried for love, for loss, for the empty spot in her heart that Jack would never fill.

If anything was to happen between you and Jack, it would have happened by now . . . He loves Jenni. Hearing the words being softly uttered by Charlotte had brought home to her more than anything else how much she was deluding herself. And when, in the sanctuary of her room, she was all cried out, she decided there wasn't much point in hanging around, inflicting more pain on herself. She just had to make her getaway without anyone, except Charlotte, knowing why.

There wouldn't even be an empty space at the gala dinner that evening, she thought hollowly as she lifted her YSL dress out of the wardrobe. Jenni had arrived. Serena had told her when she phoned her to ask if she wanted to join her and Charlotte in the Spa, but Kim had pleaded a headache and declined.

All she needed was a good excuse to leave. She had her flight booked, thanks to her BlackBerry, and just had to talk to Charlotte. Once more she picked up her mobile, hoping that Charlotte was back from the Spa.

She was, and picked up the call immediately. 'Kim. How are you?'

'Fine. Can you talk?'

'Hold on a minute.' Charlotte understood immediately that Kim didn't want anyone overhearing their conversation.

'I can talk now. I'm in the library and there's no one around. Kim, dear, are you okay? Would you like me to drop up to you, or do you need anything brought up?' Her voice was so full of concern that Kim felt the tears threatening again.

'No, I don't need anything thanks.'

'Look, I'm really sorry—'

'Charlotte, it's fine, you were right. I needed an injection of reality, but it's going to take me a while to come around. Thing is, I don't think I can stay here playing happy birthdays with Jack, especially now that Jenni has arrived.'

'Yes, I heard she was here,' Charlotte said quietly. 'Although I haven't seen her myself.'

Probably because she was in bed with Jack, Kim thought sourly, more determined than ever not to witness their loved-up faces at the dinner that evening.

'But you can't just leave, Kim. I feel terrible now . . . I certainly didn't mean for you to cut short your weekend,' Charlotte went on.

'Don't feel bad. I need to put space between me and Jack and now is as good a time as any to start. I just wanted you to know that I have a flight booked and I'm leaving for the airport in half an hour.'

'Kim! You can't go back to Dublin alone, especially this evening.'

'I'm not going to Dublin. I'm flying to Malaga and heading up to visit my parents. I've already called them and they're expecting me.'

It was the perfect solution, Kim had decided when she knew she had to get away from La Mimosa. Her parents' simple home nestling in the ochre hills of Spain wouldn't resonate with Jack's presence. They would welcome her with their usual warm-hearted affection. Luckily she had already cleared her diary for the early part of next week, thinking she'd be recovering from La Mimosa, so she could stay with them for a few days, basking in their unconditional love while she decided what to do with the rest of her life.

'I'm so glad you're not going home alone,' Charlotte said.

'I don't know what to say to Serena and – um, Jack, to explain why I'm running off . . .' Kim laughed nervously. 'I can't seem to come up with anything suitable.'

'Let me think about this . . .' Charlotte said.

After a short pause she went on, 'Why not simply say you have an offer too good to refuse? They don't need to know the details. They won't ask. Serena is still missing Paul and Jack is—'

'Otherwise engaged,' Kim supplied.

'I don't know if I'm glad or sorry that I planned this weekend, Kim. My advice is to be mysterious. That way you'll be leaving with your head held high.'

'Yeah, I could try that. Go out with a Mona Lisa smile on my face.'

'Good for you! It'll work out, I promise. You'll find someone of your own to love, someone who loves you as much as you deserve. How are you getting to the airport?'

'I'm going to ask Reception to order a car.'

'I've a better idea. Why don't you let Laurence take you? In the hotel's helicopter? He wasn't sampling any wine this afternoon.'

Laurence, in the helicopter. A swift, speedy and noisy departure. Surely better than a slow drive down the avenue from La Mimosa, before retracing the journey she'd made only the day before, looking at Jack's profile against the stunning scenery while the weekend stretched ahead like a golden present waiting to be unwrapped. And there was something about Laurence that was solid and reassuring. If she shed a tear or two en route to the airport, it wouldn't really matter.

'That's perfect, thank you.'

'I'll arrange it. Come down and join me on the

patio as soon as you're ready and I'll have some champagne waiting for you, to wish you well.'

'Thanks, Charlotte.'

It all happened very smoothly. Kim joined Charlotte on the patio and was sipping morale-boosting champagne when Serena arrived.

'What's happening, Kim? Mum told me you're leaving? You can't go now!'

'Something came up that I can't refuse,' Kim said lightly.

'It must be good if you're cutting short your weekend!' Serena looked slightly sad and envious.

'It is,' Kim forced a smile. 'Although I'm sorry to miss your birthday.'

Serena waved a dismissive hand. 'Birthdays! Who wants to be reminded of their age?'

'Age? Your best years are still ahead of you, Serena. And you too, Kim,' Charlotte said.

Kim let their talk flow over her head, her attention caught by the sight of Jack and Jenni, strolling out of a side door and heading towards the track to the beach. Jenni was wearing pink flip flops and a soft cotton dress that was almost see-through. They were holding hands as they strolled along, and it was this that lodged in Kim's throat, for the seemingly innocent body language made them look so much like a united couple, at total ease with each other. It was an ease she'd never seen between Jack and Amy.

Serena called them over. 'Hey, Jack! Jenni! Kim is leaving. Come and say goodbye.'

Kim felt her heart leap into her throat as they stopped, and almost in unison looked in her direction, looked at each other and began to walk to the terrace.

'Don't tell me you're deserting us!' Jack said, his eyes smiling at her. He pulled out a cane chair for Jenni and sat down beside her. They both had that dewy, fresh-from-the-shower look. She wondered if they had showered together.

'Kim has better fish to fry than hang out here with us,' Charlotte said, smiling gently at her. 'Something or someone has called her away but she's being very mysterious about it.'

Kim plastered her Mona Lisa smile on her face.

'Traitor!' Jack teased. 'He'd better be worth it if you're leaving us high and dry before we've blown out the candles on the birthday cake!'

'Oh, God, no candles, please, not this year,' Serena said.

'Aw, Serena, don't be a spoil sport. I can always get you a fire extinguisher if there's too many for you to manage . . .'

Jack was in sparkling form, his happiness radiating from him. Jenni was quiet but equally happy, Kim sensed. And why wouldn't she be? She had Jack all to herself. She was expecting his baby. When the lovely weekend was over, she'd be going back home with him. Kim made a determined effort to change the direction of her thoughts. Just a few more minutes and she'd be gone. In a couple of hours, she'd be in Spain and all of this would be behind her. By this time next year, she vowed, her whole life would have changed. The memories she took from this short visit to La Mimosa were entirely up to her.

Everyone came across to the helipad to see her off. Laurence was already buckled into the pilot's seat, wearing a headset. Pierre shoved her case on board. There were hugs all around, Charlotte giving her an extra tight squeeze and telling her to be good to herself. Then somehow she was sitting up beside Laurence and the door was securely closed. The blades spun and the engine roared. Laurence gave her a thumbs-up signal, pushed a lever and the helicopter began to rise. Kim looked down as the semi-circle of upturned faces and the white buildings of La Mimosa grew smaller. Her last view was of Jack holding tightly onto Harriet's left arm and leg and whirling her around in the air as though she was an aeroplane. Jenni was standing beside him, laughing.

Sunlight flashed, and beyond La Mimosa she saw the glittering sea. Then they swung in an arc and headed for the coastline and the airport.

CHAPTER 47

Wearing her turquoise silk cocktail dress, Serena joined Jack on the candlelit patio. She put her wine down on a mosaic table, finding it impossible to still her anxious thoughts. What did Jenni know that she didn't? What was Jack keeping from her? *Why* had he kept something from her? And where was Paul this weekend? Her heart twisted as she realised it had been the height of foolishness to have left him to his own devices, without even the anchor of seeing Harriet.

When Kim had left late that afternoon, Serena had been surprised with the shaft of jealousy that had gripped her on discovering her friend had obviously been offered a better invitation than La Mimosa. He must be brilliant in bed, she'd thought blackly, if Kim was passing up two nights of luxury on the Côte d'Azur. And she'd chided herself for feeling envious, it was just that she was missing Paul so much. She sat down on a patio chair and tried to calm herself. It was after ten o'clock and the fragrant evening had given way to a velvety night sky pinpricked with tiny stars.

A light, aromatic breeze riffled in off the sea, carrying scents of pine trees and lavender. Behind them, lights spilled from the windows of La Mimosa, forming pools on the patio and illuminating tubs tumbling with flowers and shrubs. Serena had already spotted Charlotte and Laurence strolling arm-in-arm back up the path from the orchard, having stretched their legs after the fabulous dinner.

It was strange to see Mum with another man, but they looked so right together that Serena could only feel happy for her. And Laurence was lovely. They seemed to fit together well. They had separate rooms and Serena was glad of that because in her present frame of mind it was bad enough having Jack going around like a horny teenager.

'Mum seems very keen on Laurence,' Jack said, as though he was reading her thoughts.

'She does. Do you mind? That someone might be taking Dad's place in her heart?'

'No, why should I? Anyway I'm not sure what place our laid-back father had in her heart. He must have been a right pain in the arse at times, rolling home drunk on a regular basis.'

'Did you love him?' Serena asked.

Jack was silent for a moment, then he said gently, 'Serena, we went through all this in those months after Dad died. That's the problem when important relationships that are far from perfect suddenly end. It leaves a terrible scar afterwards. Like you, I found Dad lovable in some ways, but annoying, undependable and occasionally embarrassing. Sometimes he was fun, other times he wasn't. But yes, of course I loved him, and I know you did too. Don't ask me how Mum kept up the happy couple front or stayed loyal to him. Anyway,' he said firmly, 'it's all water under the bridge.'

Serena sat quietly for a while. Then she said, 'Where's Jenni?'

'She's gone to bed.'

'Without you?' Serena quipped.

'I'm not that much of a sex maniac, thank you. She needs a good rest – she's feeling wrecked and thinks she ate far too much.'

'Yes, the dinner was something else, wasn't it?' Serena said. She'd missed Paul at the dinner table. He should have been there, with her and Harriet. Harriet had insisted on sitting beside Jenni, showing off yet another hair slide that Jenni had given her.

'After that dinner and the gallons of Conor's best burgundy, I feel so comatose right now that I couldn't even count to five . . .' Jack hooked a long leg under a chair and dragged it across the patio so that he could put both of his feet up.

Ask him the truth about Amy. Ask him what really happened . . .

'Jack. What really happened with Amy?' The words were out before she realised. He didn't react at first, just kept staring out into the night. The silence was so drawn out that she wasn't sure if he'd heard what she'd said.

Then he said, ultra casually, 'What do you mean?' and she knew by his tone of voice and the length of time it had taken him to answer that he was keeping something from her.

'I don't know. That's the point. I was talking to Jenni earlier this afternoon—'

'And?'

'We were just chatting. About her and Amy, and she said I should ask you what really happened.'

Another long silence. Jack sat back and clasped his hands behind his head. When he began to shake one of his feet restlessly, Serena knew he was agitated. 'Jack, you're making me nervous. What is it?'

'Oh, God,' he rubbed his face with his hands and sighed heavily. 'You really don't want to know.'

'I do. Tell me.' Something clutched at her heart. Whatever it was, it was serious. She could hardly believe he'd kept something serious from her.

'You don't want to know the kind of fool your brother has been.'

'Would it help if I said you don't know the kind of fool your sister is?'

'You were never a fool, Serena. You were always the smart girl, you still are. Not like me.'

'Jack, what is it?'

Jack stared out into the mellow night. 'You know the way you and Mum thought I was running away to La Mimosa to mend my broken heart?'

Serena nodded.

'That wasn't quite it. I was in bits after Amy

died. Remorse, guilt, anger, you name it, and my head was jumbled with it. I was a right mess. I felt like the zombie from hell.'

'Jack, you did everything you could for her.'

'You didn't know what was really going on.'

Serena felt a cold shiver. 'Why couldn't you tell me?'

Jack sighed deeply. 'You see, Serena, sometimes I felt like I was growing up in your golden shadow. You took after our ambitious, hard-working mum. I seemed more like Dad, without the heavy drinking part. But Amy just had to look at me with those little-girl eyes and I was a king. Does that make sense?'

'Kind of,' Serena said.

'It was good at the start, but after a while I began to feel that things were a little one-sided, it seemed to be always me shoring up Amy's lack of confidence. She became very high maintenance and difficult to please. I had decided to finish with her when she told me she was pregnant. So rather than be feckless like our dad, I did the honourable thing and married her, going along with her wishes that no one knew about the pregnancy until after we were married. Except I'd told you. Okay so far?'

'Yes, okay,' Serena said, her nerves on edge at his mechanical voice and her mind jumping ahead as she tried to see where this was leading.

'Soon after our marriage things got worse. Amy became quite irrational and moody. She wouldn't answer her mobile, she sometimes stayed in bed all day, blaming her pregnancy. One day she'd be withdrawn, the next full of energy. I never knew what to expect when I got home. Or what would be waiting for me at home when she summoned me.'

'Jack!'

'Sometimes she appeared to be pissed, yet I didn't think she was drinking that much. Then I went home one afternoon and caught her chopping out a line of coke.'

Serena gasped. 'You're joking.' She knew by his set face that it was far from a joke, and a lot of things suddenly fell into place.

'I begged her to stop,' Jack went on in a hard, emotionless tone of voice. 'I reminded her that she was pregnant. She said she needed the crutch of something because you and Mum filled her with anxiety and she felt she could never live up to your high standards.'

'*What?*'

'Shush and listen. I blamed myself. I was the one who'd married her. She became more clingy and tearful, looking for me at odd times. Coke made her feel good, she said. It helped her to cope with life. But of course it didn't. It made her worse. I tried to salvage what I could from our marriage. I told her she was my wife and I'd look after her and she had the baby on the way which would be very precious for both of us.'

'I really wish you had told me all this,' Serena said.

Jack went on as though she hadn't spoken. 'After a huge row, she promised me she'd turn over a new leaf for the baby's sake. I kept searching the house and her personal stuff for drugs, hoping that she had quit. I couldn't find anything and I risked going to New York because she agreed to stay with her sister Karen. Then, she lost the baby. I blamed myself for leaving her. She was devastated, of course. She said she'd let everyone down; me, you, Charlotte, and she became so depressed that I took her to Thailand. I watched her like a hawk, but somehow she managed to overdose with anti-depressants. I was terrified there might have been traces of coke in the mix and I paid handsomely to get clearance papers for her body. That was why I didn't want Paul to come out with you. I was afraid with his background that he might have copped on to something. Don't know how he didn't beforehand . . .'

Serena slowly shook her head. 'We thought she was a little too fond of the vodka, but nothing else.'

'Then afterwards, I spent a long time tormenting myself trying to figure out whether the overdose was deliberate or a mistake. I'm still not sure,' he said sombrely, 'but I've just had to learn to let it go.'

'Oh, Jack, you should have told me.'

He gave her a rueful grin that cut her to the quick. 'Do you want to hear the rest?'

'No! There can't be more!'

Jack gave her a grim smile. 'So there I was, my wife and unborn baby gone, but mixed with the shock of it all was a huge guilt trip. If I hadn't become involved with Amy in the first place, none of this would have happened.'

'You can't look at it like that.'

'I know, but it's funny the way your thoughts can take over in the dead of the night. If she'd never met you and Charlotte, or married into a family with strong, capable women at the helm, she wouldn't have needed a crutch in the first place. At least that's what I thought . . . most of the time, anyway.'

He stopped. Serena's heart gave a lurch when she saw the look in his eyes.

'Jack, what is it?'

'I was still beating myself up when her sister came over to Garryvale to go through some of Amy's personal stuff with me. I asked her out straight if she knew about Amy's coke habit. Karen crumbled and it all came out. Amy had been using it for years. It had nothing to do with me, us, our family . . . She'd gone off the rails after her parents had died. Karen tried to make her see sense, but couldn't get through to her. Amy had been well and truly hooked by the time I met her. And I also found out . . .' he paused, and dropped his head into his hands. His voice was muffled when he said, 'I found out that Amy had admitted to Karen after the miscarriage that the baby wasn't mine. She didn't know who the father was because it was the result of a one night stand when she was totally out of it.'

For a long, horrified moment, Serena couldn't believe what she'd heard. Then she sprang to her feet and enveloped Jack in a hug. 'Dear God! Jack! No wonder you were so cut up.'

After a while, Jack disengaged her arms. 'So now you know the truth about Amy, and your thicko of a brother.'

'Why couldn't you tell me? Why did you feel you had to carry that all by yourself?' Famous last words, Serena thought, recalling, with a chill, the way Paul had flung a similar accusation at her only a few days earlier.

Jack shrugged. 'Come on, sis, how could I admit what kind of fool I was? I was too ashamed at the same time to admit how stupid I'd been.'

'You weren't stupid,' Serena said gently, shaking her head. 'Gullible maybe, sensitive, definitely; you're a kind person and you let yourself be taken advantage of. But there's no big crime in that. I'm not the perfection you think I am. You should have told me.'

'I didn't want anyone's pity or sympathy for making a bollocks of my life. I do have some pride. Anyway, it's over now. I can think of Amy now without feeling any anger or guilt. Just regret at the way she messed up her life.'

'And Jenni knows?' Serena prompted.

'Yes, she's known from the beginning. She was great about it. She made me feel peaceful and strong again. She helped me to understand that Amy was more to be pitied than anything else.'

Easier to talk to Jenni than her, Serena thought for a moment. Yet it was often easier to unburden yourself to a stranger, rather than family, wasn't it? And at least, she realised gratefully, Jenni had been there for him in the way he needed.

'And now Jenni's pregnant,' Jack went on. 'It was an accident, but a good one. I feel so differently about us. Amy sucked me dry. Jenni lifts me up.'

'So I've noticed,' Serena admitted, smiling in the semi-darkness.

'It doesn't seem to matter that we haven't known each other all that long. I just hope I'll be a good father.'

'You'll be fine.'

'It's quite scary in a way. Parenthood.'

'Yes, it can be,' Serena said.

'Total responsibility for one little life. Quite daunting. If I do half as good a job as you've done with Harriet . . .'

Serena shook her head. 'Don't try to copy my example. I'm far from the perfect mother.'

'Harriet is a happy and extremely confident child with a great personality. What more do you want? Paul and you have given her a very stable background.'

'The stable background is falling apart,' Serena said sadly. 'Now it's my turn to admit to being stupid. I wasn't honest with Paul over something serious and I've lost his trust.'

'I wasn't honest with you over Amy, so would you say I've lost your trust?'

'Well no, they were exceptional circumstances. I can see why you spared me the details. But I deliberately misled Paul and made a fool of him. Because I was afraid of admitting I wasn't the super-efficient wife he thought he'd married.'

'Don't be ridiculous. Paul didn't marry a super-efficient wife. He married a flesh and blood Serena with warts and all. You should trust him enough to love you the way you are. I don't want to interfere, but what are you doing here if there are problems in your marriage? Why aren't you at home sorting them out?'

'I was hoping up to the last minute that Paul might have joined us for the weekend.'

'Christ, that's a bit of a tall order if you're the one who messed up.'

'Yes, but I don't know if he really wants me in his life anymore.'

'If I were you I'd be doing my damnedest to find out.'

'Maybe I'm too scared to know the worst.'

'Scared? Come on, sis.' Jack grinned, lifting a bottle of white wine out of the cooler and draining the last of it into their glasses. 'You and Paul had better get your act together before this baby arrives,' he said. 'I want a full complement of adoring uncles and aunties.'

When she'd finished her wine, Serena said good-night to Jack, joking with him even though she was still coming to terms with his shocking news. She was glad she felt warmer towards Jenni, and she saw a strength to Jack that she hadn't noticed before. They'd be okay, she thought with a lift.

She was coming around the far side of the patio towards the terrace bar when she saw them. Charlotte and Conor. Standing chatting together by the wrought iron railings, while the rest of their group, Laurence, Martine, Pierre and Diane, were relaxing on comfortable sofas, having a night cap. Conor and Charlotte were looking out at the softly lit, night-time gardens and he was pointing things out, obviously showing off the recent landscaping that La Mimosa had undergone.

Charlotte said something to her brother-in-law, and whatever way Conor inclined his head towards her, another reel of memory unlocked itself from the buried landscape of her childhood, a moment in time that had been concealed out of sight, until now.

Dizzy, Serena collapsed onto a nearby bench.

She looked across the shadowed grounds and struggled to take in gulps of air as the full implications of it all hit her in the chest like a sledge-hammer.

She was ten years old again, and looking for her mother because it was time to blow out the candles on the birthday cake. And then she heard her mother talking to Conor, telling him she was staying in Tamarisk on account of her and Jack. Feeling hot and heavy, after she'd heard her mother's words, that she'd run as far as the riverbank in her need to get away. And then Jack and Kim had found her. She'd known she couldn't tell Kim. No way. And what would be the point in telling Jack? When he'd started to joke in his mischievous way about the champagne, he'd made her laugh. It was better this way, she'd decided, scrambling to her feet. Better to pretend everything was fine and forget the whole thing.

But you didn't forget it, Serena realised, sitting alone in the moonlight, and feeling remorse for that ten-year-old child.

Traces lingered in the depths of your heart, especially if it made you feel there was so much to live up to, so much to prove, and it became ingrained in the fabric of your life.

Now, more than ever, she ached for Paul. She needed to talk to him and hear the sound of his voice.

CHAPTER 48

He shouldn't be here, Paul told himself. It was no place for a married man.

Married? Hah! As if he'd ever been truly married to Serena. But he knew in his heart that he shouldn't be here in this noisy, Leeson Street pub, because he was no match for the dozens of sexy, posing women, many of whom were eyeing him as though they were sizing him up for bed. He shouldn't be here when he was feeling so wretched, but he'd been crawling the walls of the apartment ever since Serena's shock confession, so he had to get out.

There was nobody else in her life. He was quite sure of that now. But why had she had so little faith in him that she couldn't talk about her problems? Why hadn't she been able to talk to him? Was he that much of an insensitive bastard that she felt she couldn't share her troubles with him? If anything he felt much worse and more beaten up since she'd told him the truth. And then, having pulled the rug from under him, she'd gone off to La Mimosa, in true, traditional family fashion. The Devlin family, of course. *And* she'd taken Harriet.

She hadn't even bothered to call him. She'd dialled his number and passed the phone to Harriet so that she could chat to him. And now he was propping up the dimly lit bar like an eejit, afraid to venture too far into hordes of salivating women. Even in his life before Serena, he hadn't bothered much with this kind of scene.

He took a slug out of his over-priced bottle of Corona and tried to figure out if the skinny model not much older than a schoolgirl was really showing off tits with huge nipples in a sheer, completely see-through top, or if he was imagining it from lack of sex. After a minute he realised that the huge nipples were actually circles of pink lace, glued to the sheer voile at the appropriate spot. She caught him looking at her and stuck out her tongue, rolling it suggestively between her teeth. He quickly looked the other way.

'I love you, Paul, I want to try again . . .'

He heard Serena's broken voice but words were easy to say, weren't they? It was what you did that counted. When he had time to think about it, he could begin to understand the whole Harriet bit. He knew if he'd been the one at home looking after a tiny baby that he'd have been terrified. He wouldn't have known what to do for the best and would have been helpless if Harriet cried. Okay, Serena was her mother, but babies didn't come with a manual or instructions. Instead, he'd been able to relax and enjoy his little daughter, because Serena had pretended everything was fine. There

517

was something about this that niggled him, but it was late, he was tired, and he just couldn't figure it out right now.

'Well hello . . .'

There was a throaty purr in his left ear and he felt a proprietorial hand on his shoulder. He looked down to see a set of ruby nails lightly gripping him, and looked up into a beautiful face with huge blue eyes. Eyes that were looking at him with warm concern. She was tall and dark haired and he racked his brains trying to recall where he'd seen her.

'Lucy,' she smiled. 'I met you in Kim's garden and then you were at my birthday party. I saw you leave with Kim?' she raised an eyebrow. 'It's just that I heard she sent Matthew O'Brien packing and I wondered if it was on account of you.'

'Kim? God, no,' he said, when her meaning sank in. 'Absolutely not. We're friends. Nothing more.'

By now Lucy was sitting on the stool beside him, leaning in close so that he caught her musky perfume and was treated to a very generous and inviting show of cleavage.

'Oh. That's good, in a way,' she said, fiddling with her dark hair. She had a nice voice. It was warm and full of empathy. 'I like you, Paul. I'm really sorry to hear of your bust up with Serena. You must be feeling bad about it.'

'Yes, and I shouldn't be here but I just had to get out.'

'Why shouldn't you be here?' she said softly.

518

'There's no point in sitting home alone looking at the walls and going over everything that went wrong. That would only do your head in. Especially this weekend when they're all partying over in La Mimosa. Even Kim. She told me they were flying out on Friday morning. So you're right to get out and mingle and enjoy some partying yourself. But if you really feel this isn't your scene, I know somewhere quieter we could have a drink and a chat.' Her big blue eyes gave him a conspiratorial, seductive glance that said it all.

Paul looked around the pub, where the air heaved with palpable sexual promise and said, 'Yeah, it's a bit noisy all right. I think it's time to go.'

She smiled warmly and slid off the stool. She put a hand on his arm. 'Well, then . . . what are we waiting for?'

CHAPTER 49

It had been easier than he'd thought, telling Serena the truth, Jack realised as he walked towards the lift. Things that had once seemed important, like for instance his pride and his ego, and his face-saving attempts at hiding the truth, mattered less and less compared to what was gradually taking over his life – Jenni and the baby.

He stepped into the lift and got a shock when he saw his reflection in the mirror. Staring back at him was the image of his father. Once more, he wondered what kind of father he'd be. He knew he was made of sterner stuff than Jamie Devlin but he tried to imagine himself holding a tiny baby and failed miserably. How would he know what to feel, what to do? Supposing he didn't love the baby? What if it was all a mistake with Jenni? That he was just infatuated and it was all on the rebound? She might get fed up with him. He was years older than her. So far she'd never said anything about being in love with him and he was too terrified to ask her.

In the bedroom, a lamp was burning low at his side of the bed and Jenni appeared to be asleep.

He went into the bathroom, had a quick shower and cleaned his teeth. Then, wearing his boxers, he slipped into bed just as Jenni stirred.

'Hey, I thought you were asleep,' he murmured.

Jenni gave him a sleepy smile. 'I missed you in bed.'

'I was talking to Serena. You should have called me to come up.'

'No, it's okay, I'm glad you were talking to Serena. Did you tell her about Amy?'

'Yes. You were right. She didn't ridicule me. She was just cross I hadn't told her in the first place.'

''Cos she loves you. That's one of the reasons I went back to London. When I saw how much your family care about you and love you, I realised how important family is.'

Yes, I'm lucky and you're special, you know that, don't you?' he gave her a cuddle and smoothed down her hair. When it felt slightly damp at the temples he sat up in bed, propping himself by the elbow. 'Jenni? Are you all right?'

'I'm fine,' she said sleepily. 'I just had a little indigestion. Nothing wrong with the fabulous cooking, but I ate far too much.'

'Are you sure it isn't anything else?' he felt a sliver of uneasiness take hold.

'Stop worrying,' she murmured. 'Just give me a cuddle. We have all tomorrow ahead of us. And it's your birthday. I'll have to think of something special for the birthday boy.'

'You're here. That's more than enough. Now,

sleep.' Jack clicked off the lamp and lay in the dark listening to Jenni's soft breathing as a whirlpool of memories threatened to surface.

What's wrong now?

What can I do to help?

Where does it hurt?

He put his uneasiness to one side and forced himself to think of brighter things and eventually he slept.

When Jack woke quite early in the morning, and saw Jenni sitting curled in a tub chair by the window, he was immediately alert. 'Jenni! What's wrong?'

Her face was pale. 'I guess I still have a bit of a tummy bug. It could be whatever I ate before I got here, crappy airport food or something.'

He leapt out of bed. 'Get dressed. I'm taking you to the nearest hospital.'

'I'll be fine.'

'Yes, of course you will,' he said calmly as he pulled on his jeans, checked for his mobile, his wallet. 'I'm just being extra cautious.'

'You're making me feel scary.'

'Don't be. And there's no need to alarm anyone. I'll take one of the cars, drive us to the hospital and we'll be back by the time everyone is having breakfast, okay?'

Jack felt as though he was outside of himself as they took the elevator downstairs, and a word with the night porter procured the keys to one of the La Mimosa cars. Pierre would have come with him, or Conor, or Laurence for that matter, but he didn't want to disturb them as word would somehow get back to Charlotte.

It was a beautiful morning. The air was fresh, the sun just coming up. La Mimosa looked like a white pearl gleaming in the emerald green lawns. He fastened Jenni's seatbelt and looked at her pale face and felt panic rise inside him. Dear God, if anything goes wrong . . .

Out on the road, Jack climbed the twisty incline until they reached the autoroute. Suspended between the morning sky, the rugged mountains and the great rippling bay, the car sped towards Nice. Jack never remembered being so focused in all of his life. Yet everything after that was a blur of images: the hospital car park; helping Jenni in through the door; waiting for ages. Waiting for ever, it seemed, after Jenni had been taken through to a small examination cubicle and he cooled his heels outside. At last the curtain rattled back and she was there, lying on a thin hospital mattress, her brown eyes smiling at him, her dark choppy hair at odds with her pale face.

'Told you. It was something I ate. Probably that cream bun in the airport.'

'And the baby?' he asked.

'All seems fine, but we'll know more later,' she said.

'Later?'

'They want to do a scan. Just routine, they said.'

He held her hand and felt the urge to sweep her into his arms. More interminable waiting, and they were taken down a long, narrow corridor and into a small room. Once again, he waited outside until she was settled. When he went in, she was lying on a small bed. Two midwives were present, chattering away in French, one of them making notes on Jenni's chart and the other busy with a machine beside the bed.

'Jack! I think they're not sure of the heartbeat,' Jenni told him.

His own heart somersaulted. They stared at each other for a long time. Jenni's face was set and resolute. She looked like someone who was trying very hard to be brave, and Jack melted.

'Listen to me,' he said, leaning over the bed, heedless of the midwives bustling around, getting things ready and flicking switches. 'I love you no matter what.' He wished he could take her out of here, whisk her back to La Mimosa and make everything right again.

'Guess what,' Jenni said, 'I always thought it would be somewhere more romantic when I said this, but no matter what, I love you too.' Her eyes were steadfast and strong, lifting him up and away from the tiny hospital room. They were smearing a gel over her stomach and running a small probe across it. The screen showed dark blobs and varying shades of grey.

Then, at last, one of the midwives pointed to the screen and said in English, 'See? There is the head and a little heart . . .'

There was a roaring in Jack's ears. Something

swam in front of his eyes. To his untrained eye, it was indistinguishable, but, there, on the small square screen, was the tiny shape of his child, his baby. His and Jenni's. What had he been afraid of? He felt nothing but love.

'But wait . . .' the midwife said, running the probe around Jenni's tummy as she stared at the screen.

Something ice-cold ran through his veins. 'What's wrong?'

Then both midwives excitedly pointed at the screen. 'There's nothing wrong. It is perfect. The heartbeat . . . there are *two* heartbeats . . . there are *two* babies . . .'

Twins. *Twins!* His eyes flew to Jenni's face. She was smiling at him.

'Told you I'd get you something special for your birthday,' she said.

CHAPTER 50

Serena's breakfast tray was full of tempting tastes, a small bowl of fruit, fresh yogurt, chocolate croissants and thick creamy coffee. Harriet, who was sharing her room, had already given her a big, pink card, full of misshapen kisses. She knew she would treasure it for ever. Then Harriet had scampered off to join Pierre and his son in the pool. Serena was bringing her tray out to her table on the balcony when Charlotte knocked on the door. 'Come in, Mum, I'm out here.'

Charlotte was dressed in a cerise pink kaftan and she gave Serena a warm hug and kissed her on both cheeks. 'Happy birthday, darling. You look wonderful. I'll give you your present and card later.'

'I'm being spoiled,' Serena said.

'Good,' Charlotte smiled. Then she looked at Serena's hair and frowned. 'What's that?'

Serena put her hand up to the precious pink slide that Harriet had most lovingly caught into her hair just above her ear, insisting that Serena have a loan of her special slide because it was her

526

birthday. Serena had felt moved at the tenderness in her daughter's eyes and the gentle way she'd secured the slide and had been overcome with love for her.

'Harriet wants me to wear it today. But I'm not wonderful, and I don't deserve to be spoiled,' Serena blurted, unable to keep up a front. She felt her mouth quiver, all her defences in meltdown. 'I've behaved badly with Paul. I shouldn't even be here, sitting on this sunny balcony with this fantastic day in front of me. Sorry, Mum, to dump on you like this, and on the birthday weekend.'

'It's okay. I understand you're upset about Paul. What do you want to do?'

'Could I turn the clock back?'

'Oh, Serena, there's no such thing. In a way it's just as well,' Charlotte said. 'Imagine if we all had things we wanted to change?'

'You mean if you had decided to go off with Conor?' Serena said, something inside her wanting to know more about her mother's secret love.

'Who told you?' Charlotte looked visibly shaken and Serena was immediately contrite with the blunt way she'd put it.

'I'm sorry, I didn't mean to spring it on you like this. No one told me. Years ago, I overheard you, during one of the birthday parties. I buried it away and forgot about it. Then I saw you both last night when Conor was showing you the new landscaping. Something about the way the two of you were standing together brought it all back to me. I think you were even wearing the same colour dress.'

'Serena, I'm so, so sorry you found out like this,' Charlotte said, her beautiful eyes full of pain, and Serena could have kicked herself. Why hadn't she just kept her mouth shut?

Charlotte said, her voice husky, 'Years ago, when Conor and I first met, we were instantly attracted to each other. We never did anything about it and now we're just very good friends. I remember that party because it was the only time we ever hinted at our feelings. I also remember thinking we'd been overheard, but I thought it had been Jamie.'

'Relax, Mum, it's fine. It explained a few things to me.'

Charlotte sighed. 'I guess you mean why your dad turned to drink. He sensed that the spark was missing from our marriage. The biggest regret I have is the way Jamie's drinking affected you and Jack. Jack missed strong fatherly guidance and you, my darling, worked far too hard to prove yourself to your father in an attempt to look for his attention and his love, and even though he's gone almost nine years, it's become a way of life with you.'

Serena stared at her mother for a long moment.

Charlotte's face flashed with alarm. 'What is it? What have I said wrong?'

Serena tried to gather her whirling thoughts. It had never been her father she'd been trying to impress. All along, it had been her strong, determined mother. She'd always had to get it right and was so focused on making Tamarisk a success, because she didn't want to let her mother down; her mother who had given up love and kept the family together for the sake of her and Jack. But what was the point in admitting all this to Charlotte now? It would only upset her and it wouldn't change anything that had happened.

When Serena had got over her initial shock the previous night, she'd sat in the soft moonlight having a long and honest think about her life. She was a far cry from the ten-year-old child who'd heard what she shouldn't have heard, and old enough to know that, now, she alone was fully responsible for her own actions. Nobody was perfect, not even a beloved parent, who had only ever done the very best she could for her children in the circumstances. In the grand scheme of things, her childhood had been a lot better than most.

She counted her blessings and she had so many to be grateful for. A daughter who loved her, a loyal and supportive family circle, a good friend in Kim, and a business that, with a little read-justing, would continue to flourish. She also had a husband who needed to be convinced of her love. On impulse, she'd phoned Paul, even though it was late, and refused to be worried when she got no answer. She didn't leave a message. Now, this morning, she was thirty-six years old and the only thing she could change was the rest of her life.

'Mum, relax,' she said. 'You shouldn't blame yourself for Dad's drinking.'

'It's one of the reasons why I worked hard to make Tamarisk a success,' Charlotte said in a regretful voice. 'I thought it would go some way towards redeeming my conscience with Jamie. Then recently I thought you were working far too hard as though you were following my example.'

Serena was silent for a moment. There was some truth in her mother's words, but no point in allowing Charlotte to beat herself up about it. Then she said, 'Mum, stop it. But I do need your help one more time as I try to fix my marriage.'

'Oh, darling,' Charlotte squeezed her arm and Serena saw tears in her eyes. 'I'm so happy to hear that. I'll do whatever I can.'

She flew from Nice to Gatwick, then Gatwick to Cork. She hired a car at Cork airport and pulled into a shopping centre on the periphery of the city. After that, she began to drive westwards through the countryside and the slanting sunshine, the conviction that she was doing the right thing growing stronger as she left the main roads behind and took side roads through jaw-dropping, beautiful landscapes. She'd left Harriet in La Mimosa, with Charlotte looking after her and bringing her home. Thankfully, her daughter had been far too busy getting ready for another trip to the water park to pay much attention to her mother's departure. Jack and Jenni seemed to be missing, gone off for their private birthday celebration, she'd guessed, but he'd sent a text to Charlotte to say they'd be back in the afternoon in time for the party. A party that, for once, Serena was going to miss.

It was early evening before she reached her destination; a place where soaring, silent woods stretched like a lush green backdrop and a path through the meadow led to a still, calm lake. The cottage they'd stayed in on their honeymoon was gone and the wooded setting boasted three newly built traditionally designed cottages, spaced well apart. When she'd enquired earlier that day, she'd been lucky to get a cancellation for the last cottage at the end of the row. She'd left a message on Paul's mobile. Words to the effect that she was starting a new tradition, the Taylor tradition, and she was going to spend her birthday evening in the best place in the world, the place where she'd once been incredibly happy.

She hoped it would convince him enough to join her.

Serena unpacked and emptied her shopping bags. She put wine and champagne in the fridge, showered and slathered on body lotion. When she blow-dried her hair, she caught some of it back with Harriet's slide. Then she put on a pair of white jeans and a soft pink shirt over her filigree lace underwear. She sprayed her favourite scent. In the living room, she lit the log fire, more for its warm glow than for its heat. Across the mantelpiece, she arranged some scented candles and put more on the dresser in the bedroom. Then she turned back the fluffy duvet, plumped up the pillows and smoothed the sheets. Her throat went dry at the thought of sharing the bed with Paul as the hushed, inky night-time settled across the countryside.

If he came.

Back in the living room, she put on some background music, one of his favourite chill-out classical albums. Then she lit the candles, poured a glass of wine and sat in the window seat to wait.

As she waited, watching the smoky fall of dusk, some of her earlier optimism began to desert her. It wasn't going to work. She'd come here on an impetuous whim. Paul wasn't convinced she meant what she'd said. Or worse, he simply didn't care enough to come. The minutes ticked by, the hours, and then just as the night was settling, and she was about to give up hope, car headlights appeared and her heart somersaulted. She flew to the hall door and opened it. Her heart lurched at the sight of him standing in the porch, in his grey leather jacket and black jeans. His wavy hair was messy and there was dark stubble on his chin as though he hadn't waited to have a shave. Or as if, she remembered the unanswered call last night, he'd lingered in someone else's bed too long after a steamy session and got dressed in a hurry.

No. Not that. It couldn't be.

'Paul. You're here. Why?' Even as she voiced it, Serena realised that the question was unnecessary.

The most important thing was the fact that he *was* here.

'I don't know,' he shrugged, his face giving nothing away. 'I went to a pub last night and I'd women coming on to me left, right and centre. I was tempted to do something to hurt you in return.' He looked at her intently and she felt a stab of anxiety. 'But only for a moment,' he said, his gaze softening. 'Because when someone offered it to me on a plate, I couldn't go through with it. So I walked out, jumped into a taxi and went home. And do you know what was killing me?'

'What?' Their eyes locked together.

'Hell, Serena, despite all the problems between us, no woman excites me the way you do. I've been awake all night thinking about you. Thinking about everything. And I realised that when Harriet was a baby, I was able to relax and really enjoy her, because you kept all your worries to yourself. What you did afterwards . . . well I'm still getting my head around it. I wished you'd talked to me. But my life is meaningless without you, you're the woman I want to spend it with. When I got your message today, I didn't know what to do at first. Then it seemed important to hear about the Taylor tradition and see what's in it for us.'

There was a long silence. She could see by the expression in his eyes that he was as nervous as she was. Underneath her clothes and lacy underwear, her skin ached for the touch of his hands. Behind her waited the welcoming cottage with its big, deep bed, inviting fire and softly flickering candlelight. She sensed that, like her, it too was holding its breath.

'What's that?' He threw a glance at her hair slide.

'A very important birthday present,' she said softly.

He gazed at her as if he was gathering his thoughts. 'What brought you down here?' he asked.

She held his gaze, feeling strong, and more sure of what she was going to say than she'd been about anything in such a long time. Feeling, too, a fizz of joy. 'I came,' she said, 'because I love it here. It's a place where I'm not Jack's loyal sister, Charlotte's good daughter, Harriet's perfect mother, or the busy director of Tamarisk. It's a place where I can just be me, Serena Taylor, and if you want, your wife and lover.' She reached up and stroked his cheek.

He smiled at last. Stepped inside. When he pulled her close to him, her senses thrummed.

He said, in a warm, seductive voice, 'Convince me.'